THE
OUTSIDER

Books by Ann H. Gabhart

The Scent of Lilacs
Orchard of Hope
Summer of Joy

THE OUTSIDER

A NOVEL

ANN H. GABHART

Revell

a division of Baker Publishing Group
Grand Rapids, Michigan

Published by Revell
a division of Baker Publishing Group
P.O. Box 6287, Grand Rapids, MI 49516-6287
www.revellbooks.com

Printed in the United States of America

Library of Congress Cataloging-in-Publication Data
Gabhart, Ann H., 1947–
    The outsider : a novel / Ann H. Gabhart.
      p.   cm.
    ISBN 978-0-8007-3239-4 (pbk.)
    1. Shakers—Fiction. 2. Kentucky—History—1792–1865—Fiction. I. Title.
PS3607.A23O97 2008
813'.6—dc22   2008006829

Scripture is taken from the King James Version of the Bible.

To my church family,
with thanks for the many prayers
and abundant love

A Note about the Shakers

At the turn of the nineteenth century, religious fervor swept the Western frontier, and thousands of people came to camp meetings such as the 1801 Cane Ridge Revival in Kentucky to hear the gospel message and find new ways to worship. Thus the Shakers, whose communities in New England were flourishing, found the spiritual atmosphere in Kentucky in the early 1800s perfect for expanding their religion to the west.

Ann Lee, believed by her followers to be the second coming of Christ in female form, founded the Shakers, or the Society of Believers, in the 1700s. The Shaker doctrines of celibacy, communal living, and the belief that perfection can be attained in this life were all based on the revelations that Mother Ann claimed to have divinely received. The name *Shakers* came from the way they worshiped. At times when a member received the "spirit," he or she would begin shaking all over. These sorts of "gifts of the spirit," along with other spiritual manifestations such as visions, were considered by the Shakers to be confirmation of the same direct communication with the Lord they believed their Mother Ann had experienced.

Since the Shakers believed work was part of worship and that God dwelt in the details of that work, they devoted themselves to doing everything—whether farming or making furniture and brooms or developing better seeds—to honor the Eternal Father and Mother Ann. Shaker communities thrived until after the Civil War when few recruits were willing to accept the strict, celibate life of the Shakers, and the sect gradually died out.

In Kentucky, the Shaker villages of Pleasant Hill and South Union have been restored and attract many visitors curious about the Shaker lifestyle. These historical sites provide a unique look at the austere beauty of the Shakers' craftsmanship. The sect's songs and strange worship echo in the impressive architecture of their buildings. Visitors also learn about the Shakers' innovative ideas in agriculture and industry that improved life not only in their own communities but also in the "world" they were so determined to shut away from their lives.

1

January 1812

The harsh clang of the meetinghouse bell shattered the peace of the night. At the sound, Gabrielle jerked upright in her narrow bed. She had not been asleep but instead had been lying very still with her eyes wide open, staring out at the grainy darkness and listening to the soft breathing of the sleeping girls around her. She had matched her own breaths with theirs in hopes of bringing quiet harmony back to her thoughts, but the gift of knowing kept nipping at the corners of her mind. Visions of men with blackened faces, corn melting, and shadows of the world flitting among the trees had troubled her thoughts all day, but it was all too vague for understanding. All she knew for sure was the sense of dread awake and growing inside her.

Usually when the gift of knowing came to her, it wasn't shrouded in so much mystery. Rather it was clear, as clear as her image in a still pool. This time a handful of pebbles had dropped in to cloud the pool. Earlier she had gone to her quiet place in the woods to pray to either rid her mind of the troubling vision or bring it clear so she could perhaps understand it. But the vision had stayed with her, as dark and murky as ever.

The bell kept tolling the alarm as Gabrielle quickly rose from her bed. Around her the younger sisters were waking and jumping out of bed to see what might be happening. Outside one of the brothers was shouting, "Fire!"

While the girls clustered around the window, Gabrielle pulled her dress over her head and found her shoes. She had no need to look out to discover what was happening, for the gift of knowing had cleared. She could see the flames whooshing through the hay and circling the posts of their harvest barn. Nathan was there in the midst of the flames crying out to her, but his voice was too faint to hear. There was no time for looking. She had to hurry to warn Nathan of his danger.

She left one of the older girls in charge before she slipped out into the hallway. It was against the rules for her to talk to Nathan without another brother or sister present, but surely tonight the rules could be broken. Nathan would be rushing out to the fire in his usual reckless way. She had to stop him before he ran headlong into danger.

Already the boys were out of their rooms and pounding down their stairway. Gabrielle hurried down the girls' stairway over to the boys' side of the house. She'd stop him on his way out and make him understand the need for caution.

"Sister Gabrielle, where are ye going?" Sister Mercy's voice stopped her.

Gabrielle spun around to look at the older woman. "Oh

praise the heavens, Sister Mercy. You can help me. I must find Brother Nathan. He is in terrible danger."

Sister Mercy was frowning. "Ye know it is forbidden for you to go to the boys' side of the house. And where is thy cap?"

Gabrielle touched the dark curls that fell about her shoulders. It was a vanity to show her hair or enjoy the feel of it on her neck, a vanity she'd never been able to completely put away from her. But surely at a time like this, one shouldn't be worried with vanity. "But you don't understand, Sister Mercy. I must warn him. The fire!" Gabrielle's eyes widened as suddenly in her mind Nathan was falling among the flames. "We must keep him away from the fire."

"Ye talk nonsense, child. Our new harvest barn has caught fire. Every hand is needed to put out the fire and save what we can."

Gabrielle turned away from Sister Mercy back toward the boys' stairway. She was always obedient. It seemed only right to be so, but this time her mind would not let her rest. Some power stronger than her need to be obedient to the Shaker rules was pushing her.

"Anyway, he is gone out to help with the fire already." Sister Mercy's voice softened as she touched Gabrielle's shoulder. "Look at me, Sister Gabrielle." When Gabrielle turned to her, Sister Mercy held her candle up high to better see Gabrielle's face and asked, "Has thou seen a vision, my child?"

Gabrielle didn't like to reveal her visions. As a child it had brought her nothing but rebukes and trouble, but even among the Believers who prized and honored such gifts, Gabrielle still held them close to her. Only when she had the gift of song during the meetings could she feel completely free to share her visions. Now she reluctantly said, "Perhaps it is nothing."

"Why do ye fear this gift from the spirits, my child? Better you should learn to appreciate and use it for the good of all." Sister Mercy lowered the candle. When she spoke again, her voice was thoughtful. "I had thought to ask you to watch after the little ones while I went to help at the fire, but instead I shall stay and you may go. Remember, child, engaged in thy duty, ye have no reason to fear."

When Gabrielle started to turn away, Sister Mercy stopped her. "First you must cover your hair." She removed her own cap and handed it to Gabrielle.

"Thank you, Sister Mercy." Gabrielle stuffed her hair under the cap as best she could, curtsied, and hurried out before Sister Mercy had a chance to change her mind.

At the barn the men and women had formed a water line, but it was futile. Already the flames were reaching for the roof. Some of the brethren were pulling out what they could from the doors, but as each moment passed it was more and more dangerous to even go close to the barn. Gabrielle stopped a little away from the milling crowd of the sisters and brethren as her eyes frantically searched for some sight of Nathan.

The fire lit up the faces of her Shaker brothers and sisters in a strange unearthly way, and on each face was written the same grave concern. That barn held much of their harvest and thus their promise of plentiful provisions through the remainder of the winter and spring. Gabrielle heard someone shout, "Those of the world are responsible for this."

Gabrielle could only agree. Those of the world didn't understand the way of the Shakers, but the little they did know seemed to upset and anger some of them so much that they wanted to destroy the community growing at Harmony Hill.

Gabrielle's eyes flew through the people, not even lingering on the few strange faces. They must be people of the world come to help put out the fire or to perhaps rejoice in the barn's burning. When at last she spotted Elder Caleb, one of the leaders of the community, she ran to him.

"Brother Caleb, have you seen Brother Nathan?"

Even with the worry of the fire troubling him, he looked down at Gabrielle with steady kindness. "Nay, Sister Gabrielle. I have not. Why do ye seek him?"

"I fear he is in danger. That he may yet be in the barn among the flames."

"Nay, assuredly not. All the brethren have been told to back away from the fire. We have no desire to see anyone hurt for a bit of grain."

Gabrielle grabbed the elder's arm as he started to turn away from her. Panic squeezed a tight hand around her heart as in her mind's eye she saw Nathan sinking to the barn floor with flames all around him. "He is in the barn," she insisted.

"Control yourself, Sister. I have told you that cannot be." In the light of the flames, Elder Caleb's face held reproof as he pulled away from her.

The ominous crack of timbers giving way filled the air. Then one of the young brothers was running from the barn, shouting, "Nathan's still in there!"

Silence fell over the group. Suddenly one of the strangers broke from the crowd and yelled at the boy, "Where is he?"

The boy was almost weeping. "I don't know. He was right behind me, and then he wasn't."

Elder Caleb stepped in front of the man from the world.

His slight figure contrasted with the stranger's tall strength. "Nay, I cannot allow you to go in there, Dr. Scott. It is too dangerous. The roof is already giving way."

The man didn't hesitate. "But I must," he said as he started for the barn.

Gabrielle stepped past Elder Caleb to grab the man's arm. "He is not more than ten feet from the door a bit to the left of the center. But you must hurry. The rafters above where he lies are aflame."

The man's eyes narrowed as he stared at her intently while listening to her words. Then he turned and ran into the burning barn. In a few moments he was out, carrying Nathan in his arms like a child. Nathan's breeches were on fire, and the man's jacket sleeve erupted in flames. Gabrielle, who had trailed after the man toward the burning barn, was the first to reach them. She yanked off her scarf to beat out the flames on Nathan's legs and the man's jacket.

When others began clustering around them, the man shouted at them angrily, "Back away and give the boy some air!" The people parted to allow him to carry Nathan several steps farther away from the barn before he laid him down and knelt beside him. The man leaned down to put his ear close to Nathan's mouth.

Gabrielle held her own breath. Nathan was so still. Ever since she'd first met Nathan after he and his family had joined the Shakers, he'd seemed to be constantly moving. Even during silent prayer he could not be completely still. Now not even a finger twitched. The man raised his head up and said to no one in particular, "He's alive."

Gabrielle began breathing again as she offered up a silent prayer of thanksgiving before the man's next words brought

14

her up short. "But he's badly burned. He may yet not see the morning." The man stood up. "I need a place where I can care for him."

Elder Caleb stepped forward. "Sister Gabrielle will show you to the guest quarters, and I'll send along Sister Helen to help you in whatever way she can, Dr. Scott."

The doctor picked Nathan up again. Gabrielle walked ahead and opened the door into the small cabin they always kept ready for any strangers who came to them in need of shelter for the night. She turned back the bed for the doctor to lay Nathan down before she located a candle and lit it.

"I need more light," the doctor said.

Gabrielle set the lamps and candles about the bed as the doctor directed her. Then he asked her to hold a candle above the bed while he began cutting what was left of Nathan's breeches away from his legs.

Sister Helen came into the room and said, "Brother Caleb has sent me to assist you, Dr. Scott. I have often dosed the sick."

"Good. Help me cut away the cloth from his legs."

A tremor went through Gabrielle at the sight of the burns on Nathan's legs, and she could not keep the candle she held from flickering. Sister Helen frowned at her before she said, "Perhaps it would be more fitting to get one of the brethren to help. Sister Gabrielle is yet young."

The doctor looked up at Gabrielle. His eyes were almost black in the light as he studied her. Gabrielle looked back boldly, knowing the candle she held out from her face kept the man from seeing her clearly. She'd heard much about this Dr. Brice Scott who lived near their village. The new converts said he doctored differently than the doctors in the town, and some called him an Indian doctor. He was not old like Elder Caleb, yet not young like Nathan. She supposed he was handsome in the way the world judged a person's looks, but the Believers looked for a person's inward beauty rather than the outward lines of one's face or the shape of one's body. He had been intensely focused on treating Nathan's burns and now appeared irritated by the distraction of Sister Helen's suggestion.

"Young sister," he said abruptly. "Are you going to faint?"

The smell of Nathan's scorched skin rose up to sicken her, but Gabrielle pushed her voice out strongly. "Nay. I've never felt faint, and I wish to stay if Sister Helen will allow me to."

"Ye don't need my permission. Brother Caleb has already given it," Sister Helen said, but her disapproval was plain to see.

Gabrielle had never felt the same closeness to Sister Helen that she shared with many of the other sisters. Sister Helen seemed to take pleasure in catching the younger sisters in some wrong, and while she had not found reason to take Gabrielle to task for any wrongs, she did take every opportunity to remind Gabrielle that outward beauty was more curse than blessing. A curse Sister Helen claimed to be glad she did not have to overcome.

Just then Nathan moved on the bed and coughed. He moved his mouth and whispered something.

"What does he say?" the doctor asked.

Again Sister Helen's sharp eyes pierced the dim light to stab at Gabrielle. "He calls the young sister's name."

"Then answer him, girl," the doctor said. "If this boy lives through the night, it's going to take more than my doctoring or your people's prayers. He's going to have to want to live. Desperately."

Gabrielle put down the candle and knelt on the floor beside Nathan's head. "I am here, Brother Nathan."

He turned his face toward her and slowly opened his eyes. They were dark with pain. She wanted to lay her hand on his cheek, but Sister Helen was watching her closely. "A doctor is here to help you," Gabrielle told him.

"The fire!" His face twisted as the terror of the fire returned to his mind. "I couldn't get out. I thought I'd died and was in hell." He began coughing and gasping for air again.

"Shh, Nathan," she said as his coughing eased. "Ye are safe now out of the fire. Just lie still."

His eyes clung to hers. "Promise you won't leave me, Gabrielle. Stay here and pray for me. The Eternal Father will listen to your prayers."

"As he listens to all who pray, but I promise. I will pray for thy healing."

His eyes went away from her back to his pain. He moaned and lapsed into unconsciousness again.

Tears wet Gabrielle's cheeks, but she made no move to brush them away. She closed her eyes and shut out all the sounds around her as she concentrated on the pleas she made to the Eternal Father for Nathan. When she finally looked up again, she and the doctor were alone with Nathan. The man's eyes were watching her intently.

When Gabrielle glanced swiftly around the room to see where Sister Helen might be, the doctor said, "I sent the other sister for some medicines."

Gabrielle lowered her eyes and remained silent. It was

unheard of to be alone with a person of the opposite sex. Especially a stranger from the world.

"Is it wrong for you to look at me, young sister? Or talk to me?"

Gabrielle's eyes came up to meet his. The gentleness there surprised her. "I fear it is surely against the rules."

"You Shakers have many rules from what I've seen," the doctor said with a frown. "How long have you been in the village?"

"Six years. My mother and I were among the first group to come together in 1806."

The doctor motioned toward Nathan. "You care deeply for the boy."

"I love him as I love all the brothers and sisters in our community," Gabrielle said.

The doctor smiled a bit. "But not so much like a brother as some of the others, I dare say."

Gabrielle met his look. "Nay, rather more like a brother than some of the others. Nathan and his family were among the first converts after our village was founded. He's the brother I always wished for but never had before joining the Believers."

"And does he love you as a sister?" the doctor asked, his smile a bit wider.

"I so wish it, but I cannot know another's thoughts."

The doctor's eyes darkened as they narrowed thoughtfully. "But you can know other things."

"I know not what you mean, sir." Gabrielle felt a twinge of guilt for her lie.

"Your eyes won't let you tell even that much of a falsehood, young sister. You knew exactly where the boy was in the barn. But how?"

18

Gabrielle hesitated, but the doctor kept looking at her, waiting for her to explain the unexplainable. So she said, "It's hard to put into words for others to understand. Sometimes I have a feeling for things, and I see what is happening in my mind even though I am not there to actually see it with my eyes. I just know what is happening or will happen. Sister Mercy calls it a gift from the spirits and says I should be thankful to be so blessed."

"But you don't always feel blessed?" the doctor said.

Gabrielle tried to suppress the shiver that ran through her as she admitted, "Often it feels more a curse than a blessing. This seeing things I should not be able to see. There are evil spirits as well as good spirits."

"I don't think an evil spirit could ever touch you, Gabrielle," the doctor said softly.

Gabrielle dropped her eyes to her hands and was silent. As soon as Nathan was better, she would have to confess this conversation to Sister Mercy for it was surely a sin of worldliness.

The doctor reached out his hand and raised her chin until once more she was staring into his dark eyes. "You have done no wrong, young sister." He looked at her for a long moment before saying, "Your eyes are the purest blue I've ever seen."

"To rejoice in the color of one's eyes is a vanity," Gabrielle whispered as she drew her head back away from his touch. His fingers on her skin had pulsed with life.

He smiled again. "I frighten you, don't I, young sister?"

Gabrielle didn't answer. She wasn't sure she was frightened exactly, but his presence and his voice were very definitely disturbing her inner calm.

"You're not the first to find me frightening," the doctor

went on. "But I wouldn't doubt that you're the most innocent to cross my path for a long time. Do you know what some of my patients call me?"

Gabrielle shook her head. She couldn't pull her eyes away from his, even though she knew she should.

"Devil doctor." His laugh was short and rough. "Maybe so, but at least they're alive to call me that." He motioned toward the boy on the bed. "This one here may be saying the same, but with any luck at all he'll live to say it."

"I'll pray that it be so." Gabrielle turned her eyes from his at last.

Still she felt his eyes probing her, and she was almost glad when Nathan cried out in pain to distract his attention from her. The doctor spoke a few soft words to quiet Nathan and then held his legs gently to keep him from injuring them more as he moved. He muttered, "What's taking that woman so long to bring the medicines?"

Sister Helen entered the room without a sound and put the bag of medicines he'd requested on the table by the bed. She made no attempt to keep the contempt out of her voice as she said, "Indian cures."

Dr. Scott's laugh was again short. "Don't worry, Sister. I won't be saying any spells or chants over the boy. Nor even performing a dance to the Indian spirits." For a moment he was silent as he began mixing the medicines and applying them very gently to Nathan's burns. Then Gabrielle saw his smile sneak back before he said, "But I doubt they'd be much different than the ones I've heard you do here at your meetinghouse."

Sister Helen drew in her breath with a sharp hiss. "Brother

Caleb should have told you to leave at once. Those of the world have no place among us."

Gabrielle's eyes sought out the doctor's quickly. She knew nothing of this man, but yet she felt that if anyone could help Nathan, he could.

The doctor met her look. "Don't worry, young sister. I won't leave the boy until he's better or he's gone on to meet his Maker. I may be a coldhearted brute, but I take care of my patients." He turned to Sister Helen and said, "Get the boy some water, Sister. Tomorrow you can chase me from your village, but tonight we're going to work together to keep this boy among the living."

Sister Helen sniffed loudly, but she did what she was told. Gabrielle hid a small smile and thought the doctor wasn't coldhearted at all. She slipped to her knees to thank the Eternal Father for sending such a man to help Nathan.

2

The night passed slowly while a dark shadow seemed to linger over Nathan as he struggled to cling to life. Elder Caleb came in to pray with them. Then he touched Gabrielle's shoulder and said, "If it be God's will, our brother shall live. But if not and it is time for him to go on to the other side, he can go rejoicing that Mother Ann is there to prepare a place for him."

He meant the words as a comfort, but Gabrielle couldn't accept them. She saw the very dearness of life as Nathan fought to stay among them. "He is too young to die," she protested.

Elder Caleb showed no disapproval of her words. He only said, "The Eternal Father calls home the young as well as the old."

Dr. Scott looked up from changing the cooling compresses on Nathan's burns. "Don't give up on the boy yet. He's a tough one or he'd already be dead. He's fought this long. I won't let him die now even if I have to cut off his legs."

Elder Caleb's brow wrinkled in a slight frown. "You may

treat him, Dr. Scott, but you are only a man. God will decide if our brother lives or dies."

"Which god is that?" the doctor asked. "The one you believe lived in your Mother Ann's body?"

Sister Helen stared at the doctor with burning contempt, but Elder Caleb remained calm as ever. "We do not ask that those from the world believe. Only that they allow us the peace to believe ourselves."

"And not burn down our barns," Sister Helen added.

"I grant you're well within your rights there," Dr. Scott said. "Those who set fires should suffer the results instead of the innocent like this boy."

By morning the lines of strain between the doctor's eyes were easing. Nathan's breathing was once more regular and strong in spite of the moans that often worked out of his lips. Dr. Scott dosed him with something to make him sleep. "Sleep is the best thing for him now. His body needs a chance to heal."

The doctor leaned back and looked at the others in the room. "Sister Helen, I thank you for your help. You and the young sister can go rest. I can care for the boy now."

"I will stay with you yet a little longer," Elder Caleb said.

Gabrielle looked at Nathan and rose from his side. All night she had knelt by him, praying for him as he had asked. She turned to Elder Caleb. "May I come back to see how he is later?"

Elder Caleb's brow wrinkled with concern as he stared at her for a long moment before he gave his permission.

"Before you go, young sister, could you bring me some fresh water?" the doctor asked.

Gabrielle took the piggin and went out. When she started to

lift the full pail of water, pain shot from her hand up through her arm. She put the piggin down and looked at her hand. Her palm was an angry red. For a moment she was puzzled, but then she remembered beating out the flames on Nathan's legs with her neck scarf. Suddenly she was ashamed to be worrying about such a small pain after what Nathan had suffered. She picked up the piggin and carried it back to the cabin.

When she set the water down on the table, pain shot up her arm from her hand. She turned quickly, but not before the doctor saw her wince.

"What is it, young sister?" he asked.

"Nothing. If there's anything more you need, you may ring the bell on the table." Gabrielle moved toward the door.

"Let me see your hands, young sister," the doctor commanded.

Gabrielle turned around slowly. Elder Caleb looked at her and said, "If you have injured yourself, let the doctor treat you, my child. It is for the good of all that we stay well and healthy."

Gabrielle held out her hands without a word. The doctor took hold of her wrists and led her over to the window. "Why didn't you tell me that you had burnt your hand, young sister?" He frowned as though her pain made him angry.

"It is nothing," Gabrielle said again. "I only noticed it a moment ago myself when I picked up the piggin of water. It's such a small thing next to Brother Nathan's burns."

The doctor's eyes came up from her hands to touch her eyes. "Your suffering won't lessen his."

Gabrielle lowered her eyes and stood quietly while the doctor soaked a cloth in the medicine he'd been putting on Nathan. Then he wrapped the cloth loosely about her right hand. "This will be a terrible nuisance if you try to use your hand, but by tomorrow the medicine should have taken the fire from your skin."

"Thank you, Doctor," Gabrielle said, but she kept her eyes from his. The presence of Elder Caleb made her even more aware of the warmth of the doctor's hands on her skin.

"Come back in the morning so I can examine your hand to be sure the medicine is working." His hands seemed to linger on hers.

The bell for the morning meal rang out through the village. Elder Caleb said, "You may go now, Sister Gabrielle. When you get to the biting room, please tell one of the sisters in the kitchen to send food here for Dr. Scott."

"Yea, Elder Caleb," Gabrielle said before she hurried out of the cabin. She stopped by the kitchen and gave the sister in charge the elder's message. Then she went on to her room. She couldn't go to eat in her grimy clothes. Her scarf was scorched and ruined by the fire, and her hair straggled out from under Sister Mercy's too-small cap. She passed several of the sisters and brothers on their way to the biting room, but there was no talk between them. Nor did any speak to her in passing, though here and there eyes sought her out with a curious look.

The house was empty when she entered. Gabrielle found her extra set of clothes and began cleaning up. She wanted nothing more than to sink down on her bed to rest, but she couldn't. The school bell would ring soon, and she had to be ready to teach her small charges.

Gabrielle was only nineteen, but she had an ease for learning. Her earliest memory was of her grandmother holding a sack and pointing out the word *flour* to her. Her father and grandmother had run a store then. Gabrielle smiled at the memory of that happy time. She had followed her father around and even found the customers what they needed when he was busy.

Her grandmother had said she was ahead of her years, a special child who should be nurtured and taught everything until her curiosity was finally satiated. So her grandmother had taught her, her father had laughed with her, and even her mother, if she hadn't been happy, neither had she been especially unhappy.

Then the baby brother had died moments after coming into the world. Her beloved grandmother succumbed to a fever a few months later, and everything changed. Her father would disappear for days at a time. When he did come home, he smelled of strong drink and was full of talk of a new life, a better life across the mountains. Her mother cried and yelled and threw pots, but in the end she had little choice but to follow her husband to a place called Kentucky.

In Kentucky, Gabrielle had found a new teacher in her mother's uncle who had helped them get settled in the frontier state. Uncle Jonas, a respected lawyer and judge in the state, had never married and had little patience with children, but when he saw the quickness of Gabrielle's mind, he undertook the task of filling it with the proper education in spite of the fact he thought such knowledge would surely be wasted on a female.

After only one summer in Kentucky, Gabrielle's father had gone away again. Before the snows of winter came, they received word of his death on a Mississippi riverboat. She and her mother had no choice but to move in with Uncle Jonas. He was a cold, strict taskmaster who scorned even the smallest mistake, so Gabrielle did her best to be perfect.

Thus when she and her mother had joined the Believers, Gabrielle at thirteen was already better educated than most of the adults in the church family. Now as Gabrielle twisted her hair into a knot to stick up under her clean cap, she thought about the last time she'd seen Uncle Jonas. When they'd gone into his study to tell him they were leaving, he had turned from his desk and stared at her mother.

"I always knew you were a weak-willed, foolish woman, Martha," he'd said with no feeling at all to his voice. "Else you would have never married such a ne'er-do-well as Alec Hope." He turned back to the books in front of him. "Go then and cloister yourself among these peculiar people with their shaking dances and odd tenets if that be your desire. Outside of childbearing, what use are women to the world anyway?"

Gabrielle wondered again as she had then if her mother had really believed as the Shakers did or if she had simply been desperate to get away from Uncle Jonas, for if he was cold to Gabrielle, he was a tyrant to her mother. Whatever the reason for their coming into the community of Believers, her mother embraced the Believers' way fully and had found a measure of happiness she'd never known anywhere else.

And Gabrielle was satisfied with her life at Harmony Hill as well. The move had been good for both of them. Gabrielle had molded her life in accordance with the rules and found it easy to love her brethren and sisters as the elders and eldresses taught. She especially loved teaching the little girls, some she'd had in class now for three years.

She looked in the small mirror as she adjusted her scarf clumsily with her bandaged hand. Nay, she had never doubted her life as a Believer. She met her eyes in the mirror and knew there was no reason to lie to herself. Instead she could only wonder why there were questions and doubts this morning where none had ever been before.

Sister Mercy knocked softly on the sleeping room's door and called Gabrielle's name. Gabrielle turned away from the mirror. She would talk to Sister Mercy before she went to the schoolroom. Sins only multiplied and darkened one's soul if hidden and not confessed.

"Sister Mercy," Gabrielle said as she opened the door. "Do you have a few minutes to talk with me?"

Sister Mercy inclined her head and without a word led the way to a small room with only two chairs and a table. Sister Mercy sat in one of the small straight chairs, and Gabrielle dropped to her knees beside her. Sister Mercy touched Gabrielle's head lightly. "Ye may sit in the chair, Sister Gabrielle."

Gabrielle got off her knees, but after she sat down the words wouldn't come. She didn't know what to say that Sister Mercy might understand. Sister Mercy had been like a mother to her ever since they'd come together at Harmony Hill. She was a small, neat woman who never seemed to have so much as a thought out of place. She moved calmly and surely through each of her duties with a quick, youthful ease even though she was past her middle years.

Sister Mercy had joined the New Lebanon Society of Believers in New York more than thirty years ago without the sin of marriage to cleanse from her spirit. When the western colonies were formed, she volunteered to come help with the ministry and leadership. She found her place of service with the children who were gathered into their family, loving them while at the same time demanding they learn and abide by the rules of the Believers. The eternal salvation and the souls of the children in her charge were at stake.

She often spoke to Gabrielle of her need to grow in pureness of spirit and intelligence so that perhaps someday Gabrielle could take a leadership role in the Society of Believers. But now she looked troubled as she asked, "What is it, my child?"

"You knew I stayed with Brother Nathan through the night."

Sister Mercy bent her head forward slightly. "Under the circumstances, that was the good and proper thing to do."

"He said he thought he had died and gone to hell."

"Brother Nathan is often a careless boy and too obstinate to accept the truth. Perhaps his guilt brought forth the thought."

Gabrielle was stricken by her words. "Nay," she said. "Surely it was the fire that made him have such thoughts. And the pain. His pain is terrible to see."

Sister Mercy reached over and patted Gabrielle's hand. "I didn't mean to upset you, child. It is possible you are right. Is he better now?"

"I think so. Dr. Scott put something on his legs to bring the fire out."

"Ah, Dr. Scott. I have heard of him. He lives near here, does he not?"

"I have heard he does. I suppose that is why he was here. He must have seen the flames." Gabrielle took a deep breath and pushed out her next words all in a bunch. "I was alone with him."

Sister Mercy spoke calmly. "I knew it to be so."

Gabrielle looked at her in surprise, but then she understood. "Sister Helen has already been to you."

"She thought I should know."

"She doesn't like me."

Sister Mercy smiled. "But of course she does, child. Ye are sisters."

"Yea," Gabrielle answered, but she remembered the look in Sister Helen's eyes the night before.

"It was only her concern for you that brought her to me. She said Dr. Scott forced her to leave you alone with him, and she was fearful of what might have happened after she left. She thought him a worldly man with no honor."

Gabrielle defended him at once. "Nay, she is wrong. He is surely a good, kind man who worked a near miracle to keep Nathan alive through the night."

Sister Mercy's voice was reproving. "If there was a miracle, it was of the Lord's or Mother Ann's doing and none of Dr. Scott's."

"Yea, of course you are right, Sister Mercy. But he did care for Brother Nathan gently and with great care and concern."

Sister Mercy studied her face for a long moment before saying, "But, child, why did you want to talk to me? Have you some sin to confess? Did the man hurt you in any way?"

"He troubled my mind, Sister Mercy, and I don't understand the reason for it."

Sister Mercy let out a small sigh of relief. "You needn't worry, Sister Gabrielle. Those of the world often trouble the true believer. They have no understanding of the peace we have here. The peace that you have so abundantly, my child. The shadow he has cast over your mind will evaporate like mist in the morning sun if you remember how the Eternal Father has so gifted you with love here among us." She smiled at Gabrielle and waited a minute before she asked, "So is that all?"

Suddenly Gabrielle couldn't tell her any more. She couldn't tell her how the doctor's fingers lifting her chin had warmed her whole being. She could only beg the Eternal Father's forgiveness for such wayward thoughts in silence. Gabrielle lowered her eyes to her hands and said, "Yea."

"Then you needn't see him again. That way his worldliness cannot trouble you more."

"But I must go see Brother Nathan again," Gabrielle said and then held up her bandaged hand. "And the doctor said I should go to him in the morning to let him treat my hand again. It seems I suffered a slight burn when I helped smother the flames on Brother Nathan's legs."

Sister Mercy was deep in thought for a long time before she finally said, "Very well. Your hand needs to be treated for the good of all. I shall go with you in the morning to shield you from his worldliness. He has not the proper respect for our beliefs."

"Yea," Gabrielle said quietly.

Sister Mercy reached over and touched Gabrielle's hands again. "You see, my child, the Believers have joined together in a family as a separate society from the world where all reasons for sin are removed from our lives. Everyone works for the good of all and without the strife of the individual marriage and family. But when someone comes among us from the world he brings evil thoughts and ideas with him. That evil can touch and disturb our inner calm. But it is just a momentary thing. Nothing a true Believer needs worry about. The stranger will soon go back to the world and his disrupting influence will leave with him."

Gabrielle lowered her eyes and said, "Yea, it will surely be so."

"It will," Sister Mercy said. "Now let us pray quickly before the morning duties begin."

"What shall I pray, Sister Mercy?"

"That the doctor's worldliness has left no stain upon you."

"And for Brother Nathan's recovery? Surely that is a proper prayer this morning."

"Yea. For Brother Nathan's recovery and for his true acceptance of the Believers' way."

Later as she listened to her youngsters reciting their spelling lessons, Gabrielle felt shame for not praying as Sister Mercy had directed her. Gabrielle didn't want this Dr. Scott to go away. Not yet. She had a great curiosity about him. She wanted to know what made him speak as he did and why he used cures others disdained. She wanted to understand the sad look that had crept into his eyes as he had looked at her the night before. And perhaps her largest reason for shame, she wanted to know more about the world he'd come from.

For more than five years she'd not thought much of the world at all. It was there beyond the border of their village, but she never thought to have any part of it again. But the doctor had pushed a new feeling into her mind. A feeling that would have to be fought.

She tightened her mouth and straightened her shoulders as she pushed all such whimsical thoughts of the world out of her mind. There would be no questions for Dr. Scott. She had put things of the world behind her, and it was best if she remembered that. The Believers' life was her life, and it was a good life.

Yet as her eyes fell on her bandaged hand, she couldn't deny the tingle of excitement that pushed through her at the thought of the doctor touching her hand again. His hands held a sort of magic. They looked big and strong like the hands of one who worked the earth, but at the same time they were gentle and soft to the wounded.

Her face warmed at the thought and then once again she felt shame. Such thoughts were surely a sin. Yet another sin she would be unable to confess to Sister Mercy.

She curled her fingers into a fist and was glad for the pain that took her mind away from the doctor.

3

Brice Scott sat by the boy all through the day, sometimes dozing in his chair but always rousing at once to dose the boy with more of the sleeping medicine whenever he moved or cried out. Then he would replace the compresses on the boy's burns. The ones on his arms and face would amount to little. In time the red might even fade from his skin. The burns on the boy's legs were different. He'd always carry the scars of them and perhaps even the pain. Still, Brice had hopes the boy might regain the use of his legs if he had a strong enough will. It would take courage for him to stand on his feet and walk again.

At least he'd live to have the chance. Not all who were burned so badly could hope for that. Brice frowned. He didn't want to think about little Amy Sue, but the sight of the boy's charred skin kept bringing up her memory. She'd been four when she'd caught her dress tail on fire, and she was the only one of his stepbrothers or sisters that Brice had any feelings for. Maybe that was because she was yet a baby when they brought him back from the Indians.

Brice hadn't been at the cabin the day she had been playing too near the fire while her mother washed their clothes. By that time he'd been plenty old enough to hire out to a neighbor. But they said she ran, and the flames wrapped her in a shroud of death before anyone could catch her to put them out. He got to her before she died, but there'd been many times when he wished he hadn't. He never forgot her face twisted in pain as she tried to reach for him to hold her.

He didn't stay for the burying. He walked out of the cabin and away. His father had died the year before, and his stepmother was ready to marry again. He had no reason to stay.

Being on his own had been hard at first, but Brice knew if he just kept pushing forward, doing whatever had to be done, the world would make room for him. His years with the Indians had taught him that. He'd lived with them for almost five years before a group of hunters had come into the Indian village and traded for him when he was twelve.

In the end, it had been the fever that had decided his future. He'd never been sick in his life, but suddenly one morning the grippe shook him with chills and burning flashes that threatened to eliminate all his problems of how he was going to live.

A settler was kind enough to take him in and send for the local doctor. As soon as Dr. Andrew Feeley walked through the door, Brice knew what he wanted to do with his life if he survived the fever. There was such an air of assurance and confidence about the little man as he put a cooling hand on Brice's brow and proceeded to bleed him quickly and capably. His very presence seemed as good as his treatment, and Brice wanted to be able to walk into a sickroom and make the air more hopeful just because he was there. He wanted to be able to do something besides watch when something happened as it had to little Amy Sue.

The boy on the bed moaned and brought Brice back to the Shakers' log cabin. The sleeping tonic was wearing off and the boy was trying to open his eyes. It was time to see if he was ready to face his future. Brice held a glass to the boy's lips to let the cold water trickle into his mouth.

The boy sputtered and coughed, but the water brought him fully awake. For a moment, confusion filled his eyes, but then his eyes touched Brice briefly as he searched the room.

Brice said gently, "She was here all through the night, son, but with the morning she had to leave."

Suspicion filled the boy's brown eyes as he spoke slowly and carefully. "Why do you think I was seeking someone?"

Brice smiled. "And you weren't?"

Again the boy looked around the room. "Are we alone?"

"We are," Brice said. "Elder Caleb was here, but he said he had work to do. Something about plans for a new barn."

A look of horror twisted the boy's face. "The fire. I didn't think I'd ever see another sunrise." He looked at Brice again. "Who are you?"

"Brice Scott. Dr. Brice Scott. And you're Nathan, but they didn't tell me your last name. Or do any of you people in this place have last names?"

Nathan's mouth turned up in a half smile. "Oh, we all have last names. We just don't use them much. Mine's Bates. Nathan Bates."

Brice sat back in his chair and studied the boy. "Well, Bates, what do you have to say for yourself?"

Nathan stared back at the doctor as if puzzled by his

36

question. Then instead of answering, he asked his own question. "Am I bad burnt?"

"You want to see?" Brice didn't wait for an answer. He pulled off the covering he'd laid over the boy's legs and helped him raise up to look.

Nathan sucked in a quick breath, but he didn't flinch away from the sight of the burns. After a moment, he said, "I guess it's no wonder I'm hurting some."

Brice was heartened by the boy's calm acceptance of the angry, oozing skin on his legs. "I'll give you another dose for the pain in a little bit," he told him.

"That's okay, Doc. It's not so bad I can't handle it." Nathan lay back on the bed and stared up at the ceiling for a long time before he spoke again. "You think I'll be able to do much walking anymore?"

"I'll be honest with you, Bates. It'll just be according to how much you want to."

"I'll want to. A lot. A Shaker that can't work doesn't make much of a Shaker." Nathan frowned. "Not that I plan to be a Shaker all that much longer."

"What do you plan to do?"

Nathan looked quickly around the room again before he lowered his voice. "I wouldn't want the others to know. At least not yet. But I'm not aiming to stay here much longer. I've been planning on leaving ever since my pa brought us over here and said we had to start being Shakers. I knew that very day this couldn't be no kind of place when they made me give up Jack."

"Jack?"

"My dog. Best hunting dog you'd ever want to see, but then

the Shakers don't hold much with dogs or hunting. Believe in growing what you need."

"Then why haven't you left already if that's what you want to do? You look old enough. What are you? Nineteen? Twenty?"

"I'm twenty, and I'll be leaving soon. I'd have left already except for Gabrielle." Nathan looked at the doctor quickly as if he'd told more than he intended on telling.

"Gabrielle?" Brice said. "That's the young sister who was here last night."

"So she really was here. I thought I saw her a time or two, but then I wasn't sure I might not be dreaming. Or just wishing I saw her."

"She was here." The boy's face lit up at Brice's words. "She has a beauty about her."

"She is beauty," Nathan said simply. "I'm going to marry her."

Brice kept his eyes on the boy. "I've heard Shakers don't hold with marriage."

"They don't hold with a lot of things."

"The young sister seems a devout Believer."

Nathan waved off Brice's words. "I'll make her see that it's better to be part of the world than here among the living dead."

"The living dead? I don't know that I'd call them that. They seem good enough people. Kind, gentle, industrious."

"But dead," Nathan insisted. "They even say they're dead to the world, and I aim to be part of the world."

Brice couldn't argue with him on that. A person couldn't shut out the problems of the world just by turning his back on it. He ought to know. He'd tried doing just that a time or two himself. He mixed some powders in a glass and held the boy's head while he drank it down. "You'd best be resting. The days ahead will be hard, Bates, and if you plan to walk you'll need to build up your strength."

Nathan swallowed the bitter liquid without complaint. "I'll walk, Dr. Scott. You don't need to worry about that," he said after Brice took away the cup.

The boy slowly relaxed as the medicine eased his pain. If Brice could keep the fever away, he'd make the boy get up tomorrow. Else his legs might tighten up too much to move. Even so, although it would be difficult, Brice didn't doubt the boy would do as he said and walk. His youth left little room for fear or he wouldn't have been in the burning barn to begin with.

"Gabrielle." Nathan called out the young sister's name in his sleep.

Brice frowned. He'd taken a liking to the boy while they talked. Now he couldn't keep from feeling a bit of pity for him, because in spite of the boy's cocky sureness, Brice doubted the young sister would go with him when he left the Shakers.

Brice stood up and went to look out the window. Not that the boy wouldn't go on living even without the girl. A man didn't die of a broken heart. Life had a way of edging on through the pain, and it would for the boy the same as it had for Brice.

Why today were all these things he'd put out of his mind coming back to haunt him? He hadn't thought about little Amy Sue for years, and he practiced not thinking about Jemma. At first not thinking of Jemma had been survival after he'd once again walked away from his life.

He should have said something to Dr. Feeley after all the

man had done for him. He not only took Brice in and apprenticed him to learn medicine; he let Brice wed his only daughter. A smile touched Brice's lips as he remembered those months of happiness with Jemma that lit up his life like sunlight reaching into a dark cave.

Jemma was special. If as the boy said, the young sister was beauty, then Jemma was joy. Everything was bright and fresh to her, and laughter lived in her sun-specked green eyes. Their love had been young and innocent, and Brice had thought it would never end. But a fever had crept up on Jemma. Each day her father had treated her, bleeding her to let out the sickness. Each day Brice had watched her grow weaker until the joy was gone from her eyes and face and nothing remained but a shell of the beautiful girl he loved.

He was beside her when she pulled in her last breath. He wanted to force his own breath into her, make her come back to him, but death kept its hold on her. After her hand grew stiff in his, he kissed her cold lips one last time and left without a word to Dr. or Mrs. Feeley. It wasn't right, but he couldn't bear seeing them put Jemma below the ground.

For a year he'd wandered without purpose except to keep going away from his grief. Then one day he found himself in Philadelphia in front of a school of medicine and knew the desire to be a doctor had not left him.

With a quick shake of his head, Brice turned away from the winter's early twilight and his thoughts. It did no good to dwell on the past. It couldn't be changed no matter how many times a man wished it differently.

He stood over the boy and listened to his steady breathing. Brice would do as he'd done since he started back on the road to being a doctor. He'd take on his patient's pains and push away his own. And this boy would have plenty enough to share.

Brice yawned and stretched back his arms. He hadn't been out of the room all day, and he felt confined. He was used to walking in the woods around his cabin every evening to gather roots and let the air clear his mind.

With a quick look at the boy, Brice stepped out into the cool air. He waited on the step when he saw Elder Caleb and another man approaching the cabin.

"We've brought your evening meal, Dr. Scott," Elder Caleb said.

The thought of food made Brice's stomach growl, but he needed to stretch his legs more. "Thank you, Elder. I'll eat it later, but now I wonder if you or one of the others here could sit with the boy while I work up a little appetite with a walk."

Elder Caleb's eyes were understanding. "Of course. I should have sent someone over to relieve you hours ago, but there were so few hands and so much to do."

"That's all right. I wouldn't have wanted to leave the boy before now anyway. But he seems a bit better this evening. When he wakes again, he'll need some thin gruel to eat to begin building his strength."

"Very well. I'll send Brother Matthias to see to it at once."

Brice started to move away, but the elder's voice stopped him. "I must ask you to remember that you are a visitor in our village, Dr. Scott. You are not to disturb any of the sisters or brothers. We have rules of behavior that we expect you to respect as long as you're here."

Brice turned around. In spite of the elder's soft, even tone, Brice heard the warning in his voice. "What do you mean?"

he asked. Brice had never liked to talk in circles. Whatever the man was trying to tell him, Brice wanted it straight out and clear before him.

The elder continued calmly. "We ask not that ye believe as we do. Only that you not defame us while you are among us."

Brice remembered comparing the Shakers' dances with the Indians' the night before. He held back a smile as he said, "I apologize if I upset Sister Helen with my words."

"Your words and behavior were disturbing to Sister Helen." Elder Caleb watched him for a long moment before adding, "And to young Sister Gabrielle. Sister Helen tells me you were alone with Sister Gabrielle."

"No harm came to her from me." Irritation rose inside Brice. The man was chastising him as if he were a child.

"That may be. Even so, I must ask you not to let this happen again, or I will have to insist you leave our community and not return."

Brice clamped down on his irritation. "As you say, Elder. But I won't leave my patient until I know he's going to be all right. Only then will I go."

Elder Caleb inclined his head in a nod. "I think we understand one another, Dr. Scott. I trust you to be an honorable man." He turned away from Brice and went into the cabin.

Brice walked briskly away through the cluster of buildings. He passed several people as they went along the paths quietly with their eyes averted from his. What an odd bunch they all were with the men in their plain dark suits and the women so alike in their blue or brown dresses with the large white scarves crossed over their bosoms. All the women wore long winter capes and some sort of cap on their heads. It was funny how the covering of their hair took away the beauty of so many of the women.

Then to remove themselves from the world as if they thought that would keep them from sin. Brice shook his head. Sin would surely be harder to get away from than that.

Brice had heard all manner of stories about the Shakers since he'd settled in Mercer County a little over a year ago. Some swore they worshiped the devil in sexual orgies, and another man had told him a wild story about the Shakers killing babies. But the Shakers endured the ridicule and faced down the unfounded rumors with a quiet strength that had earned Brice's respect. He'd made it plain to his patients he'd listen to no more tales about the Shakers.

Still they were odd. Different from other men who'd walked some of the same paths. Brice almost laughed at his thought. Who was he to be condemning a person for being different? It was a charge he faced often enough himself. He walked his own path, a path that frequently led away from all others. He refused to bleed a patient for any reason, though he knew some of his patients called in another doctor who was freer with the lancet as soon as he was gone. Some things he just felt were wrong with medicine as it was commonly practiced, and so he found his own ways, his own cures. If that made him different, so be it as long as his patients lived to talk about his odd ways.

He'd walked a little ways into the woods around the village, barely noticing where his steps were leading him. It was almost dark and he was about to turn back to the cabin and his supper when he caught the flash of something white in front of him through the trees. Surely the townspeople hadn't come back to torment these gentle people again so soon.

Walking silently as he'd learned to do while with the Indians, he inched forward. When he realized it was one of the sisters' caps he'd seen, he stopped. For a minute he thought perhaps he'd caught a couple meeting out of the elders' sight, and he started to turn away. Then he saw the sister was alone, and his curiosity was aroused. Without moving he watched the woman kneeling in a position of prayer. All at once he felt like an intruder on a very private, even sacred scene. He wanted to slip away, but instead he stood stock-still for fear the woman might hear him and be startled.

After a moment she stood up, and he caught sight of the white rag around her hand. It was the young sister. She glanced over her shoulder as if she sensed him there, but he edged behind a tree out of her sight. She hurried through the trees and was gone.

He wanted to call out to her, to walk with her, but he'd promised the elder he wouldn't disturb her again. He'd keep his word even if he did feel drawn to the girl. There was such a purity about her and yet a mystery too. Something fluttered to life inside him that he thought dead forever. Nonsense, he told himself harshly. She was little more than a child. But when he came out of the trees, he turned and fixed the spot in his mind before he walked swiftly back to the cabin where the boy lay.

4

Gabrielle almost ran through the thickening darkness out of the woods and back to her house. She hung her wrap on one of the wooden pegs in the entry room and joined several younger sisters as they climbed up to their family meeting room for their nightly prayer service. Another few minutes and she'd have been late, and her absence noted. But it wasn't her worry of being late that had bothered her. Sister Mercy knew of Gabrielle's need to pray in absolute privacy, and she'd never spoken against it.

It was the feeling she hadn't been alone among the trees that had sent her rushing through the night. She usually prayed earlier in the day while the sun was bright, but when she'd been too busy at midday, she went on to her secret place of prayer after the evening meal even though darkness had been falling. She'd never been afraid of the dark anyway. She wasn't afraid of the dark now, only of the unknown presence she'd felt there with her in the woods.

Her prayers had been for Nathan. All day she'd longed to go see for herself how he was faring, but she hadn't asked permission, sensing Sister Mercy wouldn't approve. She didn't want to make the frown come back into Sister Mercy's eyes when she looked at Gabrielle.

After the meeting was over, Gabrielle helped the little sisters get ready for bed. The younger ones and those new to the Believers often needed an extra kind word and Gabrielle went from one bed to another with a kiss and a soft good night for the girls.

The older girls settled down to sleep at once, for they knew there would be no time for rest on the morrow any more than there had been time for rest on that day. All the children had chores besides their schoolwork. The children were taught to put their hands to work early in life.

Gabrielle blew out the last candle in the large bedroom and quietly slipped off her shoes to ready herself for bed. Around her, the children's bed coverings rustled as her little sisters settled into sleep.

There were four bedrooms like this in the house. Two on the other side for the young boys, and another here for the girls where Sister Mercy slept. The very young children slept in the nursery with other sisters to care for them.

Gabrielle was ready to lie down when she heard the soft whimpers. She tiptoed over to little Becca's bed. Ever since Becca and her parents had joined the Believers back in the fall, Gabrielle had been trying to help the child grow accustomed to her new way of life. Tiny for a child of seven, Becca had a small, round face that almost sparkled when she smiled, but that smile came rarely. Every night since she'd been there she had cried herself to sleep.

At first she'd wailed fiercely, determined somehow to make her mother appear by her bedside. Her cries had pierced

Gabrielle. She had wanted to run for Becca's mother, but Sister Mercy wouldn't allow it.

"The child will bend herself to our ways and be better for it," she'd said. "She will soon tire of making so much racket."

Becca had stopped screaming before the week was out, but she hadn't stopped crying. Her weeping had just become a quiet study of misery. Gabrielle tried to lift some of that misery from Becca's heart by holding the little girl every night until she was too tired to cry more.

Now she touched the child's shoulder and said, "Shh, Becca. It's all right."

Becca moved toward her hand, and Gabrielle gathered her up into her arms, sat on the edge of the bed, and rocked her back and forth while she whispered soothing sounds. "I'm here, Becca. Please don't cry."

The little girl lay quietly in her arms for a moment before she said, "You're nice, 'Brielle, but I want my mama. Why can't I be with Mama instead of here? I promise to be very, very good."

"I know, baby, but this is the way the elders and eldresses have decided is best. In time you will grow used to it, little one. Perhaps you will even come to like our ways as I do."

Becca tried to hold back her tears, but little sobs shook her body. These quiet tears tore at Gabrielle's heart even more than the child's earlier screams. She smoothed down the little girl's hair and kissed the top of her head. "You see your mother when she comes down to the school to visit you." Becca's mother came so often that Gabrielle was sure she didn't always have permission but simply slipped away from her assigned chores to see her child.

"But at our house, Mama always rocked me and sang to

47

me and let me comb her hair at night. Even Papa sometimes sang with us before he started going to the meetings every night. Mama said that's why he changed. Why everything changed." The little girl lowered her head and sighed. "Oh, 'Brielle, why did everything have to change?"

"Shh, sweet child." Gabrielle held her tighter for a moment as she tried to ease her pain. "It's a good life here, Becca. We have love among us all instead of just among each small family." She didn't expect the child to understand. She was too young, and her pain too sharp.

"Didn't you miss your mama when you came, 'Brielle?"

Gabrielle smiled. "I was older and accustomed to a different sort of home than you, dear one." Gabrielle laid the little girl back on her bed and kissed her cheek. "Now you go to sleep, Becca. Your mother will be sure to come see you tomorrow since she didn't come today. She loves you very much, you know." She tucked the covers around Becca's small form. "You wouldn't want her to see you with red eyes from crying all night."

"Mama's eyes were red last time she came. Do you think she cries herself to sleep too?"

Gabrielle hesitated before she answered, because in fact she was sure Becca's mother did cry herself to sleep every night. Each time she saw Sister Esther, the lines were etched deeper in the woman's face and she carried a frantic look in her eyes. The mother wasn't taking to the Believer's life any better than the child. But Gabrielle couldn't lie to the child or ignore her question. She had to answer. "Some parts of the Believers' life are hard for some to accept."

"Do you think Mama is crying now?"

"I don't know, Becca, but I'm sure she wouldn't want you to worry about her. She wants you to be happy."

"That's so hard, 'Brielle."

"It won't always be hard, Becca." The child's words touched Gabrielle and brought tears to her own eyes. "Now lie still and pretend you're floating on soft white clouds in a summer sky."

Gabrielle knelt by the child's bed and stroked her back until the little girl finally fell asleep. Only then did Gabrielle rise to her feet to go back to her own bed. Her bones ached with weariness. Yet sleep eluded her even after she lay down. She couldn't stop worrying over Becca.

Becca and her mother didn't belong with the Believers. During the years since they'd come together at Harmony Hill, Gabrielle had seen many like them. They just couldn't bend their lives to fit the Shaker molds no matter how they tried. Many left the community after a few months. Others stayed longer, but nearly all left sooner or later. Sister Esther would find a way to leave in time as well.

It had been different for Gabrielle and her own mother. Gabrielle had always been able to adjust easily to the changes in her life. When she was young, her father had come and gone in her life when it suited his pleasure, and each time Gabrielle had welcomed him without mourning him when he left. Even after the trek to the strange Kentucky country, Gabrielle found it easy to settle into her new life. She missed her grandmother who had loved her so much in Virginia, but that part of her life was over. Her grandmother had died and their Virginia life died with her.

A new life in Kentucky began. So it was when they joined the Believers. For a while it was odd to see her mother only at meetings or when they shared a work detail, but soon it seemed only right that she be parted from her and call her Sister Martha.

With the Believers, Gabrielle's mother blossomed and was filled with a peace she'd never known before. Sister Martha was one of the most devout of the Believers and sometimes at meetings was gifted with a whirling exercise. The first time her mother had broken from the group of dancers and whirled alone around the room, Gabrielle had watched with amazement. Her mother had always been careful to do nothing to bring attention in their old life. But the look of joy on her mother's face when she finally fell exhausted to the floor assured Gabrielle that whatever change had come over her mother while among the Believers was good.

Gabrielle shut her eyes and listened to the light, steady breathing of the young sisters around her. For a minute Nathan came to her mind, and she whispered yet another prayer for him. Tomorrow she could go see if he was better, but now she needed to sleep.

The next morning after the morning meal, Sister Mercy went with Gabrielle to the visitor's cabin. As they walked along the path, Sister Mercy said, "I'm not at all sure this trip is necessary, Sister Gabrielle. Surely you could have removed the bandage yourself."

"I suppose so, Sister Mercy. But it cannot hurt for us to see how Brother Nathan is, can it?"

"Brother Nathan is young and strong. I'm sure he will mend quickly."

"I pray so," Gabrielle said quietly.

Sister Mercy's knuckles had barely tapped against the door before the doctor swung the door open. Gabrielle kept her eyes on the ground, but she could feel the doctor's eyes upon her. She peeked over at Sister Mercy. The woman was staring at the doctor while her frown grew deeper.

The doctor said, "So you've come to let me tend to your hand, young sister. I wasn't sure you would."

Gabrielle looked up and met his eyes for a brief second before she looked quickly away at a spot on the wall behind him. His eyes seemed to demand some sort of answers from her to questions she didn't know. His nearness disturbed her even more with Sister Mercy beside her. Gabrielle said, "This is Sister Mercy, Dr. Scott."

Sister Mercy stared at the doctor. "You're younger than I thought you would be, Dr. Scott. I felt assured a man of medicine would of necessity be older."

"I apprenticed with a doctor at a young age before I attended a medical school in Philadelphia," the doctor said.

"I was not questioning your qualifications."

Gabrielle's throat tightened at the sound of disapproval in Sister Mercy's voice. She wouldn't have been surprised if Sister Mercy had stepped in front of her and barred her way into the cabin. Before that could happen, Gabrielle slipped past the doctor to Nathan's side. His eyes were closed and his skin so pale that the red of the burns on his cheeks stood out angrily.

"Brother Nathan," she whispered. When he didn't respond, she looked up at the doctor, who had followed her to the bed. "Is he all right?" she asked.

"You needn't look so worried, young sister. I think your brother is going to live."

"Praise the Lord," Gabrielle whispered as she looked down at Nathan with relief.

"He's not past the need of your prayers," the doctor said as Gabrielle looked up at him again. "The days ahead of him are going to be hard, at times near to impossible and filled with pain."

"Of course I'll continue to pray for him," Gabrielle said softly. "As all of us will."

The doctor reached past her to gently shake Nathan's shoulder. "Wake up, boy. You have a visitor."

Nathan slowly opened his eyes. "Gabrielle."

Gabrielle spoke quickly before he could say more. Nathan often said things Sister Mercy surely wouldn't approve. "Sister Mercy and I have come to see how you are, Brother Nathan."

Nathan's eyes touched on Sister Mercy for a moment before they came back to rest on Gabrielle's face. "That was good of you. Both of you."

"How are you feeling?" Gabrielle asked. "Is the pain too intense?"

"Nay, nothing I cannot handle. The good doctor here says I'm on the mend."

The doctor laughed. "You'll be calling me everything but good before the month is gone, Bates."

"Month?" Sister Mercy's voice was cool. "Then you will be among us for a good while, Dr. Scott?"

"A few more days," the doctor said. "Then I'll be getting on back to my cabin to see to my other patients, but I'll be coming by to check on the boy as often as I can. At least until he's able to come to my cabin for treatment."

"Some of our number are skilled in healing. They could take over Brother Nathan's treatment," Sister Mercy said.

"Are they doctors?" Dr. Scott asked.

"They do not call themselves such," Sister Mercy admitted. "But we manage well enough without the help of doctors from the world."

"I'm sure you do," Dr. Scott said. "And with most injuries that would be fine, perhaps even preferable, but the boy's burns need special care. Especially if he is to walk again." The doctor paused a moment as he looked at Nathan, then Gabrielle, and last of all Sister Mercy. When he spoke again his voice was soft with all the anger gone from it. "You needn't worry about me, Sister Mercy. I have promised Elder Caleb to abide by your Shaker rules and do nothing to upset any of you while I'm here."

"That is good to hear," Sister Mercy said, but her frown did not go away.

Gabrielle touched Nathan's hand and stood up quickly. She held her bandaged hand out toward the doctor and said, "If you could see to this now, please, I must be getting to the schoolroom to begin the little sisters' lessons."

"Come over to the window," the doctor said.

Gabrielle followed him to the light and stood still as he began unwrapping the bandage from her hand. She fought against letting his touch disturb her, but she could feel her cheeks warming. If only Sister Mercy wasn't watching her so intently.

"It's better," the doctor said as he peered down at her hand. "But not well. Burns are often slow to heal." He wrapped her hand in a fresh cloth. "Don't get this wet, and come back in the morning."

"Is that really necessary, Dr. Scott?" Sister Mercy said. "It's inconvenient for Sister Gabrielle and myself to come to the visitor's cabin at this time of the day."

The doctor looked over at Sister Mercy. "Then come at noon. It won't make that much difference."

Sister Mercy's mouth tightened. "Give me the medicine, and I will see that her hand is treated in the morning."

Gabrielle kept her eyes on her hand. She couldn't understand Sister Mercy's reluctance to let the doctor treat her hand. Surely the sister couldn't guess how the blood was pumping through her wrist the doctor was holding as if she'd been running in a race. The doctor no doubt could feel it, and it was all Gabrielle could do to keep standing there and not yank her hand away from him and bolt out the door.

Dr. Scott tightened his grip on her wrist as if he guessed her desire to escape. He kept his eyes on Sister Mercy as he said, "No." His voice was mild but firm. "I like to make sure my patients' wounds heal properly."

"We don't really need your ointments, Dr. Scott," Sister Mercy said. "We make our own medicines that are surely as good as, if not superior to, your own."

"Burns are serious injuries. Do you want to take responsibility for the young sister's hand? If the scar forms too deeply, she might lose the practical use of her fingers."

The two stared at each other while Gabrielle searched her mind for some word to say to take the tension from the room. But no words came. Whatever was happening between the doctor and Sister Mercy dealt with more than Gabrielle's burned hand. She wanted to look at Sister Mercy and tell her she would abide by whatever decision she made, but at the same time, a disconcerting desire rose inside her that made her want to return the next day and let the doctor hold her hand in his strong grasp.

She glanced over at Nathan. He was smiling, enjoying Sister

Mercy's dilemma. Gabrielle looked down quickly and tried to cool the flush that reddened her cheeks. If only the doctor would loosen his hold on her wrist, then her heart might slow its wild beating.

Finally Sister Mercy said, "Very well. We will return in the morning."

"Good," the doctor said as he finished securing the bandage about Gabrielle's hand. "Remember what I said about keeping your hand dry, young sister, and I'm sure it will be much better come morning."

"Yes, sir," she said softly, not looking up at him. When he turned loose of her wrist, she stepped back so quickly that she almost upset the bowl and pitcher on the table by the window.

After Gabrielle said a quick goodbye to Nathan, she followed Sister Mercy out of the cabin. They walked some way in silence. Finally Gabrielle pushed out the words. "If you don't wish me to return to the doctor in the morning, I can tend my hand myself. The burn is slight, hardly reason to worry."

Sister Mercy was thoughtful, but after a moment she said, "Nay. I said you would return and you shall."

Gabrielle looked at Sister Mercy's face and couldn't keep from saying, "Surely you're not afraid of the doctor, Sister Mercy."

Sister Mercy stopped on the path and turned to look at Gabrielle fully. "Nay, my child, I have no fear of Dr. Scott. I only fear for you."

"But why? He is abrupt in his speech at times, but he has shown me nothing but kindness."

"He is of the world, Sister Gabrielle, and he has noted

55

thy outward beauty. I fear he may try to lead you away from us."

"Then ye have no reason to fear, for he could never do that." Gabrielle smiled at the strangeness of the thought of leaving the Believers. Sister Mercy smiled back at her, letting a little of the sternness slip away from her face for a moment.

As they turned to walk on to the schoolroom, Gabrielle thought about the doctor. She had to admit she did have a great curiosity about him and the world he came from, but she had no thought of becoming part of his world. She was one with the Believers, and here she would stay. Her path was clear.

5

Brice stayed with Nathan for four days. Each day the boy improved and his will strengthened. On the fifth morning Nathan pulled himself to a sitting position on the side of the bed. The boy bit his lip to keep back the groans when the pain hit him. His face went ashen except for the red of the burn on his cheek. But he didn't quit. He grabbed hold of the straight chair Brice sat in front of him and stood up.

"Give yourself a minute to let your head settle," Brice told him.

"My head is spinning a mite," Nathan said as he gripped the chair. "Too much time on my back, I'm thinking."

"That and the pain. It's no shame to admitting to feeling pain, boy. Go ahead and holler. It might help."

"Can't see how." The boy bit his lip again and slowly pushed the chair in front of him as he took a step. Beads of sweat popped out on his forehead.

The boy kept moving. He made it all the way across the room and back to the bed without Brice having to help him. When the boy was sitting down on the bed again and some of the color had come back into his face, Brice told him, "I'll be going along home this morning. You don't need a round-the-clock nursemaid anymore."

"You're leaving?" The boy wiped the sweat off his face with a corner of the bed cover.

Brice dipped a cloth in the basin beside the bed, wrung it out, and put it on the back of the boy's neck. "Sure, Bates. You don't think you're the only fellow who needs doctoring in this country. Anyway, that walk you made just now was pretty good. It won't be long until you're up and going again."

"I hope so, Dr. Scott."

"You'll need to keep pushing yourself. Keep moving your legs. You can't let them stiffen up on you no matter how bad it hurts. If the pain gets to be more than you can bear, put a pinch of these powders in a glass of water." Brice placed a tin of medicine on the table by the bed before he started packing up his things. "Elder Caleb will be here with some of the men to move you over to a different house where they'll take care of you till you're stronger."

Nathan watched him a minute before he said, "You're not leaving because you've given up on me, are you, Doc? I mean, you still think I'm going to be able to walk."

"You're walking now, Bates."

"I mean without pushing that confounded chair in front of me and wanting to scream each step."

Brice turned to look at the boy. He no longer had any doubt at all Nathan would get well if some sort of fever didn't set in. "You're already doing better than I thought you would, Bates. In a month you'll probably be walking wherever you want to go, and in another month, who knows? You might even be running. But it could be you'll want to scream for a long while after that."

The boy looked down at his legs and made a face. "I can live with that. I wasn't planning on leaving here till spring anyhow."

"You'd best be thinking of staying longer than that. It might be a good while before you're able to follow a plow to earn your living. At least here you're sure of eating till your legs heal."

The boy didn't say anything, just stared at Brice.

Brice shook his head and finished his packing up. "I'll be back every day or so to see about you until you get a little better at pushing that chair around. Then you'll have to come to me. It'll be good exercise for you." When a look of relief broke across the boy's face, Brice put his hand on Nathan's shoulder and added, "Don't worry, boy. I told you I'd see that you got well, and I will."

"It's just that when I ask Gabrielle to go with me . . ." Nathan stopped and hesitated before going on. "Well, I wouldn't want to ask her if I was just half a man."

Brice frowned at the mention of the young sister. The last two days the boy's talk had been sprinkled with plans he'd made for the two of them. Yet Brice was almost sure the young sister wouldn't go with the boy when he left the Shakers. Not that it was any of his concern. He'd see that the boy got well. The boy would have to sort out the rest of his problems himself. So he only said, "It takes more than legs to make a man, Bates."

"I'll have what it takes when the time comes. You'll see. They'll all see." The boy clamped his mouth shut when Elder Caleb pushed open the cabin door.

"We're here to move Brother Nathan," the elder said. Two other men followed him inside with a stretcher.

"Good." Brice looked over at the boy. "I'll see you tomorrow, Bates."

Elder Caleb stopped Brice just outside the door to hand him a small sack of coins. "I trust this will be adequate pay for your services, Dr. Scott. We are grateful for the devotion you've shown in caring for one of our brethren."

Brice took the money reluctantly. The burning of their harvest barn was a hardship on the Shaker community, but to refuse the money might insult them. While Brice didn't understand the Shakers' religion, he had to respect their hardworking industriousness and their devout sincerity. They knew what they believed even if those beliefs seemed oddly contrary to the natural order of the world and God's plan for man. After all, hadn't the Lord himself made Eve as a helpmate for Adam in the Garden of Eden and told them to go forth and be fruitful? Still, Brice had to admire the Shakers' sure grasp on what they believed to be the truth. He had never been able to feel that kind of certainty about any spiritual beliefs.

He'd spent his time in church, read the Bible, had plenty of people preach at him both in church and out, but he'd never been able to completely set aside his doubts and step forward in faith. His stepmother told him that was because his years with the redskins had turned him into a heathen unable to recognize the touch of the Lord.

Perhaps she was right. Brice sometimes felt God was near when he looked up at the stars on a clear night or walked through the woods in the springtime or brought a new baby into the world, but then when he'd try to grab hold of the feeling to make it real inside him, it would slip away and he'd wonder if there was a God at all. And even if there was, Brice doubted he'd ever done anything to encourage the Lord to look favorably down on him.

But these people had an assurance that couldn't be shaken. Not by ridicule of outsiders or by persecution. Of course, not all their members were that rock solid. The boy would never be one of them, and probably others among them entertained some doubts. How could a man not have doubts?

Brice put the bag of coins in his pocket without opening it. "I thank you," he said as another of the brethren led Brice's horse to the cabin. Brice ran his hand down the horse's neck before he mounted. "And I thank you for the fine care you've given my horse."

Elder Caleb inclined his head in a wordless gesture of dismissal, and Brice turned his horse's head toward the outskirts of the community.

He was almost past the last building when he spotted the young sister beside the road. He smiled and tipped his hat at her. She quickly looked away from him to the ground but not before he saw an answering smile jump to her lips.

He pulled up his horse and called to her. "How is your hand, young sister?"

For a minute he thought she was going to pretend not to hear. She took one step away, but then she surprised him by turning and stepping closer to him. He slid off his horse and walked over to her.

Again she looked ready to run as she glanced around her. There was no one in sight.

Brice said, "It won't hurt for me to look at your hand to be sure it has healed properly. You know you should have come back and let me treat it again."

Gabrielle held out her hand. "It was but a small burn, and Sister Mercy felt we had too much work to do to take time to come to the visitor's cabin."

Brice held her hand and gently bent her fingers and stretched her palm. "It seems to have healed well. Still, you should be careful with it for a while until the skin is no longer so tender."

"Yea, Doctor, I have been careful." Slowly she raised her eyes to meet his. "Ye are leaving?"

"I am. It's time I saw to my other patients."

"And Brother Nathan? Will he be all right now?"

So it was her need to find out how the boy was doing that had made her dare to speak to him. He told her what she wanted to hear. "I think so. It'll take months, but he's young and strong enough to make it through the hard times ahead of him."

The young sister smiled, and it was as if a flower suddenly opened up in bloom before his eyes. He remembered the boy's words. *She is beauty.*

"Thank you, Dr. Scott. I know the Eternal Father sent you here on that night to help Brother Nathan."

"Sister Gabrielle!" The old sister's voice was sharp as she came up behind the young sister. "It is time for the morning class to begin. We must be punctual."

The young sister's smile disappeared, and she looked almost frightened as she turned away from Brice. "I beg your forgiveness, Sister Mercy. I fear I could not resist the opportunity to ask about Brother Nathan."

The old sister's face was impassive, but there was disapproval in her voice as she said, "Ye should have asked one of the elders or eldresses permission to seek out information about the condition of Brother Nathan."

"Yea, Sister Mercy. Forgive me." The young sister ducked her head.

"Very well, child. Go along to your class now. They are waiting for their lessons." The old sister waited until the young sister walked away before she looked back at Brice.

Brice smiled. "Don't be hard on the young sister. I stopped her to look at her hand to be sure it had healed as it should."

The old sister acted as though he hadn't spoken. She simply said, "Good day, Dr. Scott." He could see those words gave her pleasure before she turned and walked away.

The young sister stopped to let the older woman catch up with her. Brice watched them go on up the path to the house. The young sister's face became somber as she seemed to be bowing her head in shame while the old woman berated her. And again anger rose inside Brice as it had the day he'd bandaged the young sister's hand.

He looked back at the buildings with their austere fronts. Everything in the Shaker community was built for service. Nothing was put there without a purpose, and there were no wasted frills. Nothing was built or done just because it was pleasing to the eye, and if the young Shaker sister had the misfortune of being pleasing to the eye without even trying, it appeared that was reason for shame.

Then as he continued to stare at the buildings, he thought perhaps he was wrong. Perhaps the Shakers had their own vision of beauty. While their structures had no ornamentation, there was beauty in their very simplicity. And perhaps he was reading the old sister wrong as well. Maybe she wasn't wishing away the young sister's beauty. She just wanted to step between him and the young sister because he was of the world and she was fearful her hold on the girl wouldn't be strong enough if the girl was allowed to glimpse life outside the Shaker community.

He pushed the young sister out of his mind as he rode out of the village. It was no concern of his if she wanted to give her life to the Shakers. While he might not go along with their way of life, they had the right to live as they wished. What harm could there be in wanting to live in peace and harmony with one another as brothers and sisters? Not that he thought they'd be able to shut away the evils and injuries of the world simply by building their community behind stone fences. Peace didn't come just because one wished for it, and saying "brother" and "sister" didn't always shut out certain feelings of the heart. The boy was proof enough of that.

Brice frowned and kicked his horse into a slow gallop. He was glad to leave them behind. Ever since Jemma had died, he'd shunned any kind of emotional involvement with people. He was willing to treat their physical pains. That was all. He had enough worries of his own without borrowing theirs. Yet as he rode through the woods to his cabin, the pure innocence of the young sister's blue eyes stayed with him.

He hadn't built his cabin in town. Brice needed trees around him, not houses. If people wanted his doctoring, they knew where to find him. And they did. In spite of the stories they told on him, they kept coming after him when a loved one was sick.

He slowed his horse as he came in sight of his cabin. Smoke was rising out of the chimney and a strange man stood on the porch waiting for him.

"Dr. Scott?" the man said as Brice dismounted. When Brice nodded, the stranger held out his hand. "Alec Hope."

Brice looked the man over carefully before he took his hand. Alec Hope was small but sturdily built, although age was beginning to gnaw at the edges of his strength. His leather britches were worn bare in spots, and the deep lines on his face told the hardness of the life he'd lived. An old scar from what looked to be a knife wound ran down the side of one of his cheeks. If the man had come for doctoring, there wouldn't be much chance of him paying. Then as Brice kept looking at him, something about the man's eyes looked familiar, as though they'd met before.

Brice shook his hand. "Do I know you?"

"Could be," the man said. "I used to be around these parts some years ago."

"What brings you out to my cabin, Mr. Hope?"

"I got a problem, Doc, and I'm hoping you can help me with it."

Brice pulled the saddle off his horse and turned him into the small corral beside the cabin. "If it's doctoring you need, I'll do my best. Come on inside."

Hope followed him into the cabin. "I didn't think you'd mind if I built a fire and brewed some of your coffee while I was waiting for you."

"Not at all. Smells good," Brice said as he poured them both a cup. He sat down across the table from the man and waited. He'd learned not to rush his backwoods patients. They often had a hard time coming out with their ailments. He kept his eyes on the man's face and tried to remember where they'd met.

The man moved uneasily in his chair. Finally he said, "It ain't exactly a healing problem I got, Doc."

"Then I don't suppose I can help you, Hope. Maybe what you need is a preacher. I can direct you to the house of a good man not too far away."

Hope shook his head. "I don't reckon a preacher would help me none. Preachers is part of my problem. If you'll just hear me out, Doc, I'd be obliged."

"All right." Brice took a drink of his coffee and waited.

"They tell me in town that you been out among them they call Shakers."

"I've been caring for a boy out there for a few days."

"What kind of people are they?" The man's eyes sharpened on Brice as he waited for his answer.

"Good enough people. Different from most, but they seem content with their ways."

"I hear tell they dance and carry on. Some say they even have fits where they roll around on the floor. And they call it worshiping."

"I wouldn't know about that. I didn't see any of their worship services. What difference does it make to you anyway, Hope? What they do. You thinking about joining them?"

The man laughed. "Not me. I can't see me dancing nowheres excepting maybe in a tavern somewhere if I was in my cups." His smile died away. "But I got a wife and daughter who went to the Shakers. You see, I just come back to this part of the country to see if my girl had growed up all right, and they tell me that she's part of this bunch of Shakers."

"She'll be well cared for and brought up decent enough, I'd guess. But if you wanted to know about them, why didn't you just go straight to the Shakers? They may not welcome people like us into their village, but they don't lock them out either. They would tell you whatever you want to know."

"Well, I would have, but you see, when I took off to work on the river some years back, I sent my wife word that I was dead. I thought Martha could marry again that way, that I'd be doing her a good turn. I'd have never guessed she'd do something so crazy as join these Shakers." Hope raised his hands up and let them fall back to his lap. "I don't know that they'd even let me see them now. I mean thinking I'm dead these many years and all."

Brice set his coffee down on the table. "Let me get this straight. You deserted your family years ago, and now you've taken a notion to come back to claim them."

"No, no. You got me all wrong, Doc. I don't care what Martha does. I wasn't never right for her. But I loved my little girl. She was always something extra special. That's one reason I left. To give her a better chance. Martha had this uncle over in the settlement that was an important man. Had some money. But he hated me. I thought if I was out of the way, maybe he'd sort of adopt Gabrielle, and she'd have a chance of being a real lady like she was meant to be. But it just ain't right, her being with those Shakers."

Brice's eyes narrowed on the man. "Did you say Gabrielle?"

Hope nodded. "I think it was Martha's ma who named her that. It always was a mouthful, but it seemed to fit her even when she was just a bit of a babe."

"The young sister is your daughter?"

"Young sister? I don't reckon she's no sister of yours, Doc."

Brice frowned. "I mean Gabrielle." Now that he knew who the man was, he could see a likeness to the young sister in the color of his eyes, but the deep blue had been dimmed by age and hard living.

"You know her then? You saw her at this Shaker place?"

"I saw her."

"Then you know it ain't right her being there."

"I couldn't say about that." Brice thought of how the young sister had looked when they met on the path as he left the Shaker village. Perhaps such a combination of beauty and innocence was better sequestered from the world. "She seems satisfied with her life there."

Hope made a sound of disgust. "It's just that she don't know no better. Tell me, Doc, is it true what they say in town about the folks out there? That they don't hold with marrying?"

"That's what I've been told."

"That just ain't natural. It ain't the way the good Lord intended either. Me, I never claimed to be a religious man, but I know enough about the Bible to know Adam and Eve got together often enough. And there's that part about cleaving to your wife or some words to that effect." The man stared at Brice, waiting for him to agree with him.

Brice looked down at the coffee in his cup. "They hold different ideas than most of God's people."

Hope rubbed his chin a minute before he said, "Some of the folks in town believe they dance to the devil in their meetings. That there ain't nothing religious about it. Some say they even strip off naked when they're dancing."

"I don't believe that," Brice said.

"You ever been to one of their meetings?"

"No." Brice picked up his coffee and took another drink. "But they're good enough people. Maybe a little curious to us, Hope, but they'll bring no harm to anyone."

"In my mind they're harming my girl already by shutting her away out there. She ought to be married with babes of her own by now. She's nigh on twenty. Instead she's stuck in there to spend her life as a barren old maid."

Brice looked straight at the man. "You have to let your daughter choose the kind of life she wants."

Hope stared back at him. "I'm willing to do that, Doc, but I don't know as to whether these Shaker people are. They've got her closed up in that little town of theirs till she can't see what life might be like anywhere else."

"Go, talk to her then, Hope. Tell her she has a choice."

"I've thought about that, but I'm dead to her now. I can't just sashay in there and say, 'Howdy, here's your pa back from the dead' after all these years."

"Then I guess that's your choice." Brice started to stand up. "I don't see how I can be of any help to you."

"You don't remember me, do you, boy?" Hope smiled and shook his head. "Of course, you don't. It's been a pile of years."

Brice sank back down in his chair and stared hard at the man. A long-closed door creaked open in his mind. He was a boy again fetching firewood for the squaws. Brice heard the men before he saw them. Speaking white men's words. His words. The hunters looked thunderstruck when he stepped in front of them and spoke his white name. This was one of those faces he'd thought he would never forget. "You were one of the hunters."

"That's right, boy. And you were just a little white boy who'd almost turned pure Injun."

"I did what I had to do and learned the Indian way, but I wasn't Indian."

69

"And you were grateful that we got you away?"

Brice met the man's eyes. "I'd have left in time anyway, but I suppose I am beholden to you. I've got some money here." Brice pulled out the little sack of coins the elder had given him. "I'll pay you for the booty you traded for me."

"I don't want your money, Doc. You know that. I want your help. Help just like I give you back then."

Brice kept the money there between them in hopes the man would take it still.

But Hope didn't reach for it as he went on. "The way I see it, my little girl is in sort of the same fix you was in. You liked it there with the Injuns, but once we got you away, you liked it better. She thinks she's one of these Shakers now, but she ain't. I want you to get her away from there so she'll know that."

"How? I can't trade for her the way you did for me."

"I don't know how. But at least you can let her know she can leave. That she's got a friend out here waiting for her. Tell her whatever you want. Just let her know she don't have to stay with them Shakers."

"But what if she wants to stay?"

"She won't. A place like that is for old women like Martha who never did like living. Gabrielle's not like that. I've seen her sing to little butterflies and whirl around to a secret tune nobody could hear but her. She'll come away when she sees that she can."

Brice stared at the man a long time before he spoke. He didn't want to do it. The young sister had already disturbed a part of him that he'd thought was long dead. But the man was right. He did owe him. There was no denying that, in spite of what he'd said about leaving the Indians on his own.

They'd brought him away from the Indians while he was still white. In another few years he might have forgotten too many of the white man's ways.

Brice slowly nodded. "I'll talk to the young sister if I can. But I'm not sure it will do any good. She not only lives among the Shakers. She is a Shaker."

6

Gabrielle saw the doctor when he came to treat Nathan, but she stayed back in the shadows so he wouldn't notice her. The third day he rode into the village, she didn't see him in time to step out of his sight, but when he turned his horse in her direction, she bent her head and hurried on toward the schoolhouse. She could feel his eyes boring into her back all the way up the path, and by the time she went through the door, her heart was pounding inside her chest as if she'd been playing a game of tag with her young students.

She couldn't allow the doctor to engage her in conversation again. Sister Mercy would never be able to understand or perhaps even forgive another chance meeting. While Sister Mercy had not continued to upbraid Gabrielle for talking with the doctor, Gabrielle felt a difference between them. A difference that saddened her spirit.

From the first moment Gabrielle had stepped into Sister Mercy's presence, she'd felt a special bond with her. Sister Mercy had been more mother to her than her own mother had ever been. But now when they were together, a worried frown often crept into Sister Mercy's eyes to push aside some of the fondness that had always been there so abundantly for Gabrielle.

The day when Gabrielle had talked with the doctor and then begged Sister Mercy's forgiveness, the eldress had said, "Ye need not forgiveness from me, Sister Gabrielle. It's Mother Ann you should appeal to. And ye know that if ye ask sincerely for forgiveness and pray for a pure heart, our good mother will be sure to grant you such."

They were words Gabrielle had heard many times before when she'd run to Sister Mercy to confess a slight wrong of spirit, but Sister Mercy's voice had not sounded so kindly or forgiving in Gabrielle's ears that day. Rather she had looked at Gabrielle as though some of the doctor's worldliness might be clinging to her. The stain of worldliness was not easily shed.

So Gabrielle had prayed to Mother Ann for forgiveness in hopes that the forgiveness of Sister Mercy would follow, but her prayers seemed to fall back to her unanswered. Gabrielle had never felt the same comfort praying to Mother Ann as she did to the Eternal Father. It was a lack in her life as a Believer that troubled her spirit even though Sister Mercy continually assured her that Mother Ann did hear all prayers and wanted to drop balls of blessings on their community.

As the days passed and even though Gabrielle did pray sincerely for a simple spirit that only thought of service to the Lord, she began to wonder if Sister Mercy was right and she had been touched by the doctor's worldliness. Wasn't she having doubts where none had been before? Weren't strange new feelings haunting her while questions crept into her mind that she hardly dared even acknowledge, much less try to answer?

Instead she pushed the questions deep inside her where she could almost forget them. Except when she met the doctor's eyes. Then the questions echoed in her mind and the doubts ate at her soul. So she kept her eyes to the ground away from the doctor. Better to push away the questions than to allow them to upset the peace she'd always known there with her Shaker sisters and brothers. Still she could feel his presence each time he was in the village. He seemed to linger to seek her out with his eyes as if he had questions of his own to be answered.

Gabrielle bent herself to her tasks. She set her mind to the Believers' way and did her best to put her hands to work and give her heart to God. She worked patiently with the little girls she taught, showing the same love and acceptance to those who were slow to grasp new ideas as to those who learned more easily and with joy.

Learning was a magical thing to Gabrielle. She grabbed at each new thing offered to her eagerly. She'd read all the books the Believers had, and sometimes with a pang of regret, she thought of the shelves of books her Uncle Jonas had owned. She remembered the feel of their dark bindings as she'd traced their titles with her fingers in anticipation of the secrets they would hold out to her in time. The promise of those books had been lost to her the day she and her mother had come together with the Believers.

The year before, she'd asked Sister Mercy if she could have more books. The elders and eldresses had discussed it before deciding Gabrielle's time would be better spent working with her hands. What one learned from doing a physical chore well was of equal or even more importance to whatever one might learn from a book. If there was extra time and the desire to read, she could read from the Bible or a book of Mother Ann's precepts. To soften the refusal, Sister Mercy had given her a journal to record some of the daily events of their family.

Gabrielle had already filled several volumes with the daily happenings of the village, the accomplishments of her students, and a record of her duties. When school wasn't in session, Gabrielle's hands stayed busy working for the good of the village the same as any of the other sisters, taking her turn in the laundry room, in the kitchen, or wherever she was assigned. She enjoyed working with the other sisters nearer her age and hearing their talk.

She was often touched by the new sisters' sufferings and sorrows even though she had little direct understanding of their woes. She listened closest and with the least understanding when the women spoke of their husbands and how they missed lying by their sides at night. Many of the new sisters hadn't wholly converted their hearts to the Believers' way, and they spoke of their men with the longing of something much more than brotherly love.

Once Gabrielle had dared ask a young sister about this love. "But we all love one another here. How is this love you speak of different?"

The two of them had been working together in the washhouse, scrubbing the men's clothes, and with the noise of the splashing water, there was little chance they would be overheard. Sister Cassie had paused with her hands still in the soapy water and looked up at Gabrielle. Sister Cassie was young, with eyes that shifted green to blue with her mood.

She and her husband had been married only two years when he'd decided to join with the Believers. She had had no babies, and it was a grief to Cassie that now she would never bear a child. She looked at Gabrielle with something akin to pity in her eyes. "Poor Sister Gabrielle. My life may be barren now, but at least I've known love."

"But I know love," Gabrielle protested. Her life fairly exploded with the love she felt for those around her.

Sister Cassie smiled. "True. You know love as it is here. You're much better at this kind of love than I will ever be. But I mean the love of a man and woman, bound together as one. James and I had that kind of love. It's still strong in my heart." Sister Cassie pulled a hand out of the sudsy water and held it against her bosom. "That kind of love should last forever. Till death do us part the way we promised each other in front of the preacher the day we married."

Sister Cassie bent back over her tub and blinked her eyes. Tears mixed with the sweat on her cheeks as she went on. "Now James won't hardly look at me. Says I'm the devil's temptation. Calls me 'sister.' I'm not his sister. I'm his wife."

"Maybe you should try to love as we love here," Gabrielle suggested gently.

"I've tried. Am trying. But it's not enough. If I was like you and had never known a man's love, then maybe it would be. But I don't want to live like this with the natural juices of life dried up inside me. I want to have my own cabin, my own man, and a houseful of children just like my ma did." Cassie began scrubbing the knees on a pair of trousers furiously. "I love James. Promised him I would forever, but I don't know how much more of this kind of living I can stand."

Gabrielle had no experience with the kind of love Sister

Cassie longed after. Gabrielle had witnessed no such shared love between her mother and father before her father had gone away and found death on the river, but it seemed to be the intended way for many of the world from Bible times on down. Adam and Eve. Abraham and Sarah. Isaac and Rebekah. Jacob and Rachel. Many of the converts who came into the village were married before they joined the Society of Believers.

Even Mother Ann had been married before she had recognized the true spirit inside her and the purpose the Eternal Father had for her. At times a newly converted couple came into their midst equally devoted with full acceptance of the Believers' way, but other times only the husband believed strongly, as with Sister Cassie and her husband. Then the wife was encouraged to bend her mind and will to the better way of the Believers.

Gabrielle took note of the converts who left and those who stayed and wrote of them in her journal as she sought fuller understanding of this part of life she'd never know. Marriage could never be part of a Believer's life.

Sister Mercy had explained it to her many times. "As Believers we feel the need to devote all our attention to the spiritual life and fill our hearts with spiritual love. Worldly love destroys spiritual love because there is often strife among families. Here in the Society of Believers we can worship God fully without the distractions of individual family ties. We are one family with the blessings of Mother Ann."

Gabrielle accepted that as right for her life, but sometimes when she thought of the pain in Sister Cassie's eyes or heard Becca's lonely weeping at night, she wondered if the Believers' life was right for all people.

Then the doctor had held her hand and looked deeply into her eyes, and suddenly all the questions weren't just to do with others. So Gabrielle stayed away from the doctor just as she avoided getting too near to the boilers that heated the water for the laundry. A wise person stepped back from danger. It advised as much many times in the book of Proverbs. Instead she sought her news of Nathan's progress from Elder Caleb or Sister Mercy.

Each time they told her of how Nathan was getting stronger and walking easier, she felt a growing relief. Not only for the healing of Nathan's wounds, but because once Nathan was healed, there would be no reason for the doctor to return to their village. Then she would be able to put him from her mind and the worldly questions and doubts with him. Her life was planned, and if at times she lost the absolute surety that it was the perfect life the Believers intended it to be, all the same she had no doubt it would be her way of life forever.

She wrapped herself in prayer, and any time an unworthy question or doubt slipped into her mind, she plucked it out and threw it down on the ground where she could stomp it into dust. Sister Mercy had taught her to do that when she first came into the village and missed some trivial part from her life before she became a Believer. Parts so unimportant that Gabrielle couldn't even remember them now.

This too was just a moment in her life. For this moment the sea of her emotions was rougher and the view ahead wasn't as clear. But when this moment had passed, then she would once again see her future with the Believers as it was meant to be.

On Sunday after Gabrielle dressed for the early meeting, she helped the little girls get their scarves and caps on straight.

When the meeting bell sounded, they all sang as they walked to the meetinghouse. As they came close to the building, their voices joined with the other Believers coming to meeting from the other houses. The familiar sound of the gathering song always renewed Gabrielle's spirit.

Inside they sang a hymn and then sat on the benches while Elder Caleb brought forth some Society business and spoke of the fire.

"The loss of the harvest barn is a hardship, but working through this trial will only make us stronger. We have already cleared away the rubble and will commence to build a new structure in the coming week. Soon we will be planting new crops, and in the fall we'll once again have a barn filled with the harvest of our labors. Meanwhile the Eternal Father and Mother Ann will provide for us."

"Praise God," one of the men called out.

Elder Caleb inclined his head for a moment before he went on. "As you know, Brother Nathan was badly burned in the fire. But again our Father has been kind. It now appears that in time Brother Nathan will recover the full use of his legs. Each day he grows stronger and by next week he may be well enough to attend meeting again."

A murmur of thanksgiving rippled through the Believers.

Elder Caleb said, "Later we will labor a special song for him and his complete recovery."

After a few more items of church business, the elder read from the teachings of Mother Ann. Gabrielle listened raptly for some special message that might touch her, but the words seemed to float around and away from her even though she tried to grab on to them. She'd never felt so strange in meeting before. It was as if some invisible hand was pushing her apart from the other Believers and keeping her from entering into their common worship.

When at last Elder Caleb stopped speaking and they began to push back the benches, Gabrielle was glad. Laboring the songs would surely bring her back into full fellowship with her brethren and sisters.

She did feel better as they lined up in preparation for the marches. Gabrielle took her place with the singers. She loved to sing and was gifted with a clear, melodious voice and a natural ear for the tunes of the songs. The other singers followed her lead as she sang first one song and then another. They were simple songs, songs that begged for the humble life.

"I want to feel little," Gabrielle sang. "I want to be low. I want Mother's blessings wherever I go."

There was no music other than the music of their voices and the sound of the feet of those laboring the songs as they moved back and forth and through and between the other sisters and brethren. The spirit began building in the room, and Gabrielle broke into a whirling song. The laborers moved faster across the floor and the singers lifted their hands and gave themselves to the song.

Suddenly there was a stir in the air, and one of the brethren leapt into the air and shouted. A sister fell trembling to the floor while another sister cried out, "It is the devil. We must stomp him out."

Gabrielle joined the dancers as they stomped and shook away their sins. There was another shriek, and then as quickly as the frenzied dancing had come, it departed. The Believers were once again moving orderly about the floor while those who had fallen were helped to the benches.

When Gabrielle felt the tingling strangeness up her back,

she was tempted to fight against it. She often feared giving her mind over to the power of the spirit, but Sister Mercy said she should not try to quench the gifts of the spirit. So she opened herself to the gift and whirled out away from the other singers as the song bubbled up out of her. The other Believers gathered around her. Some of them reached out to touch her in order to share in her gift.

At first she sang the melody in sounds with no words. Gabrielle, who felt as if she were somewhere far away watching someone else sing, was relieved when she heard the joy in the song. Sometimes the songs the spirit gifted her with were sad and troubled, but this melody rang with joy. The spirit was rejoicing in Nathan's recovery.

Then words were flowing into her mind and out her mouth. "There is joy in the love. The love of our Father. There is joy in our love, one with another."

Gabrielle lifted her arms upward and dropped to her knees. She sang the same words over and over as other voices began to join hers and some of the dancers went forth in another exercise.

When the song left her, Gabrielle got to her feet and went back to her place among the singers. Sister Mercy came to her and touched her face. The frown was gone from her eyes. "My child, Mother Ann has blessed you with a gift and you in turn have blessed us. You must always give yourself over to the gift and let it come freely through you as it should."

"Yea, Sister Mercy, I will try," Gabrielle said even as a great weariness washed over her. The gift did not always bring songs of joy. More often the gift seemed to tear at her with songs or messages of grief. This song had left behind no pain like shards of glass to pierce her heart, but the next one might. "The gift is not always so kind."

"We cannot choose our gifts, Sister Gabrielle, but we must receive what Mother Ann wills us to receive," Sister Mercy said sternly. But then her smile returned. "Ye are yet young, my child. Each day your understanding grows and in time you will know. Then thy gift will never be a burden but always welcome."

There was another song, and Sister Mercy drifted away from her. Gabrielle labored with the others in song until all the brethren and sisters fell to their knees and sang, "Come down heavenly spirit; descend on us like a fire. Burn away our sins and lusts. Keep us pure in thy eyes."

They sang the verse over and over as they first lifted their arms toward the heavens and then laid their faces to the floor. Then all at once the singing hushed, and as they bowed on the floor, a profound silence filled the meetinghouse.

After several moments, they got to their feet and sang a closing hymn. It wasn't until Gabrielle turned toward the door that she saw the doctor sitting in the corner. When she looked his way, his eyes were there, waiting.

Sister Mercy was by Gabrielle's side at once. "He should not be here," she said.

Gabrielle dropped her eyes to the floor. She wouldn't let his presence trouble her. As soon as Nathan was better, he'd be gone from their community for good. She would never see him again.

Sister Mercy kept talking beside her. "If he wanted to attend meeting, he should have waited until summer when we have our meetings open to the world. But not he. No, instead he sneaks in where he is not welcome. No doubt to ridicule us by carrying stories of our worship out to those in the world."

"I'm sure he means no harm, Sister Mercy," Gabrielle said softly. "He may be ignorant of our rules."

Sister Mercy's mouth tightened. "Nor does he wish to learn them." The frown inched back into her eyes.

"Not everyone can be a Believer," Gabrielle said.

"Nay. Many choose the pleasures of the lustful world instead of the rewards of eternity. In the next life they will know nothing but grief when the fires of hell burn round them."

Gabrielle's eyes shot back over to the doctor. It wasn't a thought she liked to hear spoken. She didn't want this man who'd brought turmoil to her mind to know any kind of grief in this world or the next.

7

Brice came near midday on Sunday to see to the boy because he knew it would be the meeting hour for the Shakers. He wanted to see for himself what these people did that had the county so full of gossip. And there was still his promise to Alec Hope, although he had no idea of how to make good on it.

Every time he saw the young sister she almost ran from his sight, and each time he saw her he was less sure he wanted to get involved. He'd been closed off to hurt too long to give this young sister, who was little more than a child, the chance to make him vulnerable again. But he did owe Hope and he had promised. Not to bring her away from the Shakers, but at least to talk to her. Even that much wasn't going to be easily accomplished.

He'd already been to see the boy when the meeting bell began to clang. Brice stepped up beside one of the buildings to watch the Shakers come together in the thin winter sunshine. He'd heard them singing on the nights he'd stayed with the boy, but then they'd just been an oddity. Now he was trying to understand them and why they had decided to close themselves away from the world and to deny all that was natural between a man and a woman.

He picked out the young sister easily in spite of the fact that all the women were dressed so alike. Every time his eyes touched her, he knew her at once. She was walking in the middle of a group of little girls, and her voice rose up strong and pure as she led her group in a song.

A movement in a window of the house he'd just come from caught Brice's eye. Nathan was peering out the window. Out in the pathway, Elder Caleb had also caught sight of the boy's face staring down at them. Perhaps the elder would believe Nathan had pulled himself to the window through his pain because of his devotion to the Shakers. It would go better for the boy while he was healing if the elder thought that, even if it wasn't true. Brice knew what drew the boy even before he followed the boy's gaze to the young sister.

In a straight orderly line the women and men entered the meetinghouse by separate doors. The song changed, and then all was quiet. Brice walked over to the meetinghouse and stood close to the door. He didn't want to intrude on their meeting, but he couldn't see what it would hurt for him to listen from outside the building.

Inside the elder was talking, and to Brice it sounded as though he was preaching as any other preacher was wont to do. Brice hadn't been inside a church since Jemma had died. Jemma had set great store by churches and preachers, and because he loved her, he had put on his good clothes and gone into the church house with her.

Bitterness rose inside him as he wondered for the thousandth time what good it had done her. She'd been yanked away in her youth, stolen from him. A preacher had come while Jemma had been on her deathbed and told them the Lord must have had need of an extra-special angel in heaven. Either that or the punishment for some sin was being visited upon her.

Brice had wanted to smash the preacher in the face to keep any more words from coming out of his mouth. With his hands clenched in fists, Brice had stood up and stalked outside. Jemma's father followed him out where he handed him the axe and pointed to the woodpile. Then he said, "It does no good to be angry at the preacher."

"But do you believe what he said?" Brice asked.

"I'm not a man called of God," his father-in-law said sadly. "The workings of the Lord are too mysterious for a mere mortal such as I. We can only pray for understanding."

"To understand what? That the Lord has no mercy?"

"It does no good to be angry at the Lord either, son. Fevers come. All we can do is treat the fevers as best we can and lean on the Lord whatever happens."

Brice hadn't wanted to lean on the Lord. He'd wanted to defeat the fever that was stealing his young wife. But all he'd been able to defeat that afternoon was the pile of wood that he split for the stove. Later that night he held Jemma's hands as tightly as he could, but he couldn't keep death from claiming her. And he was angry. In the months that followed, he pushed that anger into a hard ball inside him and any time some thought of the Lord came to mind, he pulled that ball out and knocked such thoughts aside.

He had no use for any show of religion. Maybe there was a God. But if there was, he didn't care one whit what happened to his people down here on earth. So what difference did it make how people decided to worship him? If the Shakers wanted to roll around in convulsions on the floor, they'd probably have as much chance of catching the Lord's favor as anybody else.

Brice was ready to turn away and leave them to their praying when the young sister's clear voice carried out to him. He stood silent while she led the others in one song after another as the sound of movement came from within the building. He had no right to enter, but he slipped inside anyway.

The men and women were marching back and forth in a sort of shuffle dance with a precision of movement. The young sister stood to the side, singing. A sudden scream from among the dancers made Brice jump. The Shakers began shouting, stomping, and jumping about until the building vibrated with their fury. Brice shrank back against the wall, afraid he was the cause of such a violent outpouring of feeling, but when no eyes touched on him there in his corner, it was obvious none of the Shakers even realized he was there. They were too intent on their dancing.

The young sister moved among the others as the violence of the dance lessened and once again the men and women were shuffling about in an orderly manner. All at once she drew away from the rest of the dancers. For a minute her face darkened, but then she looked up to the ceiling and began to sing. Now her face almost glowed, and the other Shakers ceased their movements and gathered around her. Some of them reached out to touch her.

At first her song had no words, but its lilting melody sent a shiver down Brice's spine. He recognized the joy in the song even before she began singing the words. What was it Hope had told him? That she sang to the butterflies. This could have been such a song. It might have been more fittingly sung in a sun-spotted meadow than here among these odd people.

As he watched her, long-forgotten feelings stirred to life inside him. She looked so pure and innocent, and in spite of himself, he wanted to treasure and protect that innocence. At the same time he wanted to wrap his arms around her and feel her head resting in the hollow of his shoulder. He wanted to breathe in the scent of her hair and skin. He wanted to make her his in every way a woman could be joined with a man.

He pulled himself up short and tried to clamp down on the feelings rising inside him. He tried to shove them back into the dead place inside him where he kept his memories of Jemma. He did not want to feel. Not this. But the feelings would not be controlled. They billowed out and filled every corner of his soul.

They would bring him pain. Loving the young sister would be sure to carry with it pain. He stared at her and knew the truth of that in his heart, but it was a pain he'd have to bear because the love was there already. It couldn't be denied. But could he allow his love to bring her pain?

He barely heard the rest of the songs as the Shakers finished out their service. He kept his eyes fixed on the young sister and waited for her to look his way. It wasn't until they were leaving the meeting that her eyes came to him. Then in the brief moment before she looked down, he imagined he saw a bit of welcome for him in her eyes.

But the old sister was beside her, and Gabrielle had her eyes locked on the floor while the old sister's eyes burned into him. Brice paid her no mind and kept his eyes on Gabrielle's face. So when her eyes darted back to his, he was ready to capture them. She wouldn't let him as she hurried out of the meetinghouse.

Brice followed the Shaker men out the men's door. Then he hurried to catch up with Gabrielle before she could disappear into one of the buildings and be lost to him. He would talk to her in spite of the old sister glued to her side.

"Gabrielle, I need to speak with you." He reached to touch her arm.

Sister Mercy stepped between them. "Nay, you will not disturb Sister Gabrielle. Ye are here for no good except to bring strife to our community."

"I only wish to talk to the young sister." Brice searched for words to say that would make Gabrielle look at him. "I have a message for her."

"She needs no messages from the world."

"It is from one of her family."

Sister Mercy's eyes narrowed on him. "She has no family in the world. Her family is here. She has no other except the Believers, as it is with all of us."

"And the young sister, does she not have a voice to speak for herself?" Brice pushed his voice past the old sister to Gabrielle. "Gabrielle, do you say the same?"

Her eyes came up from the ground and touched first Sister Mercy, who nodded the barest bit. Then she looked at Brice. Her blue eyes were dark as the midnight sky. "It is as Sister Mercy says. The brethren and sisters are my family."

"And is that the way you want it?" Brice asked softly.

Gabrielle started to answer, but the old sister jumped in front of her words. "You have heard what you came to hear. Now leave us be."

"What are you so afraid of, Sister?" Brice spoke to the old

sister, but his eyes never left Gabrielle. "My words carry no evil."

Gabrielle's eyes came up again, but they touched his for only a second. Then she began walking swiftly away from him while the old sister stayed to have the last word. "Evil comes in many shapes and sizes. Those are wise who can recognize it as such."

Brice paid her words little mind as he watched Gabrielle. She was running from him. He looked back at the old sister as he said, "Am I evil for the young sister?"

The old sister's face darkened and her head moved in the barest nod. "It is not my place to judge ye."

Brice's voice hardened. "I'm not so kind. I'm not the one who wishes evil for Gabrielle. It's you. You and your kind who have her locked here in this place. If you cared for her, you'd allow her to choose whatever life she desires."

The old sister held her hands out palms down and began pushing them down in front of her. She stomped her feet and said, "Get thee from me, Satan!"

Brice turned away in disgust. Not with her, but with himself for allowing his anger to make him say more than he should have. After this, he'd never get past her to talk to Gabrielle. Yet he had to find a way. He had Hope's message to give her. But that wasn't all. Now he had his own message. He wanted her to be free to sing to the butterflies again. Free to love him if that was her choice.

When he got back to his cabin, Alec Hope was waiting as he'd been every day when Brice returned from the Shaker village. The man watched Brice unsaddle his horse before he said, "No luck, eh, Doc?"

Brice wished the man somewhere else. Anywhere else but

standing there staring at him with those faded mirror images of Gabrielle's eyes. Brice needed time to think. Time to shut Gabrielle's face and eyes from his thoughts and bury those long-hidden feelings back into the deep recess of his mind. Mostly he needed time to let his anger at the old sister evaporate. After years of clamping down on his emotions, he'd managed to blow out all the stops in one day.

Brice slapped his horse's rump and closed him in the pen. As he tromped through the door, he stubbed his toe on a piece of wayward firewood. With a yell he picked it up and slung it out the door.

Hope jumped out of the way with a knowing smile on his lips. Brice was curling his hands into fists to knock the smile off the man's face when Hope reached toward the knife in his belt. "You don't want to be fighting an ornery old dog like me." His voice was soft but with an edge of warning.

"Then stop standing there grinning like an idiot." Brice stomped on into the cabin and poured himself a cup of the coffee Hope had made.

Hope waited until Brice drank down the whole cup before he said, "I'm guessing they didn't let you talk to my girl."

"They didn't let me."

"But you talked to her anyway?"

"I talked at her." Brice sat down and stared at his empty coffee cup.

"Well, what happened?"

"Nothing happened. That's what." Brice got up and paced around the room. Then he got his mortar and pestle and began grinding some medicine. He could think best with his hands busy, and the precision of his movements might calm his mind. He didn't even look up as he said, "I wish I'd never seen your girl, Hope."

Hope sat down at the table and slowly filled his pipe with tobacco. After he lit it with a taper from the fire, he looked over at Brice. "They tell me my girl is pretty."

"Pretty is a shiny stone you pick up out of a creek. Your girl is beauty." Brice echoed the young brother's description of Gabrielle.

Hope's eyes sharpened on him, but he only said, "Did you tell her what I said? Did you tell her I was here?"

"You don't understand, Hope. They won't let me talk to her. Not face-to-face like we are."

"It don't seem likely they could keep you from it, Doc. From looking at you, I'd say it'd be hard to keep you from doing whatever you set your mind to."

Brice poured the powders out of the mortar into a cloth bag. His anger was ebbing away. "I suppose I could fight with the best of them, but the Shakers don't believe in fighting of any kind. And I won't be starting in on old women." He began grinding a new bit of powder. Then he let his hands fall still a moment. "They've got the young sister protected. There's this old sister who watches her like a hawk. One look from her is enough to send Gabrielle running from me."

"Martha? My wife, Martha?"

"I don't know about your wife. But I think families are usually parted, and this old woman's name is Mercy, best I recall. She was quick to tell me that your girl didn't have any family on the outside of the village, that her family was the whole community of Believers."

"All brothers and sisters."

"So I've been told."

Hope shook his head. "I've never been a religious man, Doc. Been to a few camp meetings out of curiosity and seen some pretty strange carrying-ons, but I never heard of nothing stranger than this one. And to think my girl with my blood flowing through her is part of it. I reckon you can't get much curiouser than that."

"I went to their meeting today."

"They told me in town they only let folks come during the summer months."

"I didn't exactly get invited," Brice said.

"What'd you think of it, Doc? Did they dance the way they say, like as how they were having some sort of fits?" Hope leaned over closer to Brice.

"They danced. I guess you might say it was sort of like folk dancing and sort of like I've seen the Indians dance, and yet it wasn't like either one."

"You're talking in riddles, Doc." Hope leaned back in his chair and drew on his pipe.

"Maybe so. I guess that's because it was like nothing I ever saw before. They sang and danced, and I didn't doubt they were worshiping."

"Worshiping what? That's the question." Hope didn't wait to see if Brice had an answer before he went on. "And my girl? Was she part of all this?"

The clear voice of the young sister ringing out of the meetinghouse and pulling him inside echoed in his head. And in his heart. "The young sister took part. She sings like an angel." Brice fell silent for a moment. He was remembering how the others had clustered around her when she was singing her song. "I think the Shakers believe the angels sing through her."

"And did you think that too?" Hope asked sharply.

"No, but there is something different about her. Something that sets her apart from the others. Something that makes them guard her carefully. I've heard their founder, this Mother Ann they pray to, that she had visions and prophetic dreams."

"My girl ain't no different than any other." The words were a little too quick out of Hope's mouth and a little too loud, as though the first person Hope had to convince was himself.

Brice looked around at him steadily. "Did you know she could see the future?"

"Nobody can tell the future." Hope shifted his eyes away from Brice.

"I'm not on a witch hunt, Hope. You've no need to be so jumpy."

Hope knocked the last of his tobacco out of the pipe into the ash bucket beside the fire. Then he put it back in his mouth and sucked air through it for a spell before he said, "I reckon it did always make me a little jumpy. The way she was and all. So pretty and smart and yet marked by this curse of knowing things no mortal should know."

"A curse? I think the Shakers consider it a gift."

"It's a curse to know death is coming while there's still life in the air. I used to hear her crying in the night. The first time was when Martha was ready to birth our boy. When I asked Gabrielle what was wrong, she said she could see the baby wrapped all in white and laying in a box and he didn't cry." Hope looked down at the pipe in his hands. "I told her it was all a bad dream and to go on back to sleep."

Brice waited for him to go on, but when he didn't, Brice said, "But it wasn't, was it?"

"The boy never took a breath. My mother wrapped him in white and put him in a box and he never made the first whimper. Gabrielle didn't either. Not then when he died. She was just a little tyke. Four, the best I recall. Martha thought she should cry for her brother, but Gabrielle told her that the babe was happy. She'd seen him laughing with the angels." Hope looked up at Brice. "I heard her crying in the night after that, but I never asked her why again. If there's grief waiting down the road for me, I'd just as soon not know it till the morrow gets here."

For a long time the two men didn't speak. The fire popped and Hope leaned forward to shove a chunk of wood into the flames. Brice turned back to grinding his medicines.

He had another batch of powders ready when Hope said, "This mean you've give up trying to talk to my girl?"

"I didn't say that. Though I doubt they'll even let me tip my hat at her now. But I'll talk to her. I just don't know when or how."

"I may be moving on soon."

Brice frowned over at him. "I thought you'd come back to take care of your daughter."

"I did, but from what you say, there's not much chance of her coming away from there. And even if she did, she's well past marrying age. I 'spect she wouldn't have no trouble find-ing a younger man than her pa to put a roof over her head." Hope paused and gave Brice a long look before he went on. "But fact is, I hear there's a war brewing up in the North, and I ain't about to miss the chance to run them redcoats clear back to England. Maybe make Canada ours. Open up some good hunting grounds. So soon as they call for volunteers to form a Kentucky unit, I reckon I'll be on my way."

"Then the young sister would be better off among the Shakers."

Hope smiled and shook his head. "I never claimed to be no great shakes as a pa. I just wanted to see her free the way I've always been. If I knowed that she stayed there with them Shakers 'cause she wanted to and not just because my crazy old wife took her there, then I could go off with an easier mind even if I don't hold with the way they do. Don't you see, Doc?"

Brice didn't see, but then he wasn't seeing anything very clearly and hadn't been since he'd heard Gabrielle's beautiful voice ringing out of the meetinghouse at the Shakers' village. "All I see is that you've come to my cabin bringing me trouble."

Hope smiled. "It can't be all that much trouble to pass a few words with a pretty girl. And I wouldn't want you to get me wrong. I still want you to carry the truth about me being alive to my girl. You owe me that much."

"I told you I'd talk to her. And I will." But it wouldn't be because he owed Hope. Not now.

8

Brice waited three days before going back to see Nathan. Then it was just as he'd expected. Before he even got off his horse in front of the Center Family House, Elder Caleb was standing on the steps waiting for him.

"Good day, Dr. Scott. We've been expecting you," he said mildly. There was no censure in his eyes, but neither was there welcome.

"I came to see to the boy. Bates." Brice squared his shoulders. He'd fight against the elder's refusal.

But the man didn't refuse. "Of course," he said. "You have been instrumental in our young brother's recovery, and we are grateful. The Eternal Father uses many means to perform his miracles."

Brice hurried out his next words before the elder could turn away. "I'd also like to speak with the young sister, Gabrielle. I have a message for her from her father."

The elder showed no surprise even as he said, "Sister Gabrielle has no father in the world."

"But she does. He came to me and asked me to give her a message from him."

"You don't understand our ways, Dr. Scott." Elder Caleb's eyes were patient. "Sister Gabrielle believes her father to be dead, and even if that is not so, he remains the same as dead to her now. We've shut out the world. A father as you speak of in the worldly way means nothing to us."

"Then what could it hurt for her to know her father lives?" Brice insisted.

"Sister Gabrielle is not yet old enough to be a full covenant member, so perhaps you are right. Perhaps she should be told. I will consider it." The elder pursed his lips and stared at Brice. His eyes narrowed thoughtfully. "Meanwhile your presence in our village has been a disturbance to the peace of our family."

"I'm sorry that you think so."

"I feel you are a good man, Dr. Scott. Misguided, but with a good heart. If you were to become a Believer, your presence would be a benefit to our society."

"That could never be, Elder."

"Nay, I thought not. Ye are not ready to give up the world. Not yet anyway." Elder Caleb rubbed his chin. "As things stand I fear I must ask you to allow one of the brothers to accompany you at all times while you are in our village."

"I wish none of you harm. Especially not the young sister. I only desired to speak to her in order to deliver the message from her father."

"You must realize, Dr. Scott, that Sister Gabrielle has been with us a long time. She and her mother came together with those who formed this society over five years ago. She was hardly more than a child then, but the spirit has always been strong over her. It is our duty as her family to protect her."

"I told you I intend her no harm."

"So you say, and I believe you are sincere when you say you would not intend to harm our young sister, Dr. Scott. But just as the Eternal Father can use many means for his miracles, so can the devil for his wickedness."

"You're saying I'm God's workman and the devil's as well at the same time?" Brice frowned at the elder, whose face stayed impassive.

"As we all are or have been in the past. Except now we here at Harmony Hill have shut out the devil from our lives. We must use diligence to keep him out."

It would have been easier if Brice could have disliked the elder, but instead he respected the man and his community of Believers for the way they lived their beliefs. He stared at the man a moment before he said, "I will abide by whatever you say, Elder Caleb. But I do need to see to the boy a few more times until he's able to come to my cabin for treatment." He had little choice. And he had little chance of catching even a glimpse of the young sister now. Not with them guarding her against him.

Elder Caleb allowed a bit of relief to show in his eyes. "Of course. I will go with you to his room now. He is much improved although he continues to have a great deal of pain."

The boy was better but quiet. With Elder Caleb in the room, he seemed afraid to talk as he usually did when Brice examined him.

"Well, Bates," Brice said as he put his things back in his black bag, "you're doing even better than I thought you would. I might as well be on my way. There are sick people out there who really need doctoring."

Nathan glanced at the elder and then back at Brice. Puzzlement was mixed with concern on his face. "Am I really better, Doctor?"

"I just told you so."

"Then I need to get out of this room. I'm going crazy shut up in here."

"If the weather's favorable, I don't see what it would hurt. But you'll have a struggle up and down the stairs."

"I can do it," Nathan said.

Brice smiled and touched the boy's shoulder. "I'm sure you can. Take care, Bates."

"You'll be back?" The boy's voice sounded worried as he shot another look over at the elder.

Brice tightened his grip until he felt the outline of the boy's shoulder bone under his hand. "Sure, in a few days."

Elder Caleb followed Brice outside. Just before Brice started to mount his horse, the elder spoke. "You say that Sister Gabrielle's father from the world has come to you with a message. Correct?"

"Yes."

"And that is why you wish to talk to the sister?"

"It is."

"Very well, Dr. Scott. You tell this man to come to me, and I will arrange for him to see Sister Gabrielle if I judge that he means her no harm. You think we fear to give our young people any freedom, but we do not keep any of our sisters or brethren captive here. If one of them decides to leave us, we let them go, although it is with sadness and much trepidation and concern for their eternal soul."

Brice looked around at the elder who, in spite of declaring that he'd left the world behind, was nevertheless wise in the ways of the world. He'd easily outfoxed Brice. Now Brice could do nothing but say, "I'll tell him when next I see him."

As Brice rode out of the community, he couldn't keep his eyes from going to the building he knew served as the schoolhouse. Just briefly he caught sight of a face in one of the windows. It was the young sister. He was sure, not because he'd seen her well enough to recognize her, but because of the way she'd jumped back away from his eyes. She was afraid to let him see her, and yet he had the feeling she'd been watching for him.

As he snapped his reins to urge his horse to pick up the pace, Brice felt surer of himself than he had for days. He'd find a way to reach her and convince her she didn't belong here. The elder may have closed off one way of him talking to her, but there would be other ways. He just had to find them. The young sister wanted him to. He knew that to be true. He didn't know how he knew it, but he did.

Gabrielle turned from the window back to her classroom. The little girls were all reciting their lessons, and she was glad for the confusion of ten different lessons being spoken aloud at once. It gave her time to calm the blood thumping through her veins.

She had determined in her mind not to let the doctor bother her again, and then there she had been at the window watching for him. She seemed to sense his very nearness and to be pulled toward him as a moth to a flame. Even when he was not near in actual physical presence, his face and being often intruded into her thoughts and dreams.

Gabrielle had asked the Eternal Father to free her from this sin, but though she prayed earnestly and long, the feeling had stayed with her when she rose up off her knees. She couldn't shut thoughts of the doctor away from her. At times she felt as if her insides were dividing into two people—the person she knew who looked straight down the pathway of her life with the Believers and the other she did not know who was pulling her feet to the side to peek out the window at the doctor. She had no reason to seek him out with her eyes. He had no part in her life. Yet the sight of him made the color rise in her cheeks and stole her breath.

She turned her mind away from her wayward thoughts and concentrated on little Sister Anna's recitation. She was doing the times table and hesitated only on six times seven. Gabrielle would commend her later for her effort.

Working with the schoolgirls helped ease Gabrielle's troubled spirit. But that comfort would soon be gone, for the school season ended in a few weeks. Then she would have to apply her energy to other tasks. Those duties would surely keep her hands busy, but they would let her thoughts roam too free. She would have to pray for discipline, for right and proper thoughts.

She said such a prayer now as she walked among the girls, listening to first one recitation and then another. After a few more minutes, she set the older girls to reading silently and brought the younger ones up in a small circle around her.

Gabrielle settled her eyes on each of the children in turn. Suzy with her pretty blonde hair and dimples was a happy child but not gifted in learning. She liked best to talk. Deborah and Malinda were sisters separated by less than a year and so much alike not only in looks but in their ways as well. Whatever one did, the other copied. Together they had adjusted easily to the Believers' way.

Last she looked at Becca. Dear little Becca who had found a place in Gabrielle's heart with her tears. Gabrielle wanted to believe the patience and love she was showering on the child was helping, but if anything, Becca seemed more withdrawn than ever.

"Becca," Gabrielle said softly. "You may read the first page for us."

Becca's dark hair fell around her face as she bent her head over the book and began to read. Every word was correct, but the child read with a total absence of feeling. The words held more life while they were yet on the page.

When she had finished, Gabrielle rewarded her with a smile, but Becca kept her eyes on the book. Gabrielle spoke aloud. "That was very good, Becca. You will be ready to go into the next group before long."

Then while the other girls read, Gabrielle's eyes kept coming back to Becca. When the children filed out for a brief time of exercise before the evening meal, Gabrielle held Becca back. Gabrielle waited until all the other girls were out of the room before she said, "The sun is feeling warmer today. Spring will be here soon."

Becca stood perfectly still in front of Gabrielle, staring at the floor.

"Please look at me, Becca. It's hard to talk to your cap."

Becca's eyes came up to Gabrielle's face obediently. She didn't say anything, and every word that came to Gabrielle's mind sounded silly in the face of the child's profound sadness.

Finally she simply reached out and touched Becca's cheek. "You have learned well, Becca. I'm proud of you."

"Thank you, Sister 'Brielle." The little girl shot a quick look at the door. "Now may I go outside with the others?"

The child was not worried about missing a game of tag. She wanted to be in the yard in case her mother came to see her there. Gabrielle hoped Sister Esther would find a way to come. It had been three days since she had sought out Becca. Gabrielle feared that very many more days without the sight of her mother and Becca might actually become ill. The child troubled Gabrielle already. Her thoughts of Becca lately were rimmed with dark shadows.

"Remember, Becca, no matter what, I love you." She pulled the child close against her and held her for a minute before letting her go.

"My mother loves me more," Becca said before she turned and went out.

With a heavy sigh, Gabrielle followed her. It was a warm day for February. Gabrielle pulled in a deep breath of the air that made her imagine the grass greening and the trees budding even if it was too soon to dream of spring. A few of the children had surely caught the feel of the air and were spinning about in place until they staggered into one another. To the side, other children were playing "Mother Ann in prison," a game the elders and eldresses encouraged, but one that Gabrielle didn't like seeing her girls play. Surely there was time enough for the youngsters to learn of persecution without making a game of it, but Sister Mercy said it was good for the children to understand some of the trials Mother Ann had endured in her efforts to do the Eternal Father's will and establish the Society of Believers when she came across the ocean to America.

And Gabrielle had to admit that the children didn't seem bothered by the game. Most of them seemed happy. Many of them had shed their family ties as easily as they shed their cloaks in the warm sunshine. Then there were others like dear Becca who could not seem to find a way to adjust to the new.

Becca was sitting off by herself. Sister Esther had not come, and Gabrielle hurt for the lonely little girl. Not that Gabrielle hadn't expected it to happen. The Believers were very diligent about keeping parents and their children apart when they joined the Society to ease their adjustment to their new life. It had been four years since Gabrielle had seen her own mother other than when they were on the same duty or in meeting. Sometimes it was hard to even remember that Sister Martha had actually given birth to her.

Gabrielle sighed again and turned away from the yard. She needed to straighten the classroom to get it ready for the next day's lessons. By the time she had finished, it was time for the evening meal. When they were all lined up for their walk to the Center Family House, where they took their meals, Suzy ran up to Gabrielle. "Becca says she don't feel good. She don't want to eat."

Gabrielle looked around for the child. "Where is she?"

"She went inside to go lay down. She made me promise to tell you."

"All right. Thank you, Sister Suzy." Gabrielle looked over her shoulder toward the staircases that led to the bedrooms, but Becca was nowhere in sight. As soon as she had the other children settled at their tables, she'd come back to check on Becca.

A half hour later, Gabrielle carried back a small pot of soup for Becca. The house was quiet as she went up the stairs. Not that the children made that much noise when they were there. They'd been taught to walk quietly inside and to speak softly, but when they were present, there was always a rustle of life about the house. Now it felt totally empty.

"Becca," Gabrielle called softly as she opened the door into the bedroom. "I brought you some soup."

The double line of beds stretched out across the room. In the dim light of the winter evening, each bed cover was pulled up straight and neat. There was no sign Becca had ever come back upstairs. Gabrielle made a quick search of the other rooms in the house, but she knew she'd find nothing. The house was as empty as it felt. Outside she stood on the steps of the building and called Becca's name, but no child's voice answered her.

Gabrielle should have watched her more closely. The child had surely gone in search of her mother, but which way would she have gone? Gabrielle looked around the yard and then at the trees behind their house. She'd never once thought the woods looked the least bit menacing, but now with the early winter twilight already falling, suddenly the trees seemed to have edged closer and the shadows under them were darker and lurking with danger.

Becca would be frightened if she hadn't found her mother, and Gabrielle didn't see how the child could have done that. Even Gabrielle had no idea where Sister Esther might be working. But surely the child couldn't have gone too far. Gabrielle walked swiftly toward the woods beside the house where Sister

106

Esther usually appeared when she came to the school to visit Becca. If she hurried, perhaps she would be able to find the little girl and have her tucked safely into her bed before Sister Mercy returned with the other children from the biting room. Gabrielle had no desire to see Becca punished for wandering off.

In the woods the light was dimming fast. Gabrielle strained her eyes to see through the shadows. "Becca!" she called time and again.

No answer came back to her from among the deep shadows under the trees, but all at once Becca was with Gabrielle in her mind. The child's desperation and fear were so real that Gabrielle's heart began pounding inside her chest.

Gabrielle dropped to her knees in a layer of last fall's leaves. The warmth of the day had gone with the sun, and now she shivered as she shut her eyes and put her hands to her head. She had never sought the gift. Rather she had always tried to shut it out. Often she had prayed the Eternal Father would remove it from her just as Paul had freed the slave girl in Macedonia from her fortune-telling spirit in the Bible. Gabrielle told no fortunes. Most of the time when the gift came, it simply showed her something happening, but at times whatever the gift showed had not yet occurred.

That was the way it was with her first memory of knowing what she should not know when she'd seen her baby brother in his burial box. For a long time Gabrielle had worried that her dream of that happening had somehow stolen the baby's breath from him. So the knowing was not something she had ever sought; rather, she had always tried to block it away. But this time she would open her mind and seek the knowing. Becca needed her help.

At first she despaired of it working. The fear was there inside her plain enough, but she could not see Becca. She had never been able to push the gift even when it came to her of its own bidding. The visions formed in her mind as they willed. Gabrielle pulled in a deep breath to calm the fear pounding through her and let it out slowly. The gift could not be forced, but perhaps it could be welcomed.

She whispered Becca's name before she began softly singing one of their oft-used songs to ready her mind for the gift. "Come down Shaker-like. Come down holy. Come down Shaker-like. Let's all go to glory."

She didn't know when the song ceased coming from her lips. Total darkness covered her, seeping into her very soul. She could see Becca as gradually the images began lighting up in her mind. The little girl moved with determination as she walked between the trees. Her mother was surely just ahead. She only had to walk far enough. She stopped at the edge of a clearing and stared at a cabin there in the middle of the trees. A large dark shadow fell across the child. A bear. Becca screamed and tried to run, but the bear grabbed her. Terror consumed her. Gabrielle cried out and opened her eyes.

The dim light still among the trees surprised Gabrielle. She had expected the same darkness that was in her mind. She jumped to her feet and began to run. She had to get to Becca before the bear. Branches whipped against Gabrielle's face and tore at her skirt before she came to her senses and slowed to a walk. It would do no good to run madly through the woods. She had to use her head. She sorted through the images she'd seen. There had been a cabin, and cabins meant people. With the darkness of her vision gone, Gabrielle thought surely it had been a man and not a bear that had reached for the child.

She forced her breath in and out slowly to calm her racing heart as she moved on through the trees. She was beginning to think she was surely as lost as Becca when her feet found a path. In the fading light she couldn't see if it was a path made by men or nothing more than a deer trace to the river. She could only hope and pray it led to the cabin she'd seen in her mind.

When she caught the smell of smoke in the air, Gabrielle began walking faster. She hesitated before leaving the shelter of the trees. She'd been too long from the world. She didn't want to approach the cabin, but she had to see if Becca was there and safe.

Once she stepped out of the shadows of the trees, she moved quickly across the clearing and up the steps to the door. A horse whinnied softly in a pen beside the cabin. There were no other sounds, not even from behind the door of the cabin. As Gabrielle raised her hand to knock on the wooden door, she wished one of the brethren or Sister Mercy was with her.

Her knuckles had barely touched the door when it swung open. Gabrielle jumped back. For a minute the man stared at her as if he couldn't believe what he was seeing. Then he laughed and said, "This night holds many surprises. First the child and now you, young sister."

Gabrielle's eyes went to the doctor's face. There was a flush of red about his cheeks and a strange look in his eyes, and she wondered if he'd been drinking. She'd often seen her father consumed by the jug, and Sister Mercy said a drunken man was near to the embodiment of the devil himself.

The doctor put his hand on her arm. "Don't run away, Gabrielle. I won't hurt you. I would never hurt you."

His touch was gentle, and Gabrielle let him pull her into the cabin and shut the door behind her.

9

"Then Becca is here?" Gabrielle asked as she tried to peer past him into the room.

"She is." He moved a bit to the side to let her see the child asleep on the bed built into the wall of the cabin. "But you knew that already, didn't you, young sister?"

Gabrielle ignored his question. "I was concerned for her alone in the woods. There are many dangers for one so young alone at night."

"So there are," the doctor agreed. His eyes stayed on Gabrielle even as he spoke of the child. "But as you can see, she is safe. I would have already brought her back to your village, but she was crying and shaking so that I brought her in to warm by the fire while I brewed her some tea. Then she fell asleep."

"No wonder she was shaking. You looked like a bear coming at her out of the shadows that way. That would surely terrify anyone. Especially a small child lost in the woods." Gabrielle moved past the man to go to Becca. Even in her exhausted sleep, she looked sad.

When Gabrielle looked up and caught the doctor's eyes

burning into her, she realized what she'd said. A flush climbed into her cheeks. "I mean I suppose that's what could have happened."

"It's no shame to know what no one else can know, Gabrielle." His voice seemed to caress her name.

Gabrielle pulled her eyes away from his. She didn't know how to accept what his eyes offered. She crossed her arms tightly across her chest and said, "I must awaken Becca. We must go back at once."

"Do they know you're gone?"

"Perhaps by now they do. I shouldn't have come alone, but I was consumed with worry for Becca."

"With reason. The child doesn't look well. Another reason I made her the tea tonic." The doctor's eyes touched on the child and then came back to Gabrielle's face. "What will happen when they find you gone, young sister?"

"It will cause them great consternation and they will search for us."

"That's not what frightens you."

"I've no fear of my brethren and my sisters. I simply do not wish to cause them grief."

"Well said, young sister. But I've seen too many patients not to recognize fear when it sits on the face of the one in front of me. If you're not afraid of your fellow Shakers, then I must be what makes you tremble. Will you deny that?"

Gabrielle was silent for a moment before she raised her eyes to his. "Nay."

"What have I done to frighten you, Gabrielle?"

Again his voice speaking her name was almost as if he'd reached out and stroked her cheek. Gabrielle cast about for something to tell him that would hold the truth but not reveal the confusion inside her. She remembered the thought that he might have been drinking. "You are drunk."

The doctor laughed softly. "No, young sister, I'm not drunk. I save my strong drink for medicinal purposes. And that is not what frightens you."

Gabrielle turned away from him. "I must take Becca and go."

The doctor put a hand on her shoulder. "Wait. One minute more cannot hurt. I have a need to talk to you, and after you hear me out, then I'll carry the child back through the woods for you. I doubt she is strong enough to make it on her own."

"What have you to say to me? Is it about Brother Nathan? Elder Caleb has told us he is improving each day."

"That he is, but this isn't anything to do with your Nathan. It's about your father. He wants me to talk you into leaving the Shakers."

Gabrielle frowned. "You mean my father appeared to you in some sort of vision?"

The doctor smiled and shook his head. "No vision. He was here in this room just yesterday the same as you are now."

"That could not be. My father is dead. Six years now."

"He wanted you to believe that. He says he thought your mother would remarry and also that her uncle might look more favorably on helping you if he was gone."

Gabrielle tried to picture her father's face in her mind, but the years had fogged her memory. "It's been so long. I loved Papa, but I always knew each time he came home that it wouldn't be for long. When I was very young, he tried to be the kind of man my mother needed him to be, but there was something about him that our house could not hold."

Gabrielle was silent, remembering. The doctor didn't intrude on her thoughts. Finally she went on. "I never mourned for him when he left, but my mother did. At least she mourned the man she wanted him to be. Perhaps it was kindness that made him send a man to tell us he'd died on the river."

"So he claims," Dr. Scott said.

Gabrielle shook her head to clear it of the troublesome memories and smiled. "It's funny how the Eternal Father works things out. Papa would have never joined the Believers, but with him gone, Mother could. Sister Martha is one of the most contented among our community."

The doctor put both hands on her shoulders and turned her to face him. His eyes burned into hers. "And are you contented, Gabrielle?"

She wanted to look away, but she couldn't. The pull of his eyes was too strong. Neither would they allow a lie. "I was, and I will be again."

"And now?"

Gabrielle's voice fell to a whisper. "Now you trouble my mind, Dr. Scott."

The man was silent as his eyes probed hers. At last he said, "I'm glad, for you also trouble mine."

"I'm sorry. I have no desire to bring trouble to your thoughts, but for you, as for me, it will pass."

The doctor frowned. "What do you mean?"

"In time and with prayer this will all pass away from me. Then I can once again be in full fellowship with my brothers and sisters."

His hands tightened on her shoulders. "It won't pass away. Your spirit is troubled because you don't belong there with them."

113

"But I do. I must serve the Lord with all my being." She did not allow the tremble she felt inside her show in her voice.

"You don't have to shut yourself away from the world to worship the Lord. God intended for men and women to love and marry and bring forth children into the world. It says so in his book. Go and be fruitful. Isn't that what it says?"

"That is his plan for some, but not for the Believers. And not for me."

The doctor jerked his hands away from her shoulders and stalked across the room. Then he was back. "Surely there is some way I can make you see."

Gabrielle met his eyes steadily. She was sure of her words. "Nay, our feet have been set on different paths, Dr. Scott. For just this moment in our lives, our paths have crossed. But now they must go on again along their separate ways."

"I can't accept that. I won't accept that." He put his hands back on her shoulders. "Have you ever been kissed, young sister?"

The look in the doctor's eyes alarmed Gabrielle. "It's never wise to tempt Satan, Dr. Scott."

The man only laughed. "No girl should go through life without at least one kiss from a man who loves her."

Gabrielle tried to twist away from him, but he was too strong. He pulled her close, and then with one hand he tipped her chin up and gently covered her lips with his own. Gabrielle couldn't fight against his strength. She did fight against the feeling rising inside her in response to his touch, but the feeling rushed through her, breaking down every barrier she threw up against it. Her heart was pounding harder than when she had imagined the shadow in her vision was a bear, and her head was spinning as if she'd been drawn into a whirlwind. Even

114

after he raised his mouth from hers, it was a minute before she could make herself pull away from him.

When she stepped back, he let her go. "You can't make me believe that was wrong," he said softly.

Tears pushed at Gabrielle's eyes. Everything inside her felt as if it had been turned upside down, and she knew only one thing for sure. She had to get away from this man. "I must leave," she said.

"I can't make you stay. But I am here, Gabrielle. Remember that. Always I am here."

"Just stay away from me. I must never see you again."

"Shutting me away won't make you forget."

Gabrielle whispered, "I belong with the Believers." She couldn't keep the tremble out of her voice this time as she repeated the words yet again. "I belong with the Believers."

"No," the doctor said gently. "You've never belonged with them, and you never will."

Gabrielle spun away from him and reached to shake Becca awake. The doctor moved in front of her and gently picked up the little girl. Becca started to rouse up, but the doctor calmed her with a few soft words. The child's head nestled against his shoulder as she settled back into sleep.

He led the way through the dark woods without a word. Gabrielle was grateful for the silence. She needed time to straighten her thoughts out before she went back into the light. Now the night was a friend as it hid the shame on her face. She felt no shame for having been kissed. There had been little she could do to prevent that. Her shame was in the way her lips had betrayed her by yielding to the man's kiss and the way she had melted in his embrace.

Ahead of her, Dr. Scott stopped. "We're near your village.

It'll be best if you go on alone now. I suggest you simply tell the others you've been lost these hours in the woods."

Gabrielle took the child into her own arms. Becca's small frame was whisper light. Gabrielle looked toward the doctor. She couldn't see his face in the dark, but he was so near she could feel his breath on her cheek. "But that wouldn't be true," she said.

"You must do what you must, young sister. The truth you need to hold to is that you've done no wrong against your Lord or anyone else, but I'm not sure your brethren and sisters will recognize that truth." He ran his fingers across her cheek. "Remember what I said, Gabrielle. I am near. I will always be near."

Gabrielle walked away from him and out of the woods slowly. With each step she confessed her sins to the Eternal Father, because she knew as she approached the light that she wouldn't be able to confess them to Sister Mercy.

Brothers with torches moved through the darkness in front of the school family house. The alarm had been given then. It had been too much to expect that she could come back into the village without her absence being noted. She had been gone too long for that. She hesitated a moment before she took a deep breath and walked briskly on to the house. Whatever happened would have to be faced.

"I am here," she called loudly. Becca stirred in her arms but didn't waken.

Elder Caleb ran to her and touched her arm. "We are overjoyed to see you safe, Sister Gabrielle." He held up his torch to look at her face. "You and the child."

The gentle sincerity of his voice made tears prick Gabrielle's eyes. She waited for the questions, but the elder only took the child from her and led the way into the house.

As he went through the door, he called out loudly, "Praise the Lord. Our sisters have returned from the darkness."

Sister Mercy jumped up from where she'd been kneeling in prayer and ran to embrace Gabrielle. "My child, you can't know how worried we all were when night fell and you did not return to the house."

"It grieves me to have caused you worry." Gabrielle's voice was muffled against Sister Mercy's shoulder. "I'll pray for your forgiveness."

Sister Mercy touched her cheek to Gabrielle's and stepped back from their embrace. "As long as you're safe. At first, I thought you'd gone to your place of prayer, but then when you didn't come to meeting, I didn't know what to think." When Elder Caleb put Becca down on one of the chairs, Sister Mercy noticed the child and frowned. "Why is Sister Becca with you?"

"She's the reason I left," Gabrielle said as she stepped over beside the child and gently moved Becca's head until it was resting easier against the back of the chair. The child's eyes didn't open. Gabrielle looked back at Sister Mercy. "I should have told someone, but when I came from the biting room and found Becca missing, I thought I'd be able to find her quickly in the woods without raising an alarm."

Sister Mercy frowned and Gabrielle rushed on. "Yea, it was wrong. But I was so worried about Becca and night was falling. I thought of how frightened she'd surely be in the woods after dark."

"Your motives were good, Sister Gabrielle, but your actions

were wrong," Elder Caleb said. "For the good of all, you should have taken the time to get help in your search."

Gabrielle lowered her eyes to the floor in silent acknowledgment of her wrong.

The elder reached out and touched her head. "Don't let your heart be too burdened. You found the child in the woods and then your way back among us without meeting any misfortune."

Gabrielle nodded without looking up. She was ashamed at the ease with which she told only half the truth. In the space of a few weeks she'd become a different person, a person capable of hiding the truth and defying the rules she'd always so carefully kept. At last she raised her head to look at Sister Mercy and Elder Caleb and wondered why they couldn't see the difference in her.

But they were smiling. They trusted her, and Gabrielle felt even more shame for deceiving these two she loved than she had when the doctor had kissed her. She was tempted to tell them all the truth instead of just a portion of it, but overriding her need to confess was her fear of their disapproval. She'd heard Sister Mercy talk of others who'd been part of the Believers and then had left for the world or committed some worldly sin. She'd often said, "They have gone back to the pit from which we pulled them out of the mire."

Even worse than words of condemnation, they might insist she submit to constant supervision. That would mean she'd have to be accompanied at all times by another sister for six months. She'd seen one sister pushed away from the Believers by this when Gabrielle hadn't thought her wrong that great. She wouldn't take the chance that she might be so punished even though the blight on her conscience would surely be slow to fade.

Gabrielle knelt before Elder Caleb and said, "I'll pray for more wisdom should such a thing happen again."

Elder Caleb put one hand on her bent head for a moment and then pulled her up. His hands were cold and dry, and Gabrielle couldn't keep from thinking how different the doctor's hands felt. The elder said, "We must rest now. Tomorrow you and Sister Mercy can come to me and we will pray together."

"As you say, Elder Caleb. May I put Sister Becca to bed now?" Gabrielle asked. "She is very tired."

Elder Caleb looked at Becca. "The child is little more than skin and bones and much too pale. Has she been ill?"

"She hasn't been eating well," Gabrielle said.

Sister Mercy spoke up. "The child will not try to accustom herself to the life of a Believer. Her mother holds too strongly to her by visiting the school without permission. That is why I recommended Sister Esther be sent with the others to prepare the mill for the summer work."

"The child is young," Elder Caleb said. "In time she will adapt to our ways."

Gabrielle gently lifted Becca and carried her up the stairs. In their room, the other children were already asleep in their beds. Gabrielle moved quietly to Becca's bed and began undressing her. "Poor little one," she whispered. "It would have taken a miracle for you to find your mother this night."

She thought the child too soundly asleep to waken before the sun rose in the morning, but when she lifted Becca's head to ease on her sleeping dress, Becca opened her eyes. She looked around wildly.

119

"Shh, baby," Gabrielle said as she smoothed back the hair from Becca's face. "It's all right. I'm here with you."

"'Brielle?" Becca reached up her arms and grabbed Gabrielle. "I was lost. I just wanted to find Mama, but there were so many trees. And then something grabbed me. I was so scared, 'Brielle. Was it all only a dream?"

"Nay, child, but it's over now. You're here with us where you're safe."

Becca came more fully awake. "It was a man, wasn't it?"

"It was. But he did not hurt you."

"I know. I was so scared, but then he picked me up and hugged me like Papa used to and he kept holding me by the fire until I stopped shivering. I wanted to ask him to help me find my mama, but I was afraid."

"You had no reason to fear him. He's a good man. A kind man."

"I wasn't afraid of him. I was afraid to ask because I knew what he'd say." Becca was silent for a long minute before she went on. "Mama is dead, 'Brielle."

"Nay, Becca, your mother is not dead." Gabrielle stared down at Becca as she pushed assurance into her voice. "She has just been sent away to another house. She is not dead."

But the child would not be convinced. "But she is, 'Brielle. She would come to see me if she wasn't dead. I know she would."

"She will come again. Believe me."

The little girl just looked at her without a word.

Gabrielle stroked her face and said, "It's been a long night, Becca, and you're very tired. In the morning you'll remember that I would never lie to you and so you will know that your mother yet lives and will come back to see you as soon as she can."

Becca let Gabrielle lay her back on the bed. She closed her eyes, and Gabrielle pulled the covers up over her before leaning down to brush her lips across the child's forehead. In the morning she'd find a way to make Becca believe her mother was not dead. She'd explain how the elders had sent her away to the mill even though she knew Sister Mercy wouldn't approve. It seemed as if more and more she did things that Sister Mercy wouldn't approve.

Gabrielle snuffed out the candle. Just before she turned away to ready herself for her own bed, Becca said, "'Brielle?"

Gabrielle touched the child's hand and said, "What is it, dear?"

"Do we all go to heaven when we die?"

"Yea," Gabrielle said. "If we've given our hearts to the Lord and lived for him."

"Mama told me she loved the Lord and I do too. I talk to him sometimes and he comes and listens to me." Becca was quiet again for a moment, but her grip on Gabrielle's hand stayed tight. Finally she said, "If I die, will I go to heaven where Mama is?"

"Becca, your mother isn't dead. They sent her to the mill and that is too far away for her to come see you. In a few weeks she'll be back in the village with us and you will see her every day." Gabrielle pushed her words at the child, but they seemed to bounce off Becca's ears.

"It's nice in heaven, isn't it, 'Brielle? There are angels up there and everything."

Before Gabrielle could come up with a reply, Becca's hand went limp in hers, and Gabrielle's heart bounced up into her throat. Surely the child could not wish herself to heaven. Even so, Gabrielle was leaning over to put her ear to the little girl's

121

chest when she heard Becca's soft, even breathing that meant she'd simply fallen asleep.

She knelt by the child's bed and whispered a fervent prayer. "Dear Father above, watch over this your precious child. Ease her sadness and help her have reason to smile once more." She started to stand up, but then she glanced over her shoulder to be sure Sister Mercy hadn't come in the room before she added, "And please let Sister Esther come back to the village soon. Very soon."

10

As the days passed, Gabrielle settled back into the way of the Believers. The doctor's words stayed in her mind, but she wouldn't let them have anything to do with her life.

The day after she'd gone into the woods to find Becca, Elder Caleb had given her prayers to say as a penance. Gabrielle said them gladly although she doubted the prayers would rid her of the hidden, unconfessed sin. In time she might cleanse her soul of the sin of the doctor's lips touching hers, but now she couldn't. Not and face Sister Mercy's sure disapproval.

Gabrielle often caught Sister Mercy watching her closely, but Gabrielle didn't think she'd lost her trust in her. It was only concern that kept her close to Gabrielle's side, just as concern made Gabrielle watch Becca.

Becca appeared to be all right. The child had gotten out of bed the next morning as if nothing out of the ordinary had even happened. But although she did her schoolwork and her chores without complaint, she seemed to be collapsing inwardly until her body was only an empty shell.

Becca never mentioned her mother, but sometimes

Gabrielle saw the child off by herself with her lips moving in a secret conversation with no one. Sister Mercy instructed Gabrielle to let Becca alone. "It appears the child is praying. She is surely beginning to become one of us."

Gabrielle took no comfort from Sister Mercy's words. Nor did she abide by Sister Mercy's instructions to not give Becca any extra attention. Instead she took every opportunity to reassure Becca of her love and to tell the child her mother would be back among them in a few weeks. Gabrielle felt no guilt for speaking these words Sister Mercy might not approve. In the Bible, the Lord was always reaching out a hand in comfort to those he met who were hurting, and his Word made it clear that his followers were to do the same. It was just that she and Sister Mercy did not agree on how best to help Becca.

Either way it didn't seem to matter. Becca never acted as if she even heard Gabrielle when Gabrielle spoke of her mother being back among them soon. Instead she would lift her eyes toward the heavens as if she could see something in the sky no one else could see. Gabrielle prayed every day for Sister Esther's return from the mill house so Becca could see her and touch her and know Gabrielle spoke the truth about her. While she did not think the child could wish herself to heaven, all the same, dark shadowy fingers seemed to be reaching toward Becca in Gabrielle's thoughts.

Gabrielle's mind gave her no peace. If she wasn't worrying about Becca, then her own sins and doubts were troubling her. She did not allow herself to watch for the doctor to come and treat Nathan anymore, but she wanted to. She wanted to talk with him again. She wanted to hear her name on his tongue again, to feel the warmth of his hands burning into her shoulders. Even when she kept her eyes away from him and tried to shut her mind to the pull he had over her, his worldliness still touched her with questions she dared not ask.

The day Elder Caleb sent for her, Gabrielle feared he'd found out her sins. As she walked over to the Center House, she thought it might be a relief to have her soul cleansed with honesty, but when she reached the elder's office, a man sat with him. A man Gabrielle would have recognized even if the doctor hadn't already told her that her father was alive. The eyes and the smile when he saw her were the same.

She gave no outward sign that she knew him as she went to stand in front of the Elder. How different from the last time she'd seen her father when she'd run all the way down the road to be swung up in his arms and kissed and hugged while she'd giggled with delight as his beard tickled her cheeks. That seemed a lifetime ago now. She kept her head bent and her eyes on the floor as she said, "I've come as you requested, Elder Caleb."

"Sit down, Sister Gabrielle," the elder said. "This man wishes to speak with you. Do you know him?"

Gabrielle sat down and looked at her father. His smile had been replaced by a frown that etched deep lines between his eyes, and his hands moved uneasily across his lap as if he were used to holding something there. A gun perhaps. He wore rough leather garments and he brought the smell of the wilderness into the room with him. The sight of him brought a smile to her soul, but Gabrielle kept her face solemn. "He is Alec Hope, my father from the world."

It was Elder Caleb's turn to frown. "But Sister Martha said her husband was dead when the two of you came together with the Believers."

125

"Yea, that is what we believed. We were told he had died on the river. A riverboat accident."

Her father shifted uneasily in his chair. "I done explained all that to you, Reverend, sir. How I done that to make things better for my missus."

Elder Caleb stared at Gabrielle's father a moment before he said, "So you did, Mr. Hope, and since Sister Gabrielle remembers you as who you say you are, I have decided to allow you to speak to her."

"I don't need nobody's say-so to speak to my own flesh-and-blood daughter."

Elder Caleb folded his hands on the table in front of him and made no reply.

Gabrielle glanced at the elder and then spoke to her father for the first time. "Why have you come?"

"Any fool could guess that." Her father's voice was gruff with feeling. He had never been one to use caution with his words. Whatever he wanted to say, he said with no thought of the feelings of his listeners. Even without intending to, he'd often caused her mother tears. Now he went on. "I come to see you, girl."

Gabrielle finally allowed the smile to come out. "It's good to see you alive, Father. I could never think of you as dead even years after I heard it was so. And as you can see I am well. Mother and I have been here at Harmony Hill for over five years and we are content."

"Content?" Her father made a disgusted sound. "What do you mean by that, girl? You ought to have a man by now and young'uns of your own instead of growing into an old maid here."

"I am happy with the Believers' way, Father. If you tried to understand, you might see the peace such a life provides."

126

Her father shook his head. "I don't believe it. You can't be happy. Not living here like this with a bunch of people that might as well be dead. You must all be addlebrained."

Elder Caleb spoke up quietly. "I will remind you, Mr. Hope, that you are a guest in our village."

Her father mashed his mouth together a minute before he said, "All right." Then he stared at Gabrielle for a long time before he said, "I want you to know, girl, that you can come away from here with me. I'll see that you have food to eat and a roof over your head. You don't have to stay here. You can come with me where you can have a real life."

Before Gabrielle could answer, the elder asked, "Do you have a home, Mr. Hope? Or any means to provide the needs of a family?"

Her father shifted in his chair again as if a nail had suddenly risen up out of the seat to poke him. "I promised to provide for her. She won't be in want if she comes with me. My word is good."

The elder kept his eyes on Gabrielle's father as he calmly said, "You promised once before to care for a wife and yet you went away and deliberately abandoned her and a child. This child. Now you've come back to disturb this same child's life with no plans for your future or hers."

Her father angrily glared at the elder. "This ain't none of your concern, Preacher. I was talking to my girl, but you can be sure I could find somebody to take care of my girl better'n you folks here with your crazy dancing and such. I ain't the fool you're making me out to be. Gabrielle here knows that." Her father clenched his fists and half rose up out of his chair.

"It is not my intention to embarrass you, Mr. Hope," Elder

Caleb said. "I have only Sister Gabrielle's best interests at heart."

"And you think I don't?" her father almost shouted back.

Gabrielle held up her hand. While her father had talked, the memories of him and his ways had flooded back to her. He was always getting a new idea that filled him with purpose. Then as quickly as the idea had come, it faded away. Now she was that idea, but he would soon tire of being tied down with the responsibility of a daughter. In fact, Gabrielle wondered if perhaps some of the fire of his purpose was already cooling.

"Father, it was kind of you to come seek out knowledge of me after these many years, but now you must understand and accept that Mother and I are satisfied here." Why was it that she could explain things so much easier to this man, her father, than to Dr. Scott? What was it in the doctor's eyes that made her doubt the truth of what she was saying when she spoke with him, while at this moment speaking to her father she had no doubts at all?

"It don't seem right to me, girl. None of it, but if you want it . . ." Her father let his words trail away as he sank back down into his chair.

"I do," Gabrielle said firmly.

"Then who am I to say it's wrong? I reckon I never done nothing like nobody else, but I can't help believing this ain't the place for you, Gabrielle. You was always so special even as a little tyke." Now her father's eyes looked almost sad.

Elder Caleb spoke up again. "Among our people many have been blessed with special gifts, Mr. Hope, but our most precious gift is to be simple and to humble ourselves before God. So while you may think our ways strange, they are not. They are very simple. We worship by giving our hands to work and our hearts to God."

Her father didn't even glance over at the elder. He kept his eyes on Gabrielle. "You sure this is what you want? Living here?"

Gabrielle smiled at him. "Yea, Father, it is." She heard a whisper of relief in the way he let out his breath. While he might have meant it when he said he'd make a home for her, it wouldn't have been easy for him to change the way he'd lived for so many years. "What will you do now, Father?"

"I'm thinking on going up north a ways and watching to see what's going to happen up there. It looks like we might be going to have a war up in the territories, and if that happens, I'll be joining up to do some fighting."

"I do not wish you war, Father. I wish you peace and love." As Gabrielle stood up, she doubted her father had ever wanted peace. No wonder he couldn't understand the way they lived at Harmony Hill. She turned to Elder Caleb. "With your permission I will return to my duties now, Elder."

"Of course, Sister Gabrielle." Elder Caleb smiled at her as if she had just passed a test he hadn't been sure she would.

Gabrielle looked back at her father one last time. His age seemed to sit heavier on him now than when she'd first come into the room. She wanted to go to him and throw her arms around him and kiss him so they could once more feel the bond of father and daughter between them. But too many years had gone by. She was no longer the child who had tagged along beside him whenever he was home to hear all the wonderful stories about the strange places he'd been.

"Goodbye, Father," she said softly. She doubted she'd ever

see him again. For years he'd put her from his life. It would be easy for him to do so again. "Take care if this war of yours comes to pass. I will pray for you."

Outside she paused a moment on the path to breathe deeply of the fresh, cool air. The school term would be over in a week, for spring would bring much new work. Each season brought its special chores. Spring meant seed planting and berry season. Gabrielle let her eyes drift to the fields of strawberries behind the Center House building. Soon those fields would be white with blossoms and then dotted with red, plump strawberries that she would help pick and turn into row after row of glistening red jars of preserves.

Knowing what to expect from one season to the next held a certain satisfaction. None of her father's wars spoiled the peace at Harmony Hill. The Believers were against all kinds of violence and fighting. Peace was a good thing, Gabrielle thought as she pulled her shawl closer to her. But suddenly the doctor's eyes were in her mind, and her eyes shifted to the east until she was looking past the buildings toward the trees that stood between the village and his cabin. For a minute she imagined him standing there in the shadow of the trees watching her, waiting for her to come to him. What was it he had said? That he'd always be near.

She pulled her eyes away from the trees and stared down at the path in front of her as she started back to the schoolhouse and her duties. She was almost there when someone whispered her name. "Gabrielle."

Her heart began pounding as she thought that perhaps it hadn't been only her imagination seeing the doctor in the trees, but then the person called to her again. "Come here, Gabrielle."

Even as she recognized his voice, Nathan stepped out of the trees beside her on the path.

"Brother Nathan, what are you doing out here alone?" She had seen him out before but always in the company of one of the other brothers.

"I'm better," Nathan said and walked a circle around her to prove it. "And don't call me brother. You know I hate that."

"As you wish," she said. "And I am joyful to see you so much better, but are you sure you should be out here alone? What if you fell?"

"I'm practically well, I tell you," Nathan insisted. He took hold of Gabrielle's arm and pulled her away from the path into the edge of the trees. "Elder Caleb let me go over to the doc's by myself. Said he couldn't spare a man from the work on the new barn. I guess I'll be going out to help fetch stuff for them on the morrow. The doc said it'd be all right."

"That is good news."

"Even better, that means I'll be able to leave this place behind before long. The doc will help me find a job."

"He told you that?" Gabrielle asked.

"Not in so many words, but he likes me. I can tell he does. He'll help me."

His words didn't surprise Gabrielle. She'd been expecting Nathan to leave for months before he was burned. He chafed under the constraints of a Believer's life. He'd told her so often enough. But before when he'd spoken of leaving, she'd used all her powers of persuasion to convince him to stay. She'd been sure of her words urging him to avoid the temptations of the world. Now the words were no longer there inside her. She simply said, "I'll miss you when you're gone, Nathan."

Nathan's brown eyes were intent on her. His hand grasped

her arm tighter as he said, "You don't have to. You can go with me."

Gabrielle didn't know what to say. In the space of an hour she had been given two ways to leave the Believers. Was the Eternal Father testing her?

Encouraged by her silence, Nathan rushed ahead with his plans. "We could go tomorrow. The doc will help us, and then we can find a preacher and get married."

"Commit matrimony?" The very words were uncomfortable on her tongue.

"Nay, we'll just be getting married like folks do every day."

"But we're Believers, Nathan."

"I've never been a Believer, Gabrielle, and I'm not staying in this godforsaken place another week."

His words banged into her ears. "How can you say that, Nathan? God is all around us."

"Maybe so, but I'm not wanting to talk about God right now. I'm talking about you, Gabrielle. About us. You have to go with me. You have to."

"I cannot." Gabrielle didn't want to hurt Nathan, but the words had to be said. "I'm sorry, Nathan, but I can't leave Harmony Hill. This is my home."

The color rose up in his face and then drained away, leaving the burn scars a bright pink on his too-white cheeks. He still wasn't ready to hear the truth of her words. "I'll come back for you when you're ready, Gabrielle. I promise to take care of you. I love you, Gabrielle. I've loved you ever since the first day I laid eyes on you. I thought you loved me too."

His pain hurt her. She tried to explain. "I do, Nathan, but

as a brother. I know not this other love that men and women in the world share."

"Come with me, Gabrielle, and I'll teach you."

"No love can be taught and I fear especially the kind of which you speak. Love must come from the heart," Gabrielle said as gently as she could.

Nathan's hand dropped off her arm to hang limply by his side. His whole body seemed to sag. "I can't believe this. All the nonsense I've put up with here in this place even to almost burning myself alive for a measly sack of corn."

"I never told you I'd go away with you, Nathan, and you surely can't blame me for the fire."

"I'm not blaming you for the fire. Only that I was in it. Do you think I'd have stayed in this place a year if it hadn't been for you?" He was almost yelling. "Four years of my life I've wasted here because I thought you'd come away with me. Because I thought you loved me. And now you say nay as though I'd offered you nothing more than a sip of water."

"That's not true, Nathan." She reached out to touch his hand, but he jerked away from her angrily.

"What do you know about truth? You're as bad as the rest of them around here, going around pretending to love everyone, but it's all just a sham. You never cared nothing for me."

She wouldn't argue with him. He was too upset to accept anything she might say. So she stood there without a word and let him throw his words at her.

"And I thought you were so good, so pure, so beautiful. I didn't think you'd turn on me like some kind of snake."

Tears pushed at Gabrielle's eyes, but she blinked hard to keep them back. She didn't want Nathan to think she was softening and might yet change her mind. It would be better for him to go away hating her.

All at once his stream of angry words ran out. His voice broke as he said, "You did care for me. I know you did."

Gabrielle didn't say again that she loved him as a brother. Instead she said, "If I weren't a Believer, then things might be different." She wasn't sure her words were true, but it was the only gift she had to give him. "Goodbye, Nathan."

"I can't say goodbye, Gabrielle." He stared at her a long time before he turned and started away. He went a few steps, then stopped and, without turning around, said, "Don't watch me leave. It's bad luck."

He slowly limped off into the woods. Gabrielle watched him only a moment before she went back to the path. Tears streamed down her cheeks. She wiped at them with the corner of her scarf and wished she could believe she'd see him again.

11

Brice wasn't surprised when he saw Nathan back at his door. "What are you doing here, Bates? You should have been back at Harmony Hill hours ago."

"I was," Nathan said. "I came back."

Brice pulled the door open to let him in. He'd been expecting the boy to show up like this for a week or more. Nathan had never been a Shaker, and the time had come for him to shake off their restraints. But there was more. A stab of misery went deep in the boy's eyes. "You asked the young sister," Brice said. It wasn't a question, but a statement of fact.

"She said she loved me—like a brother." Nathan's voice was rough as he spit out the words. He angrily swiped at the tears that popped up in his eyes.

Brice mashed his lips together to keep from saying he'd warned the boy about the young sister. Nathan's pain was too fresh, too deep. Then in spite of the sympathy he had for the boy, a breath of relief swept through Brice. He couldn't have fought the boy for Gabrielle, but now as long as his only rival was the Shaker life, he'd never give up. He'd already made her admit her doubts. In time she would come away from the Shakers. The last thought echoed in his mind, and he remembered Nathan saying the same with just as much hope and sureness.

Brice pulled a chair and stool close to the fire. "Sit down, Bates, and put your legs up. You've been on them too long today already."

"I don't care. I wish you'd just left me there in that barn," the boy said, but he sat down and obediently put up his feet.

"It was Gabrielle who told me where to find you in the barn, and burned her own hands putting out the fire on your pants legs. She does care for you, Bates."

The boy leaned his head back and shut his eyes. "So she said. Like a brother." He was quiet a long time before he went on. "You know, Doc, I thought I knew all about pain. What with the way my legs are and all. But the way I'm hurting now makes all that other seem like child's play."

Brice frowned at Nathan. "I've seen plenty die with burns no worse than yours, but nobody ever died of a broken heart, Bates. You won't either."

Nathan opened his eyes and looked at Brice. "You got medicine for everything else, Doc. What you got for this kind of hurting?"

Alec Hope stepped up into the door that Brice hadn't closed. "I reckon the doc might not give you what you're needing, boy, but I got just the thing here." He came over to the fire and pulled a flask out from under his shirt to hand the boy. "Fixes up whatever ails you every time."

"At least till the morning sun shows up on the horizon," Brice said, but when Nathan reached for the flask he didn't try to stop him. The boy had to learn on his own.

Nathan tipped the flask back and took a swallow. Then he started gasping and coughing. Hope reached over and grabbed the flask before the boy could spill any of its contents. "The squeezings appear to be a mite strong for the boy." He looked up at Brice. "Who is he anyway? He puts me in mind of them at the place I just come from. He one of them Shakers?"

"He was," Brice started, but the boy swallowed hard and found his voice.

"Not anymore I'm not. If it's any business of yours."

Brice kept his eyes on Hope. "So you went to the Shaker village?"

Hope sat down in the other chair and left Brice standing. "I did. Not that it done me a bit of good."

"They didn't let you see her?"

"I seen her, all right. Talked to her too. But that dried-up old preacher sat there and wouldn't leave us alone. If I could've got her alone, I'd a made her see that that ain't no way to live."

"Then she wouldn't talk about coming away with you." Brice hadn't thought she would, but there'd been that chance.

"Nope. Claimed she was happy living there like that. Leastways that's what she said with that old preacher watching her." Hope took a swig from his flask and stared at the fire. "She was even prettier than I remembered. She's all grown up now and not a thing like she used to be when she was a little tyke. Sitting there so solemn and all. And she wouldn't even hug my neck. She always used to run and give me a big hug when I come home."

"That was a long time ago, Hope. You couldn't expect her to be the same little girl she was then."

Hope took another long swallow from his flask. He wiped

his mouth on his sleeve. "I reckon as how you're right, Doc, but I just can't get used to the idea that she wants to stay there. I don't claim to know all that much about religion, but the way they're thinking about it just can't be right." He looked over at Brice. "Can it, Doc?"

"To our way of thinking. But to their way of thinking, no other way is right," Brice said.

Nathan had been watching them while they talked and now he spoke up. "Did you say Hope, Doc?"

"That's right, Bates. You and this old woodsman have something in common. You both asked the young sister to leave with you and she turned you both down. She doesn't seem to want a husband or a father." Or a doctor either, he added silently. He could pretend not to be part of their misery, but he was. And just as apt to fail to reach her as they were.

"You can't be Gabrielle's father. She told me her pa was dead."

"So I was, and I might as well stayed that way for all the good it done me or her for me to come back. But my bones have been aching some when I get up in the morning and I got to thinking about how I was getting on in years and I got to wondering how her and her mother had got along after I sent them that message that I'd drowned. I was even thinking maybe I had some grandkids that would want to sit on my knee and hear some stories. Just foolishness on my part, and I reckon I had whatever grief I got today coming. I weren't never much shakes as a pa. Not that Gabrielle ever held that against me." Hope looked at the boy and handed him back the flask. "But what about you, boy? What did you have to do with my girl?"

"I loved her," Nathan said simply before he tipped up the

138

flask and took a careful swallow. He hit his chest with his fist, but managed to keep from coughing.

Brice thought it a good sign that Nathan used the past tense. He would heal. His love hadn't gone so deep that it couldn't be cut out. He was young. There'd be other girls with no opposition to marrying and settling down with the boy.

"I reckon as how you ain't the only one," Hope said. Brice looked quickly toward the man. Hope met his look steadily for a moment before he went on. "I mean, it'd surely be easy for any red-blooded man to fall for my girl."

Nathan stared sadly at the flask in his hand. "I never thought she'd say no." Then he tipped it up to take another drink.

Hope pulled his pipe out of another pocket and lit it with a taper from the fire. "Well, I reckon it's the truth, boy, when I say that many a man was sorry a woman said yes as the years went by. There ain't nothing like a woman to try and tie you down."

"I wanted to be tied down with Gabrielle," Nathan said.

"My girl is sure enough special, but still and all, a woman is a woman. And it ain't always a good idea to settle down so early on in life. I mean, you're just a boy and there's a lot to see out there where womenfolk ain't a mind to go."

"But I had it all planned out. Been planning how we'd go away and start on our own for years." Hope's liquor was beginning to make the boy slur his words. He tipped up the flask again, and this time drank it down clean.

"What you aiming to do now, boy?" Hope asked.

Nathan swallowed hard. "I don't rightly know. I guess I'll be having to get work somewhere."

Brice spoke up. "I could take you on to learn medicine,

Bates. I've never thought about an apprentice, but there are times when one might come in handy."

"That's mighty nice of you, Dr. Scott, but I don't think I'd make any kind of doctor. I like being outside, not in sickrooms. But if you'd let me stay on a spell, I could fetch things for you and take care of your horse. Just until my legs get some better."

"What's wrong with your legs, boy?" Hope asked.

"He was in the fire they had at the Shaker village a while back," Brice said.

Hope reached over and yanked up the boy's pants leg. He made no face at the sight of the still angry-looking burns, but he said, "I'm thinking if I ever need doctoring, I'll know where to come." Hope sat back before he went on. "But that's too bad, boy. I was thinking maybe you'd be wanting to go with me when I left."

"And where would that be?" Nathan asked.

"Can't say for sure." Hope pulled on his pipe before he went on. "Wherever my feet take a notion to lead me. But most likely I'm going to head up north to see what's going on with the redcoats. I've heard fighting might break out up there just any day now, and if it does, I'm aiming to be in the middle of it."

"They haven't declared war yet," Brice said. "I saw a newspaper just last week."

"But they will," Hope said. "They'll have to. The way them British scoundrels are taking our boys off'n our ships like it's their right. And then the Injuns are getting a mite too brave up in the territories. It's time we went up there and taught them a thing or two."

140

"A war?" Nathan sat up a little straighter in his chair and leaned toward Hope.

"Where you been, boy? Hiding in a hole somewheres?" Hope asked.

"I might as well have been," Nathan said. "The Shakers don't hold with fighting, so there wouldn't be much need in them talking about a war unless it was going on right here around them where it might cause problems with their crops or something."

Hope stared at his pipe and shook his head. "I just can't figure them people out. Any man ought to be proud to stand up and fight for his country."

"I could go with you." Nathan sounded eager. "My legs aren't that bad off. Are they, Doc? You said yourself I could start working."

Brice put a hand on the boy's shoulder. "Easy does it, Bates. Wars aren't all that exciting. Sometimes it's just a good place to die. But even so, there isn't even a war on yet. Just a bunch of rumors flying. You'd best stick around here with me for a while and let your legs get some stronger before you march off with an army."

"Sure, boy." Hope pulled on his pipe again before he added, "Like the doc here says, they ain't even said for sure there's gonna be a war yet. There'll be plenty of time to join up later on, I expect."

Nathan stared at the fire. "I'm no good for anything. Gabrielle wouldn't have me and now you say the army won't either."

He started to tip up the flask again, but Brice reached and took it away from him. "I think you've had more than enough, Bates. You're beginning to sound foolish. You'd best go to bed and sleep it off." Brice handed the flask to

Hope who stuck it back in his shirt. "You aiming to stay the night, Hope?"

"Naw, I've been bedding down in a barn over at the settlement. And I'll be wanting to get an early start come morning. I just come by to tell you I was leaving." He stuck his pipe in his mouth and reached for his hat.

Outside Brice's horse whinnied and they heard boots on the steps. Hope stood up and said, "Sounds like somebody might need your doctoring, Doc."

But when Brice swung open the door, Elder Caleb and another Shaker man stood there. Brice wasn't surprised to see them, but he'd thought they'd wait till morning. "Good evening, sirs," he said. "Is there something I can do for you?"

"We seek our brother," Elder Caleb said. "Brother Nathan was to have come to you for treatment this afternoon. He did not return to our village."

The elder's face was stern and unforgiving. He was ready to do battle with Brice for the prize of the young brother, but Brice had no wish to battle with the old elder for the boy. That fight would have to be won by Bates himself. Brice opened the door and stepped back. "He is here."

The two men moved past Brice into the room. The elder's eyes swept around the room, stopped briefly on Hope, and then landed on Nathan. "We had concern for your safety, Brother Nathan."

Nathan looked up. Hope's liquor had turned his cheeks red and now gave his tongue courage. "I decided to leave your grave out there and start to live. And living feels good."

Elder Caleb looked at him for a long moment before he fastened his eyes on Brice even though he spoke to the boy. "I fear you have sought bad counsel, my brother."

"I gave him no encouragement to leave your people, Elder. He needed none," Brice said.

"The same way you have not encouraged young Sister Gabrielle to wonder about the world, Dr. Scott?" the elder said.

"I couldn't encourage her to do anything." Brice tried to rein in the anger rising inside him. "You won't let me talk to her."

"From the first night you came into our midst, there has been nothing but discord. It would have been better if you'd never come."

"Then the boy here would have died."

"Perhaps, although the Eternal Father saves those he chooses to save. But even so, it would have been better for our brother to have died with his salvation in eternity assured than to live with only the fires of hell as a reward."

"I'm not sure the boy would agree," Brice said.

The elder looked back at Nathan as he said, "Leave us so that we might talk with our brother alone. There is yet time to help him see the error of his path into sin."

Brice didn't move until Nathan looked up and said, "They're bound and determined to have their say, Doc. I might as well get it over with."

The elder knelt beside Nathan and shut his eyes in prayer. The other Shaker stepped in front of Brice and said, "You need have no fear that we will harm the boy. He is our brother."

"Come on, Hope. We won't freeze out on the stoop." Brice led the way outside and pulled the door shut behind them. "I must be a fool letting them run me out of my own house," he said as he walked down the steps.

Hope followed him. "Best to let them do their talking and

get it out of their system, but I'm thinking they ain't going to make much headway with the boy. His mind's done set agin them, and I got a feeling when that boy sets his head there ain't no changing it. I reckon that's why my girl turning him down went so hard on him."

"I tried to tell him once before she wouldn't come away with him, but he didn't want to hear it. I'm not sure there's any way of getting her away from there short of stealing her away."

"There's an idea," Hope said. "I never thought of that, but it works sometimes with little white kids who've grown up Injun. It worked with you."

"I lived with the Indians, but I hadn't turned Indian." Brice looked toward Hope. "And I wasn't kidnapped away. You bought me."

"I ain't sure we've got enough money to make them give up my girl."

"No." Brice moved out into the yard and sat down on a stump. He didn't want to be close enough to hear what they were saying in the cabin. Hope followed him. "It wouldn't work anyway. Your daughter wasn't stolen or bought into the Shakers, and she can't be stolen away or bought back. It's just not that easy."

"I guess as how you're right." Hope put his pipe in his mouth and squatted down beside Brice. He puffed on his pipe a few times before he said, "Me and the boy, we done give up. We tried and she said no. I don't figure on trying no more, and the boy's done got the sound of war ringing in his ears."

"And whose fault is that?" Brice said.

"I was just trying to get his mind off'n his troubles. I wasn't meaning no harm to the boy."

144

"He'd be better off with the Shakers than following you off to war."

"Could be you're right. Could be my girl is better off there than with me too."

"Could be," Brice said.

"And could not be, right, Doc? So what do you say? Have you give up?"

Brice stared at the cabin. The light of the fire and candles seeped out through the cracks in the chinking between the logs to be swallowed up by the dark. Had he given up? He hadn't been to the Shaker village for days, hadn't even been close to Gabrielle since the night she'd come to his cabin for the child. He'd been busy. There'd been sickness in the town. He'd nursed two children through the fever, but he'd lost the third in spite of everything he'd done.

Still, even while he was fighting the Grim Reaper for the lives of the little ones, Gabrielle had been with him, a gentle whisper in his mind. Now with the darkness around him, it was easy to bring her image up before him. Even her sweet, clean scent was there overriding the smell of Hope's pipe. He could never give up. Yet when he was brutally honest with himself, he could see no hope that he'd ever again feel the soft surrender of her lips under his.

"Well, Doc?" Hope asked again. "Have you?"

"I don't suppose I can give up, Hope. I owe you."

"That don't matter all that much now anyhow, does it, Doc?" Brice couldn't see Hope's face in the dark, but he could hear the smile in his voice as he went on talking. "What was it you said about her once? That she is beauty. That says a lot." Hope knocked his pipe out against the stump and stood up.

"I guess I'll be getting along now. Could be I'll be back down this way in a few years."

Brice reached for Hope's hand in the dark and clasped it firmly. "Good luck to you, Hope."

"I reckon if there's any luck to be had, I'm hoping it goes with you, Doc." Hope turned and disappeared into the trees.

Brice looked back at the cabin. The sound of the elder's voice in a kind of chant leaked out through the chinks along with the light. Brice started to get up and go inside to put a stop to the whole bit. But then he settled back down on the stump. If the boy was going to make it on his own, he might as well start now.

Brice shut his ears to the sounds coming from the cabin and looked up at the sky. The moon was late rising, and the sky was full of stars. He liked seeing the stars and had cleared away a few more trees than necessary when he built his cabin just so more of the sky would be open. After his mother had died when he was five, he used to look up at the stars and imagine her sitting on one of them watching over him from heaven. And then when the Indians had taken him, he'd been relieved to see the same stars above his head there so his mother could keep watch over him. Thinking about her eyes on him helped him hang onto the truth of who he was.

His mother had been a churchwoman. She'd prized her Bible above all else. He could still remember the feel of her hand on his head as he knelt by his little bed and said his bedtime prayers. Then it hadn't been hard to believe in the Lord. The Lord was in his heaven and all was right with the world. Even when a lot had gone wrong with the world, he'd been able to keep imagining the Lord cared about him.

But then Jemma had looked at him and the joy had leaked

out of her eyes along with the blood her father let out of her arm in an attempt to cure her of the fever. A good, loving God wouldn't have taken that kind of joy away from the world. The world was a cruel place and religion didn't make it one bit less cruel. There was nothing there above him but stars. Nothing in the dark around him but more dark and maybe a bear or a panther. No Lord. No angels. A man had to make his own way.

Guilt pricked him as he stared up at the star he'd always imagined his mother sitting on. She'd be disappointed that he'd let his heart turn so cold.

A long while later the cabin door opened. Nathan laughed as the two Shakers stepped outside. The man in the back pulled the door shut and cut off the boy's laughter. After a moment, Elder Caleb asked, "Are you here, Dr. Scott?"

Brice got up off his stump and said, "I'm here."

They came down the steps and across the opening to where he stood. "We will leave now."

"Without the boy?" Brice wanted them to feel their failure as he'd been feeling his own failure to reach the young sister while he waited in the dark.

"The liquor Alec Hope gave him has confused his mind. We will come back tomorrow when his mind is clearer," Elder Caleb said. The other man, a couple of steps back, kept his head bent as the elder spoke with Brice.

"Come if you want. He'll probably be here," Brice said. "But I doubt it will make any difference. The boy has made up his mind."

"I fear you helped him along this path to destruction." It was too dark to see the elder's face clearly, but the condemnation in his voice was strong.

147

"I only treated the wounds on his body. Not his mind."

"So you say." The elder's voice was quiet but firm as he continued speaking. "Nevertheless it would be best if you stayed away from our village from this day on."

Brice studied the man's shadowy face in the dark. "What if you have sickness?"

"We have medicine to treat our own. You bring a worse sickness with you, Doctor, than any we could have. A sickness of the spirit for which you desire no cure. You are no longer welcome in our village." Elder Caleb turned away and gestured to the other man.

Brice stood still as they walked away from him. An odd pain sprang up inside him as he felt them moving in front of his image of Gabrielle and taking her away into the night with them. He pulled her image back, but he couldn't keep from wondering if he'd ever see her again except in his dreams.

12

Spring 1812

For weeks after he left, Nathan's hurt look haunted Gabrielle, and she wondered what she could have done to ease his pain. She'd known for some time that Nathan had a more worldly feeling for her than she did for him, but she had never imagined he would ask her to go away with him and commit matrimony.

Gabrielle hadn't told anyone she'd seen Nathan leave. Not even after they began to search for him. Nathan was gone. He would never come back. And she had grieved for him as the brethren spread out through the woods to search for him. Of course she knew where he'd gone. To the doctor's cabin. Elder Caleb must have thought the same, for Sister Mercy told Gabrielle he had found Nathan there and spent hours talking with him in an attempt to make him see the folly of leaving the Believers.

"I regret to say he shut his ears to the truth," Sister Mercy had said. "Our former brother was never one to admit an

149

error in his ways. He refused to humble himself and learn to love the simple life."

"He was a good worker while he was here, and perhaps he is doing what he thinks right for himself." Gabrielle defended him. She regretted the words as soon as they were out.

Sister Mercy looked at her sharply. "What one thinks is right and what is truly right are often quite different things. I know you were close to our brother who has now left us for the world, but you mustn't let his wrong thinking confuse you."

"I will not."

Sister Mercy's eyes narrowed on Gabrielle for a moment before she said, "That is good to hear. There have been times lately when I have not been sure some bit of worldliness had not wormed its way into your thoughts, Sister Gabrielle."

Gabrielle lowered her eyes. "I have prayed that it not be so."

"Yea, child, prayer is the right and proper thing to do when we have spiritual turmoil." Sister Mercy paused a moment before she went on. "And it's no wonder you've felt some confusion of thought with the way that Dr. Scott did his best to upset you. If you ask me, the fault for our poor doomed brother's fall into sin lies completely on that man's shoulders. He has surely been filling the boy's head with lies all the time he was supposed to be treating his burns."

Gabrielle mashed her lips tightly together. She dared not say a word in the doctor's defense even though she felt he was being misjudged. The strange feelings that even the mention of the doctor's name brought out in her couldn't be trusted to words.

Sister Mercy didn't seem to notice as she kept talking. "I

suppose we can only say good riddance to the both of them. Our former brother will get what he deserves in the world and you don't have to worry about that doctor bothering you anymore. He won't be showing his face around here again. Elder Caleb has made sure of that."

So added to Gabrielle's grief over Nathan being lost to her forever was the thought that she would never see the doctor again. She tried to be glad, to know it was what the Lord intended. As she had told Dr. Scott, their paths had taken their separate turns and were now leading away from one another.

One day followed another, and as she went about her assigned chores, she kept telling herself it was for the best. She could put the unsettling feelings the doctor had awakened in her mind aside and pull close the quiet peace of the simple, uncluttered life of the Believer.

But it wasn't that easy. Although it had been almost a month since she'd seen the doctor, his face was still as clear before her as if he were standing in front of her. His dark eyes challenged her to face the questions she dared not even allow to surface in her mind. And time would never make her forget the warmth that had rushed through her when his lips had covered hers. Even thinking about it made her insides soften until she thought her heart might melt like butter sitting in the sun.

Gabrielle shook her wanton thoughts away and bent back down to her work. School had been out for some time. Gabrielle had been assigned to first one duty and then another. This week she was in the strawberry patch. The crop promised to be bountiful. Already the sisters had put up more than two hundred jars of the sweet preserves. Some they would save for their own table, but the rest would be sold to those of the world when the brethren went out on one of their trading trips.

As Gabrielle straightened up to rest her back for a moment, she was grateful to be working out in the warm sunshine on such a beautiful day. The trees were leaved out and the grass was lush and green. The white blossoms of their apple trees had given way to small apple buds. Everywhere she looked things were growing and promising nature's bounty.

It always seemed something of a miracle the way the bleakness of winter could so quickly become the full promise of spring and early summer. Gone were their worries of making it through the winter after their barn had burned. Already the ground was beginning to yield up its harvest, and it would continue until winter brought its cold back, months from now.

Here in the strawberry patch, she and five other sisters were filling basket after basket of the red plump berries. Scattered among them were several young sisters helping to pick or to fetch new containers when one was full.

"Is your basket full, Sister 'Brielle?"

Gabrielle's eyes settled on the little girl. It was the first time she'd been on the same duty as Becca since the school term had ended. Becca's face was flushed with the heat of the sunshine. She looked very tired.

"Yea, Becca." Gabrielle picked out one of the large ripe berries and held it out to Becca. "Why don't you eat this one?"

"Sister Sadie says the baskets won't fill if we put the berries in our mouths." Becca took the strawberry from Gabrielle and laid it back in the basket.

"She wouldn't care if you ate one."

152

Becca shook her head and turned away. Gabrielle watched her carry the basket to the end of the patch. She moved as though each step took a special effort, and Gabrielle felt the worry spring up inside her. She had been checking on Becca every night even though the child no longer shed tears at bedtime. Now Becca went to bed and lay still and quiet till morning. When Gabrielle spoke to her, Becca answered with as few words as possible. She seemed to have gathered a cloud around her that kept everyone else away.

Gabrielle had asked Sister Mercy's permission to take the child to see her mother, but Sister Mercy had refused. "It's best this way, Sister Gabrielle. The child is growing accustomed to our ways. You yourself say Sister Becca no longer cries at night. In a few days she will be as happy as any of the other children."

But Gabrielle could only wish Becca was still weeping. Tears would be easier to deal with than Becca's silent misery.

Gabrielle bent down and began filling the new basket with berries. She silently offered up a prayer as she had many times in the past days that Sister Esther would return from her duty at the mill soon.

That night when they went to the evening meal, Becca was once again missing. But this time when Gabrielle returned to look in their sleeping room, the child was lying in her bed. She had folded the cover back neatly as she had been taught and lined her shoes at the foot of the bed, but she wore the same dress stained by the day's work in the strawberry patch.

"Becca, are you sick?" The child's face was red against the white of the pillowcase, and she stared up at Gabrielle with glassy eyes. Even before Gabrielle touched her she knew the child's fever was high. Still the heat of her forehead surprised Gabrielle. The child had no ordinary illness.

Becca turned her head to look at Gabrielle. "'Brielle, I see spots." She lifted her hand as if to catch one of the spots and then dropped it heavily back down.

"Oh my dear little one, why didn't you tell me you were ill?" Tears pushed at the back of Gabrielle's eyes, and she wanted to gather the child up to her breast and hold her tight.

"I had to pick the strawberries. Sister Sadie said so," Becca said. She grabbed at Gabrielle's arm. "But now I'm tired. Can you make the bed stop going around, 'Brielle, so I can go to sleep?"

"The bed's not moving, sweetheart."

"But it is," Becca whispered. She touched her lips with her tongue but the moisture was gone at once. "It's pushing me up at the ceiling. I don't like it, 'Brielle."

"I'll kneel here and say a prayer. Maybe that will stop it."

"Are you praying for me, 'Brielle?"

"Yes, dear." Gabrielle kept her hand on the little girl's cheek as she shut her eyes and begged the Eternal Father to take the fever from Becca.

She looked up when Becca moaned. "My head hurts, 'Brielle. My head hurts so bad."

"I'll go get someone to help you, Becca." Gabrielle started up off her knees, but Becca reached for her.

"Don't leave me alone, 'Brielle. I'm scared." Becca clutched Gabrielle's hand. "I know Mama's waiting for me up there in heaven, but I'm still scared."

"You're going to be all right, Becca. We'll send for a doctor."

"The man who held me by the fire said he was a doctor. I liked him."

"He'll come help you now. You don't have to be scared, little one."

Becca shut her eyes, but she didn't turn loose of Gabrielle's hand.

Gabrielle knelt by the bed again. One of the children would be back soon. She would send her for help. She couldn't leave Becca alone.

Sister Mercy came looking for Gabrielle first. "You were not at the evening meal," she said as she came into the room.

Gabrielle whispered a quick amen and stood up. "Sister Becca is very ill, Sister Mercy. I dared not leave her alone. I was waiting for one of the children to return so that I could send for you."

Sister Mercy was all business as she came to the child's bed. She examined the child with the practiced thoroughness of one who had cared for many children through all sorts of illnesses. She looked up at Gabrielle and said, "We must move Sister Becca out of here to a separate room at once."

"What do you think it is?"

"That is hard to say. Many sicknesses carry with them a fever, but we must do what we can to keep whatever it is from spreading to any of the other little sisters."

Sister Mercy turned her eyes back to Becca. Gently she smoothed the child's fine hair back from her forehead. "Rest easy, Sister Becca. We are going to move you to another room where it will be quieter while you get well, my child."

Gabrielle gently scooped up the child into her arms. Becca's body burned against her. "We will take her to the sickroom," Sister Mercy said as she gathered up the covers from Becca's bed.

Once Sister Mercy had the bed ready in the sickroom,

Gabrielle laid Becca down. Sister Mercy quickly lit candles to light up the small room. Then she pulled a chair up to the bed and sat down. Concern filled her eyes as she studied the child. "I wish we could somehow shut out sickness from our families as we have other worldly ills." She raised her eyes to Gabrielle. "Run, fetch her a clean nightdress so she'll be more comfortable."

Gabrielle hadn't gone two steps before Becca cried out. "'Brielle, where are you? You promised to stay with me. 'Brielle?"

"Shh, little sister. Sister Gabrielle is here with you." Sister Mercy stood up and motioned Gabrielle back to the bedside. "You stay. I'll get the nightdress and send someone for Sister Helen to mix some herbs to treat the child's fever."

Sister Mercy left the room quietly, and Gabrielle sat down by the bed. Becca's breathing was so soft and shallow Gabrielle might have thought she had fallen asleep except for her wide-open eyes. Then she called again. "'Brielle, where are you?"

"I am here, Becca." Gabrielle moved closer to her and took hold of the child's hand.

"I'm so hot, 'Brielle. Why am I so hot? Have you put me beside the stove?"

"You have a fever, little one. Sister Mercy has gone to find some medicine powders to help you. Why don't you close your eyes and try to sleep? When you wake up, you may feel better."

"I wish Mama could be here. She used to sing me songs and tell me stories when I was sick."

"I could sing to you."

Becca shook her head a little. "It wouldn't be the same.

Mama knew which songs were my favorites without me even having to tell her."

"Your mama will be here tomorrow, Becca. I promise." Gabrielle wasn't sure how she'd do it, but somehow she'd make them let Sister Esther come.

After Sister Mercy returned and they'd gotten Becca into the nightdress, Gabrielle said, "Don't you think it would be well for us to send for Sister Esther?"

She expected Sister Mercy to disagree, but instead Sister Mercy looked long at the child before she said, "I'll have Elder Caleb send someone for her at once. I fear you are right in thinking the child has not accustomed herself to the Believer's life. The sight of her mother might be a comfort to her." Sister Mercy put her hand on Becca's forehead again for a moment. When she looked back up at Gabrielle, her eyes were sad. "It is not a time to deny the child."

"Can you ask the elder to send for a doctor as well? Dr. Scott's cabin is nearby, isn't it? It wouldn't take long for someone to fetch him."

Sister Mercy's back stiffened at the mention of the doctor, but she only said, "We'll wait for Sister Helen."

Sister Helen needed only a moment's look and touch before she opened the small parcel of medicines she carried and selected a brownish powder. She mixed it into a bit of water and said, "Be a big girl and drink it all up."

Becca looked at Sister Helen and clamped her lips shut. Gabrielle raised Becca's head with one hand and took the glass from Sister Helen. "It might make the bed stop spinning, little one."

Gabrielle tipped the glass up until the liquid touched Becca's lips. The child let it dribble into her mouth and then swallowed. After Gabrielle eased her back down on the pillow, Becca pushed at the covers on her. "My blanket is all bumpy and scratchy, 'Brielle."

Gabrielle folded the cover back away from her face. "There, there, sweet child. It's just the fever making you feel so odd. Close your eyes and try to rest."

"All right, 'Brielle. I'll try."

"It could be scarlet fever," Sister Helen said softly. "The potion I gave her might cool her fever, but it doesn't always work with these kinds of fevers."

"Could a doctor help her?" Gabrielle asked. She was sure Dr. Scott could if only they'd send for him. Just thinking about him helped to ease the worry growing inside Gabrielle.

"It's hard to say," Sister Helen said. "Perhaps."

Elder Caleb came into the room. "I have sent for the child's mother as you asked, Sister Mercy. Are you sure it could not have waited until daylight?"

"Sister Becca is very ill," Sister Helen said. "She fairly burns with fever."

"Elder Caleb, will you send for a doctor?" Gabrielle should have let Sister Mercy or Sister Helen speak first, but she couldn't stop her words. "Dr. Scott might be able to help her."

The elder's eyes on her were stern and his voice cold as he said, "Not Dr. Scott."

"But he helped Brother Nathan when it seemed nothing could," Gabrielle insisted. She wouldn't have spoken out so boldly if it hadn't been so important, but Becca needed the doctor.

"The one of whom you speak has chosen not to be our brother anymore, Sister Gabrielle. We will not speak his name in this village again. And you can be assured the man who led our former brother astray will not be allowed to come back into our village to cause more trouble." His eyes were unrelenting.

Gabrielle bowed her head and was silent. Nothing she could say would change the elder's decision. Even if it meant Becca's life.

Suddenly the elder's voice was gentle again as he reached out and touched Gabrielle's head. "There are other doctors, Sister Gabrielle. I will send for one from the town at once. We won't deny our little sister whatever care she needs, but you must realize, my dear sister, that it is the Eternal Father who holds our fate in his hands, and we must accept and abide by his will."

"May I pray for my little sister's life?" Gabrielle asked. "She is very dear to me."

"As she is dear to us all. Of course we'll pray and ask Mother Ann's intercession. There is no wrong in that," the Elder said.

It seemed hours before the doctor came. Then even after he entered the room carrying his small black bag, Gabrielle felt no relief. He was thin and not very tall, and his face was narrow and frowning. "Most things can wait till morning, you know," he said crossly as he bent to look at Becca. Still, in spite of his angry manner, he was gentle as he began examining the child.

While he felt for Becca's pulse, Gabrielle bowed her head to pray for the doctor, but her words of prayer were swallowed up by the darkness of the scene that suddenly filled her mind. She looked up at the doctor. He was listening to Becca's heart while Sister Helen watched. Nothing had changed. Perhaps it was only her worry for Becca that had put the picture in front of her eyes and not the gift of knowing. She shook her head to clear away the disturbing vision, but when she closed her eyes again, the image was relentlessly there. In her mind the doctor was pulling the sheet up over Becca's face.

"What is it, Sister Gabrielle? You look faint," Sister Mercy said.

"I must talk to you." Gabrielle pulled Sister Mercy a bit away from the bed. "We must not let this man treat Becca."

"Nonsense," Sister Mercy said. "You were the one who asked that we send for a doctor. Now that he's here we must let him do what he can for the child." She pulled away from Gabrielle and went back to stand by the doctor. "Can we assist you in any way, Dr. Adams?"

"The child is gravely ill," the doctor said as he reached into his bag and pulled out his lancet. "I'll have to bleed her at once."

The sight of the long tapered blade made Gabrielle shiver. She looked quickly at Sisters Mercy and Helen, but they didn't seem concerned. Gabrielle spoke to the doctor. "You must not do that."

The doctor looked up at Gabrielle. "It's the best treatment for such fevers, miss. It will let out the poison inside her. You do want her to get well, don't you?"

"Of course we do, Doctor," Sister Helen said. "Pay our sister no mind. She is distraught."

Gabrielle appealed to Sister Mercy. "If you don't send him away, Becca will surely die."

Sister Mercy studied her for a moment before she asked, "And if it were Dr. Scott, would you be begging us to make him leave?"

Dr. Adams made a sound of disgust. "That yarb man! He let a child die just last week because he refused to bleed him."

Gabrielle didn't even look around at Dr. Adams. She kept her eyes on Sister Mercy. She didn't like going against the others, but the truth in her vision could not be ignored. She spoke to Sister Mercy. "I don't know. I only know if you allow this man to do as he wishes, Becca will die."

Sister Mercy frowned, but when she spoke, her voice was gentle. "The fever may take the child as you fear, Sister Gabrielle, but we have brought in the doctor to perhaps turn death back. So it is only right that we allow him to use his knowledge and skills to treat our young sister in whatever way he thinks best." Her voice hardened. "Now, mind your place and do not interfere again."

Gabrielle lowered her eyes and went back to stand by Becca's head. It would be futile to argue more. She wished fervently that she had picked up Becca when she had first found her ill and carried her away through the woods to Dr. Scott's cabin before Sister Mercy had come searching for her. Even now she wanted to grab Becca and carry her away from this man with his lancet, but they would stop her. All that would happen was that she would be put out of the room and would not be allowed to stay with Becca.

A sick feeling rose inside her as Sister Helen positioned the basin beside the bed and the doctor pierced Becca's arm. As the doctor probed to find a vein, Gabrielle wanted to push her arm in front of Becca's and allow her blood to flow for the child. But instead, Becca's own blood began running down her arm and into the basin. It took an interminable amount of time before the doctor was satisfied with the puddle of red in the basin and stopped the bleeding.

The room was silent except for the ticking of the clock on the wall behind them as they watched the child. After a few minutes, the flush receded from Becca's face and she began turning her head. Her eyes flickered open and then shut.

The doctor looked up at Gabrielle. "See. The child is better already."

But the darkness of the knowing pressed down on Gabrielle. She said, "I fervently pray that you are right and I am wrong, Dr. Adams."

13

It was near dawn when Sister Esther rushed into the sick-room. Her cap was missing and strands of her dark hair had escaped the bun at the back of her neck and swirled in disarray about her face. When Gabrielle went to meet her, Sister Esther grabbed her arms and gripped them tightly. "Where is she? Where is my child?"

"She is here," Gabrielle answered softly. Sister Mercy had gone back to watch over the other children. The doctor was lying down in the next room after instructing them to call him if there was any change in Becca, and Sister Helen had dozed off in her chair on the other side of the bed as the night watch had stretched out. Sister Esther's entrance into the room didn't disturb her slumber.

Becca had been drifting in and out of sleep. At first she had seemed to know Gabrielle, but the last time she had opened her eyes there'd been no awareness at all. "She is sleeping," Gabrielle told Sister Esther.

Sister Esther dropped to her knees beside the bed. She ran her hands lightly over Becca's face and down her arms as if she needed to memorize the feel of her. She gently held Becca's hands as she looked at her and said, "She's so hot."

"Yea, but she's cooler than she was."

Sister Esther laid her head softly on Becca's chest. "Her heart is pounding so hard I can feel it against my cheek."

Gabrielle could only say, "She's very sick, Sister Esther."

"She's not so sick that she won't get better, is she?" The woman raised her head to look at Gabrielle.

She needed words of reassurance, but Gabrielle had none to give her. The knowing was still strong in Gabrielle's mind, and she saw no purpose in making meaningless promises. "I don't know, Sister. Perhaps now that you are here, it will give Becca the strength to fight off the fever."

Anguish filled Sister Esther's eyes. She shot a look over at Sister Helen who was sleeping so soundly she was snoring a bit. "You don't know what it's been like these last few weeks. I've tried. I've really tried to live the Believers' life. But I love Becca so much, and I know she needs me. You know that's true."

"I've been praying for your return to the village. Becca has been very sad since you've been gone." Gabrielle kept her voice soft, not much more than a whisper.

"You could never understand what I've been through, Sister Gabrielle. Not unless you had a child of your own."

"I love the children under my care."

"I know you do, and I have thanked the Lord every day that you were here with Becca. I've seen your concern, your caring, but you've only borrowed these children. It's different when you've borne them and suckled them." Sister Esther's eyes went to Becca's face. "Becca was our miracle child. We'd already lost three babies, and when she was born she was

164

so tiny I lived in fear we'd lose her too. We prayed then and promised we'd do whatever God wanted us to if he would only let her live."

Sister Esther was quiet for a moment before she went on. "That's why I couldn't refuse to join with the Believers when Jason said it was God's will for our lives. I'd made a promise to God, just as Hannah in the Bible made a promise and had to surrender Samuel to Eli, the priest. I often think of her and how she could only go see her son once a year. How hard that must have been even though the Lord blessed her with more children. But I could not be like Hannah. Here among the Believers there is no chance for more children for me."

Gabrielle put her hand on Sister Esther's shoulder.

Sister Esther kept her eyes on Becca. "And perhaps I could not be like Hannah in another way as well. We weren't here three days until I knew I wouldn't be able to uphold my part of the covenant we made with God. I couldn't give up Becca. Not my miracle baby. But I had no money, no place to go away with her. So what choice did I have except to do what they said, Sister Gabrielle, and pray the Lord would show me a way to keep living?"

"I don't know," Gabrielle said.

Sister Esther gently stroked Becca's cheek. "I know what I'm going to do now. As soon as Becca is better, we're going to leave this place. We'll make our way somehow even if Jason stays. Do you think that is wrong?"

"I could not find it in my heart to condemn you, Sister Esther," Gabrielle said with a quick look over at Sister Helen to be sure she was not overhearing their talk. Gabrielle sent up a little prayer of thanksgiving that Sister Helen was such a sound sleeper. "But first we must help Becca fight off the fever. She told me you used to sing to her when she was sick. It might help if you did so now."

As Sister Esther began a soft lullaby, Dr. Adams came into the room to check on the child. He looked at Gabrielle and said, "You have to admit she's better."

Gabrielle met his eyes boldly. "She is very weak."

"I may not have bled her enough. A blister might help."

"It would help if you'd go away and leave the child alone," Gabrielle said.

The doctor frowned. "You should be silent about things you have no knowledge of."

Sister Esther looked from the doctor to Gabrielle, but she kept singing.

Becca stirred in her sleep and her eyes flickered open. For a moment, Gabrielle wasn't sure she was seeing her mother there by the bed, but then Becca smiled and said, "'Brielle. 'Brielle!"

"Yes, little one," Gabrielle answered.

"I see Mama." Becca's voice was excited.

"Of course you do, dear. I told you she'd be here before morning."

But Becca didn't act as if she heard Gabrielle's words. "She's come for me like I knew she would. I'm not afraid anymore. Mama's holding my hand."

"Yes, dear, she is holding your hand. She's right here beside your bed. Reach over and touch her face." Fear rose inside Gabrielle as she realized what the child meant. Gabrielle grabbed Sister Esther's shoulder. "Talk to her, Sister Esther. Tell her you're here with her."

"Becca, Mama's here, sweetheart. I won't leave you until

166

you are well, and then we'll go somewhere so we can be together all the time."

Becca smiled. "I know. It's pretty here, Mama, isn't it? Everything's so bright, and I feel like I'm floating. Look, Mama, that must be an angel!"

"Becca!" Sister Esther cried.

Becca's eyes clouded for a moment, but then she was smiling again. "Hold my hand tighter, Mama. Don't let go. I knew you'd come for me."

The spirit left Becca quietly. Her earthly body made no attempt to cling to the breath of life. Sister Esther stared at her child for a long moment in disbelief. Then as if she was sure Gabrielle could somehow make it not so, she looked up at her. Tears wet Gabrielle's cheeks as she shook her head.

"No!" Sister Esther screamed. She grabbed Becca's limp body up close to her chest. "You can't die, Becca! No!"

Sister Helen had awakened and she stepped up behind Sister Esther to put her hands on her shoulders. "The child is gone from us to a better place, Sister. Come, let her lie in peace." She began to ease Sister Esther's arms away from the child's body and pull her away from the bed. Sister Helen looked at Gabrielle and said, "Help me comfort our sister, Sister Gabrielle."

But Gabrielle couldn't take her eyes from the doctor as he listened for Becca's heartbeat. Slowly he pulled the cover up over the child's face that still carried the trace of a smile. Gabrielle had fought the vision, but it had done little good. Her request had brought the doctor there and now Becca was dead.

Dr. Adams wouldn't look at Gabrielle as he gathered his instruments. He snapped his bag closed. "If you'd called me earlier, I might have been able to save her. There wasn't time to let all the poison out of her."

"The child lies dead. Her fate has passed out of our hands." Gabrielle's own words seemed to tear a hole in her heart.

When he was gone, Gabrielle pulled back the cover and looked down on the child. Dear Becca. Would she be happy in heaven without her mother? Softly she kissed her forehead before she pulled the cover back over the little girl's face. There was nothing more she could do for her. She turned to see how she might comfort her mother.

Later she and Sister Esther prepared Becca for her burial. Sister Esther had insisted, saying, "It's a mother's duty. I got off my birthing bed and wrapped my other babies in strips of my wedding dress. I can do no less for Becca."

They washed her gently and carefully as though she might yet feel their touch. Outside the house, they could hear the brethren hammering as they prepared Becca's coffin. But Gabrielle wouldn't think about them putting the child in the ground. Not yet. Now she would concentrate on helping Sister Esther. After they had dressed Becca, Sister Esther turned away from Gabrielle and reached up under her dress.

"I'm glad Sister Mercy left us alone. She wouldn't understand, but I think you will, Sister Gabrielle." Sister Esther held out a small rag doll. "I kept this for Becca when we came. She always loved her dolls, but of course she had to give them up when we came together with the Shakers since the Society doesn't allow such toys. So I made her this special tiny doll and hid it in the hem of my dress for her to play with when I came to see her." Carefully she tucked the doll down inside Becca's dress next to her heart.

Tears filled her eyes when she looked around at Gabrielle. "Do you think the Lord took her because I said I was going to leave the Believers? Because I planned to break my covenant with him?"

"Nay," Gabrielle said gently. "Becca was very sick. Fevers take many children from their mothers."

Sister Esther looked back at Becca and softly caressed her cool cheek. "What did she mean when she said I had come to get her and that she wasn't afraid anymore?"

Gabrielle hesitated. The truth would only add to Sister Esther's pain.

When Gabrielle stayed silent, Sister Esther said, "Nothing you can say can make me hurt more than I'm already hurting, Sister Gabrielle. And I must know."

Gabrielle couldn't deny her the truth. "Becca got lost in the woods a few weeks ago. She'd never gotten used to you not being with her, and when a week passed without you coming to see her, I suppose she decided to go looking for you. I went after her and found her unharmed." She didn't say where. There was no need, and Gabrielle didn't want to think about Dr. Scott. Not now while she was so sure he could have helped Becca live.

"Poor dear. She'd have never made it to the mill even if she had guessed the right direction to go. It is too far."

"Yea, you are right. When I brought her back to put her to bed, she was asleep. I don't know. Maybe she had a dream. Anyway, she woke up while I was putting her nightdress over her head. She asked me about going to heaven, what you had to do to go there. She was sure you had died and gone to heaven already, Sister Esther, and that was why you hadn't come to see her."

Sister Esther kept her eyes on the child as she said, "And what did you tell her, Sister Gabrielle?"

"I told her where you were. At the mill house and that you'd be back soon. I told her the same thing many times after that as well, but I was never sure she heard my words."

"She wanted to die, didn't she, Sister Gabrielle?"

"She was too young to want to die."

"What does age matter? She thought I was dead, and so she died to be with me." Sister Esther's voice was barely above a whisper.

"Nay, Sister Esther. She died because she had a fever. We cannot wish ourselves dead any more than we can wish our loved ones back to life once their spirits leave their bodies."

But Sister Esther didn't seem to hear Gabrielle's words any more than Becca had. The silence was heavy in the room before Sister Esther said, "If I had taken her away, she would still be alive."

"You can't know that. There are fevers in the world as well."

"But I can know it, Sister Gabrielle." Sister Esther kept her eyes on Becca's face. "I know it in my heart."

When at last she stood up, Sister Esther seemed smaller than when she'd first come into the room before dawn. It was as if she'd shrunk into herself. "I have to put on a clean dress before the funeral. You will stay with her, won't you, Sister Gabrielle, until I return? I wouldn't want her to be alone."

"I won't leave until you return," Gabrielle promised.

The room was very quiet after she left. And empty. Gabrielle looked at Becca's small body laid out on the bed. There was none of Becca left there. She had gone on. Gabrielle wished she could be sure the little girl was happy in heaven. Suddenly she remembered the vision she'd had as a child of her baby brother in heaven. At the time Gabrielle hadn't understood why her mother had been so upset when she had told her about the vision. Her little brother had been happy. But now she knew. A mother could not surrender a child to heaven so easily.

Sister Mercy came into the room. "Where is Sister Esther?"

"She went to change into a clean dress."

"Good. The brethren are almost ready." Sister Mercy stood over Becca's body. "She was always so tiny. It seems a shame that our sins are put on those so small."

"What do you mean?" Gabrielle asked.

"I have heard Sister Esther speak of the babies she lost, and now this one." Sister Mercy shook her head. "The Eternal Father has ways of punishing us for our sins. Sister Esther never surrendered herself to the humble life as she was meant to."

"You think the Eternal Father punished her by letting her children die?"

"We cannot know the Father's ways, but Mother Ann also lost four children. The Lord revealed to her that the death of those children was his way of telling her the life she was living was wrong. That marriage is a sin and that she must forsake that sinful union and devote all her energy and every thought to worshiping God."

Gabrielle knew Mother Ann's story, as did every Believer. Before it had seemed right. Mother Ann's babies had died because she had been chosen by the Eternal Father to reveal a better way for his people to live, but Gabrielle couldn't accept the same thinking when it came to Becca. "Many others commit matrimony and their children live," she said now.

Sister Mercy looked at her. "It is not for us to question the ways of our Eternal Father, child."

Gabrielle wanted to ask her if she'd never had questions, but she didn't dare. Perhaps Sister Mercy's faith was too strong to have ever entertained doubts.

Sister Mercy seemed to guess what Gabrielle was thinking. The older sister came to her and touched her cheek. "Your faith is being tested now, my child. It is often thus when one we care for dies. When I first became a Believer, there were times when my worldly past bothered me with those things I had tried to cast away from me. You must do as I did. Pray to Mother Ann to help you. She will send you love and faith enough to carry you through any sort of tribulation."

Gabrielle bowed her head. "Yea, Sister Mercy. I'll pray for such love and faith."

Sister Mercy kissed the top of Gabrielle's head. "Just as the young sister was very dear to you, so you are to me, Sister Gabrielle. It won't be long before you will be of age to be welcomed into the circle of true Believers with the Center Family. I know you'll be ready to serve as Mother Ann wants you to."

"Yea, Sister Mercy. I pray so." But even as she spoke the words, Dr. Scott was before her and she couldn't shut away his image.

Sister Esther slipped into the room just as the meeting-house bell began to toll. Sister Helen followed her in and said, "It is time. The brethren have brought the box."

Carefully they placed Becca's body in the coffin. Then several of the young sisters carried the coffin out to the graveyard where the other Believers had already gathered. Gabrielle stayed by Sister Esther's side. When Elder Caleb finished reading from the scriptures, his eyes sought out Gabrielle to begin the funeral song.

Gabrielle swallowed hard and pushed out the words. "Our sister is gone. She is no more."

The others joined in, and they made their slow way through the funeral song. Gabrielle had led the song before when one of their number had passed on to paradise, but never had she felt the words pulled out of her so painfully.

"We now hear the solemn call. Be prepared both great and small." Her voice almost faded away, and she couldn't come back as strongly as she usually did for the last line. "O death, where is thy sting? O grave, where is thy victory?" But she sang every word.

Esther didn't sing. Nor did she shed any tears even when the brethren began to nail down the coffin top. She watched them intently as if to make sure it was done properly.

Gabrielle was standing so close beside Sister Esther that she felt the tremor pass through her as the brethren lowered Becca's coffin down into the ground. She put her arm around Sister Esther's waist, but the woman didn't appear to notice.

Elder Caleb picked up the first handful of dirt and let it fall on the box. "From dust we came. To dust we will return."

Slowly, one by one, the brethren and sisters filed past the small grave, dropping in handfuls of dirt. Brother Jason stared down at the small coffin a bit longer than the others before he dropped his handful of dirt. Then he looked over at Sister Esther, but she kept her eyes fastened on the open grave with no notice of him there. He turned and followed his brethren away from the graveyard.

When they were the only ones left, Gabrielle spoke softly into Sister Esther's ear. "It's time to leave."

Sister Esther shook her head the barest bit. "Nay, I will stay until it's finished."

So they watched as the two brothers shoveled in the remaining dirt. When at last they had it smoothed over and picked up their shovels to leave, Gabrielle felt a kind of relief. At last it was over.

Sister Esther made no move to leave.

After a moment, Gabrielle said, "She is not here, you know. You heard her, Sister Esther. She said she was with the angels."

It was a long time before Sister Esther spoke. Then her voice was flat and empty. "Yea, you are right, Sister Gabrielle. Becca is not there in that cold grave. I am. I feel as if every clod of dirt fell on my face. They didn't bury Becca. They buried me."

14

There was no rest from their duties. Idleness was the parent of want and was not entertained in the Believers' life. So even on the afternoon of Becca's funeral, Gabrielle went back out to the strawberry patch. She was glad for the work. Keeping her hands busy helped block a little of the sadness. As she filled her baskets with the plump berries just as she had the day before, it was hard to realize she could no longer look up and see Becca among the little girls in the patch.

"Sister Gabrielle," a child's voice cried.

A raw touch of grief shook Gabrielle, but she straightened up and pushed a smile across her face for little Suzy, who stood at her side. "What is it, dear?"

Suzy had tears in her eyes as she held out her hand. In her palm was a velvety blue and black butterfly. One of its wings moved weakly, but the other was crumpled and useless. "I didn't mean to hurt it, Sister Gabrielle. I just wanted to touch it because it was so pretty."

Gabrielle knelt beside her and gently lifted the butterfly

into her own hand. "Don't cry, Suzy. I know you didn't mean to cause it harm."

"But will it be able to fly again?"

Gabrielle carefully placed the butterfly on a strawberry leaf. "Perhaps. After it rests."

Suzy looked from the butterfly to Gabrielle. "Does it know I didn't aim to hurt it, Sister Gabrielle?"

"I'm sure it does, Sister Suzy, but from now on you must remember that some of God's creatures are better left untouched. Butterflies are meant to fly free and not be captured by our hands."

After Suzy dried her tears on a corner of her apron and ran back with the other children to gather more strawberry baskets, Gabrielle watched the butterfly wobble as it tried to balance on the leaf with its injured wing. She'd told the child it might fly again, but she didn't really believe it. Butterflies were so fragile. Still little Suzy had not meant it harm.

Just as the Believers hadn't meant to hurt Becca.

The pain gathered in a hard knot inside Gabrielle as she wished for the power to change things. She wanted to see the butterfly fluttering through the air again. She wanted to wipe away the night before and have Becca back beside her with her serious eyes and solemn face. She wanted to see the smile that had surely lit up Becca's face whenever Sister Esther had pulled the little doll out of the hem of her skirt for the child. And then Gabrielle was angry because she had no such power.

The anger pushed through her and then was gone, leaving in its wake a dark, sad place. It did little good to be angry at what could not be changed. The Lord gave and the Lord took away.

Becca was dead just as the butterfly would surely die. Gabrielle grieved, but her grief did not change the truth.

With a heavy sigh, she bent down to pluck more of the red berries off the strawberry vines. Would she ever be able to eat one of the sweet strawberries with pleasure again, or would the very sight of them always bring sadness to her mind?

❧❧

June came and brought warmer days as summer set in with its busy season. Gabrielle asked to be assigned to the same work details as Sister Esther.

Sister Mercy agreed. "Perhaps you will be able to help her. Sister Esther continues to resist the Believers' way. It would seem after our little Sister Becca passed on that she would see the need for our peaceful way of life."

"Grief weighs heavily on her now," Gabrielle said.

"There is no need to grieve for the child. Sister Becca has gone on ahead of us to a better life in heaven. We've worked to make our community here a kind of heaven on earth, but we know heaven will be even finer." Sister Mercy's face shone with a look of rapture as she went on. "Just think of all the saints who'll come to meet us. Mother Ann herself will take our hands and lead us to see the Christ and the Eternal Father. Yea, our little Becca has gone to a joyous home."

"Sister Esther can't see that as clearly as you, Sister Mercy. She needs special understanding now."

"That is true. I fear she strays farther from the truth of the Believers every day. I think she even holds us to blame in some way for the death of our little sister. As if we didn't do all we could for the child. Elder Caleb prayed all through the night until he heard the child had breathed her last. Sometimes

177

the Eternal Father grants us the grace to heal and sometimes he does not."

Gabrielle looked down at the floor. She couldn't keep from wishing the Lord had somehow seemed fit to spare Becca. And though she tried not to let the thought come into her mind, she could not keep from believing that if they had called Dr. Scott instead of the other doctor from town, Becca might have survived the fever.

Sister Mercy touched Gabrielle's shoulder. "Sometimes it is hard not to grieve the passing of our dear ones' earthly bodies. I will pray that your grief goes quickly, my child."

"My grief is slight next to Sister Esther's."

"I pray for her already. Remember, my child, the soul that suffers is stronger than the soul that rejoices."

"Yea, Sister Mercy. I will pray for growth in my spirit to understand such things."

She had so many things to remember, and it seemed just as many that she needed to put away from her mind. It was as if a wind were blowing her first one way, then another as she tried to listen to her conscience. Before the fire had brought the doctor into her life, things had been clear to her. Everything was easily seen as black or white, right or wrong. Now there was a shading of gray across her mind. At the same time, while her faith had been shaken by doubts and questions, she didn't want to disappoint Sister Mercy and the other brethren and sisters she loved so dearly. In time the shading would fade away, and she'd once again see her life's aim in clear light.

Right now she had to put aside her own sorrow and help Sister Esther. After the funeral, Sister Esther had withdrawn into herself much the same as Becca had done before she had died. Gabrielle didn't try to force Sister Esther to come back into life. It hadn't worked with Becca, and Gabrielle had no reason to think it would work for Sister Esther. Surely time and the quiet, undemanding love of her sisters would help her heal.

Gabrielle was with her as much as possible. They worked in the garden one week, the laundry the next, and then they were assigned to the kitchen. Sister Esther went about all her duties with a dull, steady sameness. Nothing Gabrielle said seemed to make a difference, so each day Gabrielle prayed Sister Esther would receive help from within her own spirit.

With Sister Mercy's consent, Gabrielle continued to go to her place of prayer in the woods. She never spoke her prayers aloud there. The words would have clashed with the quiet peace of the place. Instead she offered her prayers in thoughts or at times simply emptied her mind in hopes the will of the Eternal Father would be made clear to her. Even with the confusion of the unanswered questions in her mind, she continued to feel a special tranquility with the trees towering around her.

Now that summer chores were heavy upon them, she often had to wait until evening to seek her season of prayer. She went during rest time and found her prayers renewed her more than a nap could have.

For a week the days had been humid with always a threat of a storm rumbling in the distance but sliding by to the north or south. Finally a storm had passed through their village during the early afternoon, lashing their buildings and crops with wind and rain. When it was over, the sky cleared and the cooled air felt fresh and clean. Gabrielle started to pray in her room because of the wet grass and trees, but the sparkle of the newly washed world beckoned to her.

It had been a long day. Kitchen duty was Gabrielle's least-liked assignment since the kitchen was always so hot in the summer, with the heat of the day made ten times worse by the cooking fires and the ovens. Plus, since Gabrielle had no talents as a cook, she was always given the most tedious chores. She tried to work with a cheerful heart, but there had been times during the afternoon when she had hoped never to see another potato or bean. So it was a relief to be outside even if the slightest breeze did bring down showers of raindrops off the trees to dampen her clothes as she walked into the woods.

She rejoiced in the fresh green scent of the woods as she sat down on a large, flat rock in the small opening. She did not wish to get mud on her dress since she wouldn't have time to change before meeting. She would kneel and pray later in her room. But now she breathed in the freshly washed air and opened her mind to the reality of God and the wonders of his creation.

She'd been there only a few minutes when she began to feel uneasy. Something was different. Suddenly she remembered the night last winter when she'd prayed for Nathan after the fire. Then too she had felt this uneasiness as though she weren't alone.

Perhaps one of the sisters or brethren had followed her. It was not unknown for couples whose hearts were not fully committed to the truth of the Believers to arrange clandestine meetings in the woods. To discourage such forbidden trysts, there were watchers who noted the comings and goings of their brothers and sisters and reported to the elders and eldresses.

Two couples had just left the village the day before. In the spring and summer there were many from the Gathering Family who found they could no longer abide by the rules of the Believers. Their commitment to the way of the Believers was too weak. Elder Caleb called them "winter Shakers." They came for a warm house and plentiful food during the hard months of winter, but as soon as spring came they were gone again.

Others managed somehow to sneak past the eyes of the watchers as something foreign to brotherly love sprang up between them. Whether they were caught or whether they weren't, such forbidden trysts usually ended the same with the couple running away to the world.

So Gabrielle thought one of the watchers might have seen her going to the woods and followed her to be sure her purpose was innocent. Some among the Believers enjoyed catching others in wrong acts.

Gabrielle called out, "Is someone there?" The sound of her voice reached out to the trees around her, but there was no answer.

She stood up. It wasn't really dark yet, but the shadows hung heavy among the trees. A shiver of fear crept over her. She had no fear of any of her brethren or sisters, but perhaps a wild animal had been drawn closer to the village than usual or perhaps even someone from the world.

She took a step back through the trees toward the safety of the village when someone spoke directly behind her.

"Don't run, young sister."

15

His voice stopped her in her tracks. She whirled around as he stepped out of his hiding place. Her eyes widened, but there was no fear there. Only welcome as she whispered, "Brice."

He hadn't known she even knew his given name, but the sound of it on her tongue made his heart glad. He had been well hidden. She would have never seen him unless he'd intended her to. Now he reached out and pulled her back into the shadow of the trees with him. She was too surprised to resist.

For a long moment he didn't say anything as his hand lingered on her arm. He did not want to let go of her for fear she would disappear like one of his dream images. He didn't try to pull her closer to him. Just the sight of her there in front of him was enough. At last he lifted his other hand to gently trace the lines of her nose and cheeks, down to her lips. Their softness made him tremble.

Her lips parted and her breath was warm on his fingers. Her eyes were devouring his face, and for a breathless moment he thought she was going to step into his arms. Then all at once she turned her eyes from him and tried to jerk free from his hold.

He tightened his grip on her arm. "Wait a moment, young sister. You can't always be running away."

She stopped pulling against him and stood perfectly still like a captured bird too afraid to even ruffle one of its own feathers.

"Please don't be frightened of me, Gabrielle. You have no reason to be. Ever."

She stared up at him with a flash of anger in her eyes. "How can you expect me not to be frightened when you grab hold of me like this?"

"I don't think that is the reason you are frightened, Gabrielle."

She drew in a breath and became even stiller. "What do you want, Dr. Scott?"

"To see you."

"It isn't proper for us to meet like this. You should have gone to Elder Caleb and asked him to arrange a proper meeting if such was your desire."

"I think not." Brice was silent for a moment before he said, "I have been waiting. I thought you might come to me."

"I could never do that." Gabrielle lowered her eyes from his.

"Because you don't want to?" Brice willed her to look back up at him as he listened intently for her answer. Slowly she raised her head. Even in the dim light of the woods, he would be able to tell if she lied.

"It isn't right," she said softly.

"You're not sure of that. It's just what they've told you. Do

183

you really believe that the Shakers are the only ones to know God's truth? Can the rest of the world be so wrong?"

"We cannot change the truth just because we might want to. If the truth was true before I knew you, then it remains true today."

"It was never the truth. The good Lord in his wisdom designed man and woman to love one another. We need to love one another."

"Yea, but the Lord lays different paths before each of us. I am not to be as one of the world."

"The world is not all evil." Brice couldn't keep the frustration out of his voice. He pulled in a deep breath to calm himself before he said, "I didn't come here to argue with you."

"Nor do I have any desire to have cross words with you, but to talk of this is useless. I am a Believer." She was silent for a moment before she asked, "Is Nathan well?"

He accepted the change in subject. He'd expected her to ask about Nathan. "He is well. He has not recovered his full strength as yet, but each day he grows stronger." Brice frowned. "He'd best be strong for what lies ahead of him."

"What do you mean, Dr. Scott?"

"I liked the sound of my given name on your tongue, Gabrielle. Call me Brice. You can do that much for me."

"That would not be proper, Dr. Scott."

"You must not have been worried about proper before." He smiled a bit.

Color rose in her cheeks. "You startled me."

"So I did." He looked at her for a moment before he asked, "And do I still disturb your mind, young sister?"

She looked ready to run again, but she kept her eyes on his face as she whispered, "Yea."

"And you still disturb my thoughts as well, Gabrielle. I fear you always will."

"It is not my intent to disturb the peace of your thoughts."

"Intent or not, you now live in my mind."

She didn't seem to know how to respond to that, so she again switched back to questions about Nathan. "You speak of Nathan needing strength. Is he in some sort of danger?"

"Don't you people ever get the news out here?" Brice frowned a little.

"News of the world means little to us."

"There's a war to be fought. Congress voted to fight England again a few weeks ago. All the militias are being called up to march north and take Detroit."

"Elder Caleb spoke of this war at our last meeting, but as Believers we have no part in any such battles. We live in peace with all people."

"That can be easier to say than to do. Especially if all people don't want to live in peace with you."

"Surely Nathan does not plan to go to this war. He would be better off back among us. He could come back. He would be accepted."

"Your Nathan will never be a Shaker. He never was. He only stayed because of you."

Gabrielle bent her head. "I feel sorrow for being a stumbling block in my brother's path to happiness, but I couldn't leave with him as he asked. I spoke the truth when I told him I loved him as a brother, but that was not what he desired to hear."

Brice put his fingers under her chin and raised her face up until he could look into her eyes again. "And is it true that you love me as a brother as well?"

185

It was a long time before she answered. Then the word was whispered so softly he more felt it than heard it. "Nay."

He would forever hold in his heart the way she looked at that moment, so soft and vulnerable with her blue eyes filling with a love she couldn't deny. Gently he wrapped his arms around her and kissed her. When her lips met his eagerly, he thought he'd won. At last he raised his mouth from hers and said, "That can't be wrong."

Tears filled her eyes. "But it is, Brice. I love you. I may always love you, and it is not the love of the Believers. But this worldly kind of love can lead to nothing but tragedy and heartache."

"You've been shut away from normal life too long, Gabrielle. When you come away with me and become part of the real world again, you'll understand that what we feel is not wrong. It is something to be sought after and treasured."

"Something that hurts another is always wrong."

Brice frowned. "I don't know what you mean. We've hurt no one."

"Becca died."

She wasn't making any sense to him, but he could see her sorrow. He wanted to understand. "Becca? The little girl who came to my cabin? What happened to her?"

"She took a fever. I asked for a doctor. Nay, not just a doctor. I asked that they send for you. I was so sure you would be able to heal her."

"But Elder Caleb wouldn't allow it." Brice remembered the hard look on the elder's face the last time he'd seen him.

"He would not. They got a doctor from town. As soon as he came into the room, I knew he carried death in with him. Death for Becca. I begged them to send him away, but of

186

course, they would not." Gabrielle looked up at Brice. "Don't you see? If I hadn't asked for a doctor, our prayers might have saved her. But I wanted to see you, and that was my sin."

"You were only thinking of the child."

"I can't be sure of that. I should have prayed and not let my mind dwell on worldly desires."

"She might have died anyway. There's been fever in town. I lost a child to it last month. Sometimes there is nothing you can do to fight off the fever."

"Was it because you bled him?"

Her words stabbed his heart. Memories of Jemma's last days flashed into his mind as Dr. Feeley had desperately bled her in a vain attempt to save her life. He shoved aside the thought of Jemma's blood draining into the basin taking her life with it and said, "Some of the family thought the child died because I did not."

"The doctor they called bled Becca. I wish it could have been my arm he pierced instead of hers."

Brice spoke gently. "No doctor or any amount of prayer will save every child who takes a fever. Death is something we have to accept."

"But Becca was so small. She never had a chance at happiness."

"What about you, Gabrielle? Do you want a chance at happiness?" He stared down at her intently.

She spoke in little more than a whisper. "I am happy. And content here with my brethren and sisters." She sounded as if she were trying to convince herself as much as him.

"I don't believe you. You are not happy. I can look in your eyes and see that what you say is not so."

She looked at him without speaking, and after a moment

he went on. "I'm offering you true happiness where your thoughts do not have to be troubled. Where you can walk on the path of love and family in a truer sense than you've ever known. I'm offering you my love." He spoke the words, baring his soul, pushing his love toward her. Now it was up to her. He couldn't force her to accept it.

Gabrielle could almost feel his love flowing through his fingers to her. It found an answering surge of desire within her, and suddenly more than anything in the world she wanted to be part of this man's life.

He must have sensed her desire. "You can come away with me right now," he said. "There's nothing back there for you."

Could he be right? Could she desert her brethren and sisters so easily? Then Sister Mercy's voice was echoing in her head. *"You are a true Believer, my child. Mother Ann has given you many gifts. In time you will learn to use them well for the good of all in the Society."*

Who should she trust? Sister Mercy or this man whose very touch made her tremble with desire to step away from everything she'd always held true. A hint of despair leaked into her voice as she said, "But I am a part of them. They are my family."

"I'll be your family, Gabrielle. And our children."

Gabrielle closed her eyes to try to sort out the jumble of thoughts flying every which way in her mind. She tried to think of her future, to call on her gift of knowing to show her the true way, but all she could see in the darkness of her mind was the doctor with a gun. She opened her eyes. "You are going to this war?"

He was silent for a moment and she sensed his uneasiness. Finally he said, "I'm a doctor. It's my duty to go with the militia."

"You come here to disturb my peace and ask me to walk away from my brothers and sisters when you are going to this war." Her voice was flat.

"I won't be leaving right away, and I will see that you're taken care of while I'm gone. I'll only be gone a few months at the most."

She just stared at him, hardly able to believe his words.

He frowned a little as he went on. "You can't think I want to go to war. But I cannot sidestep my duty. There are some things a man must do."

Her voice was calm and assured when she spoke. Her path was once more clear in front of her. "And so I must also do what I must. I can't go away with you, Dr. Scott. My place is here with my brethren and sisters."

His hands tightened on her arms. "Your place is with me. I love you too much to let you stay here."

"You have more strength than I, Dr. Scott. You could carry me away, but I do not believe that is what you want." The light had faded and she could barely see his face.

"No, it is not." His voice was sad. "I won't take you against your will, my love. But someday you'll know in your heart that we were meant to be together. That perhaps the Lord above wrote our names together in the stars and that is why our paths crossed. I'll wait for that day."

Gently he kissed her again and then touched her cheek with his fingers. He turned and with one step disappeared into the shadows.

She started after him and then willed her feet to stop. He

was gone. Perhaps forever, for who knew if he'd ever return from this war of his. "May the Eternal Father go with you, Brice, and keep you safe," she whispered.

She tried to say a prayer for him and for herself, but a cold emptiness opened up inside her until there seemed nothing left in her spirit, not even a prayer to cling to. She began to wonder if he had taken with him all that was alive within her.

For a long time she didn't move. The winds of temptation scattered her thoughts in a dozen directions. Then the long years of Shaker training began to seep back into her mind. She fell to her knees on the wet ground. If she couldn't pray, then she could surely sing. The words came to her lips almost against her will. "Come life, Shaker life! Come life eternal! Shake, shake out of me all that is carnal."

Over and over she repeated the words. She wasn't even sure she sang aloud. When at last she stood up, the emptiness was still inside her, but she had pushed it together into one small box of pain. She could now go on with her life. The doctor was gone out of her reach. Perhaps he'd always been beyond her reach.

As she began walking back to the house, her awareness of the things around her began coming back bit by bit. It was late. The moon was already high from the horizon. It was so bright that her shadow fell in front of her on the path and only a few stars were bright enough to appear in the moonlit sky.

The night meeting would be over by now, and Sister Mercy would be concerned. Gabrielle wondered for a moment what she would tell her. But then she knew. If she'd truly taken the path back among the Believers, then it was time to renounce her sins. She'd tell Sister Mercy the truth, or as much of the truth as she could, and beg for her understanding and mercy.

A flash of white caught Gabrielle's eyes on the path ahead of her. It was the apron of a sister. So she had been followed and watched.

16

As Gabrielle walked on toward the house, she felt betrayed somehow as if a trust between her and Sister Mercy had been broken. It mattered not that Gabrielle had in fact met a man and been tempted of the world in the woods. She hadn't set out with that intent. Perhaps Sister Mercy had always sent someone to watch her every time she went into the woods to pray.

All at once, Gabrielle was ashamed of her sin of pride. She'd thought she was above suspicion. She'd thought her gifts of love and faith had somehow elevated her above those who came from the world with their sins clinging to them like burrs from the woods. She'd been so young when she'd joined the Believers, ready to receive what they taught, and she had. But now she'd been brought low with temptation and doubts. She'd have to learn to bow and be humble until her sins were forgiven. She would take no more pride in the purity of her yesterdays.

When she went into the house, Sister Helen was whispering with Sister Mercy on the stairway. Of course it would be

Sister Helen with her small eyes that always noted the slightest misdeed and her sharp tongue that would forever remind one of this or that shortcoming. She did have a gift for mixing medicines and a wonderful memory for which herb was best for which illness, but she also had an everlasting memory of a person's wrongs and took delight in carrying tales on her sisters and brethren.

Again Gabrielle was ashamed of her thoughts. She whispered her vow to be humble and contrite.

"Sister Mercy," Gabrielle said. "I need to pray with you. My soul is weighted down with the burden of my sin."

"Of course, Sister Gabrielle," Sister Mercy said, but her voice sounded stiff and no kindness warmed her eyes. She led the way to the small room where she and Gabrielle had talked so many times before. Sister Mercy placed the small taper she carried on the table and perched on the edge of the chair.

Gabrielle knelt in front of her and bowed her head. "Dr. Scott sought me out in the woods."

"Sister Helen told me it was so just a moment ago. I am saddened to know thou has fallen to the carnal ways of the world."

"I knew not that he would be there when I went out to pray. I don't know how he knew to find me there in my secret place."

For a long time, Sister Mercy did not speak. Gabrielle kept her head bent and listened to the sister's breathing. She longed to feel Sister Mercy's forgiving hand touching her head as it had so often in the past when Gabrielle had confessed some sin to her, but Sister Mercy kept her hands folded in her lap. At last she said, "I have never known you to lie to me, Sister

Gabrielle. I have no reason to believe you are doing so now. Did you send him away at once?"

Gabrielle wanted to avoid answering her question. How could she confess to her sister mother that her heart had run after the doctor? Her cheeks burned as she admitted, "I did not. When the doctor is near me, my head is full of worldly thoughts instead of spiritual ones."

"Yea, I thought it so."

Gabrielle didn't look up. If there was disappointment on Sister Mercy's face, she didn't want to see it and know it was because of her wanton behavior. She went on. "He is gone now."

"You sent him away?"

"I told him that I must stay here with my family. That I couldn't share his life as he wished." Sorrow filled her as she thought of Brice walking away, each step going farther from her, and she felt hollow and empty inside.

"He is surely from the devil." Sister Mercy's voice was harsh. "You must pray that he has left no worldly mark upon you, Sister Gabrielle."

"Yea, Sister Mercy." Silence fell between them as Gabrielle tried to pray as Sister Mercy had instructed. She said the words in her mind, but they gathered and huddled there. The prayer found no wings to carry it heavenward to the Eternal Father.

At last Sister Mercy said, "I am very fond of you, Sister Gabrielle, and it pains me to do this. Nevertheless I shall have to take up this matter with the elders and eldresses. We must have proper behavior in our society if we are truly to live the life of the devoted Believer."

"Yea. I will do whatever needs to be done to regain full

fellowship with my brethren and sisters." Gabrielle stared at the floor as she blinked back tears.

Another long silence stretched out in the room. Gabrielle could feel Sister Mercy studying her, but she kept her head bent. Finally the older sister said, "Have you told me everything, Sister Gabrielle?"

Gabrielle didn't hesitate. The lie came easily to her lips. "Yea, Sister Mercy." If Sister Mercy could not forgive an unplanned meeting, then she would never be able to forgive a kiss. Especially a kiss Gabrielle had so completely surrendered to. She shifted uneasily on her knees in front of Sister Mercy and tried to block from her mind how good the doctor's arms around her had felt. In her heart she would ask the Eternal Father's forgiveness for her desire for carnal pleasure. Perhaps he could take the guilt of this hidden sin out of her heart.

Sister Mercy sighed heavily. "Ye have been given so many gifts, my child. Mother Ann has truly blessed you and through you, all of us here at Harmony Hill. Your gifts of song bring balls of love down to us from Mother. I suppose that's why the devil wants to tempt you away from us."

"I am not leaving the village, Sister Mercy."

"But you have been tempted."

Gabrielle was silent, unable to deny the truth of her temptation. Even now a part of her was running after the doctor.

"You must overcome the evil of temptation with the goodness of a life of purity."

"Yea, Sister Mercy. I will bend my spirit after the ways of truth." The expected words slid off her lips so easily, but would she be able to do as she said? Would she be able to stop doubting the truth as she'd known it since she'd joined the Shakers?

"Very well, Sister Gabrielle." Sister Mercy fell silent for a moment. When she began speaking again, her words were blunt. "Nevertheless I feel it is my duty to recommend you be put under constant supervision until this temptation no longer troubles your spirit."

Constant supervision. Gabrielle looked up at Sister Mercy, but the sister's face was fixed and set. Nothing Gabrielle could say would sway her to lighten the punishment. Gabrielle swallowed hard. Only a few of the Believers had ever been so watched. Most of the converts preferred to leave the village rather than to submit to this constant supervision. For however long was stated, Gabrielle would not be allowed to be alone at any time. A sister would always be at her side watching her every move, listening to her every word, controlling her every breath. At least they would not be able to read her thoughts or keep her from saying her prayers silently.

"You are too quiet, Sister Gabrielle," Sister Mercy said. "You have no reason to fear such constant supervision if you truly have a repentant spirit and nothing to hide."

"Have you lost your trust in me, Sister Mercy?"

Sister Mercy touched Gabrielle's shoulder lightly, but she didn't let her hand linger there in any kind of affectionate gesture. "Perhaps that trust is being tested just as your faith is, my child. I do not desire to do anything that would bring you pain, but I must do my duty to the other brethren and sisters."

"Yea, thy duty." Gabrielle sought out Sister Mercy's eyes, but the older sister looked over her shoulder toward the door. Gabrielle had little choice except to say, "I have no wish to be so watched, but neither do I have anything to hide. I will submit myself to the ruling of the council."

Sister Mercy stood up. "Very well. It will be done."

Gabrielle stayed on her knees. "May I stay here to pray a little longer before I go to the room with the young sisters?"

Sister Mercy barely hesitated before she said, "Nay. It would be best if you go along to bed. Already it is late."

"Yea, Sister Mercy," Gabrielle said. There would be no more favors or rule bending for Gabrielle. Sister Mercy loved her, but she couldn't forgive her. At least not yet. Gabrielle followed her meekly out of the room and up the hallway to her sleeping room.

The children under her care were in bed, most of them already asleep. Here and there a child moved under her covers. Gabrielle's eyes went to Becca's bed. Another child slept there now. A child who shed no tears and had no need of comfort in the night. And as Gabrielle did every night, she missed little Becca and felt a pang of guilt for failing to comfort her enough.

Gabrielle quickly undressed and slipped her nightdress over her head. She knelt by her bed, but prayer eluded her. Empty words bounced around in her head until she decided if she couldn't talk to the Father, she could at least talk to herself. She had vowed to be humble, and she would keep her vow. She'd submit herself to this constant supervision even though it was sure to be arduous. Still, it wouldn't last forever, and then she would be back in the full fellowship of the Believers where she would stay for the rest of her life. It was as it was meant to be.

Then the doctor's words were in her mind. *"We were meant to be together."*

Deliberately she pushed a door shut in her mind in an attempt to close him out of her thoughts. But just before the door slammed shut, he slipped through to stay with her, and in spite of her resolve to walk the path of repentance, his presence in her mind comforted her.

17

After Brice left Gabrielle, the trip back through the woods to his cabin was a long one. He'd told her that someday she'd see she belonged with him, but as the shadows of the trees closed in around him, he began to doubt the truth of that. The Shakers' hold over her was too strong, too constant. If only he could be with her where he could talk to her and see her, then he could surely make her understand. But they had her locked away from him, out of reach of his words. Soon he'd be even farther from her when he joined up with the militia, but in spite of the way that tore at his heart, he had no choice about going to war.

Maybe she was right. Maybe it had been wrong for him to ask her to come away from the Shakers when he was planning to go to the war. He could make her no real promise that he'd return. A man never knew what would happen when he stepped out on the war trail. He'd been selfish, thinking only of his own needs. His desire to carry her love with him and the sure knowledge that she'd be waiting for his return had overpowered his common sense and sent him through the woods to lie in wait of her. Now he could carry the truth of her love with him but no certainty that she'd ever be waiting for his return.

Why was it that every person he loved was taken from him? He wished he'd never let Gabrielle awaken the feelings he'd so carefully buried in his mind after Jemma died. He'd never intended to let love darken his life again. The lines of his face tightened. He'd shut her away just as he'd shut away the memory of Jemma after her death.

He tried to push all his thoughts of Gabrielle from his mind, but her beautiful blue eyes were before him full of a love she believed was wrong. He remembered the soft warmth of her skin under his fingers and how he'd wanted to touch and cherish every inch of her. The feeling was too strong to deny. He couldn't give up. Not while there was yet a chance. Nothing but death could defeat him.

When he came out of the woods into the clearing around his cabin, he spotted the boy outside waiting for him in the moonlight. He'd grown fond of Nathan since he'd come away from the Shakers to stay with him. But tonight he wished the boy were already asleep. Brice needed time alone.

"You stayed out a long time, Doc. I was beginning to fret a little," Nathan said.

"You don't need to waste your time worrying over me, boy. I learned to take care of myself a long time ago." Brice's voice was rough with the edge of anger.

Nathan didn't pay it much mind as he looked back at the woods. "You didn't take your horse."

"I didn't go far."

"All that lays over that way is Harmony Hill."

"I don't need a bit of a boy telling me where I can walk in the evening if I take a mind," Brice said with a frown.

200

"No sir, you don't, Doc, and I wasn't meaning to be doing that." The boy stared at the woods as if he could see through the trees and beyond to the Shaker village. After a long minute, he said, "It's just that I can't keep from wondering sometimes what's going on over there."

"You can hear whatever you like if you go into town and ask. There are always plenty of travelers who stay with the Shakers when they pass through. Some folks can't turn down a free handout."

"True enough," Nathan said. "But I wouldn't be hearing anything about the one I'd most want to hear about. Gabrielle."

Brice was sorry he'd been so short with the boy. He sat down beside Nathan on the steps. "Don't you ever wonder about others of your family? Your ma and pa? Are they with the Shakers?"

"Pa is. My ma, she died a few years back. I miss her some, but Pa, well, he wasn't ever the same after he got religion. I had a sister and brother, but they died of the fever when they were just little things. And Pa, I guess he the same as died to me when we joined up with the Shakers. We haven't said more than a dozen words to each other since. It's only Gabrielle I think about."

"I thought you'd about gotten over her," Brice said.

"In a way I guess I have, Doc. But in another way, I don't know if I ever will. I can't rightly believe yet that she turned me away. I'd been so sure so long that she'd jump at the chance of leaving with me."

Brice wondered for the first time what the boy would have done if Gabrielle had followed him back to his cabin tonight. He'd never told the boy how he felt about Gabrielle, not wanting to crowd in on the boy's hurt, but maybe he should have.

Brice hesitated a moment and then said, "You told me once she was beauty."

Nathan looked at him as if hearing something different in his voice, but Brice didn't turn his face away. The shadowy moonlight must not have revealed the truth of his feelings as Nathan looked away and up at the sky. "That and more. She's everything I ever dreamed of."

Brice thought of telling the boy of his own love for the young sister, but something stayed his tongue. Instead he said, "Sometimes you have to let loose one dream before you can capture a new one."

Nathan didn't say anything. Just kept staring at the moon and the few stars bright enough to shine along with it. Finally Brice asked, "How are your legs doing?"

The boy answered a bit too quickly. "They're fine. I could run five miles if I had to."

Brice reached over and grabbed the boy's leg. "That doesn't hurt?"

The boy couldn't keep from flinching a little, but he said, "Not all that much, Doc. I'm plenty well enough to be going with the militia if that's what you've got in mind."

"I'm not sure you should be going at all. I can find you a place to stay while I'm gone. You're a good worker. The Shakers taught you well, and I know this man over around Sowderville who would take you in and maybe even pay you a little for your work."

"I won't be wanting to do that. I've already decided to an-swer the militia call whether you go or not, Doc. So if you're thinking I might be a hindrance to you, I can just join up on my own. I'm old enough."

"Old enough maybe, but the question is, are you well enough?"

"I figure I can do whatever I set my mind to. Pain or no pain."

Brice had to smile a little. The boy had a stubborn streak. "Your legs don't hold you back much," Brice admitted.

"They won't hold me back fighting those redcoats either."

"War's sometimes more about dying than fighting," Brice said. The boy was too eager, too young. Younger even than most boys his same age because of the years he'd spent shut away with the Shakers.

"You ever go to war, Doc?"

"Not as a soldier. But I watched the warriors go out of the village to fight when I was a boy living with the Indians, and I saw them come back. Or I saw some of them come back. Never all of them."

"You were with the Indians?"

"For a while. They took me when I was six. Tried to turn me Indian and for a while I thought maybe they had. It wasn't a bad life. Hard, but not bad. Alec Hope and some other trappers traded for me and brought me back to the white settlements after a few years."

"No wonder Hope said you owed him. Rescuing you from the redskins like that."

"You've been listening to Hope too much. Not all Indians are bad or even against us. There will be some Indians fighting on our side as well as against us when we get up north. Not as many, but some."

"You think it'll be a long fight, Doc?"

"Who can say? Maybe and maybe not. One thing for sure,

it's a long way up there to Detroit, and through some rough country."

"I can do it, Doc." The boy's voice was eager. "I know I can. My grandpappy used to tell me I had the makings of a soldier when I wasn't much higher than his knee." When Brice didn't say anything, Nathan went on. "Aren't you excited about going, Doc?"

"I'm a doctor, Bates. Sworn to save lives if I can. I'll be doing most of my fighting with the scalpel, and I don't suppose any doctor ever looked forward to cutting off legs and arms even to save a man's life."

His words didn't dampen the boy's spirits. "When are we planning to move out?"

"Right away. There's nothing here to hold me. My patients can get along with one of the other doctors around. Some of the folks in town might be glad to see me gone." Brice laughed shortly. "Your Elder Caleb will probably do a special dance when he hears I'm gone."

Nathan laughed with him. "He didn't talk too nice about you when he was here. He thinks you planted the devil's seed in my head."

"Maybe I did, Bates." Brice frowned at him. "I doubt I'm doing you any kindness by letting you come along with me."

"I'm going whether I go with you or not, Doc. I don't aim to be left behind, but I would count it a favor if you'd let me tag along with you. Leastways till we get to where the army's gathering."

"You can come with me, but it'll be no favor." Somewhere over in the direction of the settlement, a dog howled. Then another dog picked up the lonesome sound from a different direction. After a moment Brice said, "We'll go out to old man

Moore's first thing in the morning. He owes me for nursing his little girl through the fever. He can spare us a horse."

"I'd rather have a gun than a horse."

"You'll have a gun, boy. When the time comes." Brice stood up. "First things first. Right now we both need to get some sleep before the sun comes up and catches us still perched out here on these steps like two old crows."

◬

The next morning, it didn't take long to collect the horse from Moore. It was old and low on spirit, but it would rest the boy's legs. Next they stopped at the cabin of a woman Brice had treated for hysterics last summer. She hadn't had any money or anything to barter, but she was a good hand with a comb and scissors.

"Come for your haircut, Dr. Scott?" the woman asked as she set a chair out in the middle of the yard for him. "Seems like it was just the other day that I cut it for you."

"I'm going away for a while, Tyney, so I'm thinking you might need to trim off a little more to last me till I get back. Then the boy here could use a touch of your scissors."

Tyney pulled her scissors out of her apron pocket. She lovingly ran her fingers along their edges. She'd told Brice she'd brought them with her when she'd come out of Virginia seventeen years ago as a bride. They were her most treasured possession along with the Bible that had her mother's handwriting inside. She looked at Nathan and said, "He looks to be one of them Shakers."

"He was. That's why he needs the haircut, Tyney. So folks won't see that right off. He's decided not to be a Shaker anymore."

205

"I always figured them to be a little on the strange side anyways. What with their dancing meetings and all." She pointed to the chair. "Go ahead and sit, Doc. I'll get you first."

Brice sat down and let her snip the hair off his neck. He could do it well enough himself, but Tyney had more than her share of pride. She needed a way to pay off her doctoring bill. Besides, it gave the woman a break from the monotony of her hard life, shut away from most of her neighbors by distance and trees.

She fussed over him. "I just don't see how you get along out there in that cabin of yours, Dr. Scott, without a woman to see to you. Why, I bet you haven't had a proper meal in days."

Brice smiled. "It's just that all the good women like you have already been snapped up, Tyney. Now if Sam wasn't around, we might have something to talk about."

She gave his shoulder a little shove. "Go along with you, Doc. A young man like you wouldn't have the time of day for an old woman like me."

When she'd finished cutting and combing on his hair, she brushed the loose hair off his shoulders and back before she said, "Since you're already here and all, would you mind to look at little Maysie? She's been a mite peaked the last few days, and Sam brought home news from town that there was fever going around."

"I saw her run around the house a bit ago. She looked fine. Anything special she's complaining about?"

"Nothing I can put my finger on." Tyney rubbed her hands on her apron and said, "Oh, you know me, Doctor. Sometimes I worry when I ought to be praying, but Maysie's my only little one. You know the boys are all about grown, and it don't look likely that the good Lord will be blessing me with any more young'uns. It'd just make me feel lighter if you'd give her a look over before you go."

Brice touched her arm. "Sure I will, Tyney. I'd have been by before now if you'd let me know you wanted me to."

"I reckon I still don't have nothing to pay you. There just ain't never no leavings for extra."

"The boy here could use an old shirt if one of your boys has one he can spare."

Tyney eyeballed Nathan. "I guess as how he's not much littler than my middle boy. I'll give you his extra shirt before you go."

Nathan spoke up. "I can't take your boy's extra shirt."

Brice sent the boy a sharp look. "You let me and Tyney handle this, boy."

But Tyney laughed. "I reckon the boy don't understand how things are out here away from the Shakers' town. You go on along and look to Maysie, Doc. I'll explain things to him. Sit down here, boy. What'd you say your name was now?"

"Nathan Bates, ma'am," the boy said as he sat down.

"Well, Nathan, you see it's like this. I always was right handy with a needle and scissors, and it just so happens that I've got a piece of goods I've been wondering what to do with. I'll have my boy a new shirt whipped up in no time flat."

Brice left them alone and went around the cabin in search of the little girl. Maysie was always shy when he came around, but he had his magic ingredient in his pocket. He'd have her out of hiding quick enough.

He spotted a flash of blue behind a tree to his left, but he didn't look in that direction. Instead he settled down on the ground close by and took out the licorice stick he kept for just such occasions. No more than two minutes passed before Maysie sidled around the tree to stare at him with big eyes.

Brice broke off a piece of the licorice and put it in his mouth before he said, "I don't suppose you'd like a piece, would you, Maysie?"

She shuffled her feet a minute before she whispered, "I might."

He patted the ground beside him. "You have to sit down to really enjoy licorice."

She crept over to him and sat down obediently. He handed her the candy and studied her while he got her talking about a bird that flew past them. Finally he asked, "Has anything been bothering you? Your ma tells me you haven't been feeling as pert as usual."

Maysie sucked on the licorice stick before she answered. "I been getting all wore out."

"You mean when you've been helping your ma with the washing or fetching wood?"

"Ma don't make me do much."

"I see." Brice put his hand on the little girl's forehead. She didn't feel hot. "Does anything hurt you? You have a pain anywhere?"

Maysie looked thoughtful before she said, "Sometimes when I swallow my throat feels too little."

"Not all the time?"

Maysie shook her head.

"How about opening your mouth and letting me take a peek inside? See if any frogs are hiding out down there."

Maysie giggled before she stretched her mouth wide open.

"Nope, no frogs." Brice couldn't see any redness. He let her shut her mouth as he felt around on her neck. "How about now?" he asked. "Is it hurting now?"

"Uh-uh," she said. "Mostly it just hurts when I'm feeling wore out, and I'm not wore out now."

Brice smiled and kept talking about whatever came to mind. The licorice. An ant crawling by. The wind in the trees around the little cabin. The child was young for hysterics like her mother had had even though the symptoms were some the same. Even so, he didn't like the look around Maysie's eyes. He had to agree with Tyney. The child was peaked, but he couldn't be sure what was causing it. If he hadn't been leaving with the militia, he'd plan to check on her every few days to see what developed before he gave her any medicine. But he was leaving.

After a while, Brice patted the little girl on the head and said, "I guess I'd better be moving on." He reached into his pocket and pulled out another licorice whip. "I'll be leaving some medicine with your ma. Now it doesn't taste as good as this, but you be a big girl and swallow it down for your ma and that will make you both feel better."

Maysie clutched the licorice close to her and watched him with big eyes, her shyness falling back over her as he stood up.

When Brice went back around to the front of the cabin, Tyney had finished Nathan's haircut and had him wearing the new shirt. She'd given him her boy's best. That was easy enough to see, and Brice hoped the boy had had the sense to be grateful without embarrassing her again.

Tyney smiled at him. "The boy here looks like any other boy now, don't you think, Dr. Scott?"

"You've got a way with the scissors all right, Tyney. I don't know how I'll make out without you up north."

"You going north, Doc?"

"Afraid so. Me and the boy here are going with the militia now that Congress has declared war."

"War!" Tyney spat out the word. "That's all Sam and the boys talk about these days. As if we hadn't seen enough wars whilst we been in this place." She looked up at Brice. "But I reckon I don't begrudge them that do go a doctor to see to them up there."

"I hope you can keep your boys home," Brice said.

"Oh well, they don't none of them want to listen to their old mother. But what about my little one? Maysie?"

"I don't know, Tyney. She does look pale." Brice took a bottle from his saddlebags. "This tonic might help her. It could be that she'll be back to her old self in a few days." Brice didn't want to worry Tyney when he really had nothing to go on, but at the same time he had to caution her. "But if she doesn't get to feeling better, you take her on to another doctor. There's one over toward Danville that has good hands."

"You talking about McDowell? The one that cut on that poor woman and on Christmas Day at that." Tyney clucked her tongue. "I couldn't hardly believe that story when I first heard it. Him cutting her open and all."

"She lived, Tyney. That's the important thing to remember."

"I reckon that had more to do with God's will than with what he done. Anyhow I've heard tell he's a poor fever doctor."

Brice smiled a little. "They say the same about me."

"Maybe they do, but I know better, Doc. I don't know nothing 'bout this McDowell except what I don't want to know."

Brice sighed. "All right, Tyney. Dr. Johnson in town might

do just as good." He was the least dangerous of the doctors around and had a kind heart. "The time might come when you need him before I get back, and then again it might not. Most likely Maysie will snap right out of whatever's bothering her."

Tyney looked at the bottle in her hand. "I'm beholden to you, Dr. Scott."

As he rode away, Brice had an uneasy feeling about the child and Tyney too if Maysie were to really take sick. It was proving harder to leave behind his patients than he'd thought.

"She was a nice woman," Nathan said. "Appeared to set a lot of store by you, Doc."

"I doctored her through a rough time a while back." Brice hoped if she needed help again she'd be able to find it while he was gone. But he couldn't worry about maybes. He knew he'd be needed where he was going.

Then the thought of Gabrielle pushed in to join his worry about Tyney and her little girl. He was deserting Gabrielle in her time of need. The child's death was a heavy stone in her heart, and she had wanted to lean on his strength and love. She had wanted to put her hand in his and let him lead her away from the Shaker life. He had seen it in her eyes. Yet he had walked away and left her there. What else could he do? He'd offered her everything he had and she had turned him down. Because of the war. She hadn't been able to understand that a man had to answer the call of his country in times of war whether he wanted to or not.

By the time he came back from the North, Gabrielle could be far beyond the reach of his love. The old sister would have complete power over Gabrielle now. She would pull Gabrielle back into the Shaker way and build a wall around her that

Brice might never be able to breach. A deep sorrow spread through him. If only he wasn't so bound to duty.

Brice turned his horse north. "Time to be finding the militia, boy."

Nathan let out a war whoop, but Brice settled into a dark study. Each step his horse took tore at him as he longed to turn back to his cabin, back to Gabrielle before it was too late.

18

July 1812

It took less than a week for Gabrielle to grow weary of the constant supervision. Every waking moment Sister Helen was at her side and even at night she lay in a bed pulled close to Gabrielle's and blocking her path to the door in such a way that Gabrielle was obligated to shake Sister Helen awake if she needed to go to the privy in the night. Gabrielle had been moved from her room with the little girls in the Children's House to the East Family House in order for Sister Helen to watch her.

Gabrielle tried to bear it with a humble mind and a contrite spirit, but as each day passed, her spirit grew more and more restive under Sister Helen's constant eye. Gabrielle had suffered the public humiliation of being accused of wrongdoing at the meeting. She'd made no sound of defense because she was guilty of what they said. In her heart she knew she carried even worse carnal sins. She had willingly offered her lips to the doctor and had desired his arms around her.

Her intention had been to submit to her penance willingly to show her desire to once again be in full fellowship with her brethren and sisters. But she had not expected them to assign Sister Helen to watch her. Gabrielle's heart had sunk when she heard who would be watching her. It was surely another test of whether she could truly humble her spirit since Gabrielle had always had to struggle to feel any kind of proper sisterly love for Sister Helen.

Before Sister Helen had come together with the Believers at Harmony Hill, her gift with herbs had made her a sought-after midwife in the area. She often talked of the babies she'd helped bring into the world and sometimes seemed to especially enjoy telling of the babies she'd caught in her hands who had never drawn breath and how the tiny infants had surely been doomed by the sins of their parents.

Sister Helen claimed Mother Ann had visited her with a special revelation when the Shakers had come from the east to first teach their beliefs at her brother's barn. She'd known at that moment her purity of spirit and body without the touch of a man to soil her had been the Lord's plan so that she would be better fit for her work with the Believers. From the very beginning of their village coming together she had not only seen to the physical ills of the community but also undertook the duty of watching over any new converts to be sure they did not stray from the Society's precepts.

She reminded Gabrielle of this often during their first days together. "There are many gifts of the spirit. Not all of them have anything to do with singing or laboring the songs."

"Yea." Gabrielle was determined to agree with her and

not let the woman's ill attitude entice Gabrielle into allowing her tongue to lead her into more trouble by saying what she thought. Sister Helen had no ear for the melodies of the Shaker songs and her dancing was clumsy although it was said she worked long hours practicing the steps in her room. Gabrielle closed her eyes a moment and summoned all the kindness she could find in her spirit. "We could practice the laboring of the dances together if you wish."

Sister Helen's face went dark with anger as she glared at Gabrielle and practically spat out her words. "I need no help from one such as you. You've always thought you were so fine, so gifted. I guess now it will be seen which of us has the greater gifts of the spirit."

Gabrielle lowered her eyes to the ground and managed to keep her voice even and calm. "I meant you no insult, Sister Helen. It was just a thought since we are to be together so much for the next few months."

It would do little good to match Sister Helen's anger with her own, although at times Gabrielle felt as if she might break into a thousand pieces if the woman did not quit staring at her or picking at her with her words. Sister Helen harped on and on about how she would have never allowed carnal thoughts to worm into her mind and separate her from the love of Mother Ann and cause her to fall into disgrace. She would have never thought of meeting a man in the woods. And certainly not one so full of the devil as the doctor.

She managed to bring these points to light often as she and Gabrielle went about their assigned duties. Now once again Sister Helen began to browbeat Gabrielle with her words. "It looks as if, Sister Gabrielle, that you should have been able to see the wrong spirit in that Dr. Scott after he led our wayward brother away from us and into sin."

They were working in the garden, weeding and hoeing to keep out the summer weeds. It made Gabrielle's back tired and her hands calloused, but nevertheless Gabrielle liked the feel of the dirt in her hands and the strong sunlight on her back that made the sweat run in rivulets down between her breasts. Best of all she was outside where she could look up and see the trees against the blue sky and hear the birds sing as they went joyfully about their natural duties.

When a breeze sprang up, it carried not only the smell of new mown hay but also the sweet scent of honeysuckle and roses and other flowers blooming around the buildings. Their blossoms supplied nectar for the Society's bee swarms and thus were useful as well as beautiful. Now Gabrielle concentrated on filling her head with the sweet smells as she answered Sister Helen softly. "The doctor doesn't believe as we do, but he is one of God's children just as we are, Sister Helen."

"You may have fallen to his level, Sister Gabrielle, but I can assure you that I have not."

Gabrielle kept her eyes on her hoe as she pulled the dirt up around a bean plant. She had no desire to speak of Dr. Scott with Sister Helen. Actually there was nothing she cared to speak of with Sister Helen. And that too, the lack of sisterly affection for this woman beside her, was a sin.

But Sister Helen would not let her by so easily. "You were in the shadows there among the trees with him for a long time. What did you do?"

"I've told you already as I told Sister Mercy." Gabrielle leaned down to weed out some grass growing around the roots of the bean plants. When she stood up, she let her eyes slide across Sister Helen's face. "We talked. I asked him of our former brother's health, and he asked me to go away with him."

"Why didn't you go?" Sister Helen sounded as if she wished Gabrielle had gone.

Gabrielle pulled her hoe through the dirt before she answered. She wished she didn't have to answer at all, that she could just put all her attention on the beans in the row before her. But she could feel Sister Helen waiting for an answer, so she simply said, "My place is here with my brethren and sisters."

Sister Helen snorted, but to Gabrielle's relief, she left off her questioning and went back to hoeing the beans. She would ask them again. She was trying to coerce Gabrielle into admitting some worse sin. A sin that might forever put her out of fellowship with the Believers.

After a while, Sister Helen said, "You don't talk very much, do you, Sister Gabrielle? Or perhaps you talk best with those from the world."

A line Gabrielle had heard in meetings came to her mind. "None preaches better than the ant, and it says nothing." As soon as the words were out, she knew she shouldn't have spoken them aloud. Sister Helen would surely report to the elders and eldresses that Gabrielle wasn't humbling her spirit as she should in the face of her wrongdoing. Still when she looked up and saw the sister's face, a smile slipped through Gabrielle. A smile she did not dare let touch her lips or sneak into her eyes as she bent back to her hoeing.

So the days passed. Each one a bit harder to bear than the one before. Gabrielle prayed for the ability to feel love for Sister Helen or at least the strength to endure her presence with a quiet inner peace. But she felt no answer to her prayer, and she remembered Elder Caleb saying charity bore a humble mind. Perhaps the fault was within her. Every day when the sun went down, Gabrielle would sit during their rest time and resolve to be more humble on the coming day.

She no longer wrote in her journal as she knew Sister Helen would insist on reading any word she wrote as she wrote it. Rather she sat in silence and gathered her thoughts to her. She held them close and they made a wall of sorts against the never resting eyes of Sister Helen.

Many of her thoughts could not have been written in a journal at any rate. Journals were written to be read, and her thoughts could only be hidden. The doctor often walked through them, bringing the comfort of the memory of his touch. At first she had tried to shut him out, but as the misery inside her grew, she began to welcome him instead.

Sometimes Sister Helen would ask her sharply, "What are you thinking of, Sister Gabrielle, that brings that look to your face?"

Gabrielle always answered, "I am praying, Sister Helen." At times it was true, and other times she only whispered a quick prayer asking forgiveness before she spoke. But the truth didn't seem to matter as much now as bearing the constant presence of Sister Helen with the least amount of distress.

Mealtimes brought some relief for Gabrielle. Sister Helen was at her elbow as always, but there were also the other sisters of the East Family. They knew her shame, but since many of them were struggling with their own acceptance of the Shakers' ways, their eyes didn't condemn her. No conversation was allowed at the eating tables, but sometimes a smile spoke as well as words.

Each time she went into the biting room, Gabrielle quickly searched the tables for Sister Esther. Sometimes Esther would look up at her and accept her smile. Other times she kept her eyes to her plate as if she wasn't even aware of the others in the room. Then Gabrielle would wish she could sit beside her and offer her whatever help she could. But that was not allowed. It was what Gabrielle regretted most about her constant supervision.

She had pleaded with Sister Mercy to allow her to continue on the same work duties with Sister Esther, but Sister Mercy hadn't even hesitated before she refused. "You have shown yourself in need of help, Sister Gabrielle. Can we expect the lame to lead the lame?"

"I feel I can still be of help to Sister Esther," Gabrielle had said as she looked down at Sister Mercy seated at the narrow table she used as a desk in the small room where they had shared so many talks. Sister Mercy had not given Gabrielle permission to sit down.

Sister Mercy sighed and laid down her pen as though irritated to have her work interrupted. She frowned at Gabrielle. "Perhaps you could have been if you had not allowed worldly thoughts to creep into your own head. Now you must think upon your own sins and work toward repentance and cleansing in your own life."

"That doesn't make the problems of my sister go away or mean that my love for her might not be a comfort to her."

Sister Mercy stood up and leaned across the table toward Gabrielle. "Until you have once again gained the inner peace of the true Believer, your presence would only be a hindrance to the spiritual growth of Sister Esther."

"May I at least speak to her during times of rest or at the meetings?" It seemed a reasonable enough request.

Yet Sister Mercy didn't even consider it. "Nay, Sister Gabrielle. Ye will do well not to make requests out of keeping with your present situation."

Gabrielle shrank back from the coldness of her words. Gabrielle had disappointed Sister Mercy by falling away from the teachings she had showered on her these many years, and Gabrielle wondered if they would ever be close again even after she stepped back into the full fellowship after serving her penance. Gabrielle bowed her head a bit as she said, "I will pray for your forgiveness, Sister Mercy."

Sister Mercy's voice was sharp. "It is not my forgiveness you need. It is the Eternal Father's."

"Yea, I have already asked his forgiveness. He knows my sin, and yet I feel I have not lost his love." Gabrielle kept her head bent as a thankful prayer rose in her heart for that truth.

"And Mother Ann's?"

Gabrielle had never been able to pray as easily to Mother Ann as she could to the Eternal Father. She sang the songs of Mother's love, but yet some part of her seemed unable to reach out to Mother Ann. It was always the Eternal Father or his loving Son she felt received her prayers, but she looked up at Sister Mercy and said, "I pray daily for her love and forgiveness as well."

"Ye will do well to remember that saying you are sorry is not always enough. Nay, sometimes it takes much more."

"Yea, Sister Mercy," Gabrielle had said. She'd asked more than Sister Mercy was able to give. In time the old sister might forgive Gabrielle, but there would always be this hurt between them.

So she didn't speak with Sister Esther although she longed to. She could only pray for her, and many times her prayer was for the sister to leave the Believers. Then Sister Esther might be able to start a new life away from the sad memories of this village. She might have another child who would bring her joy.

But Sister Esther did not leave. Each night she looked a bit thinner and paler. When others of the Believers spoke to her during the meetings, she often seemed confused as if she could not understand the words reaching her ears.

One night at meeting in spite of Sister Mercy's orders to the contrary, Gabrielle found a seat along the wall bench beside Sister Esther. Sister Helen had gotten caught up in the exercising of the songs, and for the moment she'd forgotten about Gabrielle.

Sister Helen never watched her quite so closely during meeting. They each had their parts as they labored the songs. Gabrielle was usually among the singers and Sister Helen among the dancers. Sister Esther did neither unless one of the other sisters took her hand and led her through the motions of the exercise. Even then she couldn't keep the steps or turns in her mind, and usually they allowed her to return to the bench that held the old and the infirm.

"Sister Esther," Gabrielle said. "How are you?"

"Gabrielle," Sister Esther said, awareness coming to her eyes. "Where have you been?"

Sister Esther had been too deep in her own misery to even notice Gabrielle's trouble. Gabrielle smiled and touched her hand. "I've been near. They've assigned us to different duties."

"They must have known how I longed to talk to you and decided to keep us apart." Sister Esther moved her hands about in her lap in quick, meaningless gestures. "I have a need to talk about my Becca, but no one will talk to me about her. They say I should forget. That I should turn my grief over to Mother Ann."

"They are surely trying to help you, Sister Esther."

The woman sighed. "Perhaps so, but it doesn't, you know. I can't forget Becca. She was part of me. My gift from the Lord. He gave me Becca and I did not take care of his gift."

"That is not so. You loved Becca just as the Lord surely meant for you to do, and now she will always be in your heart." Gabrielle took both of Sister Esther's hands into hers to still them. "But now you have to quit punishing yourself for her death and go on with your own life."

"I have no life." Sister Esther's voice was flat and void of feeling.

"But you do. You have a life here with the Believers." Gabrielle glanced around to see if anyone could hear her words. Everyone was absorbed in the song, so she went on. "Or you could leave and find a new life in the world."

Sister Esther didn't seem to hear. "Becca calls to me. Did you know that, Sister Gabrielle?" Without waiting for Gabrielle to answer, she went on. "I hear her voice and see her beckoning to me. And when I don't go to her, I hear her crying."

Gabrielle searched her mind for something comforting to say, but she found no words. She held Sister Esther's hands tighter and shared her sorrow silently.

"She cries, Sister Gabrielle, and I can't go to her. I never could stand to hear her crying. I used to hold her all day and rock her when she was a baby because she would cry. But now I can't hold her. I can't reach her at all. And she keeps crying."

Gabrielle spoke around the lump in her throat. "It is only a dream, Sister Esther. Becca is in heaven. In heaven with the angels there is only happiness."

Sister Esther's eyes came up to stare at Gabrielle. "And weren't we going to be happy here, Sister Gabrielle? Weren't all our troubles supposed to be gone? Weren't we to love one another and make a heaven on earth? And didn't my Becca die anyway?"

"We are only human. We haven't the power of the Eternal Father to solve all problems and heal all sickness."

"The Believers only make problems. They solve nothing."

"We have love one for another. We have love for you."

"Tell me, Sister Gabrielle, do you think Becca would have died if we had never ventured into this supposed paradise on earth? Your truthfulness would be a kindness to me."

Gabrielle hesitated. How could she answer her? Finally she said, "Who am I to know when death will come?"

Sister Esther smiled sadly. "You know, Sister Gabrielle. You know the truth, but you are afraid to admit it or speak it aloud. I knew it was wrong the first night we were here when they took Becca from me and she cried. I didn't go to her then, and now I cannot."

Gabrielle didn't say anything. There was nothing she could say. Words and phrases shot through her mind, but all of them faded away in the face of Sister Esther's grief.

Sister Esther didn't seem to notice Gabrielle's silence as she said, "But if she keeps crying, I will have to try. You understand that, don't you? I will have to try."

Sister Helen stepped in front of them. "Sister Gabrielle, you are not in your place with the singers. Are you ill?"

"Nay." Reluctantly Gabrielle let go of Sister Esther's hands and stood up. Sister Esther's hands began their nervous dancing about in her lap again. Gabrielle looked straight into Sister Helen's eyes. "Sister Esther isn't well. Someone needs to sit with her."

Sister Helen stared at Sister Esther for a moment. Then she looked back at Gabrielle. "It is nothing. She'll snap out of it as soon as she confesses her sins and gives her obedience to the Believers' way."

"She needs someone with her," Gabrielle insisted. Then she softened her voice and said, "I humbly seek your permission to speak with Elder Caleb about her."

Sister Helen's eyes snapped angrily. "There's nary a thing humble about you, Sister Gabrielle, and there never has been. So you want to go over my head to the elder. Elder Caleb has no time for one in disgrace."

Gabrielle refused to back down. "Our sister needs special consideration. Surely you have compassion for her."

Sister Helen's face reddened and her hand came up as if she might strike Gabrielle. But then she seemed to remember she was in meeting where they were only to show love for one another and not anger, and she said, "Of course I do. I'll see that someone takes care of Sister Esther. You need not remind me of my love for my sisters."

"Nay, of course not," Gabrielle said meekly. But she didn't feel meek. Her spirit would not humble before Sister Helen no matter what she did, and suddenly she was tired of trying. Still she had to endure Sister Helen's presence for months more. It was either that or leave, and even if she had wanted to leave to get away from Sister Helen, she had no place to go.

Brice was in her mind with his words promising to be there if she needed him, but the words had no truth in them. He'd gone away into the region of war. Nathan had gone with him. She'd heard it from Sister Helen.

Gabrielle knew nothing of wars. She knew only that men fought and men died. Her gift of knowing nudged at her with images of guns and soldiers, but she pushed the gift away, fearing what she might see. Perhaps her visions were nothing more than dreams just as she'd told Sister Esther hers were when Becca called to her.

Gabrielle looked over her shoulder at Sister Esther and felt somewhat relieved when another of the sisters went to help her up and held her arm as they left the meetinghouse. Gabrielle walked with her head bowed beside Sister Helen. She'd give the woman no further cause to report her unwillingness to bend her spirit and repent.

It wasn't a dream that brought Gabrielle instantly awake just before dawn. She heard a scream. Gabrielle's heart pounded as she sat up in bed and looked around. The room was dark, but she could see the shape of Sister Helen in the bed next to her. Gabrielle waited for her to move, but she slept on as though the scream had not shattered the peace of the night. No one in the room moved, and slowly Gabrielle realized the scream had sounded only in her own mind.

Although the air coming in the windows carried the warm, dry feel of summer, Gabrielle shivered. Sickness gathered in the pit of her stomach and dread filled her being as the gift of knowing captured her. Gabrielle could not keep the knowing from washing over her. The scream was gone, but where it had ripped through her there was a wide streak of raw pain. She saw Sister Esther's face. Her features were strained and oddly twisted.

Gabrielle rose from her bed and held her breath as she silently edged past Sister Helen's bed. She had to go to Sister Esther. But where? Gabrielle shut her eyes and probed the vision. A chill crept through her, turning her fingers ice cold as her breathing grew so shallow it almost stopped. But she saw Sister Esther. She was standing on a chair, and there were pots and a fireplace and strips of towels.

The kitchen. Gabrielle opened her eyes. For a moment she was too weak to move, but then she was in the hall, running, pulled by an urgency she didn't even understand.

She was almost to the bottom of the stairs when she heard a clatter of something falling, and again the scream seared through her, burning away her breath. Each step on toward the kitchen was like pushing through a vat of syrup, and it seemed to take an eternity for her to reach the kitchen doorway.

"Nay, Sister Esther," she cried, but it was too late. The chair lay sideways on the floor and Esther dangled halfway between the floor and the rafter she'd looped the strips of towels over. Her head lay in an odd angle against her shoulder.

The gray light of dawn began to filter in through the window, but Gabrielle wished for the dark of midnight to return and shut out this horror. She closed her eyes, but the same image was there in her mind. She had no way to escape it.

She found a knife and forced herself to right the chair. She hugged the woman close against her as she cut through the knotted towels. Gently she lowered her sister's body to the floor and then fell down beside her.

She could do no more. She had no strength left to go after Sister Helen. She could only hold Sister Esther's lifeless hands and hear her words. *"Becca cries for me."*

The minutes passed, bringing the full light of day ever nearer while Gabrielle's innocence withered like a tender wildflower hit by the hot, dry wind of truth.

19

They wouldn't bury Esther beside Becca. Gabrielle begged them to, but they were unrelenting in their refusal.

"Our fallen sister cannot be placed among the other Believers, Sister Gabrielle," Elder Caleb explained patiently. "It was a sin for her to take a life, even her own, and since there is no way for her to ever confess that sin and gain forgiveness, she can never be a part of the Believers again, even in death."

"She was ill." It was useless to argue, but Gabrielle could not stop her words. "Sister Esther was sick with grief."

"She should have prayed or sought the help of the ministry. Mother Ann suffered much grief too, through the loss of her babies and the sins of her husband and the persecution of the world once the Eternal Father had revealed his plan for her life. Suffering is never a reason for sin."

"Mother Ann had the sureness of her beliefs to help her endure those sufferings. Sister Esther had nothing but the cry of her lost child in her heart."

Elder Caleb frowned. "She could have had more. She had only to ask. While true commitment may not be easy for everyone, it is possible when one allows Mother Ann to guide the way."

"Yea, Elder Caleb." Gabrielle bowed her head. Without looking up, she asked meekly, "Would it be possible to move Becca's body then?" Sister Helen drew in her breath sharply at the audacity of Gabrielle's request.

"Nay, Sister Gabrielle." Gabrielle had expected him to be angry, but the elder's voice was kind. He reached over and touched her shoulder. "My child, your spirit is troubled. Perhaps that is why you aren't seeing as clearly as you did or as you will again. You wouldn't wish to remove the child from the family of God for eternity just because of a few short years she spent here on earth with her mother. Don't you see, Sister Gabrielle? In heaven family relationships will matter even less than they do here among us. That's why we as Believers must leave our worldly relationships behind us and learn to live as loving sisters and brethren."

"I have done that, Brother Caleb, but Sister Esther could not. I only wished that she could find some peace now after life."

Elder Caleb smiled at her. "Ye have a compassionate heart, my sister, but you are young yet. With years you will grow in understanding and then your compassion will serve you in good stead among our family of Believers."

"I'm sorry to be a trouble to you," Gabrielle said. "I will pray for more understanding."

"If you pray with a humble heart, ye will receive, my child. Remember, when your spirit is troubled it is a gift to be simple, to cast away the trappings of the world that confuse our faith."

So Sister Esther was buried in a graveyard apart from that

of the Believers. The funeral was short and without song. There could be no celebration of this death. Only a handful of the Believers were there at all. Gabrielle had been allowed to go with Sister Helen's constant eye watching her.

It had been Sister Helen who'd found Gabrielle still cradling Sister Esther's head in her lap that morning. She'd looked on Sister Esther's broken body and said, "You were not to leave your bed without awakening me, Sister Gabrielle. I will have no choice but to report this."

Gabrielle had stared up at her for a long time unable to speak because of the emptiness in her soul. At last she said, "Sister Helen, don't you care that our sister lies here dead of her own hand?"

"She was a foolish woman, but her foolishness gives you no excuse to break the rules of your supervision. There can be no reason for that."

Gabrielle looked down at Sister Esther then and gently pushed her eyelids closed. She knew Sister Helen was still talking to her, but she shut her voice away until it was only an annoying noise, something like the buzz of an insistent mosquito. Inside her a wind was blowing, changing her until she felt like a tree bent out of shape by the force of a storm.

Finally Gabrielle raised her head when Sister Helen grabbed her shoulder. Anger filled Sister Helen's eyes and her mouth made shapes of words rapidly. But Gabrielle refused to hear what she was saying even though she knew she'd have to do what Sister Helen wanted.

Gabrielle carefully placed Sister Esther's head on the floor and stood up. She wasn't the same person who had followed the gift of knowing down the stairs. The storm winds had blown and passed, but she was still bent. She wondered if the next storm might break her.

"It doesn't seem right to leave her here alone," Gabrielle said. "Will you not allow me to stay with her while you get help?"

"Nay, Sister Gabrielle. You have not been listening to me. Come now and be quick. I have had enough of your slowness this morning." Sister Helen slapped her smartly on the back as one might strike a reluctant mule.

Gabrielle hadn't had the strength to fight against Sister Helen's demands, so she had followed her. She left Sister Esther's spirit there in the bleak early morning light. She'd known it was wrong even before the scream pushed through her once more. It was fainter than it had been before, but it still carried much pain.

Now as Gabrielle watched the brothers push the dirt in on top of Sister Esther, she felt the pain again. Somehow she should have kept this from happening. If only she'd been able to reach her sister with words that would have helped her see some goodness, some ray of hope in the future. If only the knowing had come to Gabrielle sooner. Then surely she wouldn't be here watching Sister Esther's grave filling and remembering the words the woman had spoken while they watched the brothers fill Becca's grave. The dirt was falling on her face just as she'd said then.

Sister Helen touched her arm almost kindly. "It's time to go, Sister Gabrielle. The grave is filled."

Gabrielle looked up with a bit of surprise. For a moment she'd forgotten that she wasn't alone, that she couldn't be alone for yet five more months. She took a deep breath while her mind once more accepted Sister Helen's presence. Then she chanced her disapproval by saying, "I want to go to Becca's grave before we return to the house."

Sister Helen frowned and hesitated, but when Gabrielle began walking toward the other graveyard, she didn't stop her. She muttered under her breath and followed along.

Gabrielle was glad not to have to speak again. She had pulled up as much of Sister Esther's spirit as she could to carry with her to Becca's resting place. The grass was fresh and green on Becca's grave and a small bush of yellow roses gave off the sweet scent of summer. Gabrielle knelt and opened her arms. She shut out all the sounds and sights around her and prayed that somehow the Eternal Father in his mercy could heal the wounds made on these two she had loved and failed.

She couldn't see them in her thoughts. The gift had gone dark when Esther died, leaving only the cold barrenness of truth. But she had to believe the Eternal Father was more merciful than the Believers. On earth the Believers had condemned Esther and Becca to separate places, but she prayed that in eternity they would be together.

As they left the graveyard, the evening shadows were long. She hadn't noticed so much time passing. It was little wonder Sister Helen was hurrying along in such a huff.

The bell rang for evening meeting. Sister Helen looked back at Gabrielle with a deep frown. "Now see what you've done. The biting room will be closed. We might as well go along to meeting."

"Could we not go on to the house? I am very tired."

"Nay, Sister Gabrielle. We shan't miss meeting. Tonight we must labor long in song to keep away the touch of Satan that has come sneaking near to us this day."

Gabrielle sighed.

"It isn't like you to wish to miss meeting, Sister Gabrielle. You have always shown great gifts of the spirit in laboring the songs." Sister Helen's voice made that sound like a reason for shame. "Ye might be so gifted again this evening."

"Nay, I think not." Gabrielle wasn't sure she'd ever feel the gift again, especially not the gift of a joyful song. No joy could come from the dark sorrow soaking through her being.

They got in line with the others who were already singing the gathering song as they walked toward the meetinghouse. Gabrielle didn't join in at first, but when she noted Sister Helen's eyes upon her, she opened her mouth. The words came of their own will from long years of habit. They had nothing to do with the thoughts in her mind.

Habit carried her through the night as she dutifully sang and labored the songs. She even tried to listen when Elder Caleb spoke, but though the words met her ears, she didn't hear.

Some of the Believers touched her during the meeting and offered a quiet word of encouragement, for they knew she'd been the one to find Esther. Gabrielle received their touches, but they didn't reach into the darkness inside her. They were kind, but they forced no answering touch of life to flow back from her to them. Even as she sang the song begging for faith to put all that was carnal away from her, she knew the touch she longed for.

But she wouldn't allow herself to think about him. Not during meeting. She couldn't remember ever wishing meeting would end as she did now. Usually meeting filled her with peace and renewed love for her brothers and sisters. But on this night she couldn't fill up with the blessings of the meeting or receive the balls of love from heaven. Her spirit was drained. It was as if she'd been yanked out of the simple world she knew where she'd gone forth in exercising the songs and loved so easily and been dropped in a strange new place where everything looked the same and sounded the same yet was so different.

Not only did Becca's and Esther's absences haunt Gabrielle, but where once she'd seen only unity and contentment at the meetings, now she saw doubts and pain in many of the faces around her as they went through the exercises of their worship. She saw how some of the sisters' eyes sought out their husbands among the brethren. She noticed the times when the mothers would find reason to drift in among the children and the special smiles that lit their faces when the children exercised their songs. She recognized the strain on many of the faces as they struggled to do what they couldn't do any more than Esther had been able to.

Still there were many who were truly content. They'd found the perfect peace all sought. If they'd ever known struggles, they'd conquered them and put them behind them. Gabrielle's eyes went to her mother, Sister Martha.

Sister Martha felt her look and raised her head with a smile. She'd aged little in the time they'd been with the Believers. Rather, her face had filled out and brought her an illusion of youth.

Sister Martha stood up and made her way across the floor. Gabrielle watched her and thought how odd to know one's mother as only a sister.

Even after her mother touched her and spoke softly to her, Gabrielle felt no return of their past relationship. She felt no nearer her than any of the other sisters who had offered their encouragement and love during the evening.

"I've been praying for you, Sister Gabrielle," her mother said.

"I need your prayers," Gabrielle responded humbly.

"Yea, I know, my sister. There have been many moments of trouble in my life, but they have now all passed away from me. They can for you too if you appeal to Mother Ann."

Gabrielle spoke before she thought. "Do you ever think of the time before we joined the Believers, Mother?" It was the first time she had called Sister Martha mother in years. The word sat oddly in the air between them.

It was a long moment before Sister Martha answered. "The past is gone from us, Sister. We have only the present and the future."

"Can we ever put aside the past completely?" Gabrielle said.

Sister Martha backed a few steps away from her as if to keep Gabrielle's doubts from touching her. "I have already," she said firmly before she went back to her place across the room. She had no desire to be pulled into Gabrielle's troubles.

Gabrielle was relieved when at last meeting was over. She followed Sister Helen meekly to their room to prepare for bed. Helen's words of reproof bounced against her ears. Whenever the woman paused to take a breath, Gabrielle said, "Yea, Sister Helen. I will try." But she couldn't have said five minutes later what she'd promised to try to do.

At last Sister Helen's light snores replaced her words, and Gabrielle let out a long sigh. It was only August. She was to be watched until the middle of January. The days and weeks stretched out before her in endless misery. What had she tried to tell Esther? That there could be good in the future if only she looked. Was that just yesterday? It seemed a lifetime ago.

Now she herself needed help. The doubts were strong inside her, too strong to be pushed aside or hidden in a dark corner of her mind to be faced on another day. They were before her now and she had to deal with them.

Doubt. There could be no doubt if faith was strong enough. The elders were always saying that was so, saying doubt should be pushed from one's mind like the finger of Satan it was. And she'd not doubted before. Not before the fire. The fire had brought the doctor, and the doctor had brought questions. Was he right? Did the Lord intend men and women to marry? To go forth and be fruitful? Or did he intend some of them to live in perfect peace and harmony as brothers and sisters?

Marriage caused strife among God's children. She'd been witness to that truth between her own parents. There had never been peace between them. Suddenly Brice's voice was in her mind asking, but had there ever been love?

Gabrielle didn't know. She'd never seen love between them, but perhaps when their marriage was new there'd been love. Love didn't bring peace anyway. She was proof enough of that. She finally knew the love she'd heard the other sisters speak of. It wasn't a brotherly love that tore at her and made her want to forget her faith. Nay, there was no peace with this love.

The voice was speaking quietly in her mind again. *"That is because you deny the love."*

Then all the voices came. Elder Caleb's told her to give her heart to God. Sister Mercy reminded her that the soul that suffers becomes stronger. And all the others who'd offered her advice and love. They whirled about in her mind until they became just a great clamor and made no sense at all.

She opened her eyes and stared at the darkness. She

couldn't listen to them all. Slowly they backed away until there was only the faint echo of their voices in the wind. But one voice remained as strong as ever. *"We were meant to be together,"* he whispered.

Becca and Esther were meant to be together, mother and child. Becca had been Esther's miracle baby, the answer to prayer. Yet they'd been pulled apart and nothing was left of their lives but the grief in Gabrielle's own heart. For a moment she wished for the gift to show her beyond the threshold of death. If she could see Becca and Esther together, then she could rest, but at the same time she shied away from what the gift might show her. The gift didn't always bring what she wished to see. It brought only truth, and she wasn't sure she could bear that.

Again the voice was a whisper in her mind. *"Don't let them destroy you, Gabrielle. I love you."*

She was so tired. She couldn't hold the thoughts of him away. "Brice." Her lips moved without making a sound in the dark. "I need you."

He came to her then out of the dark corners of her mind, and his memory comforted her. Once more she felt the strength of his arms around her, and they held away this pain that had eaten away her innocence. He was there with her and yet so far away. The memory of his love was like a shadow. There, but too illusive to hold on to.

She longed for him to really be there beside her. To touch her, to kiss her, to tell her she belonged with him. And there in the dark of the night she felt no shame for her desire. Nor did she feel any condemnation from the Lord when she offered up a prayer for Brice's safety.

20

All around Brice the men were restless in the camp. They'd been gathered longer than a month moving from place to place while waiting for some orders to march to the north. The politicians and generals haggled while the men sat in camp sharpening tomahawks and knives and rubbing their guns until they knew every scratch and nick on the barrels.

The men had shown up in the camps ready for battle. They brought their own horses and guns and wore an almost identical uniform from home of a hunting shirt with a fringe border and Kentucky jeans. A leather belt held a pocket for their tomahawks while another strap of leather across their shoulders held the powder horns and a bullet case and a sheath for the butcher knife no Kentuckian would go to war without.

Brice had been given a commission as surgeon in the second regiment of volunteers. He'd encouraged Nathan to stay with him as his assistant, but as soon as they reached camp, the boy had enlisted in the regiment for six months on his own.

Once the men had enlisted there was nothing to do but wait for orders and talk about fighting. They chased the British clear off the continent with their words and brought the Indians to their knees. If ever a word of doubt crept into the talk, it was mashed and smothered by the war fever that raged from man to man.

Nathan caught it as soon as he got to the camp. Brice did his best to keep him on an even keel, but he had no antidotes for war fever.

"It's going to be easy," Nathan said one night when he came by to talk after supper. "All the men are saying so. If they would just let us go on, we could take Malden, and then Upper Canada would practically fall in our laps."

"It sounds good when it's just talk." Brice leaned forward to take the pot off the fire and pour himself some coffee. Some of the men were already bedded down. Others sat clustered about a fire here and there. Now and again a laugh would drift out of a group to be lost into the night.

"We can do it. All they've got to do is say go."

Across the way the light of a lamp sifted out through General Winchester's tent flaps. Brice took a drink of his coffee. "Appears the general may be making plans."

Nathan spat into the fire. "He couldn't lead his way out of town. If you ask me, we'd have already been north if we had a leader that was some use. And they say he's from Tennessee. Looks like they could have found a Kentuckian for us."

"The men don't seem to be overly fond of him. He's a strange bird at times."

Nathan laughed. "You heard what some of the men did to him, didn't you? Putting that porcupine skin in just the right spot. He'll be checking things twice and then again before he goes to the outhouse again."

"I didn't have to hear." Brice bit his lip to keep from smiling.

"Don't tell me you were the one who had to pick out the quills?" The boy almost fell over from laughing so hard.

"The general didn't think it so funny. If he ever finds out who did it, he might have them shot." Brice looked over at the boy. "You weren't in on it, were you, Bates?"

"Nay, Doc." The boy slipped back into his Shaker talk. "I didn't have anything to do with it, but I guess I can enjoy it just the same."

Brice studied him in the light of the fire. He wasn't the same boy who'd come to his cabin with Gabrielle's refusal a fresh wound in his mind. He'd grown. His life was spreading out in his new freedom. Still his legs were weak. His limp had been worse in the last couple of days. "Are your legs hurting you more than usual?" Brice asked.

"Maybe some," Nathan answered carefully. "But nothing I can't stand. You know, Doc, I curse my foolishness every time I think about running back into that fire."

"A man acts without thinking things through sometimes, Bates. Else there'd be a lot of things we wouldn't do." Brice gave him another long stare. "It wouldn't be a shame to you if you decided not to go when we move out. Not if you're not able."

"Not go?" Nathan jumped back a little from the fire in surprise. "How could I not go? I've signed up. It's my duty now."

"I'm afraid the march north is going to be too arduous for you."

240

"I'm going if I have to crawl," Nathan said. "Don't you see, Doc? This is the way I've always wanted to live. To be a part of what's happening. To be where men are alive and full of purpose."

"I didn't say you'd have to go back with the Shakers, boy. There's other ways of living besides that. And besides this."

"I guess as how you're right, Doc, but I like this way. The men, they've mostly accepted me. They don't care if I used to be a Shaker or not. Most of them don't even know it, and that suits me just fine. They judge me by the way I am right now, and when we go to fighting they'll be judging me then by my courage."

"All right, Bates." Brice threw the dregs of his coffee into the fire. "But if you get to hurting worse when we're on the march, let me know. I can fix you something to ease it a bit."

Brice was starting to stand up to head for his bedroll when Nathan asked, "Don't you want to go, Doc? I mean, don't you like being here in the army?"

Brice kept his eyes on the fire as he answered, "I guess I'm older than you."

"You're not that old. What? Twenty-eight, twenty-nine? Why, there are some men here past forty, and they're just as eager to be on the move as me." Nathan hesitated for a moment before he went on. "Is it because you were friends with the Indians when you were a kid? Is that why you don't want to fight them?"

"We weren't friends. I was their captive. I learned their ways and got along, but I was always their prisoner."

"Then what is it? You surely aren't chicken, are you?" When Brice turned to stare at him, Nathan rushed on. "I mean, I never saw you act like you was scared of anything, Doc, but ever since we left Mercer County you've been so quiet and broody. I thought maybe it was because you didn't want to fight."

Brice turned his eyes back to the fire. The boy was so young. He couldn't see anything except the day ahead. "I don't look forward to the fighting, Bates, but I don't recall ever being accused of being a coward. At least up till now."

Nathan protested. "Now I didn't exactly say that, Doc."

Brice waved his hand. "It doesn't matter. I'll do my share of the fighting when the time comes, but I'll be fighting more against gangrene and death than against the British or the Indians."

Nathan didn't say anything and after a minute, Brice went on. "I never said I was anxious to go to war. And I can't say as how I've caught the war fever that's sweeping the camp, but I'll do my duty as a doctor."

"I'm sorry, Doc. I never really thought you were chicken."

"I told you to forget it, Bates. And I guess you're right about me being in a foul mood. I just keep thinking about those I've left behind who might need me and now they won't have anybody to turn to."

"You mean like Tyney and her little girl?"

"And others." Brice pulled in a long breath and let it out slowly. Without looking away from the fire, he said, "You'd best be getting some rest, boy. The troops are going to parade for the governor tomorrow. They say Senator Clay will even be here for a speech."

"You going to turn in too, Doc?"

"In a little bit, Bates. When the camp quiets down."

But Brice sat by the fire until the embers turned gray while Gabrielle walked through his thoughts. She was so real to him. He could almost hear the whisper of her breath, and he longed to be able to pull off the Shaker cap she wore and let her hair tumble down around her shoulders.

Something about her was so pure and innocent that the thought of it almost hurt. Living with the Shakers had shielded her from life until the real world was a strange and foreign place to her. Yet now she had cast her eyes beyond the boundaries of the Shaker village and had some questions about her path. He wanted to be the one she came to for answers. But he wouldn't be there. He'd be far away in a war that could have been fought without him. He hadn't had to volunteer.

Gabrielle would surely fight her own war while he was gone. The Shakers would be there with their songs and dances and words to bind her to them, but there'd be no one to plead his case. There'd be no one to tell her how much he loved her, how his heart felt hollow without her to fill it. He couldn't keep from wondering which war was the most important, and he hated the sense of duty that kept him with the army.

He could only hope she wouldn't close her mind completely to him before he made it back to Mercer County. Then he wouldn't take no for an answer. She'd come away with him and they'd build a life together as they were meant to. He had to believe she'd listen to him when he returned, but for now he'd have to be content with the memory of her lips against his and the truth of her love for him that she hadn't been able to hide.

Nearly every man in the camp had turned in for the night before Brice stood up and left the ashes of the fire. Then as he bedded down outside the medic tent, Gabrielle stayed with him. Something about her worried him. Perhaps she had caught the child's fever. He felt drawn to her, but he couldn't go even though the miles between them weren't that many. He'd put his feet on this path away from her and he couldn't turn off it now. The sun was pushing light over the eastern horizon before he finally slept.

❧

The next day, the detachment made a fine showing of strength as they paraded past the governor. Old Governor Scott came down off his viewing stand and marched with them for a ways in spite of an old wound that caused him to limp badly.

Brice marched with the men and thought Gabrielle would be marching back at the Shaker village. To a different tune to be sure. There would be no talk of war there. The elder would speak of peace and love for all. He would preach about the oneness of their spirits.

As Brice looked around at the men who were loudly cheering every word Senator Clay or the governor spoke, he thought these men might have more unity of spirit here than the Shaker brethren and sisters. Here the men were united in their fervor to march to war. There at the Shaker village the wars were different, but they raged in the individual hearts nonetheless.

Another cheer went up around him. Brice pulled his thoughts back to the words of Senator Clay. He tried to absorb some of the enthusiasm for fighting that was hanging in the air around him, but he felt out of step with the men.

The troops would have marched that day without pay, without anything but the word from the old governor or the fiery senator. But by the next Tuesday when they drew two months' pay in advance, the men began muttering some complaints about not receiving the promised allowance for clothes. On Wednesday when they moved out, finally marching north, the weather turned bad. Rain fell on them nearly every step of the way and dampened the war fever as the men plodded along the muddy roads.

Brice checked and rechecked his saddlebags and packs to be sure they were staying dry. He didn't have enough medical supplies for such a long march in the first place, so he wanted to be sure not to let what he did have ruin before the army even reached the war theater. He hunted up Nathan from time to time. The boy was pale but hadn't lost his eagerness for the march.

When they finally reached Newport six days later, the rumor swept through the camp that the old governor had pushed through a special order giving Indiana Territory Governor William Henry Harrison control of Kentucky's militia. He might not be a Kentuckian, but he'd proved his worth at the battle of Tippecanoe.

But that wasn't the only news waiting for them. Nathan came around to where Brice was going through a new supply of medicines as if it were gold. "Did you hear?" the boy asked.

Brice straightened up. "I've been too busy counting doses to pay much mind to anything else, but from the looks of your face it can't be good news."

"News has come down from the Northwest. From Detroit. Hull surrendered."

"Are you sure you got that straight? Seems hard to believe."

"You can believe it." A man spoke up behind Nathan.

Brice looked past the boy to see Alec Hope. "When did

you get here, Hope? I didn't see you back in the camp at Georgetown."

"I get kinda restless sitting around waiting for orders. My captain lets me roam about whilst nothing else is going on. So I came on up here ahead of the rest of the company."

"I thought maybe you'd decided to let this fight pass you by," Brice said.

Hope looked genuinely shocked. "Why, Doc, I'm a Kentuckian!"

"No lacking of Kentuckians around here," Brice said with a smile.

"A pure shame old Hull weren't one. Then I reckon as how he wouldn't have been so quick to lay down his guns and give up the fort. He should have tried to hang on till we got up there," Hope said.

"The way we're moving that might take a while." Brice looked down at his box of medicines.

"If they'd just give the word, I'm ready to move right now," Hope said.

"You and the rest of the men, but seems like you're readier to move out than the government is to supply us for the march."

"One good thing," Nathan said. "We'll be having a new leader."

"General Winchester is still here," Brice reminded him.

"Not for long," Hope said. "Harrison's on his way. Then there won't be no more of this shilly-shallying. We'll move all right 'cause I don't know a man among the whole lot of us that wouldn't follow Harrison to fight the devil hisself if that's what he asked us to do."

"I've had enough of fighting the devil," Nathan said. "I'm ready to go on up and get Detroit away from the Tories."

Hope looked at the boy, seeming to remember all at once who he was and where he'd come from. "My girl, Gabrielle?" he said as he turned back to Brice. "You left my girl there with them, didn't you, Doc?"

"I left her there, Hope."

Hope stared at him a long minute before he said, "I know you done your best, Doc. I guess trading the Injuns out of a long-legged boy is some easier than fighting religion. I won't hold it against you if you've give up on it."

"I said I left her there, Hope, but I didn't say I'd given up," Brice said quietly. "I'll be going back after this war is done."

Brice felt Nathan's eyes on him, but he didn't look around at him. The boy would just have to think whatever he liked.

With Hull's surrender making them the only army in the Northwest, orders came for the men to make a swift march to Fort Wayne. That fort was all that stood between the British and the more populated territories to the south. With General Harrison leading them, the men marched out eagerly.

Where before they'd marched through rain, now the sun beat down on them mercilessly. By the third day after they left Piqua, the water was gone. All through the ranks, men staggered from the heat and at each puddle, no matter how small, men dropped on their bellies, waved away the flies, and drank. At St. Mary's they got a fresh supply of water and moved on toward Fort Wayne in battle formation, but when they reached the fort three days later there was no sign of war activities.

The army set up camp to wait for the generals to decide their next move, and rumors started swirling again. When it was confirmed that Winchester had been put back in command of their troops, the men were ready to march home, but General Harrison appealed to their patriotism. The men grumbled but moved out behind Winchester north to a point close to the old Fort Defiance. They'd come through woodland all the way, and the men had been on edge watching the trees for any sign of the enemy.

They set up camp on a bluff overlooking the old fort. That night Alec Hope sat on his haunches around the cooking fire and told Brice and Nathan how he'd been with General Wayne back in the 1790s when they'd finally secured Kentucky's borders and made it safer to settle in the Ohio and Indiana territories.

"We had all this around here cleared then." Hope waved his hand about him. "It sure don't take long for the brush to overtake a woods again."

"It's been eighteen years," Brice said.

"You don't say," Hope said, scratching the new growth of beard on his chin. "Then I reckon we've been lucky to keep them redskins back this long."

Later after Hope had finished telling all about that first campaign, Brice watched Hope and Nathan walk away. They made an odd pair, but maybe the old woodsman would be good for the young innocent. The boy needed someone to help him out here in the wilderness. It was going to take a lot of work to clear the ground and set up any semblance of a fort here.

Brice turned back to setting up his tent. He wanted to be ready because these men didn't need a battle to need a doctor. Later he'd go out in the woods to hunt some roots and bark that might supplement his meager supply of medicines. The other doctors in the army laughed at his Indian cures, but a lot of the soldiers sought his concoctions to ease their ills.

So Brice gathered his roots and left his lancet in its case. He didn't mind being different.

He was used to doing things his way, and now he chafed under the restrictions of army life. Too many orders came down through the ranks that didn't make sense to him. And here in the middle of this woolly wilderness with only a half ration of food and the mosquitoes and flies tormenting them, he couldn't keep from wishing he was back in his cabin with nothing but the wind to keep him company.

The thought had no more than touched his mind till Gabrielle was there in his thoughts to prove it false. She fit there beside him. He could never again be complete without her. Yet she had turned him away, and he had no sure hope she wouldn't turn him away when he did go back and seek her out once more.

Perhaps she had run on up the path that took her away from him forever and his memory no longer troubled her mind as hers did his. He straightened up from tying down his tent and looked to the south while thoughts whirled around in his mind like leaves pulled up into a dust devil. It would be easier if he could push Gabrielle out of his head and close her away as he had Jemma after her death. But he'd been so young then, not even as old as Nathan was now. He'd thought he loved Jemma more than life itself, but it had been the love of a boy. He wasn't sure he could push aside this feeling he had for Gabrielle no matter how many miles or how much division there was between them. He'd have to learn to live with it.

He was glad when someone spoke behind him. "Sorry to bother you, sir."

Brice turned to look at the soldier, who had blood oozing

down his shin. The man grimaced and said, "My tomahawk slipped."

"Sit down on that pack and put your foot up," Brice said as he got his bag. He peeled away the man's britches from his leg and started cleaning the wound. "Looks like you could have told the difference between a bush and your leg, soldier."

"It appears I could have been more careful," the man agreed.

"What's your name?"

"Kerns, sir. Seth Kerns. I told the captain it weren't nothing to worry about, but he said he'd see enough blood when the time come and that he didn't see no sense in having to look at me bleeding now."

Brice looked up at Kerns. He was built small with a little-boy look to his face. "Does your mother know you joined up with the army?"

Kerns smiled. "I'm older than I look. Be twenty next month. And my ma didn't want me to join up but she knows I'm here."

"Well, hang on while I put in a stitch or two to hold your leg together." When Brice had finished stitching and bandaging the kid's leg, he said, "You'd better take the rest of the day off."

"I don't know as how I could do that. I mean, my captain had me come over so you could fix me up to go back to work. And you see how I ain't very big and all. I got to prove to them I can do my part. You understand, Doctor?"

"You aren't going to prove much by bleeding to death, Kerns. Tell you what. You give me your axe, and you can take my place here as doctor. Just sit down and prop that foot up

250

and give it a chance to quit bleeding. If anybody needs me, you can let out a yell."

"I don't know about that, sir. My captain—" he started.

Brice interrupted. "What's your captain's name? I'll explain things to him."

"Belding. Captain Belding. He's that one yonder with the red hair, cutting twice as many bushes as everybody else."

Brice picked up the axe and tomahawk and walked down the hill. It'd do him good to be busy. He wanted to be so busy he couldn't think about things he could do nothing about.

He glanced back at the boy, who'd settled down and put his foot up the way Brice had told him. He must be a magnet for helpless innocents. First Bates and now this boy. If he didn't watch himself, he'd start feeling responsible for Kerns just as he worried over Nathan. He kept telling himself not to get so involved with his patients, but yet here he was with Kerns's axe, chopping Kerns's bushes.

21

Autumn 1812

October brought unseasonably cold rains. The miserable weather along with low provisions started putting out the patriotic fires of a lot of the men. The regulars burrowed in to stick it out, but the militiamen weren't used to the discipline of army life. They'd signed up to whip the British and go on home. Not sit in camp through a cold northern winter.

Just enough supplies worked up through the woods to keep the men from starving. Then fever hit the camp, and Brice and the other doctors worked night and day to keep as many of the men alive as they could.

"If only the sun would come out," one of the men said when Brice examined him inside the fort the men had finally gotten raised.

"Maybe there's nothing down here the sun wants to see anymore," Brice said as he mixed some powders in water to dose the soldier. The wet weather had been unrelenting and just that morning the rain had been mixed with snow. "But as long as you can tell the sun isn't shining, then you're well enough to give up your spot inside here to somebody who's really sick."

"That'll suit me, Doctor. This being sick is more vexing than being hungry," the soldier said. "And I'm bound to feel better out in the open. Seems like there's just bad air in here."

So the fort that had looked so good to them just a few days ago now seemed to be a place to sicken and die. It was hard to scrounge up dry wood for fires, and the mud was ankle deep inside the walls while the sick filled the blockhouses and spilled out into the open. The order was given to relocate on a high-level terrain across the Maumee River, but the fever followed them. Every day they carried more men out to be buried.

As the days grew colder and they started seeing more snow than rain, they tried two more camps before they finally found ground downriver a ways that was almost dry with plentiful firewood. Brice hadn't had much time for sitting around the fire at night since the fever had hit camp, but a few days after the move, Nathan and Hope caught him taking a few minutes to brew a pot of coffee. It wasn't real coffee, just some boiled bark and roots, but after the day he'd had where the fever had won more than he did, Brice welcomed its hot, bitter taste.

Nathan took one look at Brice's face and squatted down at the fire without a word, but Hope wasn't the kind to let a man be. He poured a cup of the brew, took a swallow, and said, "That's enough to put a frown on anybody's face."

"Maybe we'd better just leave the doc alone, Alec. He's looking like things might not have gone too well for him today." Nathan shifted on his haunches.

"Things ain't going too well for nobody in this godforsaken woods," Hope said. "But I'm guessing the doc here's been keeping score and from the looks of him the score ain't too good. That right, Doc?"

Brice made himself answer. It didn't change a thing for him to sit alone in the dark and grieve over the men he'd lost. "Not good. We put four more Kentuckians in the ground today."

"It ain't right. We done got Kentuckians spread out under the ground all through this woods and we've yet to see our first redskin. It just don't make no sense. Tell me, Doc. How many does that make all told?"

"At least a hundred."

Hope shook his head and stared at the fire. "I never thought General Harrison would let us get in such a shape. Not doing nothing but sitting here wishing for food. I reckon old Winchester's still got too much say in what's happening."

"Even generals can't stop the fever," Brice said.

"They could get us some food and let us go on and fight instead of sitting here on our hands starving to death," Hope said.

"They've been sending out details to bring in food," Brice said.

"And what do they bring back?" Hope snorted in disgust. "A handful of hickory nuts and wild fruit that's nothing but mush. I've lived many a day better than that in the woods."

"Then why aren't they sending you out to get food?" Brice asked.

"That'd make too much sense. Ain't nothing we've done since we set out on this march made sense." Then Hope let out a short laugh. "Course could be my captain might have more sense than I'm giving him credit for. Could be he knows that if he let me out of camp I might just take a notion to find out if Kentucky's still down there to the south somewheres."

"You wouldn't desert the army, would you, Alec?" Nathan sounded shocked.

"Shh, boy. Don't be saying that so loud. You're apt to get me shot." Hope looked around before he lowered his voice and said, "But I learned a long time ago that if I don't take care of Alec Hope, ain't nobody else going to."

"You've been doing that a lot of years, haven't you, Hope? Taking care of yourself and not worrying too much about anybody else," Brice said.

Hope stared at him across the fire. "You're talking about my girl again. I done told you, Doc, I left so things would be better for her. Who could have ever dreamed up something like them Shakers coming along?"

Brice dropped his eyes to the fire. He had no right to try to shame anybody for running off and leaving Gabrielle behind.

"Besides," Hope went on, "I heard out of her own mouth that she was happy there. I guess that's all a pappy could want. His daughter to be happy."

"But she doesn't belong there." The words slipped out before Brice could stop them.

"You won't get no argument about that from me, Doc. It's her you've got to convince," Hope said.

Brice shifted uneasily as he felt the boy's eyes on him. He shouldn't have brought up Gabrielle. None of them could do a thing to help her now even if she did realize the Shaker life wasn't for her. "I'd better go see to my patients," Brice said shortly as he stood up.

He left them by the fire and walked back toward the sick area. He needed to stay busy. When he sat down, he thought too much and sometimes it was better not to think. Just to do.

"Dr. Scott," a voice called to him as he went through the camp.

"Why aren't you sleeping, Kerns?" Brice asked crossly, but he was really glad when the young soldier stepped up beside him.

"I can't sleep, sir. I was wondering if maybe you wanted some company while you made your rounds."

Kerns had taken to hanging around Brice since he'd patched up his leg. Sometimes he'd walk along with Brice for half an hour or more without saying a word, but Brice was always glad to have his company.

"Come along, Seth. If you aren't afraid of the fever."

"I've about decided I must not be big enough for the fever to latch on to," Kerns said and then added shyly, "and you, sir, I can always learn something watching you. I guess being a doctor's about the grandest thing anybody could be. If I was to be a doctor it wouldn't matter so much that I wasn't as big as most folks, as long as I knew what medicines cure what ailments."

"Being a doctor doesn't guarantee that you'll know that, Seth. Sometimes all a doctor does is stand there and watch death claim its prize." The faces of the men who'd died the last few days jumped before his eyes, and Brice started walking faster as if trying to keep ahead of death.

"But more get well than die, don't they, sir?" Kerns was almost trotting to keep up.

Brice pulled in a steadying breath and slowed his steps. "I wish I could believe that. I really wish I could believe that."

"You will, sir, on another day. I've been praying about it. Do you pray, sir?"

"Not since I was a boy."

"You should." Kerns glanced over at Brice, then up at the night sky. "It can be a heap of comfort knowing the Lord is there with you, helping you."

Brice looked up too. Clouds hid the stars. "I haven't seen much sign of his help in these parts."

"That's just because you haven't been looking, sir. Even them that's been dying, the Lord was right there holding their hands, bringing them on into paradise if they looked toward the Lord."

"You some kind of preacher?" Brice peered over at the young soldier.

Kerns smiled. "No, sir. But it gives me comfort knowing the Lord is with us out here in this wilderness. I thought it might make you feel lighter in the spirit knowing that too."

Brice shook his head at Kerns. "You ought to be sleeping instead of trying to preach a grouchy old sawbones out of a sour mood."

"I know, Dr. Scott, but it looks like the only time I get sleepy is when I'm out on watch."

Brice frowned. "That could be dangerous."

"I try to stay awake. I think about David in the Bible and try to recite some of those psalms he must have thought up while he was out there guarding his daddy's sheep, and I pray. But sometimes it don't seem like anything helps. It's just so lonesome and cold out there. And there hasn't been the first sign of any enemy."

"I guess they're just hanging back to let the fever get us first."

"It's not as bad as it was, is it?"

"Hard to say. Not as many new cases are reporting, but the ones who are sick aren't out of the woods yet. We don't have the medicine to treat them."

Brice ducked inside one of the sick tents and checked some of the men while Kerns waited outside. When Brice came out of the tent, he looked at Kerns in the flickering light that came from the campfires and said, "So you think you might like to be a doctor?"

"I didn't exactly say that, sir. I don't suppose I'd have enough book learning for that. There wasn't any school roundabouts our farm back home. My ma taught me some, but Pa didn't have much use for book learning."

"It's never too late to learn, Seth. You could still do it if you want. Plenty of doctors back in Kentucky never saw the inside of a medical school anyway. They learned from being apprenticed to a doctor."

"Do you think, sir—" Kerns started, then hesitated before going on. "I mean, I wouldn't want to impose on you, sir, but you think I might be your apprentice? I don't have much money, but what I do have I'd give it all to you for the chance."

Brice put his hand on the boy's shoulder. "That's not a half bad idea, Seth. Tell you what. After this war's over and we're headed back south, we'll talk about it. It might be good to have somebody to roll my pills."

In the flickering light from the fires, Brice could see the smile spreading across the boy's face. "I'd like that, sir."

"You'd best go on along and get some sleep before your turn at watch comes up again."

"Yes, sir," Kerns said.

Brice watched Kerns walk away into the night. He'd never wanted an apprentice, even though he'd offered the chance to Nathan when he left the Shakers, but he didn't wish his words back now. He liked Kerns, and every man ought to have a chance to do what he wanted in life.

As Brice ducked into another tent to see to his patients, his mood turned dark again. Too many of these men wouldn't get that chance. They'd never leave these woods.

22

The fever let up some as they went into the cooler days of December. Hope said it was because there wasn't a man in the camp healthy enough to get sick. The men dubbed the camp Fort Starvation and then set about the business of surviving the northern winter as best they could. Sometimes that meant breaking a few army rules, and court-martials became as common as hunger pangs.

The more fortunate wrongdoers merely had to ride the wooden horse while those others who had wandered out of camp in search of something to eat were accused of desertion and drummed out of camp. Brice argued their cases, but the officers said they had to keep the rope tight to maintain discipline.

"I'm not asking you to relax your rules," Brice said. "Only your punishments. If you send a man out into this wilderness without warm clothes and some kind of provisions, you might as well put a bullet in his head. It might be kinder."

"True enough, but then the next man may think twice before breaking the rules," one of the captains said.

"A starving man is ruled by his stomach," Brice said.

A colonel from the regular army spoke up. "Have you ever been in the army, Dr. Scott? The real army and not the militia."

"No sir."

"Then may I suggest you leave the disciplining of the troops to those who know what they're doing and stick to dosing fevers?"

Brice stared straight at the man and said, "I took an oath to save lives and work against death no matter how that death comes."

"Then I fear the theater of war is not the place for you, Dr. Scott. Many men die in war," the officer said.

Even though Brice knew he was stepping out of line and onto dangerous ground, he couldn't hold back his words. "Death at the hands of our enemies is a far reach from death of our comrades at our own hands."

The colonel's face tightened. "You're dismissed, Dr. Scott. Let this be your last appearance in this tent."

Brice glared at the man for a full minute before he ducked out of the tent. It was wrong. He knew it was wrong, but he was part of this army. He the same as the next man had to fall in line under the officers and do as he was told.

As Brice walked back through the camp, men huddled in tents and crude lean-tos called out greetings to him. Some of the men were fashioning moccasins out of green hides. They wouldn't do much good, but it might be better than being barefoot in the snow. Brice had already treated some frostbite.

Brice raised his hand in greeting, but he didn't feel like talking to anybody. He doubted even young Kerns could talk him out of this black mood. Nor pray him out of it. Brice looked up and toward the woods where the last boy had been sent to his death. Maybe the Lord would help the boy. Didn't he help innocents? But if so, Kerns would have to do the praying for them. Brice had no prayers in his heart.

By the middle of December the food began running out and the men were close to mutiny when some men brought in a herd of hogs. Hope ran by Brice with his knife already out of its sheath. "At least we've finally got something to use our knives on."

For a few days things were better, but the meat didn't last long. There still wasn't any flour, and the cold was unrelenting. Brice steered clear of trouble and shut his ears and eyes when the officers made a half-starved boy ride the wooden horse or sent a man out of camp because he went searching for roots or bark to eat or shot a man for sleeping at his post. He told himself it was the same as losing a soldier to the fever. He couldn't stop the dying either way. It wasn't right, but they had nothing else in this camp of starvation. Why should he expect there to be justice?

Then one morning just as Brice was getting up, Nathan came by his tent with bad news plain on his face. "What is it, Bates?"

"You know the Kerns boy. The one who's took up with you lately."

Brice's chest tightened until he thought he might not be able to breathe. He forced out the words. "Go on."

Nathan blurted it out. "They caught him sleeping at his post this morning."

Brice sank down on his heels and worked at making his fire burn. He wished fervently that he did remember how to pray. Without looking up, he said, "What are they going to do with him?"

"The same as the others. They've done picked the men for the firing squad."

"Without even a hearing?"

"I don't know about that, but it wouldn't do him no good. They found him sleeping. No amount of words is going to change that."

Brice stood up and brushed off his hands on his pants as he started off.

"Where you going, Doc?"

"To find his captain."

It wasn't hard to find the boy's captain. The big, redheaded man was pacing back and forth in front of his tent. He stopped when he saw Brice. "I figured you'd be here when you heard."

"You can't let them shoot the boy," Brice said.

Captain Belding raised his hands in the air and let them fall. "Wish to God I could prevent it, but there's nothing I can do."

"There has to be something."

Captain Belding stepped closer to Brice. "Look, don't you think I'd change this if I could? I like Seth. But I can't change the rules. Seth fell asleep on lookout."

"They don't have to shoot him. A flogging would do as well." The boy could live through a beating.

"It's not that simple, Dr. Scott. When a man is on lookout, he has the lives of every soldier here in his hands. The enemy could have got right by Seth last night and we could have all been massacred in our bedrolls."

"But that didn't happen."

"But it could have," Captain Belding insisted.

"Then there's nothing you can do?"

Captain Belding looked sad as he shook his head. "Nor you."

"I can't accept that."

"You'll just get yourself in trouble. How's that going to help Seth?"

"I've been in trouble before. I expect I will be again."

"It won't do any good," the captain said as Brice turned away.

The captain was right. The officer in charge was curt with him. Kerns was a soldier with a soldier's responsibilities. He'd have to live with the consequences of his lapse of discipline.

"But he won't be living with anything," Brice said. "He'll be dead."

"You are dismissed, Dr. Scott." The officer glared at him.

Brice had no choice but to leave or be charged with insubordination. He walked slowly to the tent where they were holding Kerns. The guard at the entrance moved over to let Brice duck inside. Brice sat cross-legged on the cold ground beside the boy. He couldn't think of a thing to say.

But Kerns smiled and reached out to touch him. "Dr. Scott, it's right good of you to come see me, sir."

Brice still couldn't speak. His throat was closing together and he felt closer to tears than he had since he'd watched Jemma die.

"Don't worry, sir. Leastways, not about me." Kerns dropped his eyes to the ground as his smile faded. "I got myself into a fine mess this time, and I'll have to pay for it. But it's all right."

"It's not all right," Brice almost shouted. "There's nothing right about any of it."

Kerns looked up at Brice again. "Don't take on so, sir. I knew better than to fall off to sleep. I did my best with the psalms and I even sung some to myself. Wrong kind of songs, I guess. Didn't nothing help last night. I just couldn't keep my eyes open. It was so cold I think my brain must've froze up or something."

Kerns was quiet for a long time. Then when he did start talking again, his voice was somber. "I guess as how I'll be able to sleep forever now. You do believe in God, don't you, sir?"

"I don't know. I guess so, but I've never spent a lot of time thinking about it," Brice said.

"You don't have to think about God to know he's there, Dr. Scott. He's everywhere, in every blade of grass and every bird's song."

"Even here in Fort Starvation?"

"Even here. I don't exactly understand how, but he's here with me now, and it's a comfort, sir, even knowing what's going to happen to me in a little bit."

"I wish I could make things different, Seth."

Again it was the boy who comforted him. "I wouldn't want you to worry yourself, sir. I never expected to go home anyhow. Though I didn't figure on being shot by my own. I'd thought it would more likely be a redcoat that got me."

They sat quietly for a moment before Kerns said, "Would you do me a favor, Dr. Scott?"

"Anything, Kerns."

"Would you write my ma a letter? Tell her I loved her and that I died from the fever. No reason for her to know the truth. It'd just go that much harder for her."

"All right, Seth. I'll tell her how good and brave you were."

The guard stuck his head in the tent and said, "Sorry, kid, but it's time."

Kerns moved to stand up, but Brice stopped him with a hand on his shoulder. "You'd have made a good doctor, Seth. Better than me."

"Thank you for saying that, sir, but I don't think there could ever be a better doctor than you."

Brice followed him out of the tent. He didn't want to watch, but he couldn't leave the boy now. As soon as Brice stepped away from the tent, Nathan was beside him. He didn't say anything, but he stayed by his side.

It was over in seconds. The sound of gunfire filled the woods, and then all was silence. Brice went to Seth.

"Is he dead?" Captain Belding asked behind him.

"Yes." Brice gently closed the boy's eyes.

"We'll bury him," Captain Belding said. "He was one of ours."

Brice stepped back out of the way as two men from Belding's company picked up the boy's body.

"All we can do now is pray for his soul," Captain Belding said.

"I think it's the rest of us who need the prayers. Not Seth." Brice looked at the captain and then to the men carrying the body away.

He wouldn't watch them bury Kerns. If there was a God the way Kerns said, the boy had already slipped out of his body and had gone on to his reward. Brice started back through the camp. He didn't even realize Nathan was still beside him until he said, "I'm sorry, Doc. Kerns was a good man."

266

"It's over now, Bates. Finished and done. There's nothing we can do about it."

Nathan walked a ways in silence before he said, "Maybe there's something I could do for you, Doc. Get you something to eat or drink?"

"If there was anything to get." Brice stopped walking and looked at the boy beside him before he said, "You don't have to worry about me, Nathan. I just need some time alone right now."

"Sure, Doc. I can understand that. But if you need something, you know, to talk or anything, I'll be around." He let Brice walk on alone.

Brice would have liked to walk right out of camp and away from it all, but instead he went back to his tent. A man could be alone no matter how many people were around him.

But as he sat in front of his tent he realized he wasn't really alone, nor did he want to be. Gabrielle was there with him almost real enough to touch. He could see the concern for him flooding her pure blue eyes, and then he could almost feel her touch him gently with her love.

She was hundreds of miles away, and yet she was there beside him. She couldn't make him forget Seth had died a needless death, but her presence there in his mind made him believe he could live with that truth.

What was it Seth had said about the Lord? That he'd been with him in the tent waiting with him to face death. And somewhere deep inside Brice, a door inched open and a prayer slid out into his mind. *Dear God, help us. Help us all.*

23

Yea, Sister Helen. Nay, Sister Helen. Whatever you say, Sister Helen. The words slid off Gabrielle's tongue with ease. Sister Helen's voice was a constant drone in her ears, but Gabrielle listened only enough to determine whether yea or nay was the proper answer. The months had edged by drearily from the steaming hot month of August through the crisp days of autumn.

The bountiful harvest months of September and October had been a blessing to both the village and to Gabrielle. All able-bodied workers went to the fields and garden plots to harvest the end-of-the-season crops. Gabrielle had thrown herself into the work of picking the beans left on the vines to dry and digging the sweet potatoes. If the day was warm, Sister Helen often had to rest in the shade a while at midday. And while she was not out of Gabrielle's sight, she was at least too far away to count Gabrielle's every breath.

Other sisters were then free to step up beside Gabrielle and speak of the wind in the trees, the bounty of their harvest, what they might have on their table that evening in the biting room. Quiet talk that meant nothing but that was somehow soothing to Gabrielle's ears after so many weeks of Sister Helen's faultfinding.

After the gardens had been stripped of every useful product, she and Sister Helen were sent into other fields to help harvest the seed crops for sale in the spring to the people of the world. The work was tedious, especially with the smaller seeds such as the tobacco seeds where Gabrielle could hold more seeds in one hand than were needed to grow plants for several acres. She liked separating out one of the seeds and holding it on her fingertip. She'd stare at it and think of the mustard seed the Lord had spoken about to his disciples in the Bible. *If ye have faith as a grain of mustard seed, ye shall say unto this mountain, Remove hence to yonder place; and it shall remove; and nothing shall be impossible unto you.*

The tobacco seed was not much more than a black speck on her finger and even tinier than a mustard seed. Silently she asked the Eternal Father to give her the faith of that tiny tobacco seed so that she could keep praying, keep singing, keep feeling some measure of joy. She liked repeating the last phrase of the Lord's words. *Nothing shall be impossible unto you.*

If only she knew what things the Lord wanted her to see as possible. Enduring Sister Helen's constant presence by her side? Using her hands to serve and her mind to worship here at Harmony Hill forevermore? Ridding her mind of thoughts of the doctor? Finding in her heart the proper sisterly love for Sister Helen?

Every morning when the rising bell rang, and Gabrielle sat up in her bed and looked down at the heavy string connecting Gabrielle's wrist and Sister Helen's, she thought the

269

last might be the most impossible. Sister Helen had insisted they be tied together at night ever since the morning Sister Esther had hanged herself and Gabrielle had been drawn to the kitchen by the scream that had torn through her soul.

When Gabrielle had promised not to go from the sleeping room again without waking Sister Helen, Sister Helen had scoffed at her vow. "If you were trustworthy, Sister Gabrielle, you wouldn't be under constant supervision to begin with. But ye are not trustworthy, and therefore you must submit to whatever I decide you must do to satisfy the rules of constant supervision. And I can't be staying awake all night to make sure you aren't slipping out to meet someone of the world."

So Sister Helen had tied the string to Gabrielle's arm. "And don't think you can untie it without me knowing. I will know."

The string was a constant irritation, a constant reminder of her fall from grace among the Believers. The first few nights she had feared the string would drive her into madness, but then every time she had felt the irritation of the string, she'd said a prayer in her heart and recited parts of 1 Corinthians 13. *Charity suffereth long, and is kind.* And she was thankful for the scriptures she had committed to her heart. The Bible verses comforted her and kept her sane when she could not sleep.

And slowly, prayer by prayer, the Eternal Father helped her find a way to keep loving her brethren and sisters even though Sister Helen still stood on the outside of her charity. The Lord did help her mash down her ill feelings toward Sister Helen so that she was open to learning from her when Sister Helen began gathering her medicinal herbs.

Sister Helen carefully guarded her knowledge of the physic

herbs and cures even though the elders and eldresses had often urged her to teach one of the younger sisters her healing secrets. She claimed none of the sisters had shown the aptitude or proper dedication to be so entrusted as yet and that she was praying Mother Ann would send her one so gifted.

She certainly had no thought of sharing any of her knowledge with Gabrielle, but at the same time she had not wanted to give over the watching of Gabrielle to any of the other sisters. She said when she started a duty, she was bound to see it through no matter how arduous that duty proved to be. So when the first frosts signaled the coming of winter, she had to begin gathering and drying the herbs and roots she might need before spring even though Gabrielle was at her side.

Again Gabrielle felt the answer to prayer lifting her spirits. When she followed Sister Helen into the woods, Gabrielle could feel her spirit billowing out inside her once more. She hadn't realized how much she had missed her times of prayer among the trees. She'd thought she had simply sought her prayer place among the trees because of the solitude, but now helping Sister Helen gather her roots, Gabrielle realized her spirit needed the sight of the trees towering over her head. She needed the smell of the fallen leaves and the acorns and squirrels. She needed the sight of fluttering wings as the birds flew between the branches.

She needed the feeling of stepping nearer the doctor. Even though she knew he was not at his cabin, for Elder Caleb said the militia was still in the North, she felt closer to Brice in the woods. She stood in the shadow of the trees and remembered the warmth of his body standing beside her, the gentleness of his hands, the love in his eyes. And she felt no shame for her thoughts even after Sister Helen frowned at her and told her to quit dragging her feet.

"We're not out here just to take a saunter through the woods. We have work to do, Sister Gabrielle." She handed Gabrielle a trowel. "Now I don't want to put up with the first bit of contrariness. You dig where I tell you and don't ask a lot of useless questions."

"Yea, Sister Helen," Gabrielle said quietly. "Show me where to dig."

So even though she did not want to share any of her knowledge, Sister Helen nevertheless had to show Gabrielle where the roots were. Then while feigning a lack of interest, she watched to see how Sister Helen labeled the roots. Gabrielle had never felt drawn to mixing medicine potions or doing physic healing, but she was open to learning. Besides, the handling of the roots made yet another connection in her thoughts to Brice. Wherever he was with the army, he too was surely digging his own roots for healing.

On the second day in the woods, Sister Helen led the way deep into the woods, claiming to be searching for a specific root. Gabrielle realized long before they reached the clearing around the doctor's cabin where Sister Helen must surely be leading her and why. Sister Helen was watching her sharply, hoping to catch her in some fault, but Gabrielle had had much practice in the last weeks of hiding her feelings, so when she saw the cabin through the trees, she simply said, "Are we close to the settlement?"

"Nay, Sister Gabrielle. Ye know that is not true."

"It has been many years since I have been away from our village. I have forgotten the directions to the settlement." Gabrielle turned innocent eyes on Sister Helen before she looked back at the cabin. Vines were growing up on the steps and some of the poles on the small corral next to the cabin were fallen and broken. "It doesn't look as if anyone has been here for some time," she said. "I hope they didn't encounter misfortune."

"Only the misfortune of going to war. Of course that could mean he has died."

"Oh?" Gabrielle didn't allow Sister Helen's words to touch her mind. She would know if the doctor had died. She didn't know how, but she was sure she would. She looked at Sister Helen. "How is it you know who lives here?"

"Don't try pulling your innocent tricks with me, Sister Gabrielle. We both know whose cabin this is. You may think you can lie to all the others, but I know you. I know the sin in your heart. I saw your sin when you stepped into the shadows with that heathen doctor."

"Yea, Sister Helen." Gabrielle kept her face expressionless. "I would never try to lie to you. It would be useless."

"Your heart is black with the sin of deception," Sister Helen said.

Gabrielle didn't lower her eyes. "I have no desire to deceive you. I only have the desire to pay my penance and regain the trust of my brethren and sisters."

"You have desire, all right. The wrong kinds of desires. I see them burning in your eyes."

"I know not of what you speak."

"So ye say, Sister. So ye say. But I have seen many of the world. I can smell worldly sins on one such as you."

Gabrielle just stared at her a moment before she said, "Should we not be seeking out the roots you need before night begins to fall?"

Sister Helen's face turned dark red, and Gabrielle thought for a moment the woman was going to strike her. Instead Sister Helen turned on her heel and stalked back into the trees away from the doctor's cabin without another word.

Gabrielle followed her without looking over her shoulder at the cabin. She had no need to look at it. The doctor was in her heart. Not in the deserted cabin. And somehow she knew that wherever he was, he was suffering just as much as she was.

24

Winter 1812–13

Christmas passed in the woods with hardly a notice. Even after one of the men went through the camp carrying his Bible and beating on a coffee pot as he reminded them it was the Christ's birth date, nobody paid the day much mind. There was no joy to be had in Fort Starvation.

And certainly no joy in Brice's heart. Not since the army had shot Kerns. Yet he knew if Kerns was alive, he'd be standing there singing one of those Christmas songs his ma had probably taught him and reciting the Christmas story. Somehow Seth had managed to carry joy with him in spite of all that had happened, even to death.

When orders came before the first of the year to move up to the Rapids, Brice was glad to have something to think about even if that was only how to move their sick through the snow. After a couple of days of marching, the weather turned against them with fury. For two days they sat huddled in camp by whatever fire they could keep going as the wind swirled the snow around them in deep drifts until many of the men were crouched in snow caves.

They inched forward through the snowstorm on the third day, but by mid-afternoon they had to give up the march and make camp. Brice pushed out a spot in the snow for his tent. Then he joined the other men scavenging for bark or bushes, anything to keep them off the snow while they tried to sleep. As he trudged through the deep snow, he thought of how as a boy he'd run through the snow in the woods, spoiling its pristine whiteness with his tracks and laughing when the trees dropped snow down on his head and shoulders.

Now he couldn't imagine ever taking pleasure in snow again. No matter its beauty, this scene around him would always be etched in his mind. Horses too far gone to pick at the brush the soldiers brought them. Men reaching hands out for warmth to flames flickering and spitting as the snow kept falling. Other men too cold and tired to do anything but sit and stare as they waited for death's horse to take them from their misery. Brice had always heard death rode a dark horse, but surely this time death was sheathed in white. There was no beauty here.

A week later they reached their rendezvous only to find the other armies weren't coming. General Harrison sent word for Winchester to fall back, but with nothing to fall back to except more starvation, they pushed on. The men cheered when they saw the first village, but the French settlers, who came out with white flags to welcome them, looked worried as they told how the British were threatening to punish any villages that gave aide to the American soldiers.

The night was so cold their breath froze in the air. Still, the men had purpose now. Under Colonel Lewis, the army was up and moving early the next day across the ice of Lake Erie and on to Frenchtown. Villagers kept passing them going south to escape the conflict sure to come.

They were within three miles of Frenchtown when the enemy discovered them. The men lined up in battle formation and stood in the snow as their battalion commanders read the colonel's orders of the day.

"Soldiers! Your ancient enemy is before you. The wrongs that he has inflicted upon your country are fresh in your memory. That country calls upon you this day to vindicate her honor and her interests by inflicting upon him condign punishment. In the hour of battle remember what the Patriot Orator said to you at Georgetown: 'You have the double character of Americans and Kentuckians to sustain.' Do so, as I feel assured you will, and all will be well."

With these words ringing in their ears, the men surged forward. The British waited until they were less than a quarter of a mile from the town to fire on them with their howitzer. It went well over their head, and the men kept moving forward. The next shot was nearer target, but some of the men in the ranks began crowing like roosters to make fun of the British artillery.

The drummers began a long drum roll as the troops crossed the slippery ice of the River Raisen in the face of the enemy fire. Once across the river they had to fight their way through a dense growth of cane, but the men pushed on into Frenchtown and the enemy force retreated.

Just as the men were ready to celebrate, they heard firing off in the woods, so they had to reform their lines and move back into the battle.

Brice stayed in the town to treat the one casualty, a Captain Hickman. He took over the first house he came to and worked to save the man's leg. For a while he heard the firing in the woods beyond, but it wasn't long before the war he fought in the house shut out all the sounds of war outside as more men staggered in with wounds to be treated.

He was working by candlelight when he finally heard the silence. No more gunfire. He didn't slow his work. If night had ended the battle for the day, more men would be brought to his door now that there was time to worry about the wounded. At least they had the confiscated store of British medicines and bandages to use.

Hope was one of the last to come in. Brice looked him over and said, "You don't look too much worse for the wear."

"I'm too ornery to kill," Hope said before he pointed to the bloody rag wrapped around his upper arm. "This ain't much more than a scratch, but I come along to make the boy happy."

"Is Bates all right?"

Hope's smile went clear across his face. "The boy would've made you proud, Doc. He stepped up to the challenge and showed he's a true Kentuckian for sure."

Brice took the wrapping off Hope's wound. "How'd the fighting go?"

"We pushed them back some." The smile slid off Hope's face. "We might have chased them clear out of the country if we'd only had the strength. We was just too weak to chase them on."

"How did you keep on fighting after it got dark?" Brice asked.

"Well, by then a lot of the officers had fell and most of us were on our own. Course Kentuckians don't need nobody to lead them into a fight. We know how to do woods fighting, and you'd be surprised, Doc, how often you can find your target if you just wait for them to shoot and then aim at the flash in the dark."

Brice probed the wound on Hope's arm. "This could use some stitches."

Hope pulled his arm away from Brice. "Now don't be doing nothing to me that'll take too long."

"The fighting's over for today, Hope. What's your hurry?"

"I reckon you've been up to your eyeballs in bandages in here and don't know what's going on outside. We won the day and now the colonel says we get to reap the rewards. Seems the redcoats left a pile of food behind when we showed them their way home. I tell you, Doc. We're going to eat tonight."

Brice wrapped a clean bandage around Hope's wound. "You'd best get going then and let me get back to those who need tending."

"You should come on out and help us eat up that good British beef. I hear they even have cider and apples." Hope winked at Brice as he stood up. "Not to mention them fine French ladies that's volunteered to serve up the food. A man can get a mighty hungering for the sight of something in skirts after months in the wilderness."

Brice followed him to the door and watched the soldiers drifting from house to house. The men were shouting, but then the soft tones of a woman's laugh carried across the town square to Brice. Something grabbed at Brice's insides and he took a step out the door. Then he stopped. It wasn't the sight of just any woman Brice hungered after. It was Gabrielle.

Behind him, one of the wounded men moaned, and without regret, Brice turned back to his work.

Late the next day Nathan came to the door of the cabin where Brice was checking over some of the wounded and said, "Got a minute, Doc?"

"Sure, Bates." Brice took one look at him and went out into the cold air to stand beside him. "I hear you were assigned to the detail to bring in the dead."

A tremble passed through the boy that had nothing to do with the chill in the air. Brice went back inside and brought him out a cup of the brew of roots he'd been giving the men to try to strengthen them. "Drink this," he ordered.

Nathan drank it down and made a face. "What was that?"

"Just some roots and a few tea leaves." Brice waited a minute for the boy to say more. When he didn't, Brice finally said, "You want to talk about it?"

"I don't know, Doc. I just wasn't ready for what was out there this morning."

"I doubt any man ever is."

"Then you don't think I'm feeling all sick like this because I'm a coward? I mean, I wasn't all that scared yesterday. I just kept loading and shooting till I couldn't raise up my gun. A time or two I thought I might get killed, but I never thought about dying like that."

"Indian warriors usually scalp the men they kill." Brice had seen the bodies the detail had brought in. Thirteen of them frozen stiff from the cold night and all but one scalped and stripped.

"I'd heard that, but I guess until you see it with your own eyes, you can't imagine what it's really like. I don't like thinking about dying that way."

280

Brice was trying to come up with the right thing to say to ease the boy's mind without lying to him when Hope came up to them. "There you are, Nathan. I been searching all over for you." Hope peered closer at Nathan's face. "Something wrong, boy? You're looking a mite peaked."

Brice answered for Nathan. "He was on the detail to bring in the dead."

"You just have to push that out of your head and not dwell on it, boy," Hope said.

Nathan looked over at him. "Don't you ever think about what if that'd been you, Alec?"

"No profit in that and no reason for it either. I wasn't one of them. Besides, we give them worse than they give us. You saw what we did to one of them."

"But why?" Nathan asked. "Isn't it enough to just kill them?"

Hope didn't let the question bother him. "That's just how things are, boy. You're carrying too much a load from those old Shakers, but the fact is us and the Injuns are natural-born enemies. There ain't no explaining it, and what does a fighting man need with reasons?"

"I don't know, Alec. Just seems like there ought to be a reason for dying."

"Well, and there is a reason for that. We're Kentuckians, boy, and our country's asking us to drive the enemy out of this place. A few of us is going to die in every battle, but in the end we'll make this whole blamed country ours like it was meant to be." Hope looked over at Brice. "Ain't that right, Doc?"

"I'll leave the explaining of it to you, Hope. I'll just patch up the results."

Hope took hold of the boy's arm. "Come on, boy. Ain't no use talking war to a man who don't like to fight."

"I'll fight my way, and you can fight yours, Hope."

"Don't get your dander up, Doc. I didn't mean nothing by what I said."

As Brice watched them walk away, he wondered if he'd ever see either of them alive again if the British decided to come back. The men had set up camp in the middle of the village, but the pickets thrown up around the town on three sides wouldn't hold long against a heavy attack with artillery. Brice went back inside to his patients. He couldn't worry about what he couldn't change, but he wished Seth were there to offer up a prayer for all of them.

The thought had no sooner come to his mind than it was almost as if Seth were speaking in his ear. *"You don't need me to pray for you, sir. Every man can go right up to the throne of God and offer up his own prayers. It says so in the Bible, sir."*

Brice looked up toward the ceiling but no words filled his mind. He'd spent a good amount of time in church. He'd heard plenty of Scripture. *For God so loved the world.* But how could he keep loving men even when they were shooting at other men who presumably God loved too? Brice frowned and let the worry flow back through him.

He saw the same worry on many of the officers' faces as the days passed. A few reinforcements straggled in, but no orders were given for the men to fortify their position. The river was behind them but the British wouldn't come from that direction. They'd follow the easy path of Hull's road close by to make an advance on the town with their artillery. But while it was obvious the army's position in Frenchtown was vulnerable, they had no way to retreat without leaving the wounded behind. No officer could order that kind of retreat, not and leave the wounded to the mercy of the Indians. Brice could only hope General Harrison would show up with fresh reinforcements before the British marched against them.

25

The British came first. The beating of reveille had no more than died away in the mist on January 22 when a sentry's musket gave the alarm. The men formed up, but once the British started pounding the ranks with their artillery fire, it was a total rout.

Brice and those wounded who could get to their feet watched out the doors and windows as the men out on the field began to run for the river with no sign of an orderly retreat. Beside Brice, a wounded captain muttered. "The Indians will cut them off for sure." He turned from the window to pick up his gun.

Brice looked from him to the men dying out on the battlefield. He picked up a gun from one of the beds and stepped toward the door to follow the captain out. One of the other doctors stepped in front of him. "It won't do anybody any good for you to go out there and get yourself killed, Scott. We'll be needed more after the shooting is over."

"I can't just stand here and watch them be overrun. You can handle whatever comes up."

Brice found a place along the pickets. Hope spotted him at once. "Hey, Doc. Now you're gonna do some of my kind of doctoring. Just make every shot count."

"I know how to shoot, Hope." Brice looked through the pickets and took careful aim. They were at an advantage here against the enemy. He couldn't see the retreat of the regulars now. He'd just have to hope they'd make it to the Rapids and some measure of cover and not worry about the captain's words saying the Indians would cut off their retreat.

He had no idea how much time passed as he shot and reloaded and shot again before Hope came running to get him. "It's the boy," he said. "He took a bad shot in the leg."

Brice looked down at his gun, warm from firing. He hadn't stopped to help others when they'd fallen.

"Come on, Doc. Any fool can shoot," Hope said. "You got to help the boy before he bleeds out."

Brice handed his gun to the man next to him and followed Hope to where Nathan was lying in snow turned red by his blood. A touch of a smile came to his pale lips when he saw Brice. "Hey, Doc, think you can work another miracle to get me around this one?"

"I'll patch you up best I can, but I'll leave the miracle working up to the Lord." He kept his voice crisp as he looked at the wound, but inside his heart was sinking. There was no doubt the boy was going to need another miracle.

Hope helped carry Nathan into one of the houses, but once they got the boy laid out on a bed, he said, "I'd stay and help, Doc, but I reckon we'd both better stick to what we're best at."

Brice waved him away as he worked to slow the bleeding.

When he raised the boy's head up to drink down a draught of medicine, Nathan said, "It's bad, isn't it, Doc?"

"It is, but I've seen worse."

Nathan reached out and grabbed Brice's hand. "Don't cut it off, Doc. I've done suffered too much keeping that leg to have you cut it off now."

"Easy, boy." Brice pushed him back down on the bed gently. "I'll do what I can, but I can't make promises."

"You won't cut my leg off, Doc. I know you won't." Nathan shut his eyes.

"Better to lose your leg than your life," Brice said, but the boy gave no sign of hearing.

"Just as well," Brice muttered to himself. There were times when even the dark sleep of unconsciousness was a blessing.

Brice didn't know Dr. Rowen was behind him until he spoke. "You're wasting your time, Scott. Gangrene's sure to set in on a wound like that, and you'll end up having to cut off the leg anyway. Better to do it first and clean."

Brice didn't look up. "Maybe so, but the boy deserves a chance at keeping his leg."

Dr. Rowen looked out toward the sound of battle and shook his head. "I'm not sure any of us are going to keep anything at the end of this day."

A couple of hours later, an ominous silence fell over the battleground. Some of the men behind the pickets stood and waited. Others left their position to find food. Hope came to see about Nathan.

"I've done what I can for him, Hope," Brice told him. "But what's going on out there? What's this quiet mean?"

"We beat them back, Doc. They made three charges at us, but we picked them off like flies. We wouldn't have lost a man if it hadn't been for the Injuns sneaking around behind us where they could get a clear bead down on us."

Dr. Rowen came up to them and asked, "Is it over for the day?"

"I'm doubting it, sir. They'll be back at us again most likely."

"And will you be able to beat them back again?" Dr. Rowen asked.

This time Hope wasn't so cocky. "Well, it's like this, sir. We're as good a bunch of fighting Kentuckians you're ever likely to see, but even Kentuckians can't shoot when they run out of ammunition." Hope fingered his ammunition pouch. "We'll keep them back as long as we can, and then we'll fight them hand to hand till there ain't none of us left to fight."

Just then a shout came from the fence. "The enemy's coming with a white flag."

"Now see there," Hope said. "Them redcoats are done ready to call a truce."

But it wasn't a truce the enemy asked for. Instead they demanded the complete surrender of the American troops. They had captured General Winchester and the general had sent orders for the soldiers to lay down their weapons and surrender.

The men's hands tightened on their guns as the parley went on. None of them wanted to give up their weapons. Not after the fate of the men at Fort Dearborn the year before. Those men had surrendered, stacked their arms, and marched out as prisoners of war. But the Indians had honored no agreements and the men were all killed without mercy. The men behind the pickets at Frenchtown remembered and vowed to fight to the end. If they were going to die, they wanted to do it with a gun in their hands.

Nevertheless, before the sun went down and with the British commander's promise that the Americans could keep their private property and the wounded would be protected by British guards until sleds could be sent to take them to Amberstburg, the officers agreed to the terms of surrender. Then even before the Kentuckians had laid down their guns, some of the Indians were crowding around to grab anything they could from the men. It wasn't until the men shouldered their guns that the British Colonel Proctor waved the Indians back.

As if to beat the fall of night, the British hurried the men as they marched out from behind the pickets and grounded their arms before lining up as British prisoners. The walking wounded lined up with the rest of the prisoners to move out.

Brice and Dr. Rowen were left behind to care for the men too badly wounded to move under their own power. Before Hope fell into line with the other prisoners, he slipped over to talk to Brice. "I don't like the looks of it, Doc. I wish you and Nathan was lined up with me."

"The boy's hurt too bad to march anywhere." Brice shook Hope's hand. "Don't worry about us, Hope. They're leaving guards, a Captain Elliott and three interpreters, until they can send the sleds for the wounded. And who knows? The way they're in such a rush it could be Harrison will beat them here."

"I wish I could believe you was right, Doc." Hope shifted from one foot to the other before he said, "If I don't never see you no more, and you do make it back to Kentucky safe and all, you tell my girl I loved her. I wasn't always a good pa, but I did love her."

Hope fell in with the other Kentuckians marching out as prisoners of the British. Brice watched them until they were out of sight. It was only right that Hope mentioned Gabrielle. She was the fine yet unbreakable thread that tied them together. Brice and Nathan and Hope.

The silence after the British left with their prisoners was oppressive. As Brice moved among the wounded, the uneasiness grew as night fell. But though a few Indians wandered through the houses looking for plunder, they didn't offer any threat, and the hours crept by.

Just after dark, Brice stepped outside to see the British captain mounting one of the wounded officers' horses. He looked in Brice's direction and hesitated for a bare moment before he kicked the horse and rode out of Frenchtown.

Dr. Rowen came up behind Brice. "Who was that?"

"Our guard, the good Captain Elliott."

"There aren't going to be any sleds, are there, Scott?" Dr. Rowen didn't wait for Brice to answer. "Not that it matters anyway. I've heard the British are giving their red friends a victory frolic a little ways from here. We'll be lucky if any of us see the sun rise in the morning."

"The sleds will be here," Brice said, but he was anything but sure of that.

"Maybe so, but it might be wise if all of us take a few minutes to get right with God before too much more time passes."

"You mean a deathbed confession?"

"I've heard plenty of them and I know you have too."

"Too many," Brice agreed.

"That boy, the one you tried to save his leg. He may be wanting to make one. He's come to and he's calling for you."

When Brice stepped up beside Nathan's bed, the boy opened his eyes. "Doc," he whispered. "I'm tired, Doc. I'm thinking about letting go."

Brice sat down beside him. "You can't give up now, Bates. You can find the courage to hang on a little longer."

"Courage. I've always wanted to have courage, to be brave, but I've never been sure I was. Maybe that's why I ran back into that barn at Harmony Hill. To prove I was brave." Nathan stopped and licked his lips. "Maybe that's why I marched on up here with Alec and you. But you know, I still don't feel brave. I'm still afraid."

"Even brave men feel fear, Nathan, but you don't have to prove anything anymore. You did that already out on the battlefield. You'll never have to doubt your bravery again." Brice gently laid his hand on the boy's shoulder. "But there's no need suffering. Let me give you something to help you sleep."

"Not yet. If I go to sleep, I won't ever wake up. I know that."

"Then drink half the draught. That will dull the pain some." He raised the boy's head and tipped up the cup until he'd taken a couple of swallows.

The boy lay back and looked at Brice. "You really think I'm brave, Doc? You're not just saying that because you think I'm about to die?"

"I don't lie to my patients."

"But sometimes you don't tell them the whole truth either, do you, Doc?"

"What do you mean?"

"Gabrielle. Why didn't you tell me you loved her?" Nathan's eyes were fastened on Brice.

Brice let out a long breath before he said, "I didn't want to admit it to myself at first. But then that day I saw her sing, I knew." He looked at Nathan for a long minute before going on.

"But what good would it have done to tell you? She wouldn't listen to either of us."

"But she listened more to you than me, didn't she? Does she love you?"

"I want to believe she does."

"Good, then maybe she'll listen to you when you go back to get her. I don't like to think of her growing old in that barren place."

"The last time I saw her she gave me no hope of ever listening."

"She'll listen if she loves you enough. She didn't love me enough." He shut his eyes and was so quiet that Brice thought he'd slipped into sleep. But then he said, "I can see her here, kneeling by my bed, praying for me. Do you think she knows I'm in trouble? You know, with her gift of knowing things?"

"It wouldn't surprise me, Nathan. She did love you."

"I know. Like a brother," Nathan said. When he groaned again, Brice raised his chin and poured the rest of the medicine down his throat.

If she loves you enough. The boy's words stayed with him as he walked through the wounded, stopping here and there to try to give a measure of comfort to the men who were only a step away from death.

An hour after daylight he heard horses and looked out to see the three interpreters leaving camp. Nothing stood between them and the Indians now. A fist tightened around his heart when he looked in the other direction and saw the Indians coming into the town. They might all just be a step away from death.

26

Gabrielle was up before dawn. She hadn't slept well. She hadn't for weeks. The winter nights were long and she often tired of waiting for daybreak. This morning she'd slipped out of her bed and silently pulled on her clothes without lighting a candle to keep from waking her sisters. Then she'd slipped down the stairs and out the door before the rising bell rang to go to the schoolroom to prepare the day's lessons.

The snow beside the paths sparkled in the moonlight. It was cold, but Gabrielle breathed in the air gratefully. Sometimes at moments like this when the rest of the village was sleeping or busy with their own duties, she wanted to throw out her arms and spin around and rejoice in being totally alone.

It was late January, and the elders and eldresses were allowing her to teach the young sisters again, although they often found occasion to step into her classes to be sure she wasn't being too lenient with any of the little ones. They'd even lifted the constant supervision a few weeks early. An answer to prayer. She no longer had to endure the presence of Sister Helen by her side at all times.

Gabrielle kept waiting for her life to even back out. Each time she woke up, each time she went to meeting and labored one of the Shaker songs, she expected to surely recapture some of the peace she'd once known so abundantly, but her mind would not stop questioning, not stop remembering. Ofttimes uneasiness covered her soul like a thick morning fog.

The schoolroom was cold. She could see her breath in the air as she built a fire in the small stove, but instead of huddling there for warmth, she went to the window to watch the night sky give way to dawn. The fresh blanket of snow hastened the morning light. She tried to pray, but a whirling wind of confusion wiped away the words in her mind. The prayer died before it reached her lips.

She hadn't been able to pray while Sister Helen was with her, not with all her spirit as she once had. She'd thought then that Sister Helen's presence hindered her prayers and poisoned her spirit. In the long months they'd spent together, Gabrielle had never been able to feel even a small bit of affection for Sister Helen. She had tried. Many times. She knew it was wrong to harbor such ill feeling for one's sister under God. But it would have been easier for her to learn to love a stone. Much easier.

During the last month of her supervision, Gabrielle wasn't sure her own heart hadn't hardened into stone. At the same time she had become meek and careful in her every answer until even Sister Helen had to admit Gabrielle had humbled her spirit as a true Believer should. Sister Helen had offered no protest when the elders had lifted the constant supervision even though she continued to watch Gabrielle with her hawk eyes whenever they were in the same room. She was waiting and ready to pounce if Gabrielle stumbled yet again.

Her sister was right to suspect her. Gabrielle hadn't put her worldly thoughts behind her. They were in her mind, stronger than ever, and at night when she lay down, she pulled her thoughts of the doctor to her without shame. He seemed the only real thing in her life now even though he was miles away fighting a war she knew nothing about. Elder Caleb had not mentioned any news from the North for weeks. War had nothing to do with the Believers.

With a corner of her kerchief, she rubbed away her breath from the frosty window. The sun's light was beginning to touch the horizon and stretching pink fingers into the sky. Her students would be coming into the room soon after they finished their breakfast.

Suddenly her heart began beating heavily as dread filled her. She tried to shake it away. She had no dread of the girls coming to class. She liked teaching them even though Becca's memory often saddened her heart.

She shut her eyes and Nathan was there in the center of her mind watching her. He no longer wore Shaker garb but that of a frontiersman. His face showed none of the anger he'd had when she'd last seen him. Instead he looked sad and weary. His mouth moved, but she heard nothing in her mind.

She lifted her hands to reach toward him and bumped her hand into the cold glass of the window. Nathan's image dissolved in her mind.

She opened her eyes and looked out on the quiet snow-covered paths, undisturbed by any foot and bringing a special peace to the village. Then all at once the snow was tinged with red in front of her eyes. She blinked and shook her head, but the red didn't go away. It only spread.

She stared out at the snow. The familiar bushes, trees,

and steps were gone. In their stead were houses she'd never seen before and men bleeding in the snow. Indians walked among the houses with tomahawks in their hands, but it was no battle. Men were dying in their beds. Gabrielle shuddered as a man cried out for mercy as the tomahawk fell.

Gabrielle closed her eyes to escape the vision but it mattered not whether her eyes were open or shut. Nathan was waiting there in her mind. He was no longer standing, but appeared to be sleeping. Flames rose up around him and Gabrielle cried out as if somehow she might awaken him. But his eyes stayed closed. Confusion rose inside her. Was she only reliving the earlier vision when the barn burned? But Nathan hadn't been asleep in that vision. And why were there Indians with tomahawks? No Indians had ever been to their village.

Gabrielle opened her eyes and looked out again. The vision was there frozen in front of her, and this time she recognized soldiers. Soldiers wounded and unable to defend themselves. The vision was as clear as if she'd been standing beside the beds of the wounded men in the houses. She wanted to run from the sight of these men dying, but her feet would not move.

Then the doctor stepped in front of her eyes as he too watched the men dying. His face looked chiseled out of ice. Gone were the gentle lines of caring around his eyes and mouth as each line on his face stood out starkly while he watched the Indians carrying death from house to house. Again she raised her hands, this time to reach toward Brice, but as suddenly as it had come the vision was gone.

She had no strength to pull it back as she fell trembling to her knees. Even if she could have, she wasn't sure she would want to. The darkness of terrible death spread over her soul.

"Eternal Father," she whispered. "Do not turn thy face from this thy child. Put thy hand of mercy out unto thy children and lift them away from misery."

The prayer welled up out of her heart and soul, and she prayed as she had not since Sister Esther had died of her own hand. She wanted to say "thy will be done," but she couldn't keep from praying, "Let Dr. Scott live. Have mercy on this thy child and let him live."

She heard the rising bell as though it rang somewhere far in the distance. She made no move to get to her feet. Instead she huddled there on the floor in despair, for she could feel no answer to her prayer.

When the children came into the classroom, she rose from her knees and went to her desk. She assigned their lessons and listened to their recitations, but even at her busiest moments the sight of men dying flashed before her over and over. Always the same. She had seen the middle of the story but knew not the beginning or the end.

In Frenchtown, Brice knew the story beginning to end too well. The first Indians had come into town an hour after daylight. A sudden quiet had fallen over the town, and the few men who'd stayed with wounded family members and friends to help load them on the promised sleds stepped to the doors and windows.

It was over. No one spoke the words, but they were there just the same. No sleds would come. There'd be no need for them. Lives Brice had fought for through the dark hours of night would be wiped out with a quick blow of the tomahawk, and there was absolutely nothing any of them could do as more and more Indians came into the town.

A wounded major spoke to Brice from his bed. "Are they drunk?"

"They don't seem to be, but I don't think it will matter," Brice answered truthfully.

"I never thought to die on my bed," the major said as he struggled to his feet just as a group of the Indians came inside and demanded plunder.

They gave them everything they had, even their shirts and shoes, but it wasn't enough. Without warning, one of the Indians swung his tomahawk and knocked down the major. Brice started forward, but stopped himself. He could not fight them all with nothing but a lancet as a weapon. Instead he slipped unnoticed out of the back door.

One of the Indians who spoke English was talking with the officer in charge. "Wounded all die. Others go with us," he said. As if to prove the truth of his words, a wounded man was dragged screaming out of one of the houses to be tomahawked and scalped in front of them.

Brice stayed in the shadows and eased his way to the house where Nathan lay waiting for the sleds that were not coming. Brice felt inside a pocket of his shirt for the precious packet of powders he'd saved for this day when the men were to be moved. He would not let the boy suffer anymore.

Inside the house, men wounded too badly to move off their beds called out to him, but Brice could do nothing but shake his head. Those men who lay in death's sleep were surely more fortunate than those who had no choice but to lie awake and await their fate.

Nathan wasn't awake when he stopped beside his bed, but neither was he unconscious. When Brice put the cup holding the draught to the boy's lips and raised his head to drink it down, he roused enough to recognize Brice.

"Doc? Is that you? Are we getting ready to move out?"

"That's right, Nathan. I just dosed you so you won't feel the jostle so much."

The boy's eyes cleared a bit. "Something's wrong. I hear screams."

"It hasn't been an easy night for many of the wounded."

Awareness finally came to Nathan. "It's the Indians. They've come instead of the sleds. We're all going to die." He spoke the words quietly.

Brice didn't lie. "I think you might be right."

The boy tried to move off his bed, but he couldn't. "My leg feels like an oak tree stump." He lay back and swallowed hard. "There's nothing I can do, is there? But you, Doc. You ought to make a run for it."

"There's nowhere to go, Nathan."

Nathan drew in a shaky breath before he said, "I'd take it kindly if you'd just go on and shoot me, Doc."

"I don't have a gun. None of us do."

"I guess it don't matter then. One way of dying is the same as the next once it's done and over." Nathan shut his eyes. "You ever pray, Doc?"

"I suppose every man says a prayer at one time or another, but I never was too good at it."

"Me either. That's something the Believers just couldn't teach me. I learned their songs and the steps to those crazy dances, and I bowed my head and folded my hands and said the words, but I never knew for sure whether anybody was listening or not."

"They say the Lord always listens when we pray whether we're good at it or not."

"Gabrielle was good at it. I used to keep my eyes half open and watch her praying in the meetings sometimes. You could almost see the Lord reaching down his hand to gather in her prayers." Nathan was quiet for a moment before he said, "She's praying for us right now, Doc. This very moment."

"What makes you think that, Nathan?"

"I don't know. I just know. I always did. It was like she had reached out and touched me even when we were on opposite sides of the village." The boy opened his eyes and grabbed Brice's hand. "Promise me you'll get her away from there, Doc. I know they're not evil or anything, but she doesn't belong there with them."

Brice heard the sound of men dying outside the cabin. He had no reason to believe he would outlive the boy more than a few moments at the most, but he said, "I promise to never give up trying as long as I'm breathing."

Nathan let go of his hand and lay back again. "That dose you gave me." Suddenly he smiled. "Thanks, Doc. I guess you went the gun one better."

Brice stood beside the boy's bed until he was sure his sleep was deep enough that he wouldn't wake from it no matter what happened. He looked so young there even with the hollow cheeks caused by their winter of starvation and his injury.

Perhaps Brice would have to pay for the boy's life. He'd once told the Shaker elder the boy would have surely died if Brice hadn't been there to treat his burns. The elder in turn blamed Brice for the boy leaving the Shakers, so in a way he'd just prolonged the boy's death. Brice gently touched the boy's head and whispered, "I'm sorry, Nathan."

Outside, everywhere Brice looked men were dying, and he could do nothing but watch as the tragedy unfolded. He thought of the boy's claim that Gabrielle was praying for them, and he began repeating a bit of the Twenty-third Psalm in his head. *Yea, though I walk through the valley of the shadow of death, I will fear no evil.*

As he stood there and watched the snow turning red with the men's blood, he knew a depth of helplessness he'd never known before and creeping in behind it was the bitter poison of hatred. No wonder Hope hadn't wanted to surrender. A man should die with his gun in his hand. Not stripped of his clothes, pale and bleeding and as helpless as a baby before the Indian warriors who struck them down.

His own turn came as an Indian stepped in front of Brice with his tomahawk at the ready. Brice stared at him without flinching. If death had come, then he would face it squarely. He only regretted not seeing Gabrielle one last time. As if in answer to his unspoken prayer, she stepped into his thoughts in front of the Indian warrior. She wore the Shaker dress but her cap had fallen away and her dark hair lay in soft curls about her shoulders. She was so beautiful he could hardly bear the thought of never feeling her in his arms again.

The Indian's face changed. He lowered his tomahawk. "You look strong. You come with me."

"You understand English?" Brice asked.

The Indian stared at him without answering, so Brice spoke in the Indian language he'd learned as a boy living with the Indians as he asked for mercy for the wounded men.

300

The Indian didn't answer his question. Instead he smiled and kept speaking in English. "You know sounds of the red brothers. Right to let you live."

"But the others?" Brice insisted. "It cannot help you to kill them."

"They die," the Indian said. "No more talk or you die with them."

Before noon all the men were either prisoners of the Indians or dead except for some of the most severely wounded men. But the Indians were thorough. They set fire to the two houses where the last of the wounded men lay in their beds unable to move. The flames licked hungrily at the wood and the smoke came up thick and made a cloud around them. Brice had pulled some of those men back from death, and for what? To burn to death.

Brice trembled as the first screams came from inside the house. He wanted to spring forward to help, but his death would not save the men in the houses. Then a man from inside one of the houses dragged himself to the door only to be met there by an Indian's tomahawk.

The same fate awaited each man who tried to crawl out of the flames. The others lay in their beds and died. Brice hoped that Nathan had never awakened, that he had breathed the smoke and died without ever seeing the flames leaping around his bed.

By mid-afternoon the houses had been reduced to smoldering rubble and the smell of burnt flesh hung heavily in the air. Brice counted about thirty men still standing, waiting with silent resignation for whatever might happen next as they tried not to look at the bodies of their comrades all about them.

When the other men were ordered into line to march out toward Malden, the Indian who'd claimed Brice as his prisoner motioned him aside. "You stay." He handed him a load of plunder to carry.

The other men marched out in the middle of the Indians. They kept their eyes straight ahead and didn't look back. They'd already seen too much. Even before they got out of the town, two more of the men were struck down when they lagged a couple of steps behind. He wondered if any of them would ever see Fort Malden.

When the Indian handed him another pack to carry, Brice spoke in the Indian tongue again to ask why they didn't go with the others.

"Talk too much," the Indian answered in English and banged the flat side of his tomahawk against Brice's head. Brice staggered back but stayed on his feet. To fall would surely mean instant death.

The Indian motioned for Brice to follow as he moved out of the town in the opposite direction from the other men. The Indian was taking him into the wilderness land of the Indian tribes. He'd walked this same path into captivity once before. He'd not known what was going to happen to him then, and because he was just a boy, he'd adjusted his life to fit into the Indian village where he'd ended up. But now he couldn't bear the thought of being a slave to the Indians again. It would be better to die. With each step he took behind the Indian, resistance grew in him until nothing mattered except the thought of escape.

It might not be this day or even for months, but he would escape. It was a prayer without words rising from deep inside him.

27

The Indian didn't go toward the fort or join up with any of the groups of Indians they met on the trail through the woods. Sometimes the Indian would stop to talk while the other Indians fastened their eyes on Brice and fingered their tomahawks. They wanted to kill him, but the man who'd taken him captive always shook his head as he pointed to first Brice and then himself.

Brice half-closed his eyes and pretended to be too near exhaustion to even care what his fate might be, but he grabbed on to every word he knew and turned the unfamiliar words over in his mind to try to understand what the warriors were saying. The other Indians called his captor Lone Hawk. That seemed to fit the man since, even while his friends were there beside him on the trail, his eyes were looking beyond to the woods.

When they moved away from the trail deeper into the forest, the only sounds between them were their grunting breaths as they pushed their way through the ever-deepening snow. Near the end of the first day, the Indian pulled a coat and a pair of moccasins from the plunder and shoved them at Brice. Without a word, Brice put down his load to put on the coat. When he leaned over to put on the moccasins, blood was soaking through the blanket strips he'd wrapped around his feet after an Indian had taken his shoes during the massacre.

But he had no time to worry about his feet now. He shoved the moccasins on over the blanket wrappings. When he was free again, he'd tend to them. First he had to be free.

By the end of the second day they were completely alone in the wilderness. No more Indians passed their way, and they saw no signs of camps. Lone Hawk was moving west as if guided by an inner sense of urgency. Brice followed without speaking and did his best to keep his mind trained on the direction they were moving even when the clouds and trees hid the sun and stars.

When they made camp the second night, Brice gathered wood and made the fire the way the Indians had taught him so many years ago. He cooked the rabbit the Indian had shot with his bow earlier in the day, and cleared away the snow and gathered branches for their beds.

"You make good Indian." Lone Hawk spoke the first words between them since they'd left Frenchtown. Then he added as though Brice would be glad to hear the words, "You prove brave, my tribe adopt you. You won't have to be slave."

Brice raised his eyes to stare across the fire at him. Just three days ago, this man and his kind had gone through Frenchtown, striking down helpless men without mercy. As Brice thought of the wounded men struggling to the doors of the burning houses only to be struck down by the tomahawk of a waiting Indian, it was all he could do to stay crouched there and not spring across the fire at the Indian.

The Indian smiled slowly. "You have much anger."

Brice didn't lower his eyes. "Much."

"White man worry too much about the dead. Dead are dead."

"Does the red man forget his dead?" It had been so long since Brice had spoken that his voice sounded strange to his ears.

"Red man, white man not the same." The Indian narrowed his eyes and stared at Brice. "You be red man, you might live. Be white man, you die."

Brice just stared back at him without speaking.

After a long moment, the Indian pointed at one of the piles of branches. "Sleep."

Brice obediently lay down. Lone Hawk settled on his own bed. He kept his hand closed around the handle of his tomahawk. Brice closed his eyes and breathed in and out slowly and evenly.

He had the feeling they would reach Lone Hawk's village the next day. Then the odds would be against his ever making it out of the woods alive. Brice didn't doubt the Indian meant to give him a chance to live, but it wasn't easy for a white man to prove worthy of becoming a red man. There would be gauntlets to run and other tests of his endurance and bravery.

Brice opened his eyes a slit. The Indian was just a fuzzy shape in the flickering firelight. The man might be asleep, but Brice thought he was too still, like a cat tensed ready to spring on a bird. Brice sat up to test him. Slowly he leaned over to place another piece of wood on the fire. Lone Hawk's hand tightened around the tomahawk as he raised it a bit off the ground.

Brice settled back down on the branches. He was in no hurry, but before the sun came up he or the Indian would be dead.

While the night deepened, Brice thought of Kerns and how the boy had looked death right in the eye and reached for his Lord's hand to lead him across the divide. Brice stared up toward treetops so thick he couldn't spot a single star. He wished he'd asked Seth more about praying, because there in the deep of the night as he waited and the screams of the wounded men burning in the houses echoed in his mind, he felt the need for prayer.

He tried saying prayer words in his mind, but they just circled in his head and found no wings. Perhaps he was praying for the wrong thing. As Lone Hawk had said, the dead were dead. Nothing he or prayer could do to change that. He could pray for the prisoners who had been marched away. He even thought a prayer for Hope even though he figured the old woodsman had probably already found some way to slip away from the British. Hope had chafed even under the rules of the militia. He'd make a poor prisoner.

It was hard for Brice to think of Gabrielle as Hope's child. Hope was a wild thing ruled by the woods and his desires. Then Brice remembered Gabrielle's eyes and the deep well of trusting innocence there that only the very young ever have. That kind of innocence should have been destroyed long before she even joined the Shakers.

So perhaps she was more like a wild thing than he'd thought. A wild thing born without a fear of the world, but with a special trust in the goodness of all things and all people. At least until he'd brought the doubts of the world to her. Had it been right for him to disturb her innocence? The old sister had thought not. In her eyes, Brice had brought discord and evil into the Shaker village.

But Brice had no wish to ever do anything to harm Gabrielle. He loved her. Even here lost in this wilderness, his love for her sprang up fresh and strong inside him like an ever-flowing spring. She was life to him.

He whispered the words in his head and Gabrielle was there in his mind as she'd been the last time he'd seen her. He'd felt like an intruder as he watched her come to her private place to pray. She was afraid when he stopped her. Not of him but of the feelings within herself. Then when he put his arms around her, she yielded so sweetly, lifting her lips up to meet his.

She loved him. She admitted it. Yet her words had been sure and determined when she sent him away, but Brice couldn't accept those words as final. He would make her send him away again and again if he lived to return to Kentucky. She didn't belong with the Shakers. She belonged with him.

It had been months since he'd seen her, but her image hadn't faded in his mind. He could call her forth and she became almost real before his eyes. This night as he lay in the darkness she felt even closer to him than usual.

What was it Nathan had said the day of the massacre? "She's praying for us. I always knew when she prayed for me."

And Brice understood now what he meant. He felt her prayers for him reaching out to the Lord when he could find no words to pray himself.

Poor Nathan. Her prayers hadn't saved him. Brice looked out of the corner of his eye toward Lone Hawk. He could only hope Gabrielle's prayers would do him more good.

The Indian wasn't asleep. He was waiting just as Brice was

for the moment to come between them. Brice wondered if he too was praying or if he was simply lying there anticipating burying his tomahawk in Brice's head as further proof of his bravery.

Brice shut away all thoughts of Gabrielle as he practiced in his mind what he was going to do in the next few minutes just as he did before he made the first cut with his lancet. When he had the first move clear in his mind, he even pushed that aside. In order to survive, he had to be ready to react instinctively to whatever happened.

Then it was time. The moment was no different from the last, but Brice knew the time had come.

He sprang across the dying embers of the fire and landed on top of the Indian. Lone Hawk was ready. Brice twisted to the left and the Indian's tomahawk bit deeply into Brice's shoulder. The Indian tried to pull it back to strike again, but Brice knocked his arm down against a branch. The tomahawk slid out of the Indian's hand and disappeared in the snow.

Brice's blood splattered down on Lone Hawk as they grappled in the dark. They were closely matched in strength, and if Brice had given in to the pain of his shoulder, Lone Hawk would have won easily. Instead Brice fought as if he were whole. Their breaths came in grunts and gasps as they rolled about in the snow with first one and then the other taking the advantage.

Then the Indian had his knife out of his belt, and Brice felt the point of the blade on the skin of his neck. He shifted away from it and threw his body against Lone Hawk's arm. Brice's sudden movement to the side caught the Indian by surprise when he thought he'd already won the battle. Brice came down hard on Lone Hawk's arm and drove the knife into the Indian's chest.

Lone Hawk made one last effort to shove Brice off of him, but the knife had gone deep. He fell limply back on the snow.

Brice kept his grip on the Indian as strong as ever until he was sure Lone Hawk was playing no tricks. Then Brice sat back on his heels and drew in a long breath. Finally he took hold of the hilt of the knife and pulled it out of the Indian's chest with one clean jerk. He wiped the blood off in the snow and stuck the knife in his belt before he put his ear close to the Indian's mouth and then to his chest. The man was breathing shallowly, but his heartbeat was strong. He had a chance of surviving the wound.

Surviving to kill more. Brice took the knife back out of his belt and held it above the Indian's heart. Then slowly Brice put the knife back in his belt.

He tore strips off a blanket and quickly tied Lone Hawk's hands and feet. The man was surely too severely wounded to lunge at Brice, but if Lone Hawk regained consciousness, Brice had no doubt he would try.

Brice built up the fire. Then in the flickering light of the flames, he pulled his shirt back and probed his own wound with his fingers. It was to the bone. The shock and the cold kept the pain at bay, but blood was streaming down his chest. Already he felt a little lightheaded. He almost smiled thinking that if he had a fever he'd surely survive with all the impurities in his blood leaving his body so freely.

All traces of a smile faded away. If he had any chance of walking out of this wilderness, he'd have to stop the bleeding. He wished for his bag of medicines, but they hadn't been part of

Lone Hawk's plunder. Awkwardly with one hand, Brice bound up the wound as tightly as possible. At first light he'd search the woods for the right kind of bark to make a poultice.

With his good arm, he pulled Lone Hawk back up on the branch bed. The Indian's wound was seeping blood. Brice wrapped a strip of blanket around the Indian's chest and tied it tightly. Then he covered him with one of the coats before he went through the Indian's plunder from Frenchtown. He laid aside a portion of the Indian's corn and tucked the pouch holding the rest of it inside his shirt.

Brice took the Indian's tomahawk and gun to his side of the fire and put them under his blanket. He didn't lie down to sleep but sat up and fed the fire to keep away the cold while he waited for first light.

Dawn was just sneaking fingers of gray light in under the trees when Brice left the Indian to find wood and something to treat his wound. The sun was up when he came back into camp warily, but Lone Hawk didn't rouse. Brice built up the fire and melted snow in the pot before adding the bits of bark and the one chip of root he'd been able to dig out of the frozen, snow-covered ground.

While he stirred the mixture, he felt the Indian's eyes on him, but he didn't look up at him. When the bitter brew was hot, Brice poured some into a cup and faced the Indian. The bindings on his hands and feet were tight and secure. He approached him carefully and offered him the drink. Lone Hawk raised his head and let Brice pour the hot liquid into his mouth. Brice backed away and drank the rest himself.

Lone Hawk lay back and stared at Brice with narrowed eyes. "White man not brave enough to kill Lone Hawk. White man coward."

"Our fight is done, Lone Hawk. There's no reason to kill you now. I'm leaving."

"Lone Hawk follow."

"No. You'll need to get to your village while you have the strength."

"Lone Hawk send red brothers after you."

"That's a chance I'll have to take." Brice piled more wood on the fire and picked up his pack. "I'll leave the brew for you." Brice pulled out the Indian's knife and with a quick motion cut through the strips that bound the Indian's hands.

"No need white man's medicine." Lone Hawk started to push himself up off the ground.

"Stay there. I could still kill you."

The Indian made a sound of contempt. "White man got no stomach for killing." But he stayed where he was.

"I'll kill you if I have to," Brice said softly, not taking his eyes off the Indian.

"You take gun and knife and tomahawk. White man let bear and wolf kill for him."

Brice didn't say anything as he backed slowly away from Lone Hawk until he was sure the man wasn't going to try to lunge across the fire after him. Then he turned and trotted away from their camp. Just before he got out of sight, Brice turned back and with his good arm he threw the tomahawk into a tree some distance from where Lone Hawk lay.

"Lone Hawk not forget," the Indian called after him.

But Brice wasn't sure what it was Lone Hawk wouldn't forget. The tomahawk or the promise to come after Brice. Brice left the camp behind in a few steps. He couldn't worry about Lone Hawk. He had to stay on his feet and find the

311

way out of this snowy wilderness without stumbling across any other Indian warriors.

By the middle of the day, the pain in his shoulder raged through his whole body until everything around him seemed unreal. All he knew was the pain. He struggled to keep enough of his wits about him to stay moving to the south. Always to the south, but sometimes he came to himself and realized he'd walked a circle. Each time he shook his head to clear his thinking, faced south, and kept moving. He had to keep moving or die.

At the end of the second day or what Brice thought was the second day, darkness caught him unprepared. He hadn't scouted out a good spot to make camp or even gathered any wood for a fire. Brice sank down in the snow and leaned back against a tree. He ordered himself to get up and cut pine limbs for a bed, but his body didn't respond.

It was so cold and so dark. Not just in the woods around him but inside him too. The pain from his shoulder penetrated every inch of his body and used up his last bit of strength. Brice wondered if Lone Hawk had made it to his village or if he too was sitting in the dark waiting for death.

Brice had seen many people die. Too many. But he'd never thought about his own breath stopping. A sharp sorrow pierced his heart as he thought about never seeing Gabrielle again. Was she praying for him now? Did she really love him or had he only imagined that? He wanted to call up her image, to have her there in his mind while he was breathing his last, but he could not. She was just a shadowy image far from him, away through the trees. It didn't seem right that she wouldn't come close to him in his dying moments.

He shut his eyes, but then pushed them back open. If he

went to sleep, he'd surely freeze. Then he wasn't sure whether he was asleep or awake as he stared out through the trees to see another shadow drift up beside Gabrielle. Hallucinations. He'd known many patients to have them when death lingered around them.

He shook his head and Gabrielle disappeared, but the other shadow stayed and came closer. Brice leaned forward. It was Bates or maybe Kerns and he was beckoning to him. But they were both dead. His mind was still clear enough to remember that. Maybe that was it. One of them had come to guide him over to the land of the dead with them.

Brice rose to follow the boy. Bates, he thought one minute, and Kerns, the next. He wasn't sure if his whole body followed or if only his spirit struggled up off the ground. But when he looked over his shoulder, there was nothing by the tree and the pain stayed with him. If he had died, wouldn't the pain be gone?

He followed the shadow in front of him. It seemed important to catch up with Nathan. He was pretty sure it was Nathan this time. He tried to walk faster and ran into a limb. The shadow stopped and waited until Brice started walking again before it drifted on ahead of him.

All at once the shadowy figure of the boy was gone. Brice stood very still and searched for some sight of the boy, but there was nothing but trees and snow. But not as many trees. Moonlight drifted down into the woods and pushed back the darkness. It was a moment before Brice realized what the bulky dark shape in front of him was. Even after he recognized the outline of a cabin, he wondered if it too was a hallucination like the boy. Any second he'd awaken and be leaning against the tree in the woods waiting for death's dark horse to come for him.

Until then he'd stay in the dream. He climbed the steps and pushed open the cabin door. The cabin smelled of wild animals. Brice's toe hit something soft in the darkness and the musty odor of pine needles rose up to his nose. He eased himself down on the bed. Just before he lost consciousness, he wondered if he'd wake up in paradise.

Mice running across his feet woke him the next morning. Slowly Brice pulled himself up to a sitting position, and the mice scattered and disappeared through the holes in the chinks of the logs. He was in a cabin, so what had happened the night before hadn't been all a hallucination. The cabin was real.

The cabin showed no sign that anybody had been there for a good while, maybe even before winter set in. Dirt lay thick in the cabin, and vines, now dead and frozen, had crept into the cabin from the outside to grow over a stack of wood by the fireplace. A small sack hung from one of the rafters in the middle of the room.

Brice stood up, took down the sack, and opened it. Then just to prove to himself it was real, he stuck his hand into the ground corn and let it fall off his fingers. No man would go off and leave a sack of corn meal. Not unless he died.

Brice put the sack on the floor and built a fire. Whatever had happened to the other man didn't matter now. Brice had been given a chance to live. It didn't even matter if his dream last night had been real or if he'd just stumbled on the cabin by blind luck. He was here. He had a sack of meal, and he was going to live.

He melted snow and made a thin gruel in the dusty pot that hung beside the fireplace. He ate slowly and let his body draw strength from the warmth of the food. Then he pulled the bandage away from his wound. It was bad. He'd cut off men's arms with wounds no worse.

He looked at it a long time before he laid the blade of Lone Hawk's scalping knife in the fire. He hung the sack of meal back up before going outside to break up some limbs for the fire and bring in more snow for the pot. Once he was ready, he barred the door. Then he sat down in front of the fire and waited.

When the knife blade was white hot, he carefully picked the knife out of the coals with his good hand and lay down on the floor. With no hesitation, he placed the flat side of the blade on his wound and held it there until everything went black.

28

As winter slowly passed at the Shaker village, the vision stayed with Gabrielle, always the same. Men dying in the snow. A few times late at night when it would give her no peace, she tried to step further into the vision to know more, but the gift of knowing could not be forced.

She never doubted what she saw had happened. Nathan was dead, and she remembered the boy she'd known and loved. Her sadness at the thought of him being gone forevermore was deepened by the knowledge that the last time she'd seen him, she'd hurt him by refusing his love. If only he could have loved her like a sister.

If only she could love Brice Scott like a brother. But his face was burned into her mind and her heart ran after him. Now she couldn't be sure if he lived or not. She might never know. They had parted, gone their separate paths as she had insisted they must.

She yearned for the gift of knowing to reveal what had happened to the man she loved, while at the same time she held it away, not sure she could bear the truth. Sometimes she thought she might step into insanity like poor Sister Wilma, who wandered about the village, her kerchief askew, talking to herself.

At times Gabrielle thought her heart might burst if she didn't talk to someone about the pain growing there, but there was no one. She sometimes even considered walking with Sister Wilma and talking to her just so she could have the words out in the air, but there were too many eyes still spying on Gabrielle, waiting for her to make another misstep.

Gabrielle found it hard to even speak of everyday matters with any of the sisters. She did her duties and taught the little girls their lessons. She ate what was put on her plate with no interest in what that might be and took part in the meetings as expected, but her voice no longer sang out joyfully as it once had.

She had been drawn into a vision of death. It darkened everything about her.

When the shadows under Gabrielle's eyes deepened, Sister Mercy took her aside. They sat in the same room where Gabrielle had so often sought Sister Mercy's counsel, and where Sister Mercy had pulled away from her when Gabrielle had admitted to her worldly thoughts about the doctor. At the time, Gabrielle had believed her thoughts were wrong. Now she was no longer sure.

"Sit down, Sister Gabrielle," Sister Mercy said.

There was none of the closeness that had once been between the two of them. Gabrielle had missed it when she'd first been put under constant supervision. She'd chafed against Sister Helen's presence at her side every moment, and ached for the reassurance of one of Sister Mercy's smiles. But the smile hadn't come. Nor had the forgiveness. Her disappointment in Gabrielle had been too great.

Now it was as if they were no longer the same two people who'd once closeted themselves in this room. The winds of the world had blown on Gabrielle and soiled her spirit in the eyes of Sister Mercy.

Gabrielle sat down obediently.

Sister Mercy studied her for a long moment before she said, "You do not look well, Sister Gabrielle, and I have been told you move about at night when you should be sleeping. Do you have a need to talk about something bothering you?"

"Yea, it is true I have not been sleeping as I should, Sister Mercy," Gabrielle said quietly. She had no intention of making any sort of confession of her thoughts. Not and chance Sister Helen's constant presence by her side once more. "It is nothing to be concerned about."

"It is my duty to concern myself with the welfare of all the sisters under my watch." Sister Mercy tapped her fingers on the table for a moment. "You seem to be weighted down by some burden, Sister Gabrielle."

Gabrielle kept her head bowed. Her eyes settled on the scar on her hand from the burn the doctor had treated. His hands had been so gentle.

When Gabrielle didn't speak, Sister Mercy went on. "Perhaps it is guilt over an unconfessed sin. You need only tell me your problem to take the weight of it away from your spirit."

Again Gabrielle did not answer or look up.

Sister Mercy sighed. "You have changed, Sister Gabrielle. I worry that ye have lost sight of the truth."

"Nay, it is rather that I know too much of the truth."

Gabrielle regretted her words at once. She had no desire to share her vision with Sister Mercy.

"What do you mean?" Sister Mercy asked sharply. When Gabrielle didn't respond at once, she demanded, "Look at me."

Gabrielle raised her head and looked at Sister Mercy's mouth but not her eyes. Sister Mercy said, "You have seen a vision."

"Yea," Gabrielle admitted. "A vision of death."

"For one of our society?" Sister Mercy asked with a touch of dread in her voice.

"Nay. For the army that went to the North against the British."

Sister Mercy let out a breath of relief. "You know we have nothing to do with wars and battles of the world. Ye need not worry yourself over such a vision. Men of the world always die in wars."

"Should we not have compassion?"

"Of course," Sister Mercy said quickly. "But we must continue with the duties Mother Ann has assigned us. Those of the world have chosen their paths, and we have chosen ours."

"Nathan is dead." The words slipped out of Gabrielle's mouth. She had not intended to say them aloud.

Sister Mercy frowned and shut her eyes for a moment before she said, "He too chose his path, Sister Gabrielle. He could have stayed here and had many happy years of service to the Lord. Perhaps it was the Eternal Father's punishment of his sins that doomed him to die while yet so young."

Gabrielle wanted to bend her head again and look at the scar on her hand in her lap, but instead she shifted her eyes to a spot on the wall over Sister Mercy's left shoulder.

After a long moment, Sister Mercy said, "It is surely a blessing from Mother Ann this gift of knowing you possess, Sister Gabrielle. But so too are the gifts to be simple and free from worry. The gift to trust in the goodness of the Lord and his sure providence. Those were gifts ye possessed in abundance only a short while ago, and yet now ye seem to have quenched the spirit that brought you those gifts."

The silence in the room between them was so complete that Gabrielle heard the soft rustle of a sister's skirt as she passed in the hall outside the closed door. Once Gabrielle would have promised to bend her spirit to the way Sister Mercy said was right. Once she would have promised to try to capture the simple freedom the Believers sought in their songs and prayers. But now she wasn't sure if any Believer ever knew freedom.

At last Sister Mercy cleared her throat and said, "Have you prayed for Mother Ann's love and blessings?"

"I have prayed," Gabrielle answered.

"Then you must pray more. Mother Ann has blessed you with many gifts. Perhaps this time of spiritual darkness is her way of strengthening you for some struggle you may face in the future. We cannot know. We can only accept the trials that come our way and strive to maintain our peace and faith. I too will pray for you, Sister Gabrielle."

"I need your prayers," Gabrielle whispered. She needed someone's prayers because her own seemed so empty lately.

Sister Mercy's voice softened. "Perhaps the vision is a false one, my child."

"I pray it so, but I fear that is a prayer that will not be answered. It is real. The gift does not lie."

It was near March before proof of the truth of her vision came to their village. Gabrielle was in the hallway when Sister Helen brought the news to Sister Mercy. She'd heard it from a visitor from the town.

Sister Mercy called to Gabrielle. "Sister Gabrielle, you may be interested in Sister Helen's news. The army that went to the North from here was defeated just as your vision revealed to you."

"Are there survivors?" Gabrielle's heart almost stopped beating as she waited for the answer.

"Some were taken prisoner," Sister Helen said, eager to be the one to tell. "But very few among the wounded at a place called the River Raisen. Those of the world are calling it a massacre."

"Such things have little to do with us," Sister Mercy said. "We have chosen to live in peace with our fellow man as all should do. Then there would not be such horrors."

Gabrielle bowed her head and turned away.

"It's almost time for meeting," Sister Helen called after her.

Gabrielle longed to be by herself, but as she turned to beg Sister Mercy's permission to miss meeting, she met Sister Helen's eyes. There was triumph there. Gabrielle's back stiffened, and when the bell started tolling, she followed the older sisters out to begin the walk to the meetinghouse.

As she moved her mouth in the shape of the words of the gathering song, she saw Brice's face before her as it had looked in the vision. Then suddenly the vision was shifting. The bodies in the snow were gone and only Brice remained.

Still his face was the same as though nothing could ever take the cruel look from his eyes again.

He was alive. If he had died, she would have known just as she knew Nathan was dead. He had to be alive. Maybe he was even now on his way back to his cabin. She wanted to drop out of the line of sisters and seek her quiet place in the woods to pray for him.

But even as she had the thought, Sister Helen stepped over closer to Gabrielle as they entered the meetinghouse. Gabrielle tried to ease away from her, but Sister Helen stayed by her side through their silent prayer and opening song.

Gabrielle looked straight ahead and pretended she wasn't there. The meeting wouldn't last forever. She could surely endure Sister Helen's presence that long after all the months she'd had to abide her presence at her side.

When Elder Caleb was through speaking and it was time to labor the songs, Gabrielle found a bench in the corner. She had no strength for the exercises.

Sister Helen followed her and sat down beside her. "Why are you not joining in the song, Sister Gabrielle?"

"I do not feel well this evening," Gabrielle said.

"That's too bad," Sister Helen said with a smile that belied her words of sympathy. "Perhaps I should make you a tonic."

Gabrielle bent her head. "A tonic might help."

"I'll work on it tomorrow," Sister Helen said, then paused a moment before going on. "Ye haven't had a gift of song for many months, Sister Gabrielle. Not since last summer if I recall correctly. Isn't that right?"

"I don't remember. I suppose it is if ye say it is."

"Why do ye think that is? Ye who have been so blessed with so many gifts of the spirit."

Suddenly Gabrielle was wary. Sister Helen was leading up to something, ready to catch Gabrielle in some wrong. She said quietly, "One can't force gifts of the spirit, Sister Helen."

"Ye speak the truth. Especially if the spirit has deserted one."

Gabrielle turned her head to look at Sister Helen. Were the woman's words true? Gabrielle had been in a dark valley for a long time, and she could see no paths that led out. Yet in spite of the darkness that kept her from praying and singing as she once had, she'd thought it was her face, her spirit that had gotten hidden in the fog of her troubles. She had never doubted the Lord's spirit was there as strong as ever if only she could reach out in the right direction. She'd been sure he would help her find the way out of the valley into the sunshine of his love once more and that love would scatter her darkness.

Again there was triumph in Sister Helen's eyes. It gave her pleasure to see Gabrielle brought low. Gabrielle knew she should stay silent and not answer meanness with more meanness. Yet she said, "Ye have not had a gift of song for even longer, Sister Helen."

Sister Helen's eyes narrowed, and her mouth tightened into a hard line. "Mother Ann has given us different gifts," she said.

"Yea," Gabrielle answered softly.

Sister Helen spoke sharply. "At least I have never gone to the woods to meet a man."

Gabrielle turned her eyes back to her hands in her lap. "I have paid my penance."

"Outwardly, perhaps," Sister Helen said. "But inside ye mourn for him."

Gabrielle started to speak, but Sister Helen stopped her. "Don't try to fool me with your lies the way you do Sister Mercy. I've seen enough of the world to know worldly thoughts."

"Ye cannot read my thoughts."

"But I can read your eyes, Sister Gabrielle. You know Dr. Scott went to the North with the army and that is why you don't feel like singing this night. Will ye add to your sin by denying that?"

"Nay, I deny nothing. My heart is burdened for all who died."

Sister Helen smiled again. "Thy compassion is touching, Sister Gabrielle, but I think it is the passion ye feel for the man of the world that is causing ye the most pain."

Gabrielle said nothing, and Sister Helen went on. "Why do you not answer me? Is it because ye know I speak the truth?"

"I wouldn't wish to have words of conflict disturb the peace of the meeting."

"If ye cared about the meeting, ye would be singing."

"Then I will sing." Singing would be easier than listening to Sister Helen. Gabrielle started to stand up, but Sister Helen reached out and held her arm.

"Just one more thing, Sister Gabrielle," she said. "If the spirit has left ye, maybe you should leave the Believers. It is harmful for those who doubt our truths to be among us."

"What do you mean?"

"Ye are not yet a full member of our society. You can't sign the covenant until you are twenty-one. It wouldn't be hard for you to leave."

Gabrielle felt weak. She couldn't leave the Believers. She

belonged here. "I am a Believer whether I have signed the full covenant or not, Sister Helen." But even as she spoke the words, she knew she'd been fighting the thought of leaving the Believers ever since she'd left Brice in the woods months ago.

Gabrielle pulled her arm away from Sister Helen's hold and joined the other sisters in the middle of the floor. She began to move through the exercise, forcing her mind to concentrate on each and every step.

As Gabrielle walked back to her room after the meeting, she thought how often lately she'd felt this same relief when the last song and prayer were finished at meeting. She got ready for bed without a word to the two other sisters who shared her room now, for while Sister Mercy had agreed to allow Gabrielle to teach again, she no longer trusted her to watch over the younger sisters at night.

Gabrielle knelt on the cold bare floor and quickly said her night prayers before lying down on the narrow bed. She pulled the quilt up under her chin and waited for sleep to rest her mind, but sleep eluded her. Thoughts crashed through her mind like a river swollen out of its banks by heavy spring rains.

At first her thoughts jumped from one thing to another with no order or reason. Then as usual at night, Brice was in her mind. She saw his face as it had looked the first time she'd seen him when he ran into the fire to save Nathan, and later the gentleness in his eyes when he called her young sister. She touched her hand that had been burned and knew the same tremble inside her she'd known then at his touch.

Then she hadn't recognized the love growing in her heart for him. Even later when she went to his cabin after Becca, she tried to deny the strength of her feelings for him. She'd assured them both it was a passing thing, nothing more than a stumbling block in her path. She'd thought she could stand up and continue on her way through life as she'd always planned. She belonged with the Shakers. She was a Believer.

Ever since she and her mother had joined the Society of Believers, she'd been sure of that. She was a Believer. Then why had so much confusion fogged her thinking these last few months? A bit of fear crept into her heart as she looked straight into that confusion. She was not sure she was ready to face the questions she'd avoided for so long, but there would be no more putting them off. This night she would seek the truth of what she really believed.

First there was the Eternal Father. She couldn't doubt her faith in him, for she knew he was there even through the darkness that had settled around her of late. Then there was the Christ, a man without sin of any kind who'd walked on the earth and offered compassion and love to all around him and even now these many centuries later to Gabrielle. *God is love.* That was the first Bible verse her grandmother had taught her many years before in Virginia.

And finally there was Mother Ann, the spiritual daughter of God who had established the first communities of Believers and the rules of behavior that were to guide them in making those communities a heaven on earth, free from all worldly sin. Mother Ann had left them instructions before she'd gone to be with the Eternal Father. They were to love one another only as brothers and sisters. Men and women were to stay apart except during meeting, and it was a sin to commit matrimony. There were more rules of behavior. Many of them, but Gabrielle did not resent the rules of behavior.

She thought of the love she had for her sisters and brethren there at Harmony Hill. It was good. Not that their life was without problems, but the love was there and the peace of a simple, contented life for many among the Believers. Still it wasn't so for everyone who came into the Shakers' community, and she had to admit it was no longer so for her. She knew a different kind of love now. Her love for Brice tore at her and tortured her as it pulled her away from those she considered her family. Her Shaker brothers and sisters told her that love was wrong, but she no longer believed that in her heart.

Suddenly the vision of death was before her. Now it was even more terrible because she could no longer even hope that it wasn't true. Without a sound, she slipped from her bed and went to the window. The snow was gone. Soon the grass would turn green and it would be time for planting. There was comfort in the sameness of the seasons each year. Planting, growing, harvesting, and the winter rest when the land readied itself for more planting.

Gabrielle looked beyond the clearing around their village to the shadow of the trees. The moon was bright and she wished she could slip out of the house and go find her quiet place in the woods to pray. But Sister Mercy had forbidden it.

That was where she'd last seen the doctor. He'd been waiting for her that night. Would he ever wait for her there again, and if he did, would she go with him?

After a long time she crept back to bed. She could not leave the Believers. One year couldn't change the direction of a whole life. But she wasn't sure she'd ever find the path to climb out of this valley of darkness to the peace of the mountaintop. She began reciting Psalm 23 in her mind. *Yea, though I walk through the valley of the shadow of death, I will fear no evil: for thou art with me; thy rod and thy staff they comfort me.*

29

Spring 1813

Brice lost track of the days. At first he'd been too sick to know night from day. But somehow he had kept a fire burning in the cabin's fireplace, and before the sack of meal was gone, he'd fought off the fever and begun to heal.

Now as he tramped through the woods around the cabin checking the snares he'd made, he tried to decide what month it was. Finding food and firewood had taken all his strength for weeks, but this morning he'd gone almost his complete circle back to the cabin with the pain in his shoulder nothing more than a mild irritation. Even his legs felt strong and fresh, not weighted down by fatigue and sickness. Maybe it was the new warmth in the air that filled him with fresh energy. Winter was surely on the way out since underfoot the snow was melting and the tree buds were beginning to swell. It had to be late March or early April.

He took a rabbit out of his last snare and headed back to

cook his breakfast. The cabin was hard to see among the trees until he came right out on it. Bare arms of vines had crept up over the logs, and in the summer when they leafed out, a person might easily pass by it without noticing it there at all. He'd thought he might come across a body or bones when he first explored around the cabin, but he found nothing to show what kind of man had built it and lived there and left behind his sack of cornmeal.

Brice could barely remember the dream that had led him there. In fact, added to all the dreams that had whirled around him while he fought the fever, he wasn't sure if anything he remembered was real. He could have stumbled across the cabin and then had the dream about Nathan. He'd dreamed about him often enough since then. And not only Nathan, but Seth as well. And always Gabrielle danced through his mind.

Sometimes when he had awakened in front of the fire with his fever raging, he had imagined her there with him. Only it wasn't this cabin. They were both in his cabin back in Kentucky, and the past was gone from them. He was no longer haunted by the sights he'd seen with the army, and she no longer followed after the Shaker way.

As Brice skinned and cleaned the rabbit outside the cabin, he shut his mind to the hope in those dreams. The past could never be completely left behind. It wound around them, shaping them for the future.

Above his head, the sky was a clear blue. It hadn't snowed for more than a week. Spring was definitely coming to the woods and with the thaw, the Indians would begin to come away from their winter camps and start hunting farther afield.

Brice put the rabbit in his iron pot over the fire. The winter rabbit was scrawny, hardly fit to eat, but it was food. Tonight at dusk he'd check his traps again. Then at daybreak, he'd leave this cabin and head south.

As the smell of rabbit stew filled the air, a hunger sprang up in Brice, but it wasn't a hunger the meat could satisfy. He hungered for the sight of Gabrielle. And not just in his mind as he'd pulled her up in his thoughts in the months since he'd left Kentucky.

She would have changed. No one lived almost a year without changing. He could only hope she hadn't completely shut him away from her thoughts and that she would listen when he returned to the Shaker village. He shut his eyes and imagined her in his arms, and he wished Kerns were there with him to teach him how to pray a better prayer so that the Lord might grant him this desire of his heart.

What was it the boy had told him? That anybody could talk to the Lord. That it was as easy as getting up in the morning and saying, "Good morning, Lord."

It couldn't hurt to give it a try. The last few weeks he'd felt the need to talk to someone and not just to himself. It was as if someone kept poking him and urging him to do it now. But no one was there and he wasn't sure what to do.

All his life he'd been told there was a God and some of the time he'd believed it. But once he'd outgrown the prayers his mother had taught him, he'd stopped talking to the Lord. He never had any reason to believe God would listen to him. Maybe to others, but not to him.

In churches the preachers prayed and Brice had let their words roll through his ears without paying them much notice. Seth had talked about the Lord and the Bible, and Brice had seen the boy's faith in his words. Brice's mother and Jemma had both trusted the Lord, and after he watched them die, he had fervently hoped heaven was real and all they had expected.

But he'd never thought about the Lord or heaven for himself. He'd been too busy, too sure he could do everything on his own. But now it was as if someone was hovering there beside him, waiting for him to look around and admit that maybe he couldn't. Maybe it was time for him to stop listening to others' prayers and start talking his own.

Brice looked up toward the ceiling and spoke out loud. "All right, Lord." His voice cracked and sounded rusty to his ears. He didn't know whether it was because he hadn't said anything aloud for weeks or because he felt funny talking out loud to the Lord.

Brice could see Seth smiling at him in his mind. He imagined him saying, "Go on, Dr. Scott. You might as well go ahead and spit it out. The Lord knows what you're thinking already anyhow."

So he did just spit it out. He pretended like the Lord was sitting down on the other side of him there in front of the fireplace. He hoped the Lord wouldn't mind too much that he sometimes saw Seth's face as he talked.

"I've never been much for praying up till now, Lord, but I thank you for this rabbit you've provided for me. And I thank you that I'm alive to eat it. I don't really know why that's so. Why I'm still breathing when so many others aren't, but if you have a reason for it, I'll do my best to follow through. I don't know that I can understand your ways, so you'll have to be pretty plain with me to show me what you want. I know you're there. I've watched you take people I thought would get well, and I've watched you heal people when I didn't think they'd make it through the night. So I've never denied you're there. Not completely. I just haven't ever known what you wanted me to do about it. I'm not sure I do now, but I'm ready to listen and pay attention if you want to tell me."

Brice fell silent for a minute and did that very thing. Listened. The fire snapped. Snow melted and dripped off the eaves. A crow cawed in the distance. No words came into the silence. But in the silence was peace.

"Thank you, Lord." Again Brice was silent for a moment before he went on. "In the morning I'm going south. Watch over me and let me make it back to Gabrielle. I don't know if that's something I should pray about or not, taking Gabrielle away from the Shakers, but if Seth was right, you already know what I'm feeling."

At Harmony Hill spring had touched its finger of fresh life all around. The grass was greening, and the first flowers were proudly holding up their blooms. Little leaves struggled out of buds to open up in the warm sunshine. The Believers welcomed the spring with their usual steady calm, glad the growing season was near so they could put their hands to better use in working. Crops weren't the only things growing this spring. Buildings were being started to make room for new converts.

Even with the spring departures of those who had only pretended to be converts for the winter, their number had grown. While last year after the harvest barn had burned there'd been some worry among the Believers, this spring seemed to bring with it a sure promise of prosperity and increased blessings from Mother Ann.

But for Gabrielle it was as if spring had not come. Winter stayed in her heart with its cold and dark. The school session was over. The children were needed to help with the planting. Gabrielle had been assigned to the laundry duty. Always before it had been one of her least favorite duties, but now she was glad to be in the laundry house. The splashing of the water and the slap of the clothes being scrubbed made talk among the sisters difficult and often impossible.

Gabrielle was glad. She didn't want to talk to anyone. No longer did she try to make newcomers to the Believers welcome. When Sister Mercy took her to task for not showing the proper love for her new sisters and brothers at the meetings, Gabrielle could only nod and admit her wrong.

The vision stayed in her mind. Sometimes it shifted a bit, and a new scene tried to flash before her eyes. But always something kept her from seeing clearly. Then the old vision of death would return.

Visitors from the world had told them many of the men who'd been taken prisoners in the war in the Northwest had returned to Kentucky, but many had not. No names of survivors reached Gabrielle's ears. There was no reason for them to. The Believers had no part in the war. Even if the brethren who went out among the world to sell seeds heard news of the men, Gabrielle couldn't ask, for Sister Helen or Sister Mercy would be sure to know and bring it before the elders and eldresses. Gabrielle couldn't bear the thought of perhaps being put under constant supervision once more.

So she still knew nothing about Brice other than what her vision had revealed to her. He was at the River Raisen during the massacre, and she held tightly to the belief he was alive. But she knew not where. He might even be at his cabin just a few miles away, but she could not imagine him there. Not even when she tried to call forth her gift of knowing. She could see him in no place. Only his face with the cruel lines around his eyes.

More than once she thought of slipping away and going to his cabin, but she pushed the thought away as quickly as it came. She'd made a decision to stay on the path she'd vowed to follow almost seven years before. She had to forget the doctor and push his worldliness away from her. She had no reason to believe he would seek her out again if he did return, and even if he did, she'd have to send him away again just as she had the last time.

So she tried to forget the doctor, but she might as well have tried to forget to breathe. He was a part of her. Even if she never saw him again, his memory and her love for him would go with her to the grave.

That was her sin. The sin that kept her feet from finding the path out of the dark valley and back up onto the mountain. She had promised to give her hands to work and her heart to God. The worldly love of a man kept her from the total commitment that would bring peace back to her spirit.

It was May when he came. Gabrielle was helping with the garden planting, putting beans into a row and carefully covering them with dirt. As soon as she'd opened her eyes that morning, she'd felt an oddness inside her. She'd knelt by her bed and closed her eyes without praying, thinking she might see the reason for the strange feeling in her mind. Nothing had been there but Brice, and he was always in her thoughts.

At first she thought it might be a vision when she straightened up from covering the beans in the row and looked across the way to see the man on the horse in front of the Children's House. It was Brice. She knew him at once even though he was too far away for her to see his face clearly. Gabrielle blinked her eyes and stood perfectly still to allow the vision to melt away. But it was no vision. He was there.

Her knees went weak with relief. He was alive. He had survived her vision of death. Without thinking, she dropped her container of beans, spilling the seeds out on the dirt, and walked out of the garden toward him. She had to see his eyes. She had to touch him and be sure he was real. She didn't think about why he had come or what she would tell him. Her heart and mind were too full of joy to worry about what might happen next.

30

Brice didn't see her until she moved toward him. He'd gone past the other buildings straight to the school because that's where he thought he'd find her. But when the building seemed deserted, he had looked around. That was when he saw the slight figure move away from the others in the plowed field and start toward him.

It was Gabrielle and she was coming to him. The Lord had granted his prayer. She hadn't forgotten him. He could almost feel her love rushing across the distance between them even though he could not yet see the look on her face. His love bounded back toward her.

When Brice dismounted and started toward Gabrielle, Elder Caleb stepped in front of him. "Dr. Scott. We thought perhaps you were dead. We heard of the massacre."

Brice wanted to push the older man roughly to the side, but he didn't. He had waited this long. He could wait a few more minutes. He looked at the elder and said, "Many did die, but by the Lord's grace, I survived."

"For that we shall give thanks," the elder said quietly. "But

336

why are you here? Our request that you not come to our village has not changed. You are not welcome here."

Brice answered just as quietly. "I have come for Gabrielle."

Elder Caleb frowned. "Sister Gabrielle? I think not."

"She's coming away with me." He wished he could be as sure as his words sounded that she would let him sit her up on his horse and depart this place forever. Brice looked over the elder's shoulder to where several sisters were closing in around Gabrielle, shutting her away from him. His heart froze inside him. They were going to try to prevent him from talking to her.

He stepped toward her, but two of the brothers moved up beside him to hold his arms. One of them said, "It is true we don't believe in violence, Dr. Scott, but we will protect our sister."

"I only wish to speak to her," Brice said.

"First we must be assured that our sister wishes to speak to you," the man said.

Elder Caleb had moved away to join the growing number of Shakers around Gabrielle. Brice wanted to knock aside the two men who stood next to him and push through the men and women surrounding Gabrielle. He wanted to grab her and carry her away with him. He sought her eyes, but the Shakers were blocking her from him.

Brice tensed his muscles and the men's grip on his arms tightened. He looked at the man on his left and then the one on his right. He didn't want to fight them. That wasn't why he'd come. He pulled in a deep breath and let it out slowly before he said, "And if she wishes to go with me, will you allow her to leave?"

"We force no one to stay with us, Dr. Scott, but Sister

337

Gabrielle is one of us. She has been in our society for many years. It would grieve us to see her pulled to the world and into eternal damnation. So we must surely war against it."

"Gabrielle has no worry of eternal damnation," Brice said.

"Not as long as she stays among us," the brother said. "As Believers we enjoy the eternal fruits of right living and spiritual love, but those of the world must suffer the consequences of a life of sin."

"I don't believe that."

"Many do not. That is why they must die and suffer for their wrong thinking."

Brice kept his eyes on Gabrielle. He had never planned to force Gabrielle to go with him. He was here. The next step must be hers. She'd have to come to him on her own. But could he expect her to risk eternal damnation for him? In his heart he lifted a prayer to the Lord that he would somehow assure Gabrielle of both his love and Brice's love.

The Shakers formed a circle around Gabrielle, who stood in the middle with her head bowed. She looked so small and helpless as the Shakers began walking around her, chanting, "Woe. Woe!"

"What are they doing?" Brice tensed, ready to spring to her defense. "They're not going to hurt her, are they?"

The brother beside him spoke calmly. "We'd never harm one of our sisters. There is only love here, not the anger of the world. But we must try to save her before it's too late. It is our warring gift, the way we fight the pull of the world."

"I thought you people didn't believe in wars."

"Our war is against the devil."

It was all Brice could do to keep from rushing to Gabrielle's aid as she huddled in the middle of the shouting Shakers.

They moved in a circle, stamping their feet while the terrible moaning sound of their woes filled the air. Brice picked out Elder Caleb in the circle. There was an unearthly fervor about him as he shouted out something about evil spirits. Dust whirled up around the Shakers as they stamped their feet with renewed vigor.

Brice fastened his eyes back on Gabrielle in the midst of their fury. He wouldn't move his eyes from her again. When she looked up, his love would be waiting for her.

Inside the circle, a miserable sickness spread through every inch of Gabrielle's body and settled in her soul. She raised her eyes just enough to search the faces of those marching around her. If only in one of them she could see some kindness, some regret for the misery they were causing her, but they were all caught up in the frenzy of the warring gift.

Sister Mercy stepped a bit nearer Gabrielle and stared straight at her as she shouted and stomped her feet. The sister's eyes were not the gentle eyes of the Sister Mercy Gabrielle had known and loved. A wall had gone up between them. A wall that no amount of words of confession or forgiveness would ever breach. Sister Mercy went on around the circle, shouting her woes even louder.

Each woe pierced Gabrielle like a spear. She wanted to burrow into the ground and pull the grass over her head to shield herself from the shouts of her brethren and sisters. She'd witnessed the warring gift before, had twice joined the circle to war against the pull of the world when a member threatened to leave the Believers, but only now did she

339

understand why the person in the center of the circle had looked as if the words had been blows beating him down.

Suddenly Gabrielle stiffened against the shouts thrown at her from the ring of Believers. Her heart grew heavy and then turned cold. She raised her head and pulled herself up straight and tall. A sharp pain ripped through her as something within her struggled and died. Then the pain was gone, and she knew she was no longer one with these people. She was no longer a Believer. They had warred for her, and instead of keeping her, they had destroyed her belief in their way of life.

A finger of panic touched her as she wondered if she'd lost her faith completely. She bowed her head and moved her lips in a quiet prayer that could not be heard over the shouts. "Take not thy grace from me, Eternal Father."

A gentle peace filled her. The Eternal Father had heard her prayer. He wouldn't turn his face from her even if she left the Believers in body as she already had in her heart.

Brice's words from so many months before came to her. *"We were meant to be together."* He said the Lord intended men and women to love and to marry. Slowly she turned her head to look at Brice. His eyes were waiting, and she knew the choice she must make.

Gabrielle stood silently and waited for the warring gift to die away. Though it hadn't accomplished what the Believers expected it to accomplish, perhaps it had been a gift to her by breaking completely the bond that tied her to the Shakers. She was free now, truly free just as a butterfly was free when at last it worked its last bit of wing out of the cocoon.

When the last woe became no more than a whisper in the dust, Gabrielle stepped out of the circle of Believers without

340

a word. Elder Caleb reached out a hand to stop her. "Ye must not go, child. Thy place is among us, not in the world."

Gabrielle kept her eyes on Brice as she whispered her answer. "Nay."

She stopped in front of Brice and asked, "You have come for me?"

"I have come for you," Brice said.

She put her hand into his. He lifted her up on his horse as though she were a great treasure. Her heart began to beat hard but not from fear. Rather she thought she might explode with joy.

As Brice began leading Gabrielle out of the village, his horse's hooves hitting the ground were loud in the silence. Then a fresh chorus of woes rose up, but the sound no longer touched Gabrielle. In a few minutes, they left the village behind.

Neither of them spoke as they went through the woods to Brice's cabin. Gabrielle had to duck and lean side to side to stay under the branches. It wasn't until he helped her off the horse in front of his cabin that he looked at her and said, "Nathan is dead."

"I knew it to be so," Gabrielle whispered. "I feared you had shared his fate."

"It was not far from the truth," he said. "But we won't speak of the past today."

"Then what shall we speak of?" Gabrielle asked.

"The future. Our future."

She followed him into the cabin and stood in the middle of the floor while he knelt to build up the fire he'd left banked in the fireplace. She stared at the flames as they leapt up around the wood logs, and suddenly feared she would not be able to step into that future. What did she know of the ways of the world?

As if he sensed her doubts, he turned to her and put his hands on her arms. "It's strange for you now, but it will seem right in a few days."

"Yea." She kept her eyes away from his face as she went on. "I must tell you I know nothing of men and the ways of the world."

"Gabrielle, look at me." He waited until her eyes came up to meet his. "Know this one thing. Inscribe it on your heart. I would never do anything to hurt you. Never. You must surely know that."

"I see the truth of that in your eyes."

"Tomorrow we will find a preacher and marry in the proper way."

"I never thought to commit matrimony," Gabrielle whispered.

"Marriage isn't a sin. You must believe me, Gabrielle." His eyes burned into hers. "We'll be committing no sin by joining our lives together in front of God and man. The Lord intended man and woman to cleave together and love one another."

"Yea, I do want to cleave unto you and be married," Gabrielle said. "But you say tomorrow. First we have the night."

Brice reached up and pulled the Shaker cap off Gabrielle's head. Her hair tumbled down about her shoulders. His hand trembled as he reached out to touch it, and his voice was low and full of feeling when he spoke. "You needn't worry about anything improper, my darling. A friend named Tyney will be here soon. She and her young daughter, Maysie, will stay with us tonight. But that won't stop us from sitting in

342

front of the fire together or walking outside in the moonlight while our hearts bond together as one. Then nothing will ever be able to separate us again. Not even death, for you will always be alive in my heart and I pray I will always live in yours."

"Yea, it has been so since you left and will ever be so," Gabrielle said as she stepped into his embrace. She was where she belonged, where she would always belong. Her past dropped away from her. It was sure to return at times just as Brice's would. Then together they would face the ghosts of their yesteryears, but now she just wanted to feel his love around her. To know the joy of their love.

Later after Tyney came, Brice and Gabrielle sat together on the edge of the porch. Brice draped his jacket around her shoulders to ward off the chill of the night air while inside Tyney sang a song to lull her little girl to sleep. Gabrielle couldn't keep from thinking of Becca and the songs she'd longed to hear her mother sing to her when she had the fever.

Brice must have sensed her sadness for he reached over and clasped her hands in his. "What worries your mind?"

"Little Becca and her mother. So many sorrows over the last year." Gabrielle stared out at the moonlit shadows drifting across the yard. "And then Nathan."

He held her hands tighter. "You knew when Nathan died, didn't you? He said he felt you praying for him."

"I knew. I saw the snow turn red with blood." She looked over at him and could not hold back the shiver that walked through her at the thought of her vision of death. "Is that the way it really happened?"

Brice put his arm around her and pulled her closer to his side. "Yes, but not for Nathan. He was wounded in the fighting. I gave him something for his pain and he did not waken until he was on the other side of glory."

"I'm glad." Gabrielle was quiet for a moment as she marveled at how safe she felt there with Brice's arm around her. Then she said, "Sister Mercy says it is a gift to know things I should not know. The gift of knowing. But no one would seek such a gift."

"And what gift would you seek instead?" Brice asked softly.

"The gift of joy. The gift of love."

"I would give you those if it was in my power."

"You have given me love, but I think joy must come from within. Perhaps a gift from the Eternal Father."

"I knew a boy who had that kind of joy. Even as he faced death." Brice looked away from her out toward the trees on the edge of the clearing.

"And how did he get it?"

"If he were here, he would tell you prayer and walking hand in hand with the Lord. He had much faith." Brice sounded sad as he added, "I wish you could have known him. His name was Seth."

"Seth." Without realizing what she was doing, she sought some image of the boy in her mind when there was no way she could know him. Absolutely nothing came to mind. No shadows of knowing lingering in the recesses of her mind. Nothing. Instead joy sprang up inside her. A new gift to drive out the old. She could almost feel the gift of knowing being pushed out of her and disappearing into the night.

A prayer of thanksgiving rose in her heart as she reached up to touch Brice's face. Then he had both arms around her and she lifted her lips to meet his. Her feet had finally found the path out of the dark valley to the mountain bathed in the sunshine of not only Brice's love but also the sure love and blessings of the Lord.

❧❧❧

For ye were sometimes darkness, but now are ye light in the Lord: walk as children of light.

Ann H. Gabhart and her husband live on a farm just over the hill from where she grew up in central Kentucky. She's active in her country church, and her husband sings bass in a southern gospel quartet. Ann is the author of over a dozen novels for adults and young adults. Her first inspirational novel, *The Scent of Lilacs*, was one of Booklist's Top Ten Inspirational Novels of 2006.

Index

Index

Pangalos, Gen.: minister of war 119; as dictator (1925–6) 124, 126, 141

Papadopoulos, Col George 183, 191, 202, 208, 220: leader army coup (1967) 187, 194; prime minister (1968–73) 189, 195, 196–7

Papagos, Gen.: minister for war (1936) 130, 136; Greek commander-in-chief (1941) 137, 163; leader Greek Rally (1951) 167; prime minister (1952–5) 169, 171, 172

Papanastasiou, Alexander, republican prime minister (1924), 123–4

Papandreou, Andreas, 191: and Aspida conspiracy 183, 185–6; leader of PASOK: 203, 208, 212, 214; prime minister 217-18, 220–1

Papandreou, George: prime minister of government -in-exile (1944) 148, 151; leader of national government (1944–5) 152–5; and National Political Union (1946) 158; leader Liberal Party (1958) 173; leader Centre Union (1961) 177, 178, 180; prime minister (1963) 180, (1964) 181, 182, 190; resignation of (1965) 184, 185; death of (1968) 191

Paris Conference (1922) 117

parties, political
Alliance of Progressive and Left Wing Forces 222–3
Centre Union (EK) 177, 178, 181, 184, 187, 200, 204, 206, 217, 220
Communist (KKE), 123, 130, 139ff, 145, 148, 153–4, 155, 157, 160–1, 163, 167, 204, 222, 223
Democratic Camp 166
Democratic Union 173
George Papandreou 166, 167
Greek Rally 167, 168–9, 172, 173
Liberal 157, 158, 166, 167, 173, 177
National 158
National Agrarian 177
National Democratic Union 205, 206, 223
National Political Union 158
National Progressive Centre Union (EPEK) 166, 167, 168
National Radical Union (ERE) 173, 177, 178, 179, 180, 181, 205; see also New Democracy
National Rally (Ethniki Parataxis) 221, 223

New Democracy 205, 206, **220**, 221, 223
New Forces group 204, 206, 217, 221
New Liberal 221, 223
Panhellenic Socialist Movement (PASOK) 204, 205, 206, 210, **222**, 223
Populist 157–8, 166, 167
Progressive 169, 177, 180, 181
Socialist Union of Popular Democracy 169
Union of the Democratic Centre (EDIK) 221–2, 223
United Democratic Left (EDA) 167, 169, 173, 174, 176, 177, 178, 180, 181, 204, 206, 222, 223

patriarchate 120–1, 126, 216
attitude of: to Bulgarian Church 88; to Greek uprising (1821–2) 54
corruption of 24–5
and Greek Church 72
and Greek life 23–4
vs. papacy 1
power of 19–20
status of 20
see also Church, Orthodox

Pattakos, Brig. Stylianos, leader Colonels' coup (1967) 187, 202, 208

Peace of Tilsit (1807) 46

peasantry 7, 29, 49, 67, 71, 143, 150–1

Phanariots 32–3, 41, 42, 43, 53, 57–8

Phokas, Capt., leader military coup (1922) 118

Pipinelis, Panayiotis, acting prime minister (1963) 179; foreign minister 192

Plastiras, Col Nicholas: leader military coup (1922), 118, 119; leader of abortive coup (1933) 128; leader of EDES 141; as prime minister (1945) 155–6; (1951) 167, 168

police, military (ESA) 191, 198, 208, 209

Political Committee for National Liberation (PEEA) 147, 148

presidents (of Greece): Capodistrias, Count John (1827–31) 64, 65, 67–8, 70, 71; Gizikis, Lt–Gen. Phaedon (1973–4) 197, 199; Koundouriotis, Admiral (1926) 124, 130; Tsatsos, Constantine (1975) 211

Rallis, Dimitrios, prime minister (1909) 98, 99

Rallis, George, prime minister (1980–1) 217

Index